Praise for

Laid Bare

"It's impossible not to love this story. The sex is sizzling, the emotions are raw. Lauren Dane has done it again. *Laid Bare*, quite simply, *rocks!*"
—Megan Hart, author of *No Greater Pleasure*

Relentless

"*Relentless* will sweep you away."
—Anya Bast, national bestselling author of *Witch Fury*

"Exceptional . . . an intriguing alternative world."
—Joey W. Hill, author of *Vampire Mistress*

"Hot romance, detailed world-building and a plot focusing on righting injustice make *Relentless* a page-turner. With passion and politics, Dane delivers again!"
—Megan Hart

"Spectacular . . . absolutely brilliantly written."
—*Manic Readers*, 4 ½ stars

"Pulled in from page one, readers will enjoy the delicious sensuality."
—*Romantic Times*, 4 ½ stars

"Emotionally charged, passionate and at times volatile, *Relentless* once again proves that Ms. Dane is a first-class author who is fully capable of delivering exactly the sorts of story lines that readers crave."
—*Romance Junkies*, 5 Blue Ribbons

continued . . .

"Filled with heat and erotic passion . . . *Relentless* is a do-not-miss."
—*Joyfully Reviewed*

"This terrific science fiction erotic romance is fast-paced and filled with action in and out of the bedroom." —*Midwest Book Review*

"Fiery, erotic and rich with plot, this book is definitely a keeper on my shelf." —*Night Owl Romance*

Undercover

"Delicious eroticism . . . a toe-curling erotic romance sure to keep you reading late into the night." —Anya Bast

"Sexy, pulse-pounding adventure . . . that'll leave you weak in the knees. Dane delivers!"
—Jaci Burton, author of *Bound, Branded, & Brazen*

"Exciting, emotional and arousing . . . a ride well worth taking."
—Sasha White, author of *My Prerogative*

"Fast-paced action, steamy romance." —Megan Hart

"A roller coaster of emotion, intrigue and sensual delights."
—Vivi Anna, author of *Dark Lies*

Insatiable

lauren dane

heat | new york

ROM
Dane

THE BERKLEY PUBLISHING GROUP
Published by the Penguin Group
Penguin Group (USA) Inc.
375 Hudson Street, New York, New York 10014, USA
Penguin Group (Canada), 90 Eglinton Avenue East, Suite 700, Toronto, Ontario M4P 2Y3, Canada
(a division of Pearson Penguin Canada Inc.)
Penguin Books Ltd., 80 Strand, London WC2R 0RL, England
Penguin Group Ireland, 25 St. Stephen's Green, Dublin 2, Ireland (a division of Penguin Books Ltd.)
Penguin Group (Australia), 250 Camberwell Road, Camberwell, Victoria 3124, Australia
(a division of Pearson Australia Group Pty. Ltd.)
Penguin Books India Pvt. Ltd., 11 Community Centre, Panchsheel Park, New Delhi—110 017, India
Penguin Group (NZ), 67 Apollo Drive, Rosedale, North Shore 0632, New Zealand
(a division of Pearson New Zealand Ltd.)
Penguin Books (South Africa) (Pty.) Ltd., 24 Sturdee Avenue, Rosebank, Johannesburg 2196,
South Africa

Penguin Books Ltd., Registered Offices: 80 Strand, London WC2R 0RL, England

This book is an original publication of The Berkley Publishing Group.

This is a work of fiction. Names, characters, places, and incidents either are the product of the author's imagination or are used fictitiously, and any resemblance to actual persons, living or dead, business establishments, events, or locales is entirely coincidental. The publisher does not have any control over and does not assume any responsibility for author or third-party websites or their content.

PRINTING HISTORY
Heat trade paperback edition / July 2010

Library of Congress Cataloging-in-Publication Data

Dane, Lauren.
    Insatiable / Lauren Dane. — Heat trade pbk. ed.
      p.   cm.
    ISBN 978-0-425-23526-3 (trade pbk.)
    I. Title.
    PS3604.A5I67 2010
    813'.6—dc22
                    2010006712

PRINTED IN THE UNITED STATES OF AMERICA

10 9 8 7 6 5 4 3 2 1

This one is for Renee, Mary and Fatin—
thank you for all you do

Acknowledgments

Thank you first and foremost to Leis Pederson, who took a chance on *Undercover* and has enabled me to write these Federation novels at Berkley. Futuristics are a big love, so thank you for giving me a place to draw the world of the Known Universes.

Thank you always to my husband, Ray, who, despite his own stressful and busy job, always finds a way to give me the time I need to work and deals with the chaos of deadline house.

Laura Bradford, thank you for your unending support and for all the work you do on my behalf.

Frauke at Croco Designs, you have done so much for me, created so many beautiful ads, bookmarks and websites, and you always find a way to squeeze me into your busy schedule. Thank you so very much.

Once when I was in high school, they had this career day thing where all the juniors had to go through cards to pick what they wanted to be. They had no card for writer. Probably still don't. This is something I dreamed of but figured would never happen. I want to thank my parents, who raised me to believe I could be whatever I wanted to be. Because here I am, with my unruly grammar, writing an acknowledgment in my novel. Dave and Linda, thank you for teaching me that everything worth having is worth working your butt off for. I love you.

Chapter 1

There was no sound other than heavy breathing and then an indrawn breath gone liquid. Normally, the sound would have fallen on deaf ears as he simply did his job and walked away. Then again, normally, it would have been quicker, anonymous, so the target wouldn't know what hit them, even as their life ended.

Today Daniel broke the rules and took a step closer to the ever-looming darkness. He wanted Saul Kerrigan to see his face, to know he was dying because Daniel made it so. To know he was dying because of what he'd done. Not just to the citizens of the Federation but to Daniel's sister as well.

Saul Kerrigan was a traitor.

The knife did its work as it always did. Deadly sharp, it slid between the ribs, moving unerringly toward the target. It was then Daniel paused to pull his mask away from his face. Saul's eyes widened with recognition and then fear. *Good*, even if too late.

Daniel put fingers over Saul's lips. "Shh. You don't have much time left." Those fear-filled eyes widened. "I know you're surprised, Saul. You thought you could evade House Lyons forever? Consort with the Imperium and not get caught? Thought you could torture and abuse my sister without consequences?" Daniel's voice was flat, emotionless, even as the rage painted his vision, the rage that this man had harmed the person he loved most in all the 'Verses.

He shook his head as Saul dropped to his knees, his life with the pulse of his slowing heart. His blood slid through his fingers, spilling on the hungry, dry ground at his feet.

Mockingly, Daniel sighed, squatting and resting on his heels. "Right now you're asking how I found you. How I could be allowed to harm you. You're outraged. After all, I'm unranked filth." Daniel laughed without mirth. "Just like you!"

Daniel wanted to remind Kerrigan he'd pushed Roman too far and had been stripped of his Rank. Saul was even lower on the chain than Daniel, as Daniel was a commissioned officer in the military corps.

"How far you've fallen. Since it's just you and me here, Saul, let me tell you a secret. It took me longer than my usual jobs do, but still not longer than a month standard. I knew you'd run. I told Roman that you'd never be satisfied with a simple life. I figured you'd have waited longer than this, though. Tsk. But find you I did. And now my job is done. The 'Verses will be cleaner for your stain having been removed."

Daniel wiped the blade clean on Saul's back. Saul squirmed ineffectively.

"Don't struggle so. It just speeds the bleeding. You're dying, Saul, you'd best really live these last moments. Back to what I was saying.

I found you because one of your people betrayed you. Credits do a lot of work in my business. Ah yes, *my business*, Saul. I'm not that powerless kid who nearly went to lockup because I defended my sister from your compatriots as they raped her. I'm something you can't imagine, even though you're a cruel brute and a craven liar. *This* is my job, Saul Kerrigan. You and your family made me this way. My sister would say that this is a classic case of irony. But I think it's fate. Here we are full circle. Not that it matters. You have less than one minute to live, so enjoy it while you can. I know I'll cherish this moment for the rest of my days. Which are, I'm pleased to remind you, far longer than yours."

He stood. He'd lured Saul out there to the middle of nowhere, deep into the deserts of the Edge, and here is where he'd be left. A sandstorm was due to kick up shortly, cleaning the body down to the bone.

It was over for that moment in time. There were more people like Saul. Men and women of Family and Rank who'd sold information to the Imperialists. That information had been used to kill their own people, innocent people at work or at play. Saul wasn't the first, nor would he be the last. But Daniel had felt pleasure, a sense of well-being and accomplishment as he'd killed. Normally, he'd be alarmed. Killing wasn't something he ever did for pleasure. This time it meant something personal. Yes, he'd done his job and made the Federation safer, but more than that, he'd erased a bad memory for Abbie, eradicated a threat to one of Daniel's loved ones.

After bending to be sure the job was done, Daniel tugged his mask back into place and headed away, up toward the dunes where he'd left the pack animal he'd arrived on. The conveyance Saul arrived in was already gone, disposed of by one of Daniel's people.

He'd be off 'Verse by the end of the hour, and Saul Kerrigan wouldn't be selling secrets anymore.

But someone was. Daniel's job was not over.

"*A*h, yes, do come in, Daniel. Are you looking for Abbie? She's resting upstairs. I know she'll be pleased to see you." Roman Lyons answered his own door, and it still surprised Daniel. The most powerful man in the Known Universes had nearly given it all away to marry Daniel's sister Abbie less than a year before. In Daniel's book, this made him *almost* good enough for Abbie. There was no doubt Roman was a great leader, a man Daniel would follow without question. And no doubt he was also a friend.

And now Abbie was in the early days of her first pregnancy, and Roman, though he already had two grown sons, doted on her totally. Daniel couldn't talk, really, he doted on her, too. Abbie was his best friend, the person he'd always been able to count on. In 'Verse after 'Verse of fuckups and selfish traitors, that meant something.

"Roman, good afternoon." He stepped into the grand entry, handing his coat off to Roman, who'd no doubt hand it off to some servant or other. "Before I go check on Abbie, I was just with Wilhelm, and he thought I should brief you."

Roman's gaze went hooded at the mention of his top military man. "Good. Why don't you come on through into my office. Once my lovely bride hears you're here, I'll have to fight her off for five minutes alone with you." He paused on his way through the conservatory, finally laughing with Daniel. "Yes, okay, that did sound dirty. But you know what I mean. I've been with your sister too long. I'm starting to see everything as dirty or funny. A rather amusing new way to see the world."

"She's a bad influence on all of us, Roman. Thank the gods," Daniel said dryly as they entered Roman's home office, and Roman set the security locks behind them.

Once he was back behind his desk, Roman spread his hands out, searching for words. "I've gone through this before. The pregnancy thing. It's not like I think she's weak. She's not. It's just . . ."

Ah, personal first. Daniel nodded. He knew of Roman's past and realized this was difficult for him on multiple levels. "I know childbirth contributed to your first wife's decline in health. You don't have to be The Lyon here with me, with her and your boys. I worry about her, too." He shrugged. "She *will* be fine. There's nothing else that would dare to light upon her. She's practically indestructible."

Roman lost some of the fear on his features and then sighed. "Yes. Yes. I know. She's just so small and fragile. But you're right, of course. She may be small, but she's mighty, and frankly, I can't imagine a more fortunate baby than the one she's carrying." And just as quickly, he was business again. "Tell me, then."

"It's done. I tracked him to Asphodel, though why he was there is a mystery. Some of our people are looking into it. There's something going on out there on the Edge. I won't bore you with details; Ellis says he'll be speaking to you about it when you two have your regular meeting."

"Things are in flux. I have come to believe our situation will only get much darker. I regret that I will ask you to do things, ask all my people to do things they'll be hard-pressed to get over. I regret it, but it remains true, and it remains necessary." Roman sat back and studied Daniel for long moments without speaking.

Daniel stayed quiet, letting Roman process whatever in hells he wanted to order him to do. He preferred action. Regrets never saved anyone. Then again, he didn't have the pressure Roman had.

"Because of this new challenge facing us, we're going to need new approaches and new leadership. I've let Wilhelm know you can give me my briefings in the future. He laughed and laughed and said I'd have to propose it to you since it was—in his words, mind you—*a shitty deal because Roman Lyons is a pain in the ass.*"

Daniel had no problem imagining Wilhelm Ellis saying just that. He was honored and proud of what he'd accomplished, even as he, too, felt the onset of something truly ominous. "Thank you, Roman, I'm honored. Is this because of my sister?" he joked, hoping to lessen the tension just a little bit.

Roman simply stared at him, one brow raised. "Your sister is on me all the time about sending you *away* from danger. It's a good thing your job is secret, or she'd bite my ass over this move." He grinned quickly before sobering again. "No, I think you're an incredibly qualified person. You're already Wilhelm's right hand, and your group is integral to what we do. Right now, with things so dire, we need you on the ground, and I want to hear from you directly about what Phantom Corps is doing. Our focus must shift to defense and planning for an offense. The special teams are more important now than ever."

He was undeniably pleased and flattered at such a rise in position. "Yes, sir. Of course. My schedule, as you know, can be erratic, but I expect we can work around that."

"We can. I'm quite happy to be a pain in Wilhelm's ass when you're off 'Verse."

Daniel wondered what it was between the two powerful men that had bonded them so deeply. He had his own twisty, complex and no less deep bond with Wilhelm Ellis, wasn't sure Ellis had anything but complex relationships with people. "Anything else?"

"I'm concerned about developments on the Edge. Keep me apprised of things as they happen. I want to know why that piece of garbage was out that far."

"As you're no doubt aware already, there's been a marked increase in the gun for hire biz on the Edge. More weapons violations every day. More arrests. We're watching and listening, calling in favors and trying to work it out. We agree that something is brewing, and we've got all available resources on it. I assume Ellis has his other teams on this as well."

Daniel knew there were things he wasn't told. That was how it went in their business. Though he had excellent clearance, it wasn't as high as Ellis. Still, he'd like to know what the big picture held, and he hoped this new rise in responsibilities and position would enable him to finally know more about what the hells was going on.

"I expect you'll be getting a one-on-one briefing with Wilhelm about all we're gathering now. Your new position will deem higher clearance. You'll be liaising with some of the other Corps branches, coordinating the special teams. I'll leave the details up to him; you know how much he'll enjoy drawing it all out for the drama."

Daniel nodded his assent and then jolted when the chimes on the office door rang.

Roman sighed, not without affection. "I believe your sister has realized you're here."

"It's really difficult for her, being so shy and all." Daniel opened the door, and she all but tumbled into his body, so he caught her up, carefully, and kissed the top of her head.

"I can't believe you came to see him before you came to see me." Her face had a roundness it hadn't before. Pregnancy suited her. Happiness suited her.

"Pressing business. And it's now out of the way, so I can be with you." He took her hand. "Roman said you weren't feeling well?"

"Pressing business, my pregnant ass. You two were being furtive." She snorted. She led him into the room she'd converted into an intimate family area. Mercy, the house manager, a woman who was like a member of the family, rushed in, clucked at the sight of Abbie being up, ordered her to sit and headed back out to retrieve refreshments.

"My beauty. You believe anything not directly involving you is furtive. We were working. And now we aren't," Roman said, dropping a kiss to his wife's temple.

The way she was with Roman told Daniel they were a forever match. She teased him, played with him, treated him like her mate, her man, instead of a figurehead. In doing so, she risked herself, risked exposing her soft side, knowing Roman would never use it to hurt her.

Mercy brought in a rolling cart laden with food and drink. She unceremoniously pushed Roman's feet from the low table while putting a pillow behind Abbie's back.

"She's nicer to you than she is me," Roman groused.

Abbie winked at Roman. "It's my sparkling personality. Or she has a love for nauseated, grumpy women who make gagging noises."

Mercy laughed as she left the room.

Daniel winced. "Sorry about that. Is it that bad? Can I help?"

"It's common. I'm not the only woman who's ever felt this way. It should pass as I get further along. Mercy helps. Mai, too, of course. I'm taken care of. You look handsome." She eyed him carefully. "But not handsome enough to get away with being gone a whole week without coming to see me."

He rolled his eyes and ate the food laid out for them. Of course Abbie accused him of inhaling it, but he did chew after all. A man had to eat to stay strong.

"Sorry about that. How dare I do my job when my sister is here in this palace and might have needed a back rub."

"I totally agree, Daniel." Abbie winked at him.

"Tell me what you're doing these days. Not a lady of leisure, never for you." Daniel wished it were otherwise sometimes, but Abbie was driven and committed, full of passion, and he couldn't really imagine her any other way.

"Oh you know, agitating Roman's cronies and enemies, too. Making all the Ranked listen to me. This amuses me, of course, which is a bonus. Nothing better than watching some of these tight-arsed old bastards have to politely listen to the rabble." She laughed, utterly delighted. "We're working hard, my little group. When I'm not doing that, I'm here, lolling around, having people serve me food and drink while I objectify Roman. Good times."

Roman's surprised laugh made Abbie's eyes brighten, and their connection strengthened, heated. It embarrassed Daniel even as he envied it, wanted it for himself, wanted a woman to look at him like he was the best thing ever.

"I saw the raised beds you made for Mai's kitchen garden. Very nice work."

He nearly blushed. "She needed them. I had the raw materials and the time."

"You gave her a way to garden again without overtaxing herself. It was a lovely gift, Daniel." Abbie watched him as she ate. "It's okay, you know, to be nice to your mother."

"Does that mean I can throw our father out a window?"

"Ha! No." Roman interrupted. "If my father gets to bully me and act like a right grumpy old pain in my behind, yours gets to live. Though I'd be lying if I said I hadn't imagined him with my fist planted in his mouth."

Daniel laughed this time. "My father or yours?"

"Both." Roman shrugged and grabbed a sandwich off the tray.

By the time he left, Abbie's spirits were high, and she was surrounded by people who loved her. That left him content. His other sister was newly married and happy, their mother was healthy and her business thriving and his flighty little brother had become an important man in politics. He had no real fear for himself. He'd accepted the vagaries of his job long ago. But he wanted those people he loved to be safe from harm. Knowing they were happy made it an easier task to leave them behind.

The sky was clear, stars fiery in the distance. His mind flitted briefly to those last moments with Saul. Not to the death. Not that it was ordered. Not that it was done. No, to the location, to the *whys* of Saul Kerrigan's presence in Asphodel.

He shifted course, heading to work.

Chapter 2

*E*sta hurried down the long hallway, hoping not to be noticed. She'd been at it long enough to have mastered the art, and a member of her husband's family long enough to fear failure. She'd been in the kitchens, overseeing the details for the meal her husband had ordered for twenty guests, when she'd heard something that'd made her uneasy.

One of the pantry girls had said something about making sure to have enough wine on hand for the toasts. When the gossiping had started, the word *betrothal* had come up a few times as conjecture.

Panic that her husband had finally chosen one of his monsters to marry Carina had jolted her into action.

So she found herself heading toward his receiving offices to try to speak with him on the issue. It would most likely do no good this time. She'd held him back before, but with the passing of each year and the ever increasing stupidity in her husband's choices and behaviors toward the Federation, he was listening to reason less and less.

And he needed their daughter as a bargaining chip to keep his men in line more and more.

Her heart pounded so hard she felt faint and needed to slow down her pace. And thank the gods she had, because her husband stood in the hallway, just around the corner, speaking to some of his top people. Esta wanted to avoid an audience. Ciro could be nicer when he was alone.

She ducked back, fitting herself into one of the nooks holding the tapestries that lined the walls.

Hartley Alem, one of Ciro's ministers, spoke, "I think we've got enough liberiam to move forward with tests now."

"We haven't had the time to clear the area completely yet. Give me a week more. The station is near a very heavily populated area." Esta wasn't sure who that was, but it sounded like one of the new so-called science ministers Ciro had had hanging around him of late.

"More cattle where that came from. The Imperium is crawling with people. One of them is just as good as another to mop up and clean." Alem. Esta curled her lip.

A throat cleared. "I was thinking more that witnesses would be a bad thing. Until we gather the rest of the materials we need, the lab should be able to act without being monitored overmuch."

What in the name of the gods above and below was her husband doing now?

"The longer we delay, the longer our justice will be denied," Alem argued.

"Hartley, do calm down. We'll get our results, and you can keep your program going in the meantime. Caine, do continue to move the populace away, but slowly and quietly for now. You have your week."

"Thank you, sir."

"We have an audience to take. Let's get that done. Guard! Send for my daughter. Tell her I wish to see her in my audience chambers before the hour is up."

They moved away, their speech fading as they did. Esta needed to move and move quickly.

She peeked out from her spot and then around the corner. No one was there, so she hurried down the hall and stepped into the private offices her husband worked from. Or pretended to work from while the others destroyed their 'Verses one by one, all for greed.

He had a personal assistant, but she was gone. Not surprising, considering her only job was to service him and look pretty. Better her than Esta.

She used the keypad to enter his space and closed the door. Fear kept her skin clammy, but realization that she had to act and act now kept her from bolting out of the room. Too bad Ciro didn't have a personal assistant who could service him *and* keep him organized.

His desk was a mess of data chips and files, of discs and tossed-aside reports. She grabbed several of them, including one that bore Alem's insignia. Esta wasn't sure what she'd find, but she couldn't take it all, and there wasn't time to use his reader, so she took the discs with the highest color rating for security clearance and one with the science ministry's stamp.

No one saw her leave. The halls were empty until she got closer to the living quarters and areas the public were allowed into. Not that anyone paid her any mind; she was the first wife, tossed aside after her sons had failed to rise to power.

They thought she didn't know. Or worse, that she did know and cared. She didn't care because he left her alone. She'd never had any misconceptions that he loved her. She did her duty, a duty she was born to, and bore his children. For duty and then, as she began to raise those children, for love.

It was love that kept her moving toward her personal quarters where she could secret the things she'd stolen. And love, still, for her people, that would lead her to do whatever needed doing with the information she'd found.

*D*espite the summons she'd received from her father, Carina stared out the windows of her bedroom, looking down the long, steep line of the rampart and into the courtyard below. The late afternoon suns sent warmth over her face, even through the darkened glass. A warmth she didn't feel inside. Inside she was cold. Always cold, alert, scheming, listening and keeping her mask firmly in place. The penalty for slipping was something she kept close to her heart every moment of every day.

Not many people were outside at this point of the day. The heat drove them into the shade of the arches and into the buildings. They'd congregate in the cafés and taverns until the first sunset and the heat wore away. The local taverns were raucous, filled with noise and laughter and the sharp scent of the spices used for the mulled wine. She'd always wanted to spend some time in one, but the closest she got was observing from across a square or through the plasglass.

Over the years, she'd observed life far more often than she'd lived it. Observing was her one guilty pleasure.

A muted sort of yearning stole over her, as it always did, as she continued to stare at the scene below, wondering how they felt, if any of them felt normal or whole.

What she wanted so much was the space in her life when she didn't have to pretend. Exhaustion at keeping up a false identity every waking moment had taken over her life in ways she hated but couldn't seem to stop. She searched her memories and realized she couldn't remember a time when she didn't constantly fear for her life.

She exhaled hard. It did no good to be morose, and she didn't have the luxury of it, anyway. Feeling sorry for herself never made a difference; it never made anything better. In truth, her life was far better than most; she needed to remember that.

Taking a deep breath, she sipped a glass of juice and continued to watch the scene below and mull over the changes. Earlier she'd been out, returning from the room where she taught sums to some of the local children. She stopped at a stall, one of her favorites where the couple brought in freshly farmed gourds and purri fruit. Today, though, it had been bread. Her farmer couple had been gone, and they all pretended not to notice the difference. That she went along with it had slashed through her heart. Every time something like that happened and no one spoke of it, it eroded their society even more. She was just as guilty as anyone else, and it stuck to her like filth she could not rinse away.

Something inside her was broken. The fissures had widened, and she wondered what it might be like to feel whole, tried to remember if she ever had, and failed.

The soft chimes at her outer doors rang as someone entered the suite. Carina looked up and caught sight of her mother standing in the doorway, small and fragile, wringing her hands.

Looks were deceiving. Esta Fardelle had survived marriage to a man like Ciro since the tender age of fourteen standard years. She'd managed to stay alive, managed to stay one step ahead of a brute like Carina's father because she was good at acting a part, something she'd drilled into Carina from a very early age. Because of her mother, she was alive and loved. That was something important, and she would do well not to forget it.

"Carina, your father sent for you some time ago; you can't delay much longer." She paused. "Darling, be mindful today." Those last three words put Carina on alert. What was her father up to?

Foreboding riding her, Carina stood and smoothed down the gown she'd been laced into just minutes before. She surveyed her hair, pale as moonlight, same as her mother's, making sure the curls hung just so. Her eyes, dark brown like her father's, looked back, appearing as listless as she felt. That wouldn't do. She pinched her cheeks and took a deep breath as she pulled the Carina Fardelle her father knew around her like armor. She shoved her thoughts far away and let a petulant smirk mark her lips. The woman looking back this time was arrogant, confident, spoiled and bred to be a pretty ornament.

She was always mindful, of course. But there'd been a level of activity within the walls that'd nettled her of late. People around who weren't usually around. That pig Hartley Alem and his people visited far more often. Something was happening, and she didn't know what. Given her father's insane behavior of late, it couldn't be anything good, though.

"Let's go then." She swept past her mother and out into the hall. Two of her father's finest—meaning cruelest and most loyal—soldiers escorted her everywhere, ostensibly to protect her. Carina spent most of her life making sure they felt that way instead of suspecting her. Her father would never fully trust anyone, but as long as he didn't look on her with too much suspicion, she would remain safe. People disappeared in her world all the time: the couple running the fruit stand, a neighbor you just never heard from again, a teacher who suddenly quit with no notice and left her belongings in her flat, a maid or cook. Her grandmother. One day they were there, the next they were gone. For as long as she could remember, the fear of waking up and being disappeared had lived inside her.

They walked silently down the long hall toward the rooms her father held his audiences in. More of a throne room, but that was a quibble anyway. Imperial 'Verses held him like a king, and that was just how he liked it. Not that they'd dare any other way. The sense of duty had been replaced by fear of standing out, of drawing attention and ending up in a cell somewhere. He ruled because everyone was afraid to call him out. That kind of rule never lasted.

The plasglass held back the heat of the twin suns and also protected against rockets and other incendiary devices should any attackers actually make it close enough to the inner sanctum of the complex where the Fardelles lived and worked. The insulation they provided kept the interior cool but still let in enough light to gleam over the black floors, casting the reflection of crest after crest, generation after generation of Fardelles who held the position of Supreme Commander of the Imperial Universes.

At one time in her life, she'd been proud of that. Been proud to be part of something as important as building the Imperial 'Verses and protecting its people. And then she'd begun to learn more than just what her tutors were allowed to teach. Her older brother Vincenz had left, run away from his life here, and by some accounts was somewhere in Federation Territory. His portrait had been excised from all public places, his name, his very existence erased. And then her younger brother had died after being stricken by a sudden illness that had ravaged him, leaving him dead in only four standard hours.

Her mother had struggled to hold herself together, but part of her had never been the same. She had just faded, more by the day until the vibrant woman Carina had grown up with was now a pale shadow.

None of them had been the same.

It was then that she'd begun to find bits and pieces of information from the outside. Vid clips and audio reports from the Federation government. Every few days, sometimes once a month, or nothing for long periods and then four things in one day. She'd soaked it all in and had shared with her mother, who had confessed her own divided loyalties.

She became hungry for more, for the truth of it all, even as it had cut to the bone. Sought out as much information as she could as safely as she could. The world beyond their borders flooded in, and she'd been moved, shattered, grief-stricken and then remade into someone else. Someone stronger. She wanted to take over after her father died or gave up the seat at the head of the table. Wanted to right his wrongs. She was a Fardelle who believed in duty, honor and loyalty. But he had no plans to leave any time soon, and she wouldn't be allowed to lead, anyway.

The bare fact was, she was female, and that made her unfit to rule. By virtue of her birth, she'd been deemed useless in all ways but as wife and mother.

Her brother would because he was male and she was not. Not the older brother who should rightfully lead, not her long gone Petrus who'd only been a small child when he'd died. No, the brother who had only recently learned to walk and was many years from long pants. The boy who was the child between her father and his recently appointed second wife, a woman younger than Carina who'd been chosen after she provided a male heir.

Carina hated him for that. Hated him for telling her she wasn't good enough because she was female. For telling her mother she was of no real use to him because the sons she'd given him hadn't been enough. For bullying his new wife so much she rarely said a single word and avoided all eye contact. Hated him for being the source of so much terror and suffering, and for making her be a party to it simply because of who she was.

Ciro Fardelle's entire life was primarily grand theater. Much like her own, she supposed. Only he played a life-and-death game and didn't seem to be moved by that at all. Carina had often thought her father acted like a small child who wanted cake, but as history often showed, he had so much power no one dared deny it to him. This tendency had become excessive over the last three Imperial years. Showing no indication that he understood how to pull back from this gorging of power, she despaired of the cost of his behavior.

Lacking intelligence but not cunning and merciless greed for power, his hold on leadership of the Imperium had been absolute until this ridiculous aggression he continued to show toward the Federation Universes. He'd only gotten worse as the advisors of old had given way to new men in his inner circle. And now those advisors controlled just about every aspect of governance of Imperial law all across the Imperial Universes.

The men around him were dangerous, devoid of compassion and filled with a greed for power that left her in a cold sweat when she thought about it overmuch.

In his presence she was not the Carina who had those thoughts. In truth, her life was an act, too, though she had the intelligence to understand the gravity of her behavior. She was better than her father, better than his cadre of hard men who liked to inflict pain for sport. But her noble intentions wouldn't save her if she let her guard down and made a mistake.

As she turned the corner to enter his office, she reached up, flipped her hair back over one shoulder and stood tall. A beautiful woman would never stoop. She kept her eyes on her father on that ridiculous throne and smiled with a cock of her head and a flutter of her lashes. He warmed a moment, smiling back as he stood, holding his hands out. Something deep inside her wanted it to be real, but died a bit more when she remembered it never would be.

"Darling Carina. Come in and greet Hartley Alem, I've just signed papers allowing him to court you."

Her mother's hand on the small of her back reminded her not to let go of the illusion, but it was a trial not to spit in his face or to run screaming from the room. Instead, she turned to Hartley Alem, one of her father's advisors, a man who'd engineered the bombing of several Federation outposts, a man who had his own personal torture chamber built into his home in the most inappropriately named Fortuna, a 'Verse several portals away.

It was to *this man* her father had given her like a piece of jewelry. It wasn't unexpected; after all, he'd been trying to marry her off for years. But it still shook her up. It was a vital reminder of what she was and what she meant. She was nothing but a chip to be traded. All for power. Hartley had wanted her, and her father wanted the power Hartley enabled him to keep. So he traded her away. Her mother had protected her the last three times he'd tried this, but they both knew it would happen eventually.

Obviously, this was what her mother had warned her about. Swallowing the bile that'd risen, she forged ahead. "Do you believe yourself worthy of me, Minister Alem?" she asked, astonished her voice didn't falter. He actually giggled, and nausea roiled through her. She'd never been this close to losing it before, had never felt so bereft and adrift. This was the one last thing; her limit had been reached. It sent her spinning as she furiously worked through how to feel about it. And then she began to plan.

Hartley reminded her of the flat-faced, hugely muscled dogs the stableman kept in the compound to curtail the snakes. He was big and blunt and tried to hide his true nature with frilly clothing and so much jewelry he should have groaned at the weight. His pale eyes were bright as they darted over her body, lingering on her breasts. A sheen of sweat clung to his brow, and his fingers, heavy with large jeweled rings, twitched as he held back his impulse, thank the gods, to touch her. As his wife, she'd be at his side, attending to him as little more than a personal assistant. The idea of hand-feeding him repulsed her nearly as much as his touching her in a sexual manner. It could not be her fate to be tied to this man.

"That is my sincere hope, my dear. Allow me to escort you to our meal." He held out an arm and she placed a hand on it, allowing him to lead the way to the dining room where the late afternoon meal waited.

She and her mother held the higher place of honor than Aila, the second wife, but she seemed to prefer the far end of the table anyway, and Carina envied that distance. As Carina's brother got older, he'd sit there at her father's right hand, his mother where Carina's mother now sat.

She saw her own future as she thought about how her mother would keep to her rooms more and more, her power fading as Carina was too far away to help and dependent on the whims of a brute. If she was lucky, she'd be able to convince Hartley to have her mother live in Fortuna. Most likely she'd need to get pregnant before he'd even consider it.

Internally she shuddered in disgust.

Carina just concentrated on serving the food to her father and Hartley. She hummed her agreement every few minutes and pushed her food around enough to give an appearance of eating. Hartley seemed mollified by being served by her, so he turned his attentions back to Ciro, and Carina breathed a sigh of relief.

Her life wasn't all bad. There were lovely things in her world, too. People who cared about her, took care of her. The table had been laid out beautifully. She did so love this part of their house, loved the staff who took such good care of her, had done since she was born. She sighted many of her favorites littering the menu. Roasted root vegetables with spiced oil, fresh loaves of bread, fried fish and game and sweet cakes to end with. The colors and scents dizzied her senses and she smiled, ever mindful to keep to a smirk rather than a full smile. But it pleased her, the way the table looked, the ritual of breaking bread with one's community. All this would be wonderful if it were only with other people somewhere else.

Carina desperately wanted to speak to her mother about this situation and what she was going to do about it. Fear and panic ate her insides as she kept a serene face. Her mother's eyes remained cast downward for most of the meal, just like her father preferred it, but she knew her attention was on a solution for Carina. That connection, the love and trust they had, had saved her sanity many times over her life.

Even so, the thought of that being her life, her future, a future of downcast eyes, of whatever sick, twisted bed sport Hartley preferred, of bearing children and having them be indoctrinated the way all children were, made her feel like bolting her lunch.

She pretended interest and made small talk, the passage of time slow and sticky. Thankfully, once the food had been cleared, Carina's mother stood up and smiled at her husband and then to her daughter. "I believe it's time for Carina to take her leave. She and I have plans for the evening." Esta curtsied deeply. "Thank you, dear husband, for this meal. Thank you, Aila for gracing our table." She looked down the table at Ciro's other woman and bowed. "Minister Alem, it will be our pleasure to watch you capture the heart of our daughter."

Alem took her mother's hand and kissed her knuckles. Carina desperately wanted to give in to a full body shudder. Instead, she allowed him to kiss her cheek before nodding to her father and the others at the table and following her mother from the room, her guards trailing behind them.

Her mother put a finger to her lips until she'd closed not only the outer doors to Carina's common rooms but also her bedroom. Her personal maid swept the space for listening devices on a regular basis, so she knew it was as safe a spot as any to speak openly.

Carina spun, yanking her hair free of the fripperies holding the fall of cascading curls. "No." She didn't yell, she didn't throw herself on the floor and howl, she simply said it with all her might. "There are things I am willing to endure, this is not one of them. Not without a fight."

"I had a feeling when I saw all the spirits he'd ordered served at the luncheon. But I didn't know for sure. Gods help me, Carina, he kept it from me, elsewise I'd have said. I'd planned to talk to him about it earlier, but he was surrounded by his people, and I got distracted by something else."

The last thing she wanted to do was add to her mother's list of things to feel guilty over. "I know that. I'd never think anything else. But it doesn't matter. You couldn't intervene forever. It was bound to happen at some point. None of that changes what is happening right now."

Her mother drew her into a hug, kissing her cheeks. "You are right. This will move at a fast clip. Hartley Alem will not be swayed; he's wanted you since you were but a girl, and your father will need him now more than ever." Esta began to pace.

"Now that he's gone and messed up this whole situation with the Federation you mean?" Carina whispered harshly.

Her mother swallowed hard and nodded. "The skirmishes on the border grow worse by the tide. He draws us into a war that will cost many lives. You have no idea what he's capable of. What he's planning. This is not the place for you anymore. I have something. I know where we might get some help. We should be able to buy your way across." *Across to the Federation.*

Could she do it? Be free of a man she loathed and feared since before she could walk? Be free of a system seemingly obsessed with repressing her citizens with such brutality it stole her breath? Yes.

Carina had given bits and pieces of information to Claira, her maid, for the last several years. Carina had a strong feeling Claira knew Vincenz somehow. They never spoke of it or of what happened to any of the information she passed along. It would mean torture and death for both if they were found out. But since the moment Carina had figured out Claira's leanings and she'd let slip her ability to help out here and there, Carina had felt a small bit of hope every time she'd sent a packet away.

"What is it?" she asked quietly, moving closer to her mother.

"I can't tell what it all is. The data is encrypted beyond anything I can untangle without the proper decoding program. What I could see from documents referring to the main data is that they're plans. He's building something. There are references to a laboratory. He's had those men from his so-called science ministry here. It's dire enough that he's got it in a program more complicated than I've ever seen before."

Carina's respect of her mother only grew, thinking about how long she'd been fighting back in her own way against Ciro Fardelle's tyranny. If her mother was this afraid, whatever it was, was very bad indeed.

"All right then." She'd need to move now, no matter what. This information needed to be given to the right people. "I know who I can get it to if you can't contact your source."

Her mother simply nodded. "I will see what I can do. You contact your person, too, and we'll go with whatever we can get. We cannot fail now; we have to move forward as quickly as possible. The information I have will be enough, no matter who we can get to aid us. I'd planned to get it to them anyway; *it's imperative*. This is meant to be. You must go; they need to know, and this will be the key to getting you there. The gods are watching over you, Carina. You have a destiny far, far greater than being a mere pretty bauble on a tyrant's arm."

Just what was her father doing? Did she even want to know? "Are you sure?"

"Yes."

"All right then, I agree."

"The laundry in the stables at moonrise, I'll bring it there. I've loaded it into a subdermal chip so you can carry it undetected. Even better, they can't get at the data unless you're alive, which gives them great incentive to keep you that way. You'll get it where it needs to go and deliver the message that the price for such a prize is your freedom."

"If he finds out . . ." Carina let the words trail off.

"What else could he do that would be worse than watching him trade you to a monster like Alem? Do not hesitate in this. You cannot. If you do, you will fail, and we will *all* be doomed. He won't stop. He gets worse every day. He has lost all sanity. If we don't stop him, no one will. War is coming. Can't you feel it? Even here, can't you? You. Must. Go."

Her muscles hurt from the strain of forcing herself not to shake, and she built a wall around her feelings. "We have to see how they respond. If they agree, we insist you come, too, make it part of the agreement. If it's dangerous for me, what is it for you? You're in danger as well."

Her mother shook her head slowly. "We both know this information is more than enough. It will pay your way across and then some. Which is what I shall demand. As for me coming along, it can't happen. I will stay here and keep them diverted as long as I can." She paused. "*This is my place*, Carina." She pressed her lips together as Carina's world began to fall apart. "Your path lies out there. You will save us because you are meant to. My path lies elsewhere. Here." She took a deep breath and stood tall. "I'm off. I'll see you at moonrise."

With that, Carina watched her mother leave as her heart tumbled into her belly.

Her legs gave way, and she simply slid to the floor. Could she leave her mother behind? Her innocent baby brother? Her people? In truth, she had much love for her people, not so much the nobles who fawned over her father and executed his every whim, but the everyday people she knew here in the Fardelle compound and all around Caelinus. She'd been to most every 'Verse in the Imperial territories and had met people from all walks of life. Would leaving them mean turning her back? Didn't she have a duty to them? To stay?

Carina had few options. As a female, her status was that of her father's until she married. And then it would be the status of her husband. She had no power outside that. Her father would not protect her once she accepted a marriage contract. Vincenz tried to help, tried to make change, and look what had happened to him. Though she held out hope, she wasn't entirely sure her big brother was alive any-more. Though his name had been erased, what he'd done remained burned in her father's every action. Teams of assassins still hunted Vincenz down. She had to hold on to her belief that he was out there and working hard, at least living a good life. After all, her father still had assassins on his trail. But reality told her he had a good chance of being dead, too.

The scent of her mother's perfume hung in the air, and Carina felt as if everything was slipping through her fingers like smoke.

She wanted to do the right thing. Pushing to her feet, she began to pace the small room. She'd taken the easy way before, each time when she remained silent to avoid causing a stir. She wasn't proud that she hadn't led a revolution, but she didn't have to give up. She was faced with the opportunity to act and do her duty.

Staying and marrying Alem wouldn't help them. Her father seemed set on this insanity of provoking the Federation, and war wasn't just a far-off idea, but each rise of the suns brought it closer. Her people would suffer if she couldn't do something, and it didn't hurt that she'd be far away from her father's plans to join her life with that of a sadist.

The contents of that data, even the little they did know, was ter-rifying. What had her father done? And what of her mother if she got caught?

Her mother raised her to be strong even in the face of challenges. This was the biggest one of her life, and it was up to her to make something of it.

She used the call to summon Claira as she began to pace.

Chapter 3

Carina left her guards outside the door, retreating into her bed-chamber and closing those doors as well. In the pale light she crossed to her wardrobe, pushing it aside so she could stuff herself through the small space behind it. Sucking her belly in, she pressed the depression in the floorboard, exposing a crawl space. Pulling the wardrobe back into place, she turned and moved down the narrow hall until she reached the hidden passageway just beyond.

Here it was blessedly cool, the thickness of the stone around them deflecting the heat. There had been many times she'd come here just to enjoy a few minutes of total privacy. The silence and the solace embraced her, calmed her. Reminded her how rare such things were in her life.

As children, she and Vincenz had used these secret spaces to move about the compound without notice of their parents or the guards. YaYa, their grandmother, had shown them the entrance in Vincenz's rooms. Only later did they find the one in the rear of Carina's bed-chamber.

It was impossible not to think fondly on those nights she and her brother had snuck down to the stables to give fruit to the animals and to play with the children of the staff. Oh, Vincenz, she sighed, missing him, wishing he were there to help make things right. She was really frightened of making a mistake. He'd know what to do.

But he wasn't there. There was no one else to do this but her, and she needed to buck up and do it. The Fardelle women were stronger than most knew. Her mother was taking great risks for Carina that very moment. YaYa had been the bravest person Carina knew. If they could do it, she could. She had to.

It made a depressing sort of sense that the Fardelle women were always looking for a way to escape. YaYa, her paternal grandmother, had given birth to sixteen children and had insisted on raising them all herself. There were no wet nurses or nannies. But her grandfather had removed all his sons from her care when they'd been old enough to begin military training. Later, Esta was sent there as in infant, having been contracted to marry the oldest Fardelle when he reached the age of majority, and YaYa had become Esta's mother, too.

Women didn't always fare well in their world. Her grandmother had disappeared shortly after Vincenz had escaped. One day she'd been there, running the household with her signature efficiency, and the next, she was gone.

Carina had wandered the compound, asking where YaYa had been. No one would meet her eyes. No one would tell her anything, and her father had yelled at her and made her leave the room when she'd asked him. Her mother had counseled her in very strong terms to stop asking, telling her YaYa had gone and wouldn't be back and there was nothing Carina could do about it but stay alive.

That had been the year she realized there was no one to save her. No matter how much her mother loved her, it wasn't in her mother's power to save her, should her father decide Carina needed to disappear, too. Carina needed to remember that. Needed to remember no one was safe.

There was no way she could help anyone if she stayed. If she got this information out, there were those, men who used to be part of her father's inner circle, who had a decent chance of winning in a bid to run the Imperium. It might end up saving her little brother's life.

Scared or not, she had to act.

The passageway continued to slope downward until she finally reached the crawl space in the drying lofts in the stables. Being full dark, the area was deserted, so no one saw her enter and climb down to the floor below.

Her mother wasn't in the tiny laundry room at the rear of the stables when she arrived, so Carina visited the animals, loving the quiet there, the soft sounds of a horse's nicker, or the purr of a barn cat, the soft rumble of the targas after having worked all day plowing the fields or hauling goods from town to the compound.

In those moments she felt remarkably safe and even happy. She could be a person with potential she could define for herself. But it was a fantasy, a dream made of smoke, as it was for most citizens of the forty-seven Imperialist 'Verses. Freedom shouldn't be a stolen few moments in private. It shouldn't be a fantasy.

She thought then about what they'd started out as, and felt the loss keenly.

Caelinus was mainly agricultural. Generations ago, when they'd chosen it to be the Core of the Imperium, the first supreme leader had done so on purpose. Fruit of the earth was the heart of any civilization. Therefore, it would be made the centerpiece of their new world. There would be technology and slick cities, too, but Caelinus, with her harsh environment, was conquered by her people, tamed enough to feed and house them. They were no soft lot like their distant brethren in the Federation.

This notion still appealed to Carina. This *was* the heart of her people. Pity her father didn't seem to remember that.

By the time her mother arrived, agitated and slightly out of breath, Carina felt far more resolved about leaving. They both drew into the shadows of an alcove at the rear of the stables.

"It's done." Retrieving a vial from her pocket, she screwed the lid off and shook out a small, silvery tab. The chip would be applied to her skin, the entry would take her blood into the chamber and lock the retrieval of the data to her key only. And she had to be alive for the chip to be retrieved.

"Here now. Let me get this in. You will have to leave with a moment's notice, so be ready at all times. Pack a bag and leave it in the passageway." A twinge of pain and the slither of the chip as it inserted itself into her skin and then deeper.

"This is the oddest thing I've ever felt," she whispered to her mother.

"It's safe. Your father's men use this technology all the time."

"You know a lot more than I ever thought you did. I'm sorry I underestimated your cunning."

Her mother kissed her cheek with a sad laugh. "We wait now. I will try to hold this courtship off as long as I can. They need to arrive before the nuptials take place. I can't help once Alem takes you to Fortuna. I've communicated to them that this is a matter of some extreme urgency. Nor have I revealed to them, or you, the full extent of the information. Enough to let them understand the gravity of the situation and keep you alive at all costs. The less you know, the better it'll be for you."

Carina took her mother's hands. "Please come with me. He will be murderous when he finds out."

"Let me do this. Please. Carina, I failed you so many times. I can't help in any other way. I *can't* save you from this disastrous marriage. You have no choice. If you do not leave, you will be with him, that monster, that cruel, evil man, and I will have to watch from afar as my status falls and you will be broken until you are either gone or a shadow. I can't protect you in any other way. Let me do this."

"I *will* leave, and I'll let you help me. But you can come with me and do that, too. If this information is as important as you say, they'll take us both, or they won't get it. He'll kill you!" She kept her voice down, but it was impossible to disguise her panic.

"This is my place, Carina. I am his wife. He'll know I helped you if I go. I'll stay and be shocked when you're gone. I've lived a lie for my entire life, I can continue to do so. Once I know you're safe . . . perhaps I can go later. But he watches me so carefully at times, other times he forgets I exist. I cannot know which he will do on which day. It's too risky. I can keep him distracted when you go, keep his eye on me. It's impossible any other way. Once he discovers you gone, he'll send Skorpios to find you. You will have to run, darling. You will have to hide and flee for your life. I'm too old to do that. I can't keep up. There is no other way, and I will not discuss it further. I'm expected in his chambers shortly, so I must go. Keep alert. You'll know when it's time. I love you with all my heart, Carina. You're the best thing I've ever done. Be strong and make a difference; you have a destiny far beyond this place. Live and become the woman you're born to be."

Before Carina could argue further, her mother spun and hurried away, leaving Carina alone in the dark where no one could see her tears.

"*A* blade like this one"—Daniel moved his wrist just so, producing a razor-sharp blade he could kill with in seconds—"can be secreted easily, and the material is invisible to most scans." Another movement of the wrist and the blade flew, buried to the hilt in the neck of the tactical model across the room. "Kill and be gone before anyone is aware there's a problem. You need no ammunition, no time to charge or load the weapon. A blade can be your most effective tool as long as you keep it clean and sharp."

The soldiers in the room, most of them younger than his nephews, watched. Some of them—those he took note of—moved their wrists experimentally, trying out what he'd done. *Those* were the ones he'd want on his team. He had no need of those men and women who waited to be taught. If they wanted to be Phantom, they had to do better than that.

Phantom Corps was small so it was rare to have any openings for new Operatives. But they often worked with the special teams, a good fit for both. So he knew what sort of soldier they looked for.

Wilhelm had insisted some years ago that Daniel teach knife work courses to all new military corps recruits. From that group, he passed on recommendations for those he thought would be good for the special teams. It was a wholly different kind of mental challenge, and he relished the new opportunities he'd been given over the last several standard years as he'd advanced.

He eyed a student standing a few arm's lengths away, nodding his approval of her throwing technique.

"You know you have it right when you do it without thinking. You'll have to get in closer to use a blade, which is a drawback. Still, stealth is an important weapon. Time is the enemy. Detection is the enemy. Get in. Remove target. Get out. There are no questions, there are no hesitations, there is only your mission. Hesitation will get you killed. If you're dead, you've failed your mission."

Some minutes later, as he'd been demonstrating some hand-to-hand knife work, a messenger came in with a summons. A summons he couldn't refuse.

*D*aniel held still for the retinal scan at the doorway to Comandante Ellis's offices. The panel beeped, and the door slid open, revealing two heavily armed men who nodded to him and stepped aside.

There were public receiving offices, but this was the heart of where Wilhelm Ellis *really* worked, where he commanded all of the Federation Military Corps.

The assistant stepped out from behind the soldiers and handed each of them a hard copy file. "Operative Haws, Operative Solace, Comandante Ellis wishes for you to review this information while you wait for him." Must have been important to put on paper; most of the time it was an electronic file. "Go on through. He'll be with you shortly." She indicated their path with a wave of her hand.

They settled in the comfortable (but not too) waiting area, opening the files to read the information. A silent but quite lovely woman brought out cool drinks and some light food before disappearing again. Sipping the fruit juice, Daniel sighed inwardly as he read, pretending to wait patiently. Patience was *not* one of his strongest traits, but he was trained well enough to fake it. Sitting beside him, his friend and fellow operative, Andrei, *did* have patience, though it wasn't necessarily what others would perceive as a virtue. Andrei could wait, utterly still, for hours until an opportunity to take out a target presented itself. And he did it with clarity, calm and what at first glance might seem like little emotion. Some might think Andrei either liked killing or didn't care that he killed.

Daniel knew better, of course. Andrei didn't enjoy it, but he did it well and he did it for a cause he believed in. That seemed to be enough for him, and Daniel agreed.

There were those who did like it. Those who lost the ability to draw the lines they didn't normally cross. Over the years he'd been with Phantom Corps, Daniel had known a few. Some had to be bounced out totally, while others had rotated out for some period of time and came back slowly.

Perspective was difficult to keep sometimes when one was confronted with something horrible. Each experience with it brought a man closer to the darkness lurking within everyone. Maybe it was because he was raised by a person he considered a failure at being a man, but Daniel was especially sensitive to trying to do the right thing, even when it was difficult. *Especially* when it was difficult.

It had been fascinating to end up as a mentor to these younger corpsmen and women. In all his life, he'd never felt as if he had any moral foundation, certainly not enough to pass on to others. He'd been good at tracking and killing, and he'd been satisfied with it. It wasn't until he began to take on more responsibility that he'd begun to discover there was more to himself, more to the corps than what he'd thought.

It had surprised him to discover how good he was at connecting with his people, how proud he was that they sought him out when things began to get to them. To share their burdens and ask for advice.

He was glad of that especially now as he knew the political tensions between the Federated Universes and the Imperium continued to accelerate. Things had been precarious and on the verge of exploding for the last nearly two standard years. The treason trials of those who'd collaborated with the Imperialists to bomb Federation citizens in Federation territories as well as raising money and selling munitions to the enemy had made some things worse, even as the open nature of the process had put many at ease about Family Rule. The frequency with which Daniel found himself moving farther and farther out from the Core and closer and closer to Imperial territory alarmed him. But there was nothing to be done but continue to try to stem the rising tide of war, or at the very least, ensure victory for the Federation should war finally break out.

Until then and as always, he worked to deepen his connection with those he loved and to keep his roots deep in the world where one didn't need to know the angle of a knife to the chest to kill instantly.

Just that morning he'd been laughing and eating breakfast with his mother and brother-in-law Marcus at his sister Nyna's café. Abbie had been well, and they'd all stopped over so his mother could drop off some things for the baby. Things felt normal, calm. He carried that inside him, an anchor to keep himself grounded, a shield against the darkness he knew he carried within.

And now he sat in a room accessed only by a single, guarded entrance very few knew about. Most within the government and military thought they were special assistants to House Lyons and the Office of the Comandante. That ignorance kept them safe, kept their missions safe and made Daniel's life a lot simpler when he interacted with his family and nonmilitary friends. To most he was a contractor, a consultant of sorts to the military.

Everyone had secrets. Daniel's was just bigger than most. Those who suspected, like Abbie, and those who knew were a very small and, fortunately, very honorable group who all pretended to go about their business totally unaware Daniel was an assassin.

Business indeed! He preferred to get back to his classes. The last thing he needed was to have to wait around all day to deal with Ellis. Not that his wishes mattered. Ellis called, and they came because he asked it. Any of them would give their lives for the man who'd saved those same lives at some point when they'd all been younger and in a bind.

Phantom Corps belonged to Ellis. They were his creation and existed under his power. Very few people knew just exactly what they did, and Daniel liked it that way.

Each operator within Phantom Corps had his or her own story about how they'd come to know Wilhelm Ellis, their own complicated feelings about him as well as their feelings about Phantom Corps. Not that any of them spoke about it very often. Their pasts were their own to share or not as they chose. Most didn't want to think about what landed them in that dingy little windowless room where they were all taken after they'd been remanded into the care of the military.

Daniel had been young and scared. His sister had been in the hospital, recovering from an assault that nearly took her life. She had faced reconstructive work, rehabilitation to be mobile again and years of assistance to get past the mental and emotional damage she'd suffered with the broken body.

He sat in lockup, charged with a host of crimes, all of them against Family members. No job, no one to count on and a dark future. But he'd done the right thing. He'd saved Abbie, and that was worth whatever he'd had to face.

Into that room walked a man so tall and imposing, Daniel had to fight the urge to stand and run. Instead, he'd listened as the man had outlined what he thought could be a second chance for Daniel. A chance to prove those who'd accused him wrong. A chance to rise and learn and be a leader and protector.

Daniel had listened, asked a few questions, weighed his scant options and had signed the papers. Ellis had become more than a mentor, and outside his immediate family, the first person to really believe in Daniel.

That had changed his life. Changed his trajectory, and he'd become someone better.

Phantom Corps was his family.

Enough of that. He made the choices that put him in that chair and in the end, he was satisfied with his life.

The information on the pages in his hands filled him with dread. A stillness washed through him as he began to extrapolate outward, applying the facts, adding them to what he already knew.

There was activity at the Edge. People disappearing. Mercenaries had become more rampant and in some cases, more violent. Information leaked through: something was up on the other side, and now, apparently, new information had come to light.

He'd fallen into the information so deeply, the planning and deciphering of many possible approaches, he didn't hear the connecting door open until someone spoke. "Go in now, Mr. Haws, Mr. Solace." Ellis's assistant looked to be approximately three hundred standard years old, but Daniel had no doubt the man could kill with his bare hands.

Ellis waved them to sit as he ended a comm. The man behind the giant desk with the communications console at his back was one of the most important and influential in all the 'Verses. He dwarfed even the furniture he used, but Daniel knew from experience the man could break into a building, acquire information from a sealed, guarded comm room and escape without a single sound. He may have been at least six foot eight standard feet, but Wilhelm Ellis was stealthy and graceful in ways most people never expected, which only made him more formidable. Daniel respected Wilhelm Ellis, looked up to him as he would a father. Gods knew his own father wasn't worthy of admiration or respect. But he'd certainly never make the mistake of underestimating him.

"This is going to take a while. Hold all communications unless they come from Roman Lyons himself." Comandante Wilhelm Ellis didn't look up from his work as he gave the order. It wasn't a lack of respect toward the assistant, but the opposite; Ellis just assumed it would happen and be done correctly. If he didn't, the man wouldn't have been in Ellis's employ.

He typed out a quick note before turning back to Daniel and Andrei, giving them a smile that most would have found disquieting.

"Boys, and how are you?"

"Busy these days, sir. I trust you received our debrief of the last trip to Corazon?" Corazon was a 'Verse on the Edge, teetering dangerously toward Imperial influence. They'd dealt with some local militia, people who had a decent relationship with the mercenaries running the Edge. It would be a very good thing to have them on the side of the Federation. Mercenaries often had information long before anyone else; it was just a matter of getting them to share it.

Ellis indicated the screen to his left. "I received it. Well done as usual. I hear you debriefed Roman on this and your previous mission. He seems to be satisfied with you as a liaison." From Ellis this was high praise. He motioned to the files with a tip of his chin. "Did you review those?"

"Yes, sir."

"We've evaluated it, and I've spoken to Roman." Ellis nodded shortly at Daniel. "I need you to go to Caelinus and pick up a passenger."

Daniel had a feeling it was moving in that direction. Hells, he hated these trips into Imperial territory. It was dangerous and tedious, and he had to risk exposing their people on the other side.

The file indicated the informant would be in possession of a lot of important information about Fardelle's smuggling of weapons and terrorists into Federation territory and other tactical intelligence. But that usually meant a trip to the Edge, not fully into Imperial territory. Did he just say . . . ?

"*Passenger?* We'll be extracting the informant as well?" This was a job far better suited to one of his special teams, wasn't it?

"Yes. The last packet we received is incendiary. We need to move right away to get her out. If she has even half of what our contact indicates, this could tip the balance in our favor considerably."

"Her?"

"Carina Fardelle. Ciro Fardelle's daughter."

Well now. That was interesting. That upped the risk factor immensely. But he understood the choice to send them in for her now. A high-profile target like that would be better off in their hands.

He could get in and out on his own with a minimum of damage, but dragging along some spoiled princess would add a great deal of complication to the process. He made a mental note to bring some of the tranquilizer he'd used on one of his most recent missions. Just a quick administration with a minuscule needle, and the target would be far more malleable within a breath or two. He wondered why she was giving them this information. Wondered who this Carina Fardelle was on the inside. Would she be a spy? A double agent? A whiny, weak mess of a woman he'd have to drag around? What motivated someone like her to do something so drastic?

"The intel she has will be embedded. Only safe release here with proper codes will get the data free. He's gathering materials, gentlemen. Gathering materials for what purpose we don't know, but it involves a lab and possible testing in a public place. That's all I've got for now, but that's more than enough."

Daniel and Andrei got very still but said nothing. Ellis made the choice to have them go in; they'd go. Whatever this information was, it was important enough to risk the trip. Daniel believed that implicitly.

"She's given us intel before. The mother has, too. We can trust them. To a point. Daniel, I want you to head up the mission. You'll be her contact and get her out of Fardelle's compound and back here. We have some very good inside information regarding the schematics of the compound, specifically the living quarters and Fardelle's work spaces via our friend on the Edge. It's been sent to your secured comm. Pick a team to provide support for extraction if necessary. This is of top-level importance. I don't have to tell you this information she possesses can prevent a war. I want you on this as soon as possible. Phantom Level clearance and license to eradicate all impediments to your success. All resources are, as always, at your command."

Daniel stood and gave a small bow; Andrei did the same. Phantom Level meant he could destroy, kill, bribe, kidnap, whatever he had to do. Ellis hadn't needed to say it; Daniel always had that clearance, though the saying reinforced the importance and gravity of the mission and the ability to plan it however he needed to. He liked the freedom but hated the possibilities. He tucked the folders into his case and began to plan an extraction that would either save the Federation or get him and his men killed.

Daniel left, not needing to say more. He'd go over all the details and would consult Ellis as was necessary. They were admonished to be careful and were dismissed. Daniel told Andrei to round up their team and have them meet back at their offices after his last class of the day.

He took a train back to his flat after the class, thinking through the contingencies as he traveled. It would be risky, but with the way things were on the Edge and at the Frontier, sneaking across wouldn't be that difficult. The biggest challenge would be getting her out with the hounds of all seven hells on their tail. It would be dependent on what this Carina was like. She could slow him down and get them caught, or be halfway useful. That sort of uncertainty wasn't anything he liked, but it was quite frequently part of what he did.

By rote, he headed back out, a kit bag on his shoulder. First to work, then to play and shed the part of himself he only could with his family at a name day dinner later that evening.

He'd done this job a long time. It had become his life, and he had no regrets. It gave him a direction. It made him a good man, even when he doubted himself at times. He was on the right side. He was good at it, he made a difference, and at the end of the day, what else did a man have?

A family.

Unlike Roman, Daniel didn't come home to a house filled with the chaos of children and a wife. That's what was missing at the end of every day, and the older he got, the more he realized how much of a difference that connection made in a life.

Chapter 4

$\mathscr{N}$eeding to keep busy and not think about how it'd been a standard week and no one had shown up to get her and the information, Carina had taken to using the passageways more often. Just to be able to wander and do so unobserved.

She could be nervous and jittery and who could see her?

Thinking she'd stop in and visit with the animals in the stables, she headed down that way, pausing at the cleft where she'd need to exit and realizing there were people just on the other side.

She could see them, partially, and moved to pull herself back into the passageway to go in another direction. But a sound stopped her, even as it made her heart pound in her chest. A sound, a muted gasp laden with desire so deep that even Carina, who'd never actually felt that sort of thing, understood what it was.

Her fingers dug into the rock as she pressed herself into the small crevice, keeping out of sight but able to see them better.

A man and a woman, young, barely into adulthood. Standing in the far corner of the loft, the man's back to her as they looked at one another. The woman's hands slid under the hem of his simple workman's jersey. Her face was tipped up, looking at him with raw yearning all over her features. He touched her face, sliding his fingers down her throat, and she made the sound again.

It tore through Carina's belly, tightened her nipples and brought a flush to her face. What would it feel like to want to look at someone like that? To open yourself up to your very core for someone else that way?

It was more than the way he brushed the backs of his fingers over the curve of her breasts as they heaved up and over the low neckline of her blouse. More than the darkened shadow of her nipples and the way a gasp seemed to rip from the woman's lips as her lover moved lower, flicking against them with this thumbs.

His hands would be rough, work hardened.

The woman arched into him as his hand slid into the blouse and freed one of her breasts. Carina's heart threatened to burst through her chest. She'd seen all manner of things as she'd traveled around and kept her eyes open, but never so close and so totally intimate. This couple had a connection so raw and tangible, Carina felt it from her hiding place. Felt the charge between them. It was more intimate than if he'd thrust himself into her from behind right in full view. The man craved touching his woman, and she clearly couldn't get enough, either.

Carina held a hand at her own throat as she watched, not able to move, even to touch herself. Their magic held her still as she watched, envy burning through her belly. He spoke in the woman's ear, and she laughed, low and sort of sultry. Then she grabbed the front of his pants and pulled them open, sliding her hand down into his underpants.

And then *he* made a sound. An answering sound to hers, but his was unmistakably male. Low, nearly a growl, and Carina had to let out the breath she'd held, but it was shaky.

She wanted this. Not with that man of course, but with someone who was hers alone and who looked at her, not with the sick greed Hartley Alem did, but as if she was so beautiful and desirable he couldn't stop himself from staring and wanting to touch her.

He'd already begun to lay the woman down in the loft when a clatter sounded below, and they both sat up, pulling themselves back together. Shouts sounded out, calling names, so Carina supposed someone was looking for the man. Hurriedly, he leaned down to kiss her as she tried not to laugh and reached up to fix his hair.

They left, and Carina continued to stand there for some time afterward, feeling nothing but loss.

Carina barely kept back a shudder of revulsion. She hated the touch of Hartley's hand on her forearm. Or her back, even a shoulder. Constantly on her, wanting to take up all the space in every room until she had no place to hide. It drained her, made her lose hope. What she'd have as his bride was not what she'd witnessed just hours before. This wasn't an acceptable substitute for that. She had no idea how women could stand this sort of thing, not if they knew what those two in the loft had was possible.

Her sorry excuse for a fiancé had taken to arriving every single afternoon, and she'd been ordered to attend to him under the guise of courtly flirting. Her mother had been sure to always be present as was the expectation. It was an older way to deal with courtship, but her father was old-fashioned. Enough that her mother had easily convinced him that it befitted his position to serve as example to his people, to hold up the old ways. Thank the gods he was easily led by his ego at times. It lengthened the process considerably, giving Carina time to find a way out of marrying that monster if they didn't come for her.

Of course, the monster himself was agitated by this wait and the constant supervision. He had continually tried to get Carina alone. Her mother was smarter, and it wasn't as if Hartley could complain to Carina's father that all the supervision kept him from divesting his daughter of her virgin status before the nuptials had been completed.

Status. Ha! She'd have loved to have been able to have the chance to be divested of her virginity long ago.

Since she'd reached sexual maturity she'd been watched closely. Except for those little forays through the secret passageways there'd been no opportunity to even *try* to have sex with anyone but herself. She couldn't bring anyone back there, or she'd risk exposing the only private way to move around undetected.

Even if she *had* found a way to meet someone for a secret assignation, no male worth having sex with would have dared it. Her father had people executed for far less serious offenses than fucking his daughter. The most exciting thing she'd ever shared with a boy was a kiss, and that had been deliciously fleeting.

Still, at that moment she was quite relieved for all that history. Hartley wanted to *breach her womanhood*. She shuddered at the phrase, the one he'd just moments ago uttered in her ear, his disgusting, hot breath on her skin. She may not have been an expert at love play, but she had the feeling those men who'd use the phrase *breach her womanhood* would be terrible sex partners. *This* man seemed to like that she'd been uncomfortable, which only made her want to vomit more.

"We're having a delegation from some of the outer 'Verses this evening. Carina, please do join us so that we may announce your upcoming nuptials." Her father would naturally be pleased by this news. It would give him the opportunity to be worshipped and celebrated.

She, by contrast, was not pleased. This meant she'd have to spend interminable hours with Alem as he pawed at her and made lewd comments about her womanhood to people under his breath.

Hartley gave a hearty laugh as he petted her hand and wrist. "Yes, sweet flower, do so that I may show off the bounty of my future bride to all."

Sweet flower? She managed to smile even as she wanted to sneer. She'd never met anyone who actually spoke like that. There was no way around it, so she nodded. Where was her rescue? It had been a standard week already! If they didn't hurry, she'd have to marry and consummate with this beast, or throw herself out a window to escape it.

What she'd seen earlier that day only made the vision of her future worse. Dread numbed her fingertips. She was twenty-three standard years old. A virgin. Unmarried. Trapped in a house with her mother and her insane father who'd sold her off to a crazy, violent man bent on breaching her *whatever*. It was a waste of time to feel sorry for herself. She couldn't solve anything that way, but right then she veered perilously close to self-pity.

She needed to begin to face the fact that help may not arrive until after the marriage. She'd keep an eye on the door for her rescuers, but she began to try to figure out what to do if they didn't show.

Mortimer Silas entered the Fardelle compound with an entourage and a well-practiced walk. He was a fancy man, and this place was . . . not. Caelinus was provincial for a supposed capital 'Verse. And hot. Gods, it was ridiculously hot, and he could not understand why Fardelle would choose to settle the home 'Verse here in a place with not just one relentless sun, but two. It had slowed their travel down as they could find no one willing to make the journey from the portal to the compound at full day. They'd been stuck in a receiving room until the suns began to set. The heat made his hair less attractive than normal, made him sweat. No one looked handsome covered in sweat.

He had no desire to spend a moment longer than necessary here. He'd pay his respects, gather his due and get out. Get back home and be finished with this trip.

Unfortunately, he had not anticipated the dinner being held in honor of the visiting ministers from other Imperial 'Verses. The last thing he wanted to do after the trial of just getting to Caelinus was to sit around eating horrible food, rubbing elbows with people he'd rather kill than drink with. It was supposed to be a brief meet and greet, bow and scrape thing. He hoped he had the right ensemble for the dinner. He'd beg off and keep to his rooms or find a way to leave early, but it was clearly mandatory, and this was Ciro Fardelle, after all.

He found the reality of Ciro Fardelle far more absurd than he could have imagined. A tyrant was one thing; a stupid tyrant seemingly wedded to dragging them into a war with the Federation for no apparent reason and with no chance of winning was another. He was a fool, and why they all suffered this one for so long wasn't something he understood.

Mortimer was a man who appreciated details, so he kept a close eye on things as they were brought from the guest quarters into the main hall where the family lived and where Fardelle had his offices and receiving chamber. Gleaming black surfaces did please the eye and give a grand feel to the space. If Fardelle didn't have more delusions of power than taste, the place would be far more pleasant. Everything about the compound shouted of trying too hard.

The windows overlooking the secured courtyard were large and tinted to keep the heat out but to let in the light. Plasglass, he surmised. There was fortification on the outer walls and windows facing the town, surrounding dunes and vistas off in the distance toward the portal. Armed guards patrolled in thick formation, on foot, in vehicles and on horseback. Mortimer watched, took in their rather obvious timing, as they all waited for Fardelle to swan around the room like someone who mattered.

Once they'd finally made it through the receiving line of lesser nobles and lackeys to their supreme commander, Mortimer was able to get a clear look at Carina Fardelle. Her mother and Ciro's primary wife, Esta, sat with her at the far dais.

Esta was small in stature and in presence. Once reputed to have been a great beauty, she kept her eyes down most of the time, her hands clasped in her lap as she perched in the space next to her husband. The second wife sat a bit lower, and where Esta had been small, Aila looked defeated. This was not a woman who'd schemed her way into Ciro's bed for the power and position of giving him an heir. This was a girl younger than his daughter who'd been plucked from her home and given to the supreme commander to do with what he wished. Mortimer found that . . . tawdry. Once a man settled, he should stay that way. Women were not chattel; they were precious and deserved to be honored, not demeaned. Fardelle was as poor a man as he was a leader.

They'd been informed that the evening's events were also a celebration of the betrothal of Carina Fardelle and Hartley Alem. Alem was a lump of a man with a heart as dark as any he'd ever known. What would Carina see in such a man? Was she like her mother? Aila? One of countless females across the 'Verses whose lives were simply a matter of following direction from the males in their lives? He looked at her again, contrasted against her mother, and thought not.

Carina was different from every woman in that room. Cool. Regal. Hair as pale as moonlight bound up in some ridiculously complicated hairstyle one of her retinue created for her. She looked soft, but her eyes were hard. Despite his unease about what her motivations were and the kind of person she most likely was, there was no denying her beauty. She was not petite like her mother; instead, she was long and lithe. He imagined she'd walk like music played in her head. And she was set to marry Hartley Alem, who couldn't keep his gaze off his future bride, though, to Mortimer's eyes, she did not share that enthusiasm. Or maybe she did, and that's how she showed it.

He shook his head and squared his shoulders. Whatever the case, her marital status was none of his concern. What she was like, who she was, was not his business. He was not there for that.

His man adjusted his cape as Mortimer discreetly checked to be sure his rings looked just so. The gems needed to catch the light to be their most attractive. He'd waxed down his mustache just before arriving, so he knew that would look most fetching as well. If he had to be bored and tossed in with villains and idiots, at the very least, he could look good doing it.

"Supreme Commander Fardelle, may I present Mortimer Silas, the ministerial representative from Caldara." The sergeant at arms bowed, and Mortimer stood forward, bowing deeply himself. It wasn't quite to his knees—Fardelle didn't deserve it—but it made Mortimer look regal, or so he'd always thought when he looked into the mirrors in his home.

"It is a great pleasure to meet you, Supreme Commander." Mortimer used his best, most oily voice to soothe the man before him.

Hartley Alem stood between them as Fardelle nodded and moved on.

"Of course it is. We all share that great honor. Mortimer, I'm told your delegation was waylaid earlier on the way here by brigands. I trust all is well?"

Yes that. It had worked out quite well in the end. "Just a minor inconvenience with pirates. Pirates in our own territories. I'm sure it's that rabble from the Edge coming here to terrorize us. They won't be terrorizing anyone again, I promise you. My people are all very good with weapons." There hadn't been a single person left alive.

"Good to hear. We need to be vigilant in our self-defense against the vulgarity of the Federation. Your tribute has been received, and we shall continue to endeavor to protect your people." With that canned and emotionless commentary, Alem turned and held a hand out toward the dais. "Please do meet my lovely betrothed, Carina Fardelle."

An average man would have missed the slight narrow-eyed glare of disgust, just a brief, fleeting expression before her smile settled onto her mouth but not her eyes. This was no empty-headed woman. He hadn't expected that.

She moved to them with the grace he'd predicted. Regal. This woman was no fool, but she was a queen. Impossible not to find her breathtaking. He bowed over the hand she'd extended. Smooth, cool, scented of evening flowers. "It is an honor to extend my congratulations to you in person."

Her smile never changed, but he felt the tension in her muscles and again, wondered about the woman inside this facade. "Thank you, Minister Silas. I do hope you'll be able to attend after we announce a date. Hartley still has some work to do. A lady does enjoy being courted." The comments were meant to be coy, but he wondered if that's what she'd intended. Wondered too much. Damn it, he had no call to be wondering anything about her. Mortimer would not care. She was not important here; he had to keep his wits about him, not fantasize about a woman most likely too soft and coddled to ever be of real interest to him.

Alem tittered, and Mortimer, surprised by the violence welling inside himself, swallowed hard and took a sip of his drink.

"Sweet flower, I am yours in all things." Alem looked back to Mortimer. "Are we not all but puppets to dance for our ladies? Are you married, Silas?"

"I am not, though I wait for that woman to fill my life with happiness." Mortimer's smile seemed to soothe Hartley Alem, though Carina didn't appear as charmed.

Carina sent him a last, cool look and stepped back. "If you two will excuse me, I see my mother asking for my attention. A pleasure to meet you, Minister Silas. Enjoy your stay here on Caelinus."

He bowed in response before she was swept away quickly by her mother, leaving that scent in the air and the soft swish of her gown in her wake.

He ate and drank, refused the attentions of a young male who'd been sent his way for entertainment and the young woman who followed. He liked sex as much as the next man, but he didn't like it with prostitutes and he didn't like it with slaves. He had no need to pay or hold someone in bondage to get them to open their thighs. Not that kind of bondage anyway.

He watched and learned. Found weaknesses and tucked them away. By the time he retired, he had a plan in place.

He'd need to move quickly.

*A*fter her escape from the dinner, Carina escorted her mother to her rooms, and they'd shared a cup of tea. Esta would be called to attend to Ciro when he finished with the reception, so they'd stolen those moments to try to decompress and pretend not to be concerned that the Federation hadn't shown up yet. The walk back to her own rooms was quiet. Carina ignored her guards the best she could and went directly inside, locking the door behind her.

Now finally alone, she brushed her hair and readied to sleep. She'd dismissed her attendants as she'd left for the reception, so there was no one else to worry about just then. Which was good since she had plenty to worry over as it was.

The evening had left her unsettled, impatient. Time was running out! Hartley had managed to fondle her breast at one point, squeezing so hard he'd caused her pain. At the sound of distress, he merely smiled and stepped back, licking his lips and nearly sending her meal bolting from her belly. Thinking back, she should have thrown it up all over him. But knowing him, he'd have enjoyed it.

Alone in the pale light, she realized no matter how crafty and brave she thought she might be, this was beyond her, and it could very well be her undoing.

It would do no good to pace anymore. She needed some rest, or she wouldn't be able to keep up the mask with her father. After a quick sleeping draught, she turned out the lamps and climbed into her bed. Sleep came quickly but was fraught with ugly thoughts and dreams of disappearing.

Jolting her from a nightmare, a hand touched her and then pressed against her lips. She came fully awake, thrashing until a voice whispered to her.

"Be still. Terra roses await you."

At the sound of the code words her mother had told her to expect, Carina obeyed.

"Be still a moment until your eyes adjust."

Despite the curt nature of his order, she knew he was right. Slowly, her eyes adjusted to the dim light and she saw who'd spoken.

Sharp green eyes took her in and she nearly recoiled. Him? Mortimer whatever his name was? That silly fop? They wouldn't get five steps down the hall!

When he spoke again, she began to realize her error. "We must move fast. Do you have a bag of any kind?"

This man was not the same. His voice was different. Clipped. Hard. He had none of that softness she'd witnessed earlier that evening. No, the man in her room had perceptive eyes. His movements as he checked the room were predatory. Gone were the outlandishly silly clothes, the gaudy jewels on his fingers. In that man's stead was one wearing dark clothing clinging to a body she was quite sure would be as magnificent without them as inside them.

This man was *not* Mortimer at all, and she realized this man would get her free. Hope surged through her veins.

Her dry mouth searched for words, stumbled and found her voice. "I . . . yes. My mother told me to. It's here."

He looked her up and down and shook his head. "Princess, we cannot run very fast with you in that frilly gown. Do you have pants or boots? Those slippers will be a disaster." The disdain was clear, and she felt anger rising within, hot and mighty.

She wasn't proud that her whispered reply was less than polite. "I was *sleeping*. I don't sleep in pants. It's not as if I knew you'd *finally* arrive today."

His mouth may have curved into a slight smile, but she wasn't sure if it was hope or an illusion. "Whatever you say. Sorry my schedule wasn't fast enough for you. Let's move. Get your ass dressed. We have little time. Do you have the information?" He turned his back as she got up. At least he had *some* manners.

She pushed past where he stood, taking up all the air in the room in a most disconcerting way. "My clothes are inside the passageway. The information is inside me, chipped. You can't get it without me, so don't get any ideas. How did you get in here?"

"The passageway. Clever. Your mother assured us your father and his people do not know of it. I hope for all our sakes she's right. Go on in and change. I'm going to do a few things."

She tried not to flounce off, but she probably did, and that only frustrated her more. Just as she reached the crawl space, he spoke again.

"By the way, princess, if I wanted you dead, you'd be dead. I'm not a villain; I'm your only hope of survival. Don't forget that." He turned his back on her and began to fuss with the bedding.

She stifled her urge to hit him over the head with something and instead, grabbed a photograph, one taken when she and her mother had been on holiday some years before. Once she'd squeezed into the passageway, she dressed quickly, leaving her sleeping gown behind. Carina leaned a note at the base of the wall, knowing her mother would find it eventually.

The pain of that tore through her, sending her reeling as the loss hit her. The reality of what she was doing finally registered. She might never see her mother again.

He came in through the crawl space and stood to his full height.

His gaze went to the note and then back to her face. He took the note and handed it back to her. "Don't. I know it's hard, but you can't look back. If this is found, you will endanger whoever it's for." The words were hard, but he said them almost gently as he took her elbow. "We have to run, princess. Can you do that?"

She nodded, grateful for the spark of anger he'd stoked and also that small thread of compassion in his eyes. "Yes. Physical activity is part of my daily regimen. In the future, don't call me princess, *Mortimer*. My name is Carina." It wasn't very haughty, though she tried.

He grinned, transforming his face, and an unbidden thrill rode her spine, sped her heartbeat. He was so breathtakingly overwhelming.

"All right, Carina. I'm Daniel, and we have to go." He held out a hand, and she took it, changing her life forever.

Daniel. The name fit this man far better than Mortimer.

Chapter 5

They ran. Down the darkened corridor, following it farther and farther until he finally eased her out, shouldering her pack, on the other side of the outer wall. The air outside was still warm, but the still-dark sky would provide plenty of cover. Andrei waited there, as Daniel knew he would. The others he'd had in his entourage had melted back into society. He knew if he had need to call for them again in the future, there'd be fewer. Fardelle's grasp had tightened. Security had become far more difficult to work around. Some of the operatives who helped them would be discovered; it was a basic fact of what they did. A fact he tried not to think about even as he appreciated and respected their choice to do right, no matter the cost.

They could not take horses or any sort of vehicle while in the sight of the compound. Remaining on foot would keep them quieter and less easily sighted by the spotters who would most definitely be called up when she was discovered missing. If their luck held, they'd be off 'Verse by the time her disappearance was discovered.

His cargo began to speak, but he shook his head. Her mouth firmed and her eyes narrowed, but she obeyed. He didn't dare look at her mouth any longer; he'd already been too distracted by it. All his attention needed to be on the mission. On eluding their enemy and getting to the portal. He'd shaken off Mortimer and was fully Daniel again. He needed to keep focus.

His field glasses showed Imperial troops along a nearby road. He pulled out the map and looked it over. There was no way around the path they were on. They'd been stationed on a narrow bridge over a dry gulley, far too steep to climb into and out of, and the nearest crossing beside that one would take them several hours out of the way and make it full day by the time they reached the portal. Their options were limited.

"Stay here. Both of you."

Andrei nodded once and pulled her back into a more secure location.

"Why? Is there a problem I can help with?" She kept her voice down.

"There are troops between us and the portal. I have to take care of that."

Her eyes widened. "But . . ."

"This isn't going to be easy. If you want to live and get the fuck off Caelinus, you need to let me do my job. They will, without a second thought. They're not going to let you pass; you have to know that. They'll kill us and send you back. And then what? If you want that, tell me now before I risk my life or my partner's life."

Hanging her head, she sighed heavily. Part of him felt bad for what she'd be seeing between that moment and the time she got off the transport in Ravena, but it was his job to make sure the latter happened. And his job wasn't pretty.

"They're my people. I'm supposed to protect them."

"No they aren't. They're your father's people. Those men are Skorpios. Do you understand the distinction here?" He took her upper arm, not to harm but to bring the point home. "Giving up now solves nothing. Making hard choices is the mark of a true leader. Be one now. You can't help them here."

"All right."

Trusting Andrei to keep her safe, he moved quickly and quietly to the knot of soldiers. There were only three, and if he could have managed a good diversion, he would have rather than kill. Not because he cared about them particularly. They had their job and he had his. But it made far less of a mess. Bodies were a pain in his ass to deal with.

These were Skorpios, Fardelle's shock troops, and they weren't likely to fall for that anyway.

He planned how to take them all out as quickly as possible as he crept toward them. Once he began to work, he went into his head deeply. Part of him detached, entirely focused on the details of the job. It was like he watched a vid as he managed to take one out with a knife, hitting the other in the temple and grabbing his knife to finish the job and hit the third.

With a signal to Andrei to get moving, he turned back to his work. Using the powder that would burn the bodies to little more than ash, he had cleaned up enough to cover their tracks by the time the other two arrived.

She tried not to make a big deal out of looking around, but he could tell she did it nonetheless. She was freaked out, out of her element and, he had to admit, stronger than he'd thought she'd be.

"Let's move."

Though she was pale, she nodded and kept the pace.

They had three standard hours until the first sun began to rise. This was not a time to walk. He was grateful she'd been telling the truth about being physically active daily, because she kept up as they continued their quick pace. He'd have carried her if necessary, of course, but it would have taken more out of him, and he was pretty sure he'd need every bit of strength and guile to get the hells out of the Imperium alive.

Andrei took up the rear, watching their backs, while Daniel continued to run all the options through his head. It was so automatic, his mind wandered back to her again.

Daniel knew she was on the verge of losing it. He'd probably never forget the devastation on her face when he'd told her to not leave the note back in the passageway. A note to her mother, he'd guess. Most likely it was becoming real for her. The cost of this decision. She was bound to grieve the loss of her mother. Even if she wasn't dead, it wasn't as if they could see each other again any time soon.

And the soldiers. That lay heavy on her, he knew. It should, of course, but he'd been at this a lot longer than she. Her path had been far different than his.

The woman had given up everything to get her daughter and the information out. He would not fail Esta Fardelle or Carina. Or, more important, the Federation.

He'd already discovered Carina Fardelle was a lot more than he'd first imagined, but he wasn't sure if he should be relieved or concerned. Both, he supposed. She wasn't the kind of woman he'd have to tranquilize and carry back because she fainted at the barest whiff of danger.

And damn it all, that intrigued him. Enough to make him wish she had been some silly, weak female, or at the very least, less attractive and capable, so he could stop thinking about her legs, her ass, the way she looked so caught between grief and concentration.

She was so ridiculously, utterly beautiful. A man like Alem would have taken this gift and destroyed it utterly.

He'd been thinking about how arousing the small slice of her bare legs had been when she got out of her gigantic bed earlier, when Andrei put a hand on Daniel's arm to get his attention.

They stopped, taking shelter behind a nearby outcrop of rocks. They'd be at the portal shortly; he could see the approach just off in the distance.

"What is it?" Carina asked softly. She waited for his next instructions, and he thanked the gods for it. If she was at least that malleable, his job was easier. Some of her behaviors led him to believe she was fighting off shock. Should it set in at some point, he wanted to get them safely ensconced in their room on the ship first. It would be normal for her to fall apart—most would—but it had to wait until the time when he could shut a door and keep her safe while she did it.

Andrei cut him a look, reminding him to keep gentle with her, as he handed a small container of water to Carina, who took it, sipping cautiously. The look, and truth be told, his conscience reminded him he'd been a cad for not thinking that she'd need a bit of a breather and something to drink.

"How are you feeling?" Daniel asked, pulling some dried fruit from his pocket and passing it her way. "That should help with energy."

She took it, eating calmly. "I'm feeling quite glad I am not a corpulent, lazy layabout like Hartley Alem."

She surprised him, this princess who could run like an athlete, with a sense of humor, too. He laughed quietly. "Me, too. We'd have never squeezed him into that passage. Let's stay for a little while longer, and then we need to keep going. We should be at the portal within the hour. We have a berth on several vessels. We'll decide which one to take when we arrive." He didn't want to probe on her emotional state. That had to lie untouched until it was safer to deal with. Preferably with someone who wasn't Daniel.

"All right."

Going over timelines, he looked back to her again. "When do you normally rise?" Once he'd allowed himself a look at her, he couldn't tear his gaze away from her mouth and the delicate way she chewed.

"Second sunrise. Claira is the one who comes in to wake me. She can be trusted."

"She can't hide it forever, and she's been instructed not to. The last thing we want is for her to be implicated in this. Still, we've got time then." He dug in his pack again. "Take these pills." He handed them over. "They'll darken your skin a bit. That one there," he indicated as she swallowed the pills, "will change your hair, just for a cycle or two."

She swallowed both quickly, looking wary but not hesitating.

"Thank you. For this." Her voice shook, but then evened out.

"No need to thank me. It's our job. Just follow our lead."

He stood and noted her skin was already beginning to darken. By the time they reached the spot where she'd need to change her clothing, she'd have made the transformation.

"Ready?" He held out a hand and she took it, allowing him to help her to her feet. "You're doing a good job, princess."

"Stop calling me that!"

He grinned and she locked her jaw and rolled her eyes. Good. Anger was better than fear, easier to manage and control.

"You're an idiot," she muttered, bringing a startled laugh from Andrei.

"No argument there."

And they ran again.

She must have hit her head in the passageway. There was no other explanation for why she couldn't seem to stop thinking about the strength in his hand as he'd helped her up, the way his voice had softened as he'd told her she was doing a good job.

Ridiculous to be excited by such a rude man. Though, she thought as they ran, he was so very masculine and imposing. Nothing like anyone she'd ever met before. The other man was handsome, too, mysterious and quiet, but she couldn't stop looking at Daniel. He was just, so . . . something. Big. Bold. Strong. Fearless. She admired it, was attracted to it even as it puzzled her and made her breathless.

Her muscles began to burn and ache. She killed the time and tried to ignore the fear and encroaching exhaustion by thinking of other things. But those other things were either about losing her entire life, those dead soldiers or about Daniel.

At least thinking about Daniel warmed her, made her nipples harden against the material of her blouse. She didn't need to change her fantasies, or even feel guilty about it.

Whatever he was, whoever he was, he'd unleashed something inside her, sent it rushing through her veins. At least she could blame any breathlessness or flushed skin on the running. If she lived long enough to stop, that was. Good gods, she'd not done this much physically intense activity in many years.

The first arches around the portal city meant they needed to slow down. Excitement and fear woke her up again once she'd caught her breath. She hoped she looked nonchalant as she ate up the details of what she saw all around her.

The portal city was always awake, always working. It was one of her favorite places on Caelinus, and she took every chance she got to come out and greet visitors or see off guests. It was totally different from the compound. Vibrant. Everything smelled and sounded spicy.

People milled around, but not in as great a number as they did once the suns had risen until midday. As such, the three people headed toward the departure decks weren't given more than a second glance. They were just like everyone else, leaving, arriving, doing business.

They passed an open-air fried dough booth and her smile faded as she wondered if they had anything like it on the other side. She'd miss the smell of home, miss the people, miss how they spoke, their accents, the way they looked on festival days. She would have to leave it all behind. The ache of it made it hard to get a deep breath as she struggled to hold it together.

The portal was just ahead, and Daniel stopped, steering them into a space between two outbuildings. A nearby door squeaked when Daniel unlocked it, nearly sending her out of her skin.

Andrei touched her arm briefly, calming her, ushering her inside after Daniel. The room beyond looked relatively unused. Dust covered the stacks of boxes against a far wall. There were no windows and no other doors but the one they'd just used.

Daniel strode over, handing her a bundle. "Traveling clothes and some papers. It's pretty simple: You're my sister Rina. We're on our way to Monteh to attend the harvest festival and to meet your intended. I figured it was close enough to your real name you could remember easily enough."

She'd been simmering with anger that he seemed to consider her an utter idiot, but then he turned his back and began to strip. Though she knew it was rude, there was simply no way she could stop herself from staring at the wide expanse of his shoulders tapering down to a narrow waist. Oh, gods, this was so ridiculous, but it pushed all her buttons! He stepped from his pants, and his rear was the finest she'd ever seen. Not that she'd seen a lot of bare asses in her lifetime, not on adult men anyway. But the few she'd espied over her life had given her a fair enough spectrum, and his was right at the top.

Her gaze glued to his body, her hands fumbled, but she managed to change into the simple gown he'd provided. It fit fine, and the fabric had been softened by age. Her skin had darkened, and from what she could see, her hair was now the same shade as her eyes. No one would expect to see her in the first place, but now she felt even better about their ability to remain undetected.

His muscles flexed and bunched as he moved. As he slid weapon after weapon onto his body. He was so taut and dangerous. Beautifully lethal and it stole her ability to think. His clothes fit his body well and even though she'd watched him strapping on all that gear, she couldn't tell by looking at him.

"I never thought to carry a weapon there," she said, and then he looked up. Their gazes locked, and she felt it all the way to her toes. *This* was how she wanted to look at a man. There was something there between them. It wasn't the same sort of depth of want she'd witnessed in the loft, but it was not the calculating greed she'd seen on Hartley's face either.

It had been less than a day, not even half a day since he'd been some fop bowing and scraping to her father. It seemed as if weeks had passed, as if worlds had slid between her and the woman she'd been before the first moonrise. Instead of Mortimer, or even the man who'd introduced himself as Daniel in her bedchamber, he was something else again. Capable. Aggressive. Hard. This Daniel was posing as a boot maker, he'd told her. Ha!

She'd had boots made for her over her lifetime, and none of the men who'd crafted them ever looked like Daniel. She might have worn boots more if they had.

"Ready?" Daniel, broke his gaze away from her face as he looked her up and down. He made a sound and stepped into her space, fussing with her hair. She tried to pull back, but he held on, yanking just a bit harder than he needed to, and she slapped at his hands.

"I don't appreciate being manhandled."

"Too bad. Look, you're sheltered obviously, but common people don't have that sort of hair, not the way you have it styled. What woman who had to work all day long would have the time to do something so ornate?" He took down the updo she'd created and began to braid it in the back.

It felt . . . intimate to have his hands in her hair that way. Even as she wanted to be angry at him for handling her as if she were a doll or a thing, he was gentle once she held still. She didn't get touched very often. Other than her mother and YaYa, no one hugged her tight or touched her with absent affection.

She slammed the door on that. If she went that way, she'd only end up more upset.

"There." He stood back, and she patted his work, finding it more than satisfactory.

"Do you braid your wife's hair?" Well, that was very obvious. She fought a blush and thanked the low light of the room.

He took a few more steps away and the distance yawned between them and then she felt like a fool, wondering if he'd misinterpreted what she'd said. Or interpreted it correctly.

"No. My sister has very long hair though, like yours only dark as obsidian." He shouldered his gear and motioned to hers. "Grab your pack. I can't carry it for you."

"I don't expect you to!" That bag held what little she could safely take with her. She'd hold it and keep it safe herself.

He rolled his eyes. "Stop being so offended all the time. You're a workingwoman; you'd be expected to carry your personal pack. If it were heavy, I'd take it for you. But you have to remember your role here."

It was right at that very moment when she promised herself that she would never again live a lie or use masks with people unless it was absolutely necessary. She had a big job ahead of her, and she'd be alone. She owed it to herself to be a real person, the Carina Fardelle she was when she was alone in the passageways.

"In the first place, do you have another complaint to make? I'm bored with this one now." She glared. "I'm not offended! You keep going out of your way to think I'm someone I'm not. It's vexing. It's like you want me to be offended. If I mess up, then do correct me, but you have no right to prejudge me. You don't know me enough to think me spoiled and lazy."

"Deal with it." He turned and fussed with something in his pack, so she was content to make a face at his back.

She tested the weight of her bag; it wasn't too bad. *Offended!* The only thing she was offended by was his assumption that she was offended in the first place. She hated that he thought she was a spoiled princess. Yes, she had grown up with things many others didn't have, but she wasn't so sheltered she didn't know how to carry her own bags.

"Carina." He kept his back to her.

"Yes?" she asked with mocking sweetness.

He may have snorted; she wasn't sure. "You're right. I apologize."

Ugh! He was so infuriatingly unexpected. Before she could reply, Andrei came back into the room, and the moment had ended.

This time he faced her. "We're going now. Follow my lead and remember, you're not Carina, you're Rina, and you're my sister. I'm hoping they don't find you missing for a while yet. At least until after we get checked in. But if they do, if we encounter anything danger-ous, you have to trust me and follow my lead. Have your papers within easy reach; you'll need to show them multiple times."

She clenched her fists so her nails dug into her palms, just need-ing that sharp edge of pain to keep it together. Carina needed to re-member that it was still some time until she'd be expected. There was no reason to go searching for trouble. They had enough already.

"Fine. I'm not stupid, you know. I'm educated and capable. And"—she arched a brow at him, reminding him she was more than some half-witted twit who couldn't find her way from a wet bag— "I've been to other 'Verses many times throughout my life. I've been on transports before. I'm also a qualified pilot."

He stopped so close to her she felt the heat from his skin. So close she could scent him. That male whatever he seemed to exude—and it made her heart beat faster, her breath catch and all sorts of wonder-ful things happened to her nipples and her clit. She might have been embarrassed by that even just days before, but right then, she reveled in it.

He leaned his head down, just inches from touching her. She could almost feel his lips against her temple. How could his nearness make her so befuddled? It was as if the closer she stood to him, the more fluff-headed she felt.

"I don't believe you're stupid. I do believe I know more about this sort of thing than you do. In fact, let's get this clear right now. You will give me your complete obedience in all things. Once this is over and you're safely on the other side, you can do whatever you want. But until then, our lives are on the line, and all my concentration will be necessary to get us out of here. If you can't do that, tell me now."

She had a few things to tell him all right. "You're such an ass."

He grinned, and it infuriated her. Both that he was so arrogant and pushy and that her body seemed to find those things attractive.

"I've been told this a time or two. I may not have the best manners of any man you'll meet. Then again, I'm not a torturer either. In any case, I'm the best hope you have of escaping, so let's just get to the point where you agree, and we can get going."

With a barely restrained growl, she clamped her lips and nodded. "Fine."

"Then let's move."

And they went from the quiet little room out into the city again, surrounded by noise and people. Andrei touched his forehead with a slight bow and then turned to Daniel.

"Travel safe, friend."

Before she could say another word, Andrei had melted into the crowd and she lost sight of him. She swallowed hard at the unexpected swell of emotion at the loss of someone she'd only known for a short time.

Daniel squeezed her hand a moment and tipped his chin toward the departure decks, and she took the big, scary step into her future.

Chapter 6

The chaos of the departure decks had provided plenty of cover as Daniel split off from Andrei to guide Carina to their transport. Andrei would head to the other side of the deck to meet up with a female operative, to spread their trail a little wider. As they moved through the outer edge toward where the transports were docked, Daniel noted the level of soldiers and security in the area.

Just in the last short while the activity levels all around them had increased so that there were three times as many people out than there'd been before. Carina had told him it would be busy in the two hours before the suns rose as the commerce hours started before first sunrise and closed during the zenith of the heat. Normally Daniel hated crowds because it was far more difficult to see and react to all the variables of an operation. However, just then he appreciated the extra strain on attention of those soldiers. Distracted and busy personnel at the checkpoints raised their chances of getting on board and off 'Verse without any trouble.

Their identification and destination paperwork seemed to hold up as they moved closer and closer to where the midsize transport they had booked into loomed ahead. In the time it had taken them to get through the last six checkpoints, the light was beginning to edge the darkness at the horizon.

"What's your purpose and destination?" The harried clerk at the base of the stairs up to the passenger decks held their paperwork in her hands.

"Monteh. The harvest festival. I'm a boot maker. Lots of flush farmers who need new boots." He flirted with her, and her annoyance softened. "This is my sister, Rina. I'm escorting her to meet her intended and his family."

A soldier approached and pushed the clerk aside. He grabbed the paperwork and grunted as he looked it over. Carina stiffened, and Daniel willed her to hold herself together and keep to her cover. This same soldier had been moving through the crowd, bullying and harassing people since they'd arrived. Best to keep your head down and not let his type rattle you.

"Doesn't look like your sister," the soldier said, looking at her a little too closely for Daniel's liking.

Daniel moved his body, keeping between the man and Carina. He didn't answer, it wasn't a question anyway.

"What'd you say you were doing on Fortuna?"

"Monteh. We're going to Monteh. For work and for my sister to meet her intended." Daniel wished he didn't have to play meek, wished he could plant his fist in this fool's face to stop him from pawing Carina with his gaze.

She was nervous enough without this idiot using his power to abuse her for no other reason than because he could.

Bored that he was unable to get a rise out of Daniel, the soldier tossed the papers at the clerk. "Mind your manners, farmer."

The clerk stamped the paperwork and thrust it back to Daniel with an annoyed glance back over her shoulder at the retreating soldier.

"Safe travels and good tidings on your upcoming nuptials."

Carina choked out a thanks as Daniel steered her up the steps to the entrance to the passenger berths.

She'd held up well, but the strain was beginning to show on her features. Funny thing was, it made her look far more like a regular citizen of the Imperium than she did before. Most of the people he encountered had tired eyes and an air of sadness around them.

"Here we are." He slid the key card through the slot next to their door, and it blinked green. It wasn't a large room, but it would serve their purpose. He hoped.

"Why don't you rest? It'll be some time before we arrive, and you need to sleep."

With wide, startled eyes, she looked up at him from where she'd curled up on the small bed. They shimmered with unshed tears, and her mouth had that wobble Abbie's did when she tried not to cry. Carina looked about one more upset away from weeping, but she held up. He had to give it to her, she held up.

"I don't know that I can sleep right now. I feel tired, but my mind is racing."

Something tugged deep in his belly. He knew she must have been devastated, but he was not her nursemaid. He didn't know how to be, and he wasn't sure if it would send her rocketing over the edge she was already perilously balanced on.

Usually he came in, grabbed the information or took out the target and got out. He rarely worked with people other than contacts or operatives. This was different. *She* was different. He felt for her, admired her even though he kept telling himself to stop thinking about her at all. She shook him, and he could not afford to feel sorry for her.

She was the enemy until proven otherwise, though he trusted his gut, and his gut told him she was not going to play him false. He wasn't going to take any chances until he knew more.

He bustled around, trying not to look at her again. Talking to her to pass the time and, he told himself, to keep her calm. She made a small sound, and he turned, unable to ignore her any further.

He looked. And found himself ensnared.

She was so small there, lost. Every part of him wanted to go to her, gather her up and make everything all right. Since that was utterly out of the question, not to mention totally unprofessional, he found himself trying to make her smile. "If you won't sleep, at least you can eat. Once we get started, I'll get us some food and something to drink. Are you all right until then? I have some dried fruit in my pack if you need something."

She blinked. A combination of surprise to be roused from whatever she'd been thinking of and also to clear the tears she'd tried to hide from him. He was torn between handing her a kerchief and pretending not to see it. He was transported back to seventeen standard years old, the first time he'd seen Mariella, the first girl who'd truly stolen his breath.

But he wasn't that boy, and Carina Fardelle wasn't some innocent merchant's daughter either. Though reminding himself of this point wasn't enough to make him look away from her.

She sat up, tucking her feet beneath her, and it made her look small, something she wasn't. Fragile even. "I can wait. Thank you. For everything. I know you're risking your life for me."

The tug in his belly told him they'd begun the first leg of the trip, passing through the first portal to the next 'Verse. Thank the gods he had something else to do now.

"Comes with the territory. It's my job. And if you have what you're supposed to have, you're risking your life, too."

She swallowed hard and nodded. "All you have is my word that I do. But we've helped you before, so that has to be enough."

"Fair enough. We can talk more about it later. Are you tired?" Gods, what was he doing repeating himself like a half-wit? She was *his job*! Why was he petting her and asking after her this way?

She exhaled softly, squaring her shoulders. "I don't know what I am."

"I have something to help you sleep, if you like." He told himself he offered because if she slept deeply she'd be easier to control and keep track of as he sat across from her on his bunk.

All that went out of his head when he took in how miserable she looked. "I know this is hard. Leaving your mother behind. But she did this for you. She's making a sacrifice not only for you but for everyone across the Known Universes. It doesn't make it easier, I'm sure. But not all parents are as caring as your mother. She's doing the right thing, as are you. It's very brave."

She nodded, blinking quickly to keep the tears back, and he found himself wanting to touch her, to reassure her. Instead, he pushed to his feet and busied himself setting up a few internal alarms in the small room. He needed to work, even just busywork, to keep from his imaginings about her.

With his back to her, he made sure he had his alarm keys and that all his weapons were in place before turning to face her again. "I'll be back shortly with something to eat, and then you need to rest. Don't leave the room. Don't answer the door. If anyone tries to force inside, pull this here." He pointed to a small string near the doorway. "It's an alarm, and I'll come running. Understand?"

Pale, she appeared to have reined in her upset, but it edged all around her.

"I understand."

"Do you know how to use any weapons at all?"

Her fear morphed into annoyance, and he relaxed. Maybe if he kept her annoyed, he could avoid tears.

"Of course I do. You know what I am, who I am. I've been trained extensively since I was very young. Knives and blasters. I've got some hand-to-hand experience. If I'm attacked here in this space, a blaster would be useless. Have an extra blade?" She cocked her head in his direction.

Quickly, he pulled a blade from his ankle and handed it to her, still in the sheath. "Here. Don't cut yourself."

He left before he found himself wiping the tears off her face or singing her a lullaby. He didn't stop his smile at her annoyed huff.

She ate the modest meal he brought back and tried not to think beyond that moment. Everything felt wrong, like she was in clothing that didn't fit. She looked down and realized that was partially true.

Daniel sat on the bunk across from hers and ate efficiently, like it was an assignment, too. She wondered if he ever let go. His go-to personality so far had been an efficient annoyance. And while that was comforting to a certain extent, did he just turn everything else off when he worked? Was he always this way? Did he get mad? Did he laugh? What was he like when he wasn't on a job?

Once he finished shoveling all that food into his mouth, he wiped his lips and took a deep breath. "I'm going to get some rest. I sleep lightly enough, so please don't worry about your safety." He told her this as he moved his cot to block the door. "They'll have to go through me to get to you. That won't happen."

He reached into a pocket and handed her a pill. "To help you sleep. Let go and let me do the worrying."

Consternation rippled through her. Why did he have to be so nice just when she'd worked up all that annoyance at him for being so aloof? At least it kept the tears away, and maybe he planned it that way.

She took it from his palm and swallowed before she could over-think it. She needed to trust him, and he was right; rest would be integral if she meant to keep her wits about her.

He turned and stripped out of his shirt, boots and pants. Well, now she hoped the pill didn't work too fast, because this would be too good to miss. Until he stopped at his undershirt and long underwear.

Was he really going to just stop at that? Stingy. Probably just to spite her. She might have felt a little better if she caught sight of the beauty of his body. Not that she'd been thinking of the glimpse she'd received earlier that day. Constantly.

With a stifled laugh, she finished her meal, though it tasted like nothing. She shoved the energy into her body and carefully put the wrappings into the refuse chute.

He burrowed under a blanket and turned his back to her, facing the door. She'd seen how he tucked a weapon next to the cot and still wore a knife or two. Her fear lessened enough that she didn't feel like clenching her fists every moment.

"You should sleep, Rina," he murmured, using her fake name. "You'll need the energy, and we have a long way to go yet."

She sat heavily, managing to toe her boots off and slide beneath the blankets. She left her clothes on for warmth and a sense of control. The pill began to work, edging away her angst and bringing weight to her limbs. She let go, trusting him to stand between her and any threat that came at her.

Just knowing that warmed her and let her accept the sleep she needed so much.

Chapter 7

$\mathcal{D}$aniel came awake as the static on the frequency he'd been monitoring cut out and terse orders began to filter through. He got dressed quickly and moved the cot closer to hers. He set more alarms and eased himself out into the hall, listening carefully. He hated to leave her, but she was resting, and it was safer to go alone.

The transport's hum had lessened, and Daniel knew they'd entered the outermost edge of the portal, preparing to arrive in the destination 'Verse. At the end of their hallway, he slipped into a communications room, the kind used by traveling businesspeople to keep up with comms from home without the high cost of a personal comm capable of cross-'Verse transmissions.

Though Daniel had such a personal comm, he needed to access the transport's communications system to tap into the locked channels. He could do so at this node. A quick jamming of the door panel and some magic with one of his electronic toys, and he was in. The orders on the less secured channel were exactly what he thought, a minor shadow of what the secure channel held. Carina's absence had been reported, and every ship stopping at every portal was to be boarded.

Accessing the evacuation routes noted in a ship's map, Daniel managed to plot out three ways to get off the transport should they run into trouble. And hoped for the best. He'd figured a higher troop presence into his original plans. He'd expect Fardelle to send troops out to search transports and most likely a total sweep of all buildings in Caelinus. The time they had before they'd discovered her missing gave him an edge, got them farther out. The area Fardelle would have to search would be so great it wouldn't be possible, especially early on, to thoroughly search every transport. It didn't solve all their problems, but it gave them more room to avoid detection. He needed to explain to her that it would be far more dangerous from that moment on.

He arranged for several contingencies via coded message to his team, undid his work and quickly returned to their berth.

For the second time in as many days, Carina found herself awakened by Daniel standing above her, his fingers against her lips. Once she relaxed, he leaned down to whisper in her ear.

"We're nearly finished with the arrival process. Within a short time, they'll make the announcement that we've arrived in Philos. We'll be exiting here. Imperium troops are waiting at the decks to enter the other end of the ship."

The transport's captain announced their arrival as fear flushed through her system, leaving her woozy. She willed herself to get up, and she did it, scrambling to get into her boots.

He already held her pack, which she took without a word.

"Do you still have the weapon?"

A quick check in her bag confirmed that she did, so she nodded.

He took her hand and squeezed it, the harsh mask he wore softened. "Focus on details. On the small mechanics of the larger things you do. Break it down, and don't give yourself any reason to think about anything but what you need to. That's how I hold it together sometimes."

It surprised her, but she grasped on to his advice like a shield.

Letting go of her hand, he turned toward the door. "I need you absolutely calm. Keep the weapon with you at all times, but don't use it unless I order it so or I'm not there to give that order and it's live-or-die time. They have no reason to believe they're looking for you and me; let's not give them one."

Calm? She wouldn't be. None of the people on this vessel would be if troops had boarded. That's not how it worked in the Imperium. People feared authority.

She shook her head and pretended her knees weren't weak. "Everyone out there will be jittery. If we act calm, we will make a target of ourselves. Troops being here would mean people would be taken away."

He paused. "That's an excellent point. You're absolutely correct. You're afraid, and that's normal for Rina. Be calm inside as you wear your fear appropriately, yes?"

Warmed by that small praise, she buttoned her cape but left the hood down until they got outside.

"Shall we go then, Sister?" he asked, opening their cabin door and stepping into the hall.

She followed, and he stuck to her carefully as they made their way through the knot of people moving toward the exits. The troops were behind them somewhere; she felt that as he hurried her out. She sent up silent prayers that they'd escape without anyone on the vessel being involved or getting hurt.

Even the slightly acrid air of Philos filled her with joy as they stepped onto the platform. She followed him, trusting he'd know what to do. Hoping he did.

The muddy streets were filled with police and military. Her fear didn't have to be feigned. He stuck to side streets and alleys, she was sure to avoid detection. The noise from soldiers entering buildings and of doors being pounded on began to well all around them.

"Hold there."

Daniel froze, bringing them both to a stop. A soldier stepped fully into their path from where he'd exited a building just ahead.

"Where are your papers?" The soldier looked them both over carefully. Carina hoped he'd have some sort of explanation as to why they'd exited the transport three 'Verses early.

"Here." Daniel pulled them from his bag. He took a few steps to the side, bringing the soldier with them.

"What is your business here? Where did you come from?"

"We boarded the transport two days ago in Birrden. We're stopping here to meet my sister's intended and his family. I have business with a number of shops here. I make boots."

Carina digested those details, along with the scorpion insignia on the soldier's lapel. Her stomach cramped.

"This code is more than four standard months old."

"I booked our transport when the bride price was accepted at the end of last year. It was part of the nuptial contract." Daniel seemed to have a good grasp on the basics of how things worked in the Imperium, thank goodness.

"You both need to accompany me to the portal security complex."

"Sir, we're already late. Can we not handle any problems with our code at another time? There is a security station just a short way from the guesthouse where we are staying. I can handle this before evening, once I get my sister settled." Daniel kept his eyes down.

"You'll do what I tell you, when I tell you. Until I can verify your story, you're both going to wait in lockup."

"I'm sorry to hear that." Daniel stepped forward, and before Carina had even registered what was happening, he had dragged the soldier into the narrow space between the buildings. Carina hurried after them, looking around in what she hoped was a surreptitious manner.

She heard the sickening crunch of the soldier's neck breaking. The body slumped to the ground.

"Keep watch," Daniel murmured to her as he dragged the body back behind a trash recycler.

What the seven hells she'd do if anyone actually discovered them, she didn't know. But she held on to her bag, her fingers touching the edge of the blaster, just in case.

"Let's go. It won't be long before they discover him missing." Daniel took her arm and hustled her away at just shy of a run.

She wanted to panic but concentrated on each step they took. Kept her gaze on the street and walkway, taking in details. She needed to keep herself together and help him get them out of danger. Anything else was unacceptable.

Finally, he relaxed his spine a bit, waving to a group of men standing near a conveyance just across a small square.

"Well met, Neil. I see you have Rina with you, good, good. Come along, there are brigands about. The soldiers are on the hunt, and I wouldn't want to be one of them once the troops catch up with them." The large male laughed, but it didn't reach his eyes.

She hopped up and into the cab, followed by Daniel, and they sped off.

Daniel handed them a packet of papers, and the shorter of the males handed him another. "Updated with better codes."

Daniel made no comment as he looked through them and she over his shoulder. She was to have a new name and they were married, not siblings, residents of Philos, water runners.

Each time they had to stop at a checkpoint and hand over their papers, she thought for sure they'd stop them and toss the whole lot of them into lockup. To her relief, no one questioned their papers overly much. Soon they were away from the portal and deep into the canyons where the locals worked to make building materials from the mineral-rich mud.

She started to speak once, but he sent her a look that quelled the urge. If he didn't want her to say anything, he had his reasons. No one spoke either, after the last checkpoint. Until the sun was fully up and they'd reached a wide canyon.

Once the conveyance had gone, there was no sound other than their breath and the soft shuss of sand and dirt shifting.

He perused a sheet of paper and then crumpled it up until it dissolved and there was nothing left. "Come on through here." Daniel indicated a cleft in the cliff just ahead.

They hiked for long enough that even Daniel felt it in his thighs. But finally, as the pale sun stood straight above them, he led her into a small space, barely large enough to crawl through. He hoped to the gods that she wasn't claustrophobic as they wended their way through stiflingly small, nearly airless passages, sometimes on their belly or hands and knees. For long minutes, with dirt caked in the sweat on their skin, they crept toward their destination.

"Are you all right?" he asked softly.

"Of course. I do this sort of thing every day." She snorted in-delicately. "This is horrible, and I want to harm you severely for putting me in this position," she panted from her place just behind him. Luckily he heard the humor in her tone, liked her a bit more for it.

"I'm the only one who knows the way. Don't kill me just yet," he said back to her as they kept moving.

At long last they were able to slide through what looked to be a natural gap in the wall, but what was revealed just beyond was un-expected.

Living quarters. Not overly large, but lit by glow globes. It had a kitchen, a rough-hewn table and a sleeping area.

"I . . . is this someone's home?" She turned in a circle once he'd put the pack down and slid a panel forward, and the gap was now gone, replaced by solid rock.

"Hope you're not claustrophobic."

She shuddered. "This is far more tolerable than that tiny crawl space we just went through. I'm afraid I have dirt in every part of my body. What is this place?"

"It's a smuggler's den." He shrugged. "They hide here when things get hot. Make yourself comfortable; we have to lie low for a while. We can't get off 'Verse until the soldiers go away." He looked at a pocket comm. "My contact says the 'Verse is crawling with Skorpios. Not that we needed that information; the one I killed was one. That will cause some trouble, I imagine. I tried to make it look like a robbery."

Skorpios were her father's private militia. They were his secret police. His right hand of death. When something very bad happened, Skorpios were there. She shivered a moment. There was no going back, and they wouldn't stop until she was captured or dead.

He must have seen her fear, because he touched her cheek and then drew his hand away quickly. "I know. But I'm better than they are, Carina. Do you believe that?"

She didn't know why she should, but she nodded because she did. "They know I'm with you. Or with the Federation. They won't stop until I'm dead."

"Or I kill them first. That's my preferred outcome. We're getting out of here, Carina. Not today. But we will get back to Ravena. I promise you, I will get you away safely, or I will die trying. I'm sorry you had to see that back there; I am. But you can't go back now."

"There's nothing for you to apologize for. We would have been captured and discovered. You would have been tortured and killed, and I would have been sent back home. I believe you. I trust you." Still, Carina worried for her mother. Wondered if they knew it had been her who'd helped her escape. "My mother? Any word about who found me out?"

"I don't have that much detail about anything inside the compound. We managed to get several cycles away before they discovered you gone. And then they sent shock troops. To have them out this far so fast means they must have burned out a good number of private portals to get here. If they're burned out, he can't use them again. Slows him down."

"*Burned out?*" Her stomach sank more. "What do you mean?"

He bustled about the room, starting the heating element in the hearth and swinging the kettle over it to get it boiling. Efficiently, he set his little traps, looking into every closet and behind every drawer. Finally, he stopped, poured the water into a teapot and set it between them on the table.

She didn't quite know what to do, felt like a stupid child, but pride shouldn't stop her from learning.

Daniel looked up and pointed at a chair he'd pushed out for her. "Sit, please. You don't know anything about what goes on, do you?"

His voice wasn't mocking or hard but filled with wonder and sadness. She felt it herself. The world was so much bigger than she'd ever imagined, and it broke part of her to realize her very imagination had been stunted by what her father had done.

She shook her head. "I thought I did. I'm at a loss."

"It's okay. I'll teach you. Others will teach you." He touched the back of her hand so briefly she wondered if she'd imagined it. "Portals take energy from the 'Verse and the friction from where each 'Verse meets. The portal is a controlled tear in space-time, fired as the vessels travel through, by that energy. Ingress and egress through portals is regulated very strictly for that reason. There are smaller portals, private ones like your father's, like the ones the mercenaries use. Those are centered on weaker spots, ones that are stable but can only handle a fraction of the traffic with far shorter trips. If those portals are used too much, or if boosters are used to enhance the speed of the transports, they burn the portal in their wake. It reabsorbs into the 'Verse but causes intermittent to severe trouble with the land around where the portal once stood."

"And my father has done this before?"

"Yes. Drink your tea. The larder here is stocked enough for a few days if we need that. It's one of our places to lie low if we have to come over here. Don't worry about the air supply. There are vents to the outside, complete with scrubbers to get rid of the air pollution. Smugglers have comfortable hiding places. We appreciate that. No one will find us here. You can relax for a little while at least. I'll make us a meal in a moment."

"I can do it. I'm a decent cook for a spoiled princess." She stood and put her hand on his shoulder to stay him. Their gazes locked, and a warm flow of desire pooled through her, loosened her muscles. She swallowed. "No, really, I can do it, and I want to. I want to stay busy."

He hesitated and then relaxed. "All right. Thank you. I'll be sure the beds have linens. I'm told there's a cistern here. You can't take a sit-down bath, but the water should be warm enough to clean off a few layers of dust if you'd like."

She thanked him, watching his back as he began to rustle again, placing blankets on the bed. *One* bed.

As if he'd sensed her thoughts, he spoke without turning around. "I'll sleep on the floor, near the entrance."

"That's silly. I'm sure it will be cold here in the evenings. We obviously can't have a fire. We're adults. You'll be close enough to protect me should we need it as well." She sounded very matter-of-fact, but she wasn't at all. She wanted him in the bed with her. Didn't want to be alone. Wanted the feel of a man beside her as she slept.

She walked to where he stood and put the bedding back onto the bed. "Here now. You can bathe first, while I make the meal. I won't peek." She smiled.

He cocked his head and finally smiled back. "Before I do that, I need to go out, see if I can't receive a transmission with some further information. The signal near the portal was jammed, but out here with all the smugglers and mercenaries, there should be enough boosters to get through."

He needed to be away from her for even just a short time. It was her smell, he'd decided, the way her skin and hair carried her scent, even from beneath the sweat and dust. It had woven into his consciousness and was beginning to drive him mad.

The longer he was with her, the more he admired her, found little things about her enchanting and wanted to know more, and that was not a good direction.

Right then she tried not to look scared; he saw that clearly. She'd been so strong that whole day. She hadn't made a sound as he'd killed a man right within her reach, hadn't lost her composure once, despite the number of times she'd been in danger since he'd met her. She worked through her panic and stayed sharp, even reminding him earlier about how everyone in the Imperium would have been afraid at the sight of troops.

He touched her cheek, rewarded by the smooth satin of her skin. Her pupils widened and her breath caught. He needed to stop touching her, but he didn't plan to start right then. "I won't be far. You're safe here. Only I or someone with the right instructions and codes can get this far. I'll be back before you finish with the food." His voice was husky, even to his own ears, and she smelled so good he had to fight against the urge to lean in and sniff.

Then she said, "I trust you with my life, Daniel." And he lost his footing entirely, leaning down to kiss her forehead before he'd even really thought about it. The longer he was around her, the more he found himself doing things he hadn't really thought about, which was stupid and dangerous.

But she hugged him, holding him tight, and he let go of all the supposed to bes and the should haves and instead, hugged her back. "We're going to be all right, Carina."

She squeezed him one more time and stepped back, blushing furiously even as her gaze was locked on him. "Go on and hurry back so things won't get cold. I saw some dried meat and vegetables. I'm sure I can make something for us."

Her forced cheer only made him want her more. Instead, he turned and headed not toward the door they came through, but another entrance at the side, through a closet.

Needing to get the fuck away from her presence, he quickly took the darkened passage, the glow lamps warming and casting dim but consistent light as he passed. He hoped the break from her would help him get his thoughts together and get his impulses back under control. He needed to rein in whatever it was she brought out in him before he did something stupid. Like kiss those sweet lips.

Gods above and below, he wanted her. His skin crawled with it, with the desire to touch and caress. He ached to know her taste. He was off balance and in unfamiliar territory. Not that he hadn't felt desire for women before; he had on many occasions. But never on a mission and never for a woman like her. And never with this sort of bottomless need he couldn't even begin to name.

Daniel had never had a thing for virginal young women, preferring partners who were as experienced as he. Carina Fardelle might have been braver than most people he knew, resourceful and smart, but she sure as the seven hells was *not* sexually experienced. She couldn't have been, given who she was, and her reactions to him only cemented that fact. She was out of his league and off any possible list for bedmates, and he had to let that go before he did something disastrous. He could only hurt her, and the very idea of bringing her pain seemed untenable.

Why in the 'Verses did he have this reaction to her?

He shoved it all away as deep as he could and concentrated on the tasks before him.

Once he found the communications array, he settled in and started the download of information. He logged that they were alive and on the run. There were several directions he could take, depending on what happened over the next hours, so he'd go from there, arrange to have contacts at each portal he could take. Leaving it loose meant they could change plans as necessary. He read the updates posted by his people and set the messages to send in small bursts of data so they wouldn't be tagged.

Finally finished, he leaned back in the chair and gave in to what he'd wanted to do since his first glance at the beautiful Carina Fardelle. Unzipping his pants, he pulled his cock out, slowly, squeezing at the base to prolong the pleasure.

As he stroked, hand over fist, again and again, he thought of the sweet hollow at her neck, just below her ear. He imagined the skin there would be soft, scented of night flowers, heady and sticky. Her breath would catch as he licked that spot, knowing no one had ever before, knowing he'd be the man to introduce her to sensual delights in a way she'd never forget.

He thought about what she might sound like, that cool, regal voice with just a hint of the fire she kept in her belly. One hand would slide down her perfect spine, the curve making love to his hand until he settled, cupping the weight of the cheeks of her ass. Her skin would be pale, supple, extra-sensitive to each caress. He'd pull her close, rolling his hips just enough to create delicious friction against her clit. Just a breath of intense sensation before he pulled back, letting her adjust slowly.

She'd arch against him as he moved around to unbutton the bodice of her dress, her breasts spilling into his hands. Perfect. He'd watched them that day as she'd run, knew the beauty of the curve at her neckline. He'd bury his face there, thumbs slowly sliding back and forth across her nipples, driving her toward climax, just the first of a long evening's worth.

He considered slowing down as he continued to fuck his fists, but he couldn't. He needed her, needed to taste her desire. Wanted to kiss down her belly as she trembled. Not with fear but anticipation. He needed to kiss her pussy until she whimpered. Wanted to pay homage to that sweet cunt so she'd be extra soft and wet when he was ready to fuck her. To ease her way and his. He wanted to last.

That wouldn't happen just then, in the penetrating cold from the stone that surrounded him, trailed by elite troops. All that aside, he still needed to come, and he groaned long and hard as he climaxed, the heat of it against his skin. Thinking of her beneath him.

Carina bit her bottom lip so hard she feared it would bleed. She'd followed him after she'd finished preparing the meal. She told herself she was worried about him, but if she were to be totally truthful, she wanted to see him, to be alone with him to see what he would do with her if she caught him at a weak point. She burned for him to touch her, to notice her.

But when she came around the corner, what she saw was Daniel, head back, rapture on his face as he self-pleasured.

Masturbated.

Fucked his fists.

She'd spied on men as they'd masturbated before, the sight always intensely titillating to her. But there'd been nothing in her life that could have prepared her for the sight of him there like that. She pressed her fingertips to her eyes, the vision of such intense sexuality and maleness burned into her brain like a fever. She made her way back as quietly as possible and hoped he wouldn't notice. He'd been magnificent there, taking what he needed. His cock had been beautiful in a way she hadn't expected. Hard, masculine, feral. She'd nearly swooned as he gasped. As he gasped *her name*. He'd said it, and it had been lightning to her pussy, to her heart, as the electricity of the moment had hit.

He'd come on a groan that seemed to echo between her thighs and then totally relaxed. The machines had started to hum, and that's when she'd turned tail back to the kitchen.

All this time and she'd been half convinced he pitied her and the other half of the time she thought he hated her. Obviously he didn't hate her enough to stop himself from orgasm while thinking of her.

Her hands shook a bit at the excitement in her system. She wasn't stupid. Daniel wasn't convinced she was genuine. He was wary, held back because he was a professional. Or something like that.

No, he was the kind of man who would deny himself personal pleasures because doing the right thing meant everything. That sort of person was so rare in her existence it made him powerfully more alluring and attractive to her. He would tell himself she was young and inexperienced. That the wisp of skin that created the technicality of her virginity was worth something, therefore he could not take it. Daniel was a man of substance, even as he carried more weapons than anyone could logically expect and used them with vicious efficiency.

She should respect that. Just let him get her to Ravena safely. Shake his hand as he dropped her off, and forget everything about him.

But she wouldn't. She knew this as well as she knew her own name. He'd done something to her brain so he dominated it. She craved him, and for the first time in her life she wanted to give rein to that selfishness, wanted to evoke something from him. Wanted to know he wanted her as much as she him.

She busied herself, waiting for him to come back, and when he did, striding into the room looking a bit more relaxed than when he'd left, she tried to pretend she wasn't thinking of him masturbating at all as she placed their meal out on the table.

Perhaps she should have taken the time alone to have an orgasm, too. It certainly seemed to have unknotted his spine.

She sent him a smile, pretending she hadn't just spied on him. "It's ready."

He nodded once, keeping his distance. "I'm going to wash up quickly. I'm dusty." He nearly ran from the room, leaving her confused.

She stared after him, wondering just what had happened between them just then. It was as if he couldn't get away from her fast enough. Did he know what she'd seen? Oh gods! Did he catch her spying on him and think it was about the data instead of her utter fascination with him?

*F*eeling slightly embarrassed but admittedly less distracted, Daniel peeled his sweater and undershirt away from his body. The water in the basin had been warm, most likely kept in catchments near the surface where the sun would keep it that way. The soap wasn't the most luxurious he'd ever used, nor did it burn his skin like some had. As far as hidey-holes went, this place was a good one. Secure.

Getting her to Ravena safe and soon was the only way this situation would end well. The longer they were together, the more he'd want her, want to touch her, the more he'd want to do to her everything he'd already imagined and more.

He had to keep his distance, or he would break every rule, and they'd both be damned for it. She was royalty. So far out of his rank it wasn't humorous in any way. She was innocent and soft, and there wasn't any way a man like him would be allowed to have her. Or should be.

Just a while longer, and he'd turn her over. They'd both be way better off if he kept his hands to himself.

Carina looked up when he came around the corner, cleaned up and looking less agitated, though the distance still lit his eyes. Hmpf. What was it with men anyway?

"Sit down. I brewed some tea as well. It's getting chilly in here." She smiled and gestured at a chair.

"This looks good. Thank you." He nodded toward the platters of food, and she found herself less annoyed with him, which only annoyed her again.

"You're welcome. Any news? Did you get what you needed?" She watched him, trying not to smile as the double meaning of her words hit her.

"Not totally what I needed, but it'll do for now. We'll have backup wherever we head next. They know we're on the move. We can stay here a while longer, rest up and head out again. We need to get off this 'Verse and to the Edge as soon as is safe." He hesitated and then began to eat again.

Panic hit. "What? There's more, I can tell. Is it my mother? My brother?"

He looked up, his distance gone now. "No. There's been more violence. Imperialist troops fired on Federal troops at a crowded portal station in Parron. Seven civilians were killed. The Federation has expelled the Imperial troops and their ambassador. War is only a matter of time. Which makes it even more difficult to get you back." He paused, touching her temple. "What do you have, Carina? What's in that head of yours?"

"I don't know all of it. Honestly, I don't. The things I've seen over the years have been minor compared to whatever this is. My mother was terrified because of it. He's building something, using his labs to help research it. She said she overheard my father talking about evacuating civilians around the site, whatever he meant by 'the site.' She's risking her life for it, so you'd better get me out of here."

"Do you have any insight as to why he has changed his tack with us? Our two sides haven't been friends, but the last years have been different. He's gone out of his way to be aggressive toward the Federation Universes. He can't possibly think he can win. We're bigger and have better weaponry. We have more troops. I'm not trying to put you on the spot, I know he's your father, but if we could understand his motivations or mind-set better, perhaps we could find a solution to this before it blows up in our faces."

He couldn't have had any idea how his seeking of her opinion made her feel. Most people tended to ignore her, to think she was pretty and good at knowing how to put dinner parties together. This was the first time anyone like him had ever asked for her feedback.

"It's difficult to say. My access to information is severely limited. I'm quite sure I don't know the entirety of what he's doing and has done. It started going wrong around the time my older brother disappeared. My father became more secretive, more sensitive to anyone questioning him. Some of his closest advisors left then, and even more left when my younger brother died. Precisely the wrong kind of men filled their places. He doesn't talk to me the way he would if I were male. But he oftentimes shows a sort of jealous rage, a general feeling of grievance whenever the subject of the Federation 'Verses comes up."

"If you ever want to know something, ask. If I can tell you, I will. Naturally some things will be off limits, but I understand you've been in somewhat of an information vacuum. As that sort of thing would bother me a great deal, I can understand how it might affect you."

Shiny baubles and the softest of materials would not have meant more to her than this.

"We will hole up here, get some rest. Recharge and wait. We've got a difficult course ahead of us, but I've done this a time or two before." He grinned, and she went soft inside. "If we fail, he wins. And failing makes me angry."

He shrugged and continued to shovel food into his mouth at an alarming rate. She noted that about him the day before. The way he ate, steady but in huge amounts. She'd seen enough of his body to know he didn't carry a bit of extra fat on his body. She wondered if he'd had bioengineering enhancements done.

She knew her father's Skorpios had them, and their central nervous systems had been damaged to the point of them having to take chemicals to keep balanced or die a painful death. It made them lightning fast and very eager to accept his orders, but he hadn't shown any signs of dependence or their sometimes jittery movements.

Daniel looked up, as if he'd forgotten she was there. "You're still upset. What is it? If I had information about your mother, I would tell you. I have a mother, too. Like yours, mine would risk her life for her children as well."

Oh, damn him! Just when she'd worked up her indignation that he'd not been obsessing over her like she had him, he goes and says something comforting.

"Your metabolism is very fast." She didn't know if she could talk about her mother just then. Not without crying.

"I burn a lot of calories while I'm on a mission. But that's not what you mean."

His tendency to see right through her was unsettling. "Do you have bioenhancements, then? My father's men have to take in more calories, too. They carry around special protein bars."

He snorted. "Special protein bars? Is that what they call them? Let us be honest, shall we? They carry around bricks of chems laden with stimulants because your father's labs have turned them into super soldiers. He's created an army of addicts, and he's their source. That's not loyalty. It's a dangerous line he walks. I'm not addicted to anything but good food. I work with my body. I need the calories. I'm not in the military because it's the only way I can get my drugs."

It had been the longest speech he'd given since she'd met him, and despite her offense and some shame, she found herself fascinated by the cadence of his speech. The way he spoke, like each word weighed a certain amount and they all had to fit, precise, and yet there was wildness, too, just beneath the surface.

"I apologize. It wasn't meant to insult you."

"I'm not insulted by your question. You didn't mean it to be offensive. I understand that. I told you I'd give you answers when I could, and I mean that. I'm insulted by the way humans are engineered to serve better, but in doing so, they're unmade and turned into automatons. Automatons chemically dependent on your father. To live. That offends me. I serve willingly. Others should have the same choice. There should always be a choice."

Shame made her skin hot. "I agree it's not perfect. But to assume *you* had not been pushed into a place where you chose this life, but over something worse, is somehow free choice, is to underestimate how dependency works, does it not?"

He chewed, thinking. She sat back, sipping her tea and watching him, fascinated with the way he processed information.

"I'm not a chem-head, and I don't serve tyrants because I'm a slave to a craving. However, you *are* correct that at the time I entered the military, it was a choice between that and something worse. But I *choose* to be here now. I *choose* to do my job. I don't do it for more chems; I don't do it for credits. I do it because it's what I do. I do it because it's what I'm good at, and I make a difference. I did not make a purely free choice when I entered, but staying? That's my choice, and that is what makes me different from the Skorpios. It's what makes *you* different, too, Carina."

She wished she had the courage to ask him to tell her that story. "I . . . I'm not like you. You're a soldier. You do this every day while I had a maid just for my hair. I left them all behind. Sure, I'm giving you information, but I'm saving myself from a horrible marriage. I'm not noble or brave, just desperate."

Those green eyes focused on her. His gaze roved over her features, and she felt it like a phantom caress. She struggled not to get lost in him. He was so very much more than anyone she'd ever met. She bet it would be easy to lose herself in a man like Daniel. Realized it had already begun.

"You can't believe such a thing, can you? You're allowed to want out of what your father had planned by marriage to Alem. You had helped before, and if this provides us with a way to stop a weapon he's developing before he can do any damage with it, it can tip the balance in our favor. As for my job, sure, I risk my life all the time. And you don't, not in this way. Which is why it means more that you're doing it."

He snorted a laugh and shoved another slice of flatbread into his mouth. "You're special. You're risking everything to help people. Yes, I know it gets you out of marrying that pig. For that alone your father should hang." He glared at a faraway thing before turning his attention back to her. "You're doing the right thing. The brave thing. Millions of lives on both sides may be saved because of this information you have. Don't let yourself underestimate the importance of what you're doing."

He stood and began to take the plates from the table, running them to the basin nearby as she reeled, still sitting. "I'll clear up from the meal. It's only fair. Go and wash up. There's soap near the basin. The water is relatively warm. I found some clothing you may want to change into as well."

She was dismissed as he began to work, turning his attention elsewhere. She was partly relieved. Being in his focus was confusing. He was hard to figure out.

She undid the braid he'd given her before. The color was beginning to fade back to her normally pale tone. The stone floor beneath her bare feet was warm as she managed to get wet enough to soap up.

The rinse water made her realize just how dirty she'd been, had cleaned her skin and in the offing, had made her more sensitive to the air around her naked body. There was no door here. Just an alcove around a corner from the main room.

She could hear him move around as she bathed. As she stood totally naked, her nipples hard, her pussy aching as it never had before, he was close enough for her to hear his mumbles as he turned things over in his mind.

Or she figured that's what it was; she couldn't make out words, just the feel behind them.

He'd understood her in a way she wasn't sure if she could trust. She wanted very much to to do the right thing. Knew her father had done a lot of damage in the name of the Imperial 'Verses, and as a Fardelle, she wanted to mediate that, wanted to make it better. How she could do so and not be a traitor, or at the very least, accept that she was a traitor, but for the right reasons, she wasn't sure. She wasn't sure if she would ever not feel as if she was betraying everyone she was supposed to protect.

The air had cooled, so she dried off, dressing quickly. She decided against relieving the sexual ache in her gut, not with him just steps away, right around the corner. She may have needed to be touched and to come, but she wasn't so very bold as that.

What she was, was lonely and desperately in need of some understanding and company.

With a sigh, she headed back out into the main room.

"Tell me about yourself, Daniel," she said, settling on the bed, gathering the blankets around herself.

Surprise skittered across his features. "Like what?" Instead of coming into bed with her, he grabbed a chair and moved it nearby.

"Do you have any brothers and sisters?" His nearness settled and unsettled her all at the same time.

He smiled, and she knew there was a man beneath this facade who loved people.

"I do. I'm the oldest. I've got two sisters and a brother. I have two nephews by marriage; both are adults. Good boys. My sister is carrying a baby now." He paused as if he'd been caught doing something naughty. "What about you?"

"I imagine you know most of the details." She shrugged, far more content to listen to him talking. His voice made her feel safe.

"I've read a number of reports, yes. But that's not the same as you telling me about them."

She swallowed hard around the truth of that. "I have a new baby brother. He's beautiful and very cheerful. We joke between ourselves that he got his temperament from his mother. She's younger than I am, my second mother. I had a brother who was several years younger than me. He died of a fast-spreading illness. We still don't know what it was."

The warmth in his eyes was gone in just one breath. His face closed off. Alarm raced through her.

He knew something about Petrus.

"What? Tell me. Tell me, you said you'd teach me. What?"

He didn't bother to pretend not knowing what she was talking about. "I'm sorry, Carina. Our reports indicate your brother was infected by a bioagent he'd found by accident in your father's chambers. They . . . well, that's our report of what happened."

Her eyes burned. "You're saying my brother was poisoned by something my father left lying around? He's not a good man, but he's not careless. Something like that would be valuable; he wouldn't just toss it aside for someone to find."

"Right."

She looked at him and realized what he had hinted at, what she'd said. Instinctively, she recoiled. "No. No, no, no. He wouldn't. *He wouldn't.* My brother was the only heir. Even if my father hadn't cared for him on some level, he needed an heir."

"I . . . I'm not even supposed to be giving you this much detail. But if it were me, I'd want to know." He nodded as if finishing an internal argument. "Your little brother wandered into a lab near your father's office. According to the official report, he'd been following your father around. The syringe had been put in a receptacle near where it had been used earlier to test on animal subjects. There was only a very small amount. But your brother was young, and he'd recently been ill, so it took hold."

Ice frosted through her, but she couldn't stop asking. "The rest?"

He sighed. "Once he'd been infected, they decided to study him. He was worth more to them dead than alive. There wouldn't have been time to save him anyway, I don't think. They watched the disease ravage him and studied it. The data they got enabled them to inoculate Imperial soldiers. He's built a biological warfare unit, and this was a huge breakthrough for them."

"This can't be true. It's just not. It's not even rational."

He started to speak and then shook his head before saying anything else. "Okay. You'd know better than me."

"Are you patronizing me?" She got to her knees, crawling directly in front of where he sat next to the bed. "I'm not stupid. But not everyone in the Imperium is evil either. We're not all soulless, child-killing monsters." She choked on a sob she hadn't expected.

He wasn't lying, he wasn't even misinformed. She knew it was true. Oh, she hadn't known before just moments ago, but she'd always felt the situation surrounding Petrus's death had been odd. The way her father had responded had seemed off. But he was odd anyway, and she couldn't have imagined this. Who could have imagined such a thing?

But her father did have new labs. There were rumors of people being sick with things no medic could ease. What if this thing he was building was part of it?

"I'm not patronizing you." He cupped her cheek gently, surprising them both, if the look on his face was any indicator. "I'm sorry if I upset you. That was not my intention at all."

"What are you?" It tumbled from her mouth even as her brain screamed at her to stop it.

He smiled just a little. But when he did, she caught a glimpse of the man he was when he wasn't on a mission. A glimpse of the Daniel beneath the uniform and weaponry. Without thinking, she reached up to trace his lips, and he allowed it for longer than she thought he would, finally pulling back.

Carina swallowed hard, feeling exposed, grief-stricken, confused and alone. "I apologize. That was rude. All of it. I shouldn't be surprised my father would have used my brother's death to profit from. I remember the vaccine. It was released with much fanfare. But he never said." She let out a long sigh. "It's very hard to realize your whole life is a lie."

There was no pity on his face, just sorrow and understanding. "I'm sorry."

"I have another brother," she said, needing to fill the quiet space. "He escaped. I believe he's still alive out there on the Edge. I hope he's happy and doing something to stop my father. My mother is a good person who never had a chance. And you're familiar with my father. I could spin a tale and tell you he was once a good man who changed slowly. But I'd be lying. He's always been small, petty and self-centered. Vicious. Deceitful. Brutal when bored, cuttingly cruel. There were no stories about when he took time from his schedule to come listen to me when I sang or danced in the youth troupes." The ice had settled in her chest, achingly cold and sharp. She pressed the heel of her hand there. "He let Petrus die. Who could do that?"

Daniel wished with all his heart that he hadn't told her the truth about her brother. She wore so much pain on her features he felt it as if it were his own. "I don't know. For what it's worth, my father isn't on the best father in the 'Verse list either."

Her brows knit in consternation, and he fought a smile. Better to be annoyed with him than hurt.

"Really? Aside from him obviously not being as big a villain as a man who'd plunge billions into war because he can and because he wants to, what's he so bad at? Did he toss your mother aside so he could rut upon a woman barely into adulthood to replace the sons he so casually tossed aside?"

The truth wasn't so very far from that. "He's had numerous affairs.

Most of them my mother knows about. She has her room in their house, and he has his own. They rarely speak. My father was willing to toss my sister to the wolves for more attention from the media. He's not a good man, no. He's not your father, but I wish to seven hells he wasn't mine either."

Daniel stood and paced a bit. He hadn't meant to reveal any of that. She got to him, and he wasn't even aware of it until he was doing it. This was not the way for a top-notch operative to act.

"Why do you run?" She was closer than she should have been.

"I don't know what you mean. From the compound? We had to get out of there."

"As you may have noticed, I'm not the most sophisticated when it comes to men. But I'm not stupid. Several times after you and I have shared something, a depth of emotion, you push back to put space between us. Why?"

He didn't turn. If he had, he'd have lost his resolve and gathered her to him the way he'd been wanting to all day. His control was slipping, and he was not about to embrace the weakness.

"I have a job to do, Carina. You've had a hard time, I know. I suggest we get some sleep. We might have to leave here once night falls."

She growled, surprising him enough that he turned to catch sight of her heading back around the corner. "You're lucky you're handsome, because you're not very bright," she muttered, stomping away.

He wasn't bright? He may not have been raised in a compound, but he wasn't stupid! He was set to tell her so when he realized she'd baited him, and he grinned again. She was surprising, Carina Fardelle. That might just keep her pretty little ass alive.

Chapter 8

He awoke at the time he'd set his body clock, a talent he'd discovered and then honed over his time in the military. She huddled against his back, and while he knew he needed to just get up and dress so they could leave, he lay there for a while, enjoying the soft feel of her there, snuggled against him. This was new and, he reluctantly admitted, pleasant.

She smelled good, even if she'd refused to say another word to him once she'd come back into the room after her comment about him not being smart. He'd stripped to his long underwear and she'd settled in behind him.

"Are you married?" she asked, her voice sleepy.

"Why?"

She pinched him, and he rolled away, laughing.

"Because if I'm in your bed and you're only barely dressed, I should know if you have a wife. It's only fair."

He got up, heading around the corner to clean up. "One would think it was my wife who'd deserve to know about that." He smiled, knowing she would be flustered. "So I suppose it's a good thing I'm not married."

He pulled a shirt on and tucked it into his pants before returning to the main room where she still lay beneath the nest of blankets on the bed.

"I'll return shortly. I want to check in with my people to see what's going on."

Before she could argue or worse, try to go along with him, he ducked back into the entrance to the communications array.

The news wasn't encouraging. They'd need to stay in place for another day or two. They'd discovered the dead soldier and had left a garrison behind. He wasn't worried they'd find this place, but he couldn't take a chance and be out in the open with her either.

She had wrapped a blanket around herself, bending over to put the kettle over the heat, when he returned.

"We need to stick for another day. Good thing there's enough food here. It'll give us some more time to recharge, too."

"What's happening?" She set the leaves in the pot so it would be ready once the water heated.

"They found the soldier I killed. Left a garrison here and are conducting a thorough search. We can't risk a trip to the portal just now."

She sighed. "All right. Any news from my home?"

He busied himself in the small kitchen area, slicing bread and setting it in the rack to toast it.

"Just tell me, Daniel. What I'm imagining has to be worse. Is it my mother?"

"It's your maid, Claira. She was executed. I'm sorry. I do know, at least from the reports, she was executed for letting this happen, not for being the cause of it."

Carina's eyes widened. "She died because he thought she was incompetent?"

Daniel took her by her upper arms. "Please believe me when I tell you it was better this way. If he thought she helped you escape, they would have tortured her. You have to know that. Her end would have been worse."

"It was all for nothing! She was a good woman. Kind. If I hadn't done this, she'd be alive right now."

"Carina, stop this." He put his face right in hers. "This is not yours to own. She helped us for her own reasons. She did not die for nothing. She died for everything. Everything. Do you see the difference?"

"What reasons? What do you know?"

"Seems she had a secret romance with one of the young men in town. She was barely of age to romance anyone, but he tells me she was the great love of his life. They had to keep their relationship quiet because he was from a merchant family and she a servant. He disappeared, along with his entire family. He ended up on our side, but not before enduring four standard years of daily torture and abuse. His mother died on the transport to Silesia, where your father has his prisoners processed. The camp he was in does not exist anymore. He runs a dry goods store in Sanctu."

Her eyes were wide, and she'd ceased trying to pull away. "She never told me. All those years she ferried information to you all, and she never once told me about this boy."

"She could have left. We offered her the chance on several occasions. He wanted her to join him. But she told him she had to stay to make a difference. To bring your father's regime down so he'd stop ripping families apart. She knew the risks. She was a brave woman,

Carina. Don't diminish what she did with your guilt. She chose her path, and she walked it with dignity."

Without meaning to, he kissed her forehead again before stepping back. Her taste was on his lips, damn it. He knew her now, and he couldn't wash away the sadness and salt from his mouth.

"I'm making toasted bread, and the water is boiling for tea. Let's break our fast and toast the very fine and brave Claira."

She nodded, still looking pale and lost. "Yes, yes, that's a good idea."

He wanted to make it better. She wasn't hard like him, couldn't be expected to find a way to deal with heartbreak like this.

Woodenly, she stood. "Let me help. I saw some preserves. Those will be good with the bread."

He made the tea and managed to rustle up some grains and salted meat to go with the meal.

Carina's head hurt. She wanted to cry but knew she'd totally lose control if she did. But she wanted him to know, at least part of it. What she'd grown up with had bent her thinking in ways she would probably never comprehend.

"People disappear. A lot."

Startled, he looked up from where he'd been frying the meat. "In your life? How do you mean?"

"Here. In the Imperium and in my family. It's always there in me. The expectation that one day I'll hear someone else I know or love has simply gone. It's happened to me so many times it's just something I've accepted."

She swallowed several gulps of the sweetened tea, letting it warm her.

Dividing the bread between their plates, she got out utensils, and he brought the meat over. There had been some jarred fruit, and the simple food was what she needed.

"I've prepared myself for this moment. When I heard Claira was dead or had disappeared. I always think that preparing myself will make it hurt less, but it never does. And she's so much more than I gave her credit for. I feel small for that. I never imagined she'd had this boy she'd loved and lost. I . . ." She raised her shoulders. "I don't know what to feel. It's nothing good in any case."

"I imagine it will take you time to adjust. You've lived a certain way your entire life, Carina. You can't just suddenly not be who you've been bred to be. There's no shame in that. How could there be?"

"I'm frightened that the next news I hear will be about my mother." She blurted it out, needing to say it out loud.

He covered her hand with his own. "I know. I'm sorry. I hope very much that we don't."

He didn't promise anything. He couldn't have. The entire thing was utterly out of their control. But he listened to her, and it made her drunk with emotion. It was invigorating to have this interplay with him. This getting to know him. The ease with which she got used to him, wanted his presence. Felt safe with him.

At the same time, they were in danger, and she'd just heard terrible news. It rolled around inside her. He held her hand.

"Your hands are cold. Here." He scooted over until he was next to her. Taking her hands in his, he bent his head and cupped her hands with his own, blowing warm breath over her skin.

She was utterly comforted and wildly charmed. Confused, but enjoying it, even as everything else got more dire.

"Do you know how to play cards?" he asked, as if he sensed she needed the diversion.

"Why do I get the feeling you're an expert at games of chance?" She raised her mug. "To Claira."

They both sipped.

"I promise not to bet you any money." He smiled at her, and she realized he'd opened up to her, that they'd reached a new level of comfort.

"This is a good thing, as I have none."

"Good point."

*D*aniel returned from the comm array and caught sight of her as she brushed her hair. Stroke after stroke, it gleamed in the low light of the room. When they got up and left for the portal, she'd appear different, but for that moment, he simply stared.

She looked up, and their gazes locked. The power of that connection with her hit him straight to his toes, as it did each time they looked at each other. Humbling, to think he could be so affected when he'd considered himself unshakable on an op.

He broke eye contact and moved toward the bathing alcove to change.

"Looks like we're a go. We'll head out in four standard hours. There'll be a conveyance waiting where we got dropped off. It'll be full moonrise then, so we should have plenty of natural light to travel in."

He spoke to her from around the corner and came into the room after he'd changed his clothes. "I'm going to propose we sleep for the next three hours. It's going to be a long trip, and we should be as rested as possible."

She'd changed her clothes, too, and had burrowed beneath

the bedding. The room had gotten steadily cooler, so he didn't waste any time making one last security check and getting in bed himself.

"Daniel?"

"Go to sleep, Carina." The last thing he wanted was to get back into some intimate discussion with her so temptingly close and warm. He'd folded up blankets to fit between them, but she was still very near, near enough to smell her.

At her annoyed snort, he let himself fall into sleep.

"$\mathcal{D}$aniel." She poked him. "Wake up."

"Why?" he mumbled.

"Three hours are up."

"No. I had another short dream. I had time left." He rolled to sit up, and the cold air got under the blankets.

"I don't think so. Maybe time moves differently in your 'Verse. But here we use chronos. Mine says our three hours have passed."

He got out of bed, grabbing his pants and pulling them on.

"And even if you did have a short time left, you needn't be so cross."

"I have a very good internal chrono." He went to wash his face and noted his skin had gone very pale and his hair very dark. After the pills kicked in, his eyes had gone from green to brown. He added a scar on his neck, leading up to his ear.

She barged around the corner to continue pestering him. "You're a pain in the—" Her eyes widened. "You're very good at this disguise part of the job. I should cut my hair, don't you think?"

His gut cramped at the thought. "It's very beautiful," he said before he could say something sane and professional. "I mean, you'd still be beautiful with short hair and—"

She put two fingers over his lips and froze, before moving her hand away. Then she pressed her mouth to his. He hadn't expected it, but he couldn't step away either.

Her lips were sweet, sweet as the kiss was. A soft exploration of his mouth with hers. At first. It wasn't so much innocent as it was unexpected. It snared him, much like her taste had. She was warm against him, relaxed, obviously trusting him more than any rational woman should have. His blood surged with need for her, with want, demand for more.

He fisted his hands to keep from hauling her against him, from stroking the elegant curve of her spine down to her ass. A groan bubbled from deep within his gut at the memory of the fantasy he'd had the day before. She sighed, taking it into herself.

It was when she stepped closer, her fingers digging into the front of his shirt, molding herself to his body and her tongue sliding into his mouth, that he finally found his sanity about a meter from where all the blood in his body had gathered.

"Seven hells," he gusted as he set her back from him, holding her upper arms firmly. "That can't happen again." Her mouth called to him, those luscious lips just so slightly swollen.

"Why?" She licked her lips, and he groaned.

"Stop that. Carina, this is a bad idea."

A smile played on her lips as she realized the extent of her power. Gods, he was in trouble now.

"Why? Really? You kissed me back. You're attracted to me. I can see it. I can taste it." She pressed fingers to her lips, and he struggled to breathe.

"You're my *cargo*. You have something that could save the lives of millions. You're . . . I bet you're untouched, aren't you?" He forged on without an answer. "I'm not. I'm not a nice man. I kill people. All the time. You need a nice man. A *gentle* man who can give you the life you were bred for."

She waved a hand as she turned. He took advantage of her distraction and headed back out toward the main room.

"Where are you going? I need your help with my hair," she called out.

"Tell me when to come back there." He scrubbed his hands through his hair, standing it on end.

"*Now*. Gods, did your mother drop you on your head a lot as a child?"

"You're pretty mouthy," he mumbled as he headed around the corner and found her in little more than sheer underclothes. "Hey!" He turned his back. "You're naked. I said when you were ready."

"You'll get hair in my clothes and it will itch. Cut it short." She handed him shears as he turned back around and tried in vain not to look at the shadow of dark pink nipples against the pale material.

"Are you sure about this?" He sifted fingers through it, so long and soft. Beautiful and feminine. "If you braid it, you can tuck it into a watch cap, and no one will know the difference. Women of all ranks have long hair. You don't have to cut it."

She turned, so close she brushed against him. "Women of all classes have short hair, too. Do you like it?" Tossing her head, pale burnt-sugar hair tumbled around her shoulders.

The scent of her choked him in the best kind of way. This chemistry between them was so very delicious, even if he knew anything else between them was totally impossible.

"It's lovely. It's up to you." He tried to step back, but he was boxed in, and she knew it.

"I *am* a virgin, you know. But that doesn't mean I don't have desires." She leaned in, brushing her cheek against his chest. His cock ached, the pulse as he got harder and harder was an angry throb. "I do. Have desires, that is. I've never had the opportunity to express them and certainly not with anyone like you. There's no one quite like you, Daniel."

"You'd do well to remember that, Carina." He pointed to the stuff he'd left on a ledge near the basin. "You're my sister again. We'll call you Carrie, and I am Neil. We're itinerant workers, looking to get on with the grain shipments. Do you know anything about wheat? It's a crop brought from Earth, and I know it's grown out here. We're from Suerte."

He managed to step neatly away once she'd turned to look. "I always wanted blue eyes." She began to plait her hair into two long braids as she spoke. "I'll keep it long for now. And I'm very well aware that there's no one like you. This isn't over."

She wanted to laugh when he scurried from the room. An altogether new sort of power surged through her veins. Her allure as a woman wasn't new, not really. But this sort of romantic chase, the sensual dance they did as he pretended to resist her, was something she'd never imagined, and it was thrilling.

If she had to risk her life, leave her family behind and hare off into new territory with a man like him, she planned to enjoy every moment of it.

Chapter 9

*F*our days after they'd finally left Philos safely, they were no closer to Federation territory. He'd had to put them on super-slow and off the basic path transports, crisscrossing back and forth to keep from attracting too much attention. It was tedious progress; he itched to get her back, to be assured she was safe. He had to run like hells before he did something monumentally stupid like fucking her.

Carina Fardelle and her big, sexy eyes, her constant questions and the way she was strong and so fragile all at once. She'd relentlessly thrust herself into his space whenever she could. He realized she'd begun to understand her effect on him, but there were times when she charmed him. Some little thing she'd do or say would leave him disarmed and pleased all at once.

She looked beautiful. Even as she was supposed to be some riff-raff, ranging around looking for work, she looked gorgeous doing it. Damn it. She'd trimmed her hair this time. But whatever she'd done had left it curly instead of straight. It took all his strength not to touch it.

Instead, he worked on keeping his gaze sharp for their contacts and pretended she didn't make him want to stop and sniff her like a lovesick fool. That level of concentration kept his mind actively engaged on keeping them out of trouble and not on the way she'd brushed against him earlier that morning, trying to tiptoe up and kiss him. And especially not thinking about how close he came to letting her.

He bit back a groan and redoubled his efforts to be on the lookout for trouble.

They'd arrived in Frontera and had easily made it through the checkpoint. They'd heard a rumor that the troops had been diverted to another transport that was set to arrive shortly after theirs had. He hoped that luck would continue to be with them.

Rife with thugs, the criminal element of the portal city in Frontera had been the reason many transports refused to stop for fear of losing cargo. Since his cargo was feminine, on the run from a monster and beautiful, he would have to kill anyone who thought of stealing her.

"You need to stick closer to me," he said but realized he'd sort of growled it. Infuriatingly, she turned and smiled his way, that knowing feminine smile, and he wondered where she'd gotten that from. Did virgins have that look yet? He made a mistake with her, he realized, in making an incorrect assumption that having her maidenhead in place meant she was naïve about sex. She was not. He needed to remember that.

Better yet, he didn't need to remember it at all. He didn't need to think about it in any way.

She'd begun to lose some of her fear, growing bolder in many ways. She settled into herself in some way, taking up being Carina with a sort of wholehearted enthusiasm. Though annoying at times, she was generally a pleasure to be around, even when he didn't need to be thinking about any of this at all.

"I'm within reach, Neil. You know I'm always happy to have you touch me." She broke into his thoughts. "Where is our conveyance?" She put her hand through his arm. Instead of telling everyone she was his sister as instructed, she'd told people they were married and had taken every opportunity to touch him and act like a wife.

In short, he was nearly insane with wanting her, and she had no intention of letting him forget it. His mother had a word for what Carina was becoming with him—*saucy*.

"Don't start with me, woman." He tried to be light with her, but something wasn't right. He didn't like the feel of the streets here. He felt far too exposed and wanted to get her away and safe. "Perhaps we should get back to the guesthouse. I can come out later to see if they've arrived." He steered her away from a group of undesirables who'd just materialized and most likely were the source of his agitation. He sent them a look over his shoulder as he escorted her back around the edge of the marketplace and toward the guesthouse they were staying in.

"It's getting rather warm out here anyway." She continued to hold his arm as they walked, and he continued to like it, even though he knew how stupid it was when he could not have her.

He tensed up, keeping a watch on three men who'd walked from an alleyway just ahead. The group he'd avoided a few streets over. Four more appeared, followed by one last man, and they all headed straight for them. Sound died away as the street emptied. At least he could get rid of some of his pent-up energy with a fight. Daniel felt a moment of pity for these probably illiterate morons who chose the wrong mark.

"They're coming for us," she murmured.

"Stay behind me. Use that weapon if you have to; don't you dare hesitate." He stepped ahead, putting her behind him.

"Looks like you two are a bit heavy with gear." A mouth filled with few teeth made an ugly gash of delight on the thug's face.

Daniel knew the look in the man's eyes, knew they meant to rob him and harm Carina. Neither would be allowed.

He rolled his head on his shoulders, steadying for what was to come. "You should heed my warning and keep moving. You're not going to be pleased with the outcome if you bring a fight my way." Daniel didn't speak very loudly, but the one in charge heard just fine. Whether or not he took the warning was something else entirely.

The snick and gleam of a blade triggered Daniel's sense of calm. His body relaxed as he focused. White noise rushed through his ears as a blade handle fit into his palm.

"Look here, boys, he thinks he can take us all on."

Daniel sighed and began to move. Nothing he did when he fought ever took conscious thought; his body, his reflexes simply took over and did the job. A step forward, a lunge with one arm and a step back.

One of the men hit the pavement, blood spilling from a nonlethal but debilitating slice. The scent of copper hit the air, spicing up the stench of open-pit sewers and garbage.

"Well now, looks like I was right to think I could take you all." He tipped his chin at the groaning, semiconscious man bleeding at his feet. "There's one less now. The odds keep getting better."

It was wrong, she knew, very very wrong of her to be excited and titillated by the way Daniel carried himself just then. Even worse to have her heart speed when with two movements so fast and smooth she barely noticed, there was pain, blood and debilitating injury.

She didn't care. He was masterful, and it moved her. He protected her because it was his job, yes. But at the same time, she knew it was more for him. Whatever that meant, she wasn't sure. But being protected by such a scary, fierce man was so sexy she couldn't find it within herself to feel guilty about it.

"You think you're smart? Pulling that?" The other man—the one who could have used a bar of soap and some water, the sour stink of his body wafted to her, roiling her stomach as she began to breathe through her mouth—jerked his head, and the others rushed toward her and Daniel.

The intensity of the event brought her images, sounds, scents, but no real concrete impression of anything specific.

Daniel's hair gleamed as he moved with such a grace of economy she could do little more than stare. Small movements sent men falling to the side, blood darkening clothing and the dirt beneath their feet.

Her own blade rested in her hand, at the ready if anyone got past Daniel, which appeared to be an impossibility as body after body slumped. She watched, not really alarmed, as two men flanked Daniel and one rushed past him to her.

All the years of training came back to her, and she rested her weight on her heels, slicing out and up as she blocked the blow. Or thought she did until Daniel, grim-faced and satisfied, turned with a savage grin.

"You did a fine job. Now let's get off the street before the authorities arrive." He reached for her and stopped, grabbing her tunic, pushing it aside to reveal her torso and a bleeding slit in her skin. "Why didn't you tell me?" He paled, picking her up over her protests, striding back to the safe house without another word.

"I'm fine. Really. I didn't even notice he'd got me with his knife until you pointed it out." She clung to him, loving the scent of male sweat and adrenaline all over his skin. She buried her face in his neck, glad he didn't pull away or try to tell her how bad he was for her.

The sounds around them fell away as he carried her, seemingly effortlessly, up three flights of stairs and into their room.

"Next time you get hurt, tell me immediately." He put her on the bed, one he'd refused to share with her since they'd arrived, and moved to run a bath.

"How was that not immediately? They're still bleeding on the street; it's not as if I waited hours. In any case, I don't think it's a problem, Daniel. What's your last name anyway?" She pulled the tunic and undershirt off, wrinkling her nose when she noticed all the blood.

"Keep still!" He moved back to her and began to remove her clothing. Like she was going to protest? He slid his hands all over her feet and legs, looking for any more injuries. She tried not to gasp or arch, but she'd never felt anything like this, his big hands all over her body. Her breathing sped as a peculiar sort of lethargy set in. How was it possible to feel both things at once? And yet she did.

"Are you hurt anywhere else?" he asked as he picked her naked body up and put her gently in the warm bathwater. He began to clean her up, rinsing her off, tending to the wound on her side, which had been, as she'd tried to tell him, pretty minor. Not that she was thinking very clearly as his hands romanced over her naked, wet body.

"I'm fine. I swear to you. Daniel, you stopped seven of them. Seven. That's remarkable."

"Not eight." He moved his gaze from her side to her eyes. "Not eight."

She sighed, holding his face between her hands. "*You're* remarkable. You blocked two at once, even knocked him sideways. If you hadn't done that, I'd have been hurt far worse. You saved me. You've *been* saving me."

His eyes deepened in color, darkened to a stormy green, the brown of the prior day having worn off. The moment, despite her silly chemical attraction to him, sliced into her, the pleasure of it nearly pain. "You're so beautiful. I can't imagine—" He broke off, shaking his head.

She stood before him, looking down at this epic male specimen kneeling at her feet. Water caressed her skin as she did, as she watched his gaze slide up her body like another caress, one she'd been waiting for since she took his hand that first time as they fled.

"This shouldn't be." So much emotion in that whispered sentence. She should feel bad that she'd been breaking down all his defenses against her, but she didn't. She gloried in it.

She stepped from the tub, reaching for a towel, but he was there before she could begin, drying her off instead, his gentle treatment such a stark contrast with the man outside, the man who carried death like another blade secreted on his body. He laid a bandage against her skin, wrapping linen around her torso to hold it there.

It was the contrast that set her on fire. The way he could take life with such depth of concentration and skill but dry her off and bandage her wound without even a twinge made her feel special to evoke such care from a man like him.

He tried to turn away, but she stepped in his path, dropping the towel. The room was cool, and her skin rose in gooseflesh, her nipples beading, and not just because of the temperature. Daniel looked at her, looked at her nipples and a groan escaped his mouth.

She had the sense of walking a very thin line. If she made the wrong move, he'd find his control again, and she didn't want that. She wanted him to let go, *wanted him to take her.*

The door was locked, his security measures were all in place. The bed, the bed she'd been alone in the night before because he'd insisted on sleeping in a chair near the door, was right behind her, so she held her hand out. Not to offer, but to take. She grabbed the fabric of his tunic and pulled, surprising him, toppling him onto her on the bed. Which was slightly painful because despite her cut being minor, it was still a cut and he was, oh my, he was so deliciously solid the pain seemed to recede as she lay there.

"Damn it, Car-Carrie. I'm going to hurt you." He tried to roll off, tried to see if he'd harmed her, but she wouldn't allow it. She knew if she let him slide back into caretaker mode, she'd never have him.

And she wanted him so much every cell in her body ached with it.

Instead she rolled up to her knees, pulling his tunic and under-shirt off. "You're not even bruised," she said, taking in every inch of his exposed upper body. She drew her fingertips along the scars on his chest. "What happened here?"

"Incendiary device blew as I was dealing with its creator. I have scars; he's dead. Carrie, you have to stop. You're hurt and you're naked. This combination is not something I can work with."

That he said it as he drew his palms from her hip bones up her sides clued her in. His hands on her left her brain addled, but not so addled she didn't crave more.

"You're bluffing. You want this, too. I know you do." Taking a chance, she leaned in, sliding her breasts along his chest. It backfired, of course, as it felt so ridiculously good she nearly fell over. "That's, oh, gods, that's beautiful. Is it always like that?"

Hands that had been restraining now pulled her closer. "No. No it's not." She heard the anguish in his voice and wanted to weep with joy when he allowed himself a brief kiss at her breastbone.

"More." She tugged, and they both fell back onto the bed. She looked into his eyes. "Be with me, Daniel."

"I'm going to hurt you."

"I told you, it's just a minor cut." She tried to undo the waist of his trousers, but he put a hand over hers to stay the action.

"Not just that. Everything. You are not meant for a man like me."

"Please! A man like you how?"

"You are a princess. You're soft and feminine and you deserve to be cosseted. In case you haven't noticed, I kill people."

She waved a hand. "*For* princesses. And thank the gods you do, or I'd be dead. I would venture to say many more people would be dead if you weren't a killer. As for the rest? Why can't *you* cosset me? And who says I want to be cosseted anyway? You can't just leave me this way. I feel all knotted up; I need you to fix it. I can pleasure myself. I have, every time you leave the room, and it is not enough."

"Why do you tell me these things?" he muttered, toeing his boots off.

"So you'll take your pants off?"

He jerked to a stop and shook his head at her. "Not as innocent as you appear."

"I've been begging you to help me with that! Daniel, what if I die tomorrow, and I have never been with you? Never had you inside me?" She sent him her best face, the most pitiful one that almost always worked on others when she was growing up.

"You're a menace." He shoved his pants down, and she exhaled sharply at the sight of his body so boldly exposed to her view.

"You're breathtaking." Scrambling from bed, she pressed herself to his body for long moments, just soaking him in, skin to skin. He groaned again, kissing her temple, his fingers digging into her ass to haul her closer. She tried not to smile her triumph but failed.

Her amusement melted away at the wonder of his body against hers.

So much sensation! So much feeling. Her head tipped back, and he feasted on her neck. How long had she dreamed of what this would be like? And how much was reality far better and more overwhelming than what she'd imagined?

His hands were big, sure as he cupped her ass. He was so much bigger than she was. Normally, back home, a man like Daniel would have scared her, but this one was so delicious she couldn't seem to get enough.

He shook just a bit, more like vibrated as he kissed over one shoulder and to the hollow of her throat. He wanted her so much he had to rein it in or risk scaring or harming her.

He shouldn't be doing it, he knew. Shouldn't be giving in to his nearly overwhelming desire to kiss and touch every part of her. But it was too late for that. Once he'd seen that slice, once he'd come out of the haze of worry that she'd been harmed, she'd been naked. And wet. And like a siren, she beckoned him, and he couldn't resist her any longer.

Her taste was just like her: spicy, sweet, complicated. He swirled his tongue in the hollow of her throat, licked over the delicate edge of her collarbone. She arched, made soft sounds of need as he struggled to hang on and give her pleasure.

His inner conqueror wanted to storm the gates, to thrust inside her, rut on her until they were a sweaty heap. She wasn't ready for that just yet; he knew it even as need crawled through him like broken glass.

Lowering her to her back, he secured her wrists above her head, grasping hard enough to keep her still, but not hard enough to harm. What a picture she made there, arched, her pale skin flushed with pleasure, her body more lovely than he could have imagined. Desire blurred her eyes, brought a fever gloss to them, but the mischief remained. That had surprised him about her at first, the way she teased when he'd least expected it.

"I want to touch you," she gasped out as he kissed the soft spot just beneath her ear.

"I like you in my control. Keeps you out of trouble."

She arched, rolling her hips to grind against his already aching cock, and they both moaned. Hers was surprised pleasure.

"*You* are trouble, Daniel." She smiled up at him, her eyes filled with trouble of her very own.

"So my mother and sisters tell me." He slid his body down hers, loving the way it felt, loving how those bright eyes of hers clouded again, hazed with pleasure.

"I can't possibly fuck you if I don't know your last name," she gasped out when he let go of her wrists to slide his palms down her arms, down to her breasts. The prettiest breasts he'd ever seen. Heavy and large, though the rest of her was lithe and slim. Oh, the fantasies he'd had about them, about sliding his cock between them, tasting them, touching them.

He should have lied. Told her the name he used on assignments, but she'd called him Daniel. She was naked, giving herself to him so honestly he couldn't pretend with her. "Haws." To ensure she didn't follow up, he licked across a pebbled nipple, and if she had another question, she swallowed it on a delighted gasp.

"Please. Please be in me." She writhed, driving sense from his brain.

"It's not that simple," he said around a nipple. "I can't just shove my cock into your pussy. You need to be wet, prepared so I don't hurt you."

He laughed at her pout and annoyed snort. "Trust me when I tell you this part is fun. The making you ready part entails an orgasm before fucking."

She blushed, the heat of her skin against his more than a tiny bit distracting.

After he'd paid homage to her nipples, licking, sucking, biting, he continued to kiss his way down her belly, smooth as the softest silk, before settling between her thighs. She tried to close her legs, but his shoulders made that impossible.

"Are you still with me, sweet?" He looked up the magnificence of her body and into her face.

"You're going to l-lick me?"

He sent her a mercenary grin. "More than once. I'm going to bury my face in your pussy, licking, sucking, tormenting your clit until you come all over me."

Her eyes widened, her lips parted as her breath sped and she nodded. *"Oh*. I've never done that."

Good.

He spread her open, loving the way she looked, desire darkened, glistening and swollen. All for him.

Her muscles tensed, and he petted down her thigh a moment. "You're beautiful here just like everywhere else." She was, gods, she was, and it peeled away layer after layer of his defenses. She left him exposed in a way he wasn't comfortable with and yet began to crave.

A long, gentle lick stilled any further protests from her, and he laughed inside.

She couldn't tear her gaze away from the sight of his head, bent over her pussy as he paid it homage. Each time his tongue swept through her, she melted just a bit more. Warm, languid ripples of pleasure broke over her again and again. What he did devastated her in all the best and most frightening ways.

This, this licking and ministering to her with his mouth was intensely intimate. So much trust there to expose herself to him like that and for him to take; that's what got her most. She offered herself up, and he didn't rush, didn't ravish her, he tested, tasted, enjoyed every moment. Daniel Haws *savored* her.

It was so beyond her ability to grasp, what he made her feel.

Climax approached, sinuous and white-hot, it struck when he slowly sucked her clit, something she'd never imagined before but now surely couldn't be expected to live without. She'd heard women refer to screaming when they came and had never understood the phrase. Sure it felt good to orgasm, but so good you screamed?

She understood it as pleasure barreled through her, drowning her until the sensation had such an edge she lost her moorings and a sound, deep from her gut, tore from her mouth so loudly she was sure people across the courtyard had heard it.

She hoped they had, as she lay in an exhausted and utterly sated heap. She wanted it known just what he'd done to her. Daniel kissed her hip and then moved to take her mouth. She hesitated, knowing where he'd just been, but who was she to resist him?

The result left gooseflesh, a tangle of taboo, of desire, of satiation, she tasted herself, but it was on him, so it was more.

"Am I ready now? For the fucking part?" she asked, eyes still closed as she drew lazy circles on his forearm.

"Already? Did I misjudge your reaction when I ate your pussy?"

"Oh, that's a term I'm not sure how I feel about. On one hand, it's spectacularly dirty, and with you, dirty makes me feel all tingly and warm."

He laughed, kissing her chin.

"On the other hand, it seems vulgar. Which is probably why it sounds so dirty, which is why I like it, so never mind. I'm all right with it. Really all right with it. It might be my favorite thing ever."

His grin was something she hadn't seen from him yet, something she'd never seen directed at her, ever. The smug male grin, the one that says he knows what he's done, and he likes that it's made you all silly.

"We should wait."

She sighed at his half-hearted attempts to protect her virtue. This called for action on her part. Reaching down, she grabbed his cock. *Cock.* She liked the word; it made sense, she thought as she grasped it, hard, feral, proud. His pulse beat against her palm, the way he totally gave up arguing with her once she'd slid her fist down over him.

"I've seen this. Not your cock, um." She panicked as she remembered she had seen his cock when she'd watched him masturbate several days before.

He opened his eyes, knowing she was hiding something. His muscles coiled, and it made her sort of dizzy. This was totally how women became addled with men. She got it now, but the trap was sprung! Even knowing this, even knowing utterly silly things like muscles made her loopy and giggly, she couldn't bear the idea of not having him make her feel that way.

"You've seen what?" The voice was indolent, but she heard the steel beneath.

"You're very bossy."

One eyebrow rose imperiously. "*I'm* bossy? You're ordering me to fuck you. Who's bossy?"

She couldn't hide a grin. "I never denied I was bossy, and you *will* fuck me, Daniel Haws. I demand it, and you're just a . . . a tease if you don't."

"Indignation suits you," he murmured, stroking the backs of his fingers down her body, over each nipple until she forgot what she'd been talking about. Until he reminded her. "You've seen what? A cock in your hand? My cock?"

She huffed. "I've watched. I know I shouldn't have. I watched a couple out in the courtyard. They didn't see me. She"—Carina pumped her fist up and down his cock, startled when he groaned so very loud—"she did that."

"Do you want to know the jargon for that?" He adjusted her grip a little, showed her a pace and it warmed her, made her want him even more. But most of all, she wanted to show him pleasure.

"Yes."

"It's called a hand job. Men can give them to women, too. My sister is the kind of woman who—just a tiny bit slower, yes, that's very good—my sister likes to know things, always reading, always studying. She told me once that the term came from Earth. Funny the things that survive."

She liked that he shared that bit of his life with her. It meant he trusted her.

"Have you watched a lot?" His voice had deepened somehow. The strain was evident.

"A few times. I . . . I wanted to know, and it was so beautiful, even in a courtyard under the moon."

"But dirty." He stayed her hand. "Wait, I want to be in you when I come."

"Yes, dirty, and I must tell you I heartily approve of this direction. I'm on fertility blockers. I had to in preparation for my nuptials." She grimaced, and his lip curled.

"None of that talk now. That's not going to happen. Do you feel up to straddling me? You can control how fast and deep I am that way."

"Is that how it's normally done?" Gods, she sounded like such a twit. "I mean, I know the insert of boy part into girl part stuff. But, I've seen it twice. One was a man on a woman, the other was from behind, like horses."

Daniel scrubbed his hands over his face. "You're going to kill me. Sweet, I'm no virgin. You should have a gentler man, one with more patience."

This was *not* going in the right direction at all. She scrambled over him and realized what he meant and liked that idea. "I've masturbated before. I know the mechanics of sex. I've felt desire, and I even feel it now, despite your attitude. I just have to learn more than you do. I don't think it's fair to malign that. You said you'd teach me, after all."

"I meant what the world is like, not all the sexual positions. Also, you're quite the voyeur."

"Well, you said it, and you didn't say the other thing about only the world and not sexual positions, so you'd be a cheat if you tried to take it back now. I'm quite sure honor would prevent you from being such a cad. Teach me, Daniel. I only trust you to do it."

"You're dangerous." He snarled when he said it, but made no move to get away. So she took that as a compliment. "Rise up on your knees," he said, stroking his fingertips up her thighs. "But don't think I'm fooled by your game."

She laughed, rising up and putting her hand atop his as he grasped his cock. "I didn't think you'd be fooled, but it sounded good. If you were just a bit dumber, I'd have had you. I think I have it from here." She lowered herself, just letting the head slide inside. "This part"— she circled just a bit, and sparks of pleasure arced through her in a totally unexpected way. In a really good way—"goes here."

When he answered, she had to work to understand him, because his teeth were clenched. "Yes, take it slow so your body can adjust. I wanted to stretch you with my fingers but, dear gods, it's too late for that."

This was natural, right, and she let instinct take over. She didn't need a lesson; she just needed to listen to her body and to his. Rocking her hips, she took him in deeper, and he cursed.

"Are you all right?" he asked.

"It stings just a bit, but the next time I pull up and come back down a bit, it won't hurt anymore. It will feel very, very good." This time when she pushed herself down on him, the head of him hit the whisper of skin that technically made her a virgin. It hurt then, the press of his cock into her pussy. He felt enormous.

His hands on her hips tightened. "Here, sweet, let me ease you." He slid a hand between them, finding her clit, slowly circling it. Within a few breaths, she slickened, loosened around him and the burn was gone when he thrust up just a bit, but enough to slide past that barrier.

She handled the rest, fascinated by the intensity of her pleasure as he burrowed deeper into her body. And by the way he hardened as they remained locked together this way. His belly tautened; his fingers digging into her waist would leave a mark, though not one she'd regret in any fashion. His features froze, hard with concentration.

Whatever he did to her clit, it built slow and deep, and the only way it seemed she could get more, get what she needed to scratch an itch deeper than she'd felt before, was to let him in all the way.

Daniel looked up at her. The light of the waning day tinted her skin a soft pink. Never had he touched such a fine, beautiful thing. Inside she was hotter than the surface of the nearest sun, a scalding hot glove around his cock designed to make him embarrass himself by coming three breaths after he'd gotten inside her.

The wonder on her face as she'd experienced each new thing, her utter fearlessness, the way she moved, the sounds she made, all of it dug in deep, making itself at home within him when he knew the last thing he should be getting used to was the pulse and clasp of her inner muscles around his cock. And yet what else could he do but enjoy her, because he couldn't resist her magic?

"Do you like this?" She braced her hands on his belly and ground herself against him in a circular motion that nearly blew the top of his scalp off.

He simply thrust up a bit while raising a single eyebrow. Indeed. Did she expect him to write her poetry or sing her odes? Though for more of this feeling he might find himself doing just that, or anything else for that matter, so long as she kept herself wrapped around him.

"I quite like it up here, Daniel. I'm in charge, and you're beneath me looking like a debauched divinity. And I'm the one who debauched you." She laughed, and the jiggling parts of her only made him groan.

"Once you're used to me, I'll be back in charge," he growled, and she stilled, her laughter dying on a strangled breath. He paused, worried he'd frightened her, until her eyes widened and she nodded.

"Yes, all right then. That sounds agreeable. I believe I'd like that very much."

He laughed then. Gods, she was so completely irreverent and silly at times. Picking up the speed of his fingers, he figured he'd push her into orgasm at least once more before he came. Deep inside her, her muscles fluttered, and he felt it to his bones as his balls crawled up to his body.

With one hand, he thumbed her nipple in time with the circles around and against her clit as he began to meet her thrusts with his own, careful not to push too hard.

"Oh," she gasped, her eyes sliding all the way closed, her head falling back as she came around him. Once that began, he couldn't hold it back any longer. He pressed deep and came just as her body began to relax after her climax ended. She was warm and pliant around him, a secret smile on her lips as she straightened and looked down at his face.

Gently, he helped her roll to the side, glad there hadn't been a lot of pain or blood for her. Still, she'd be sore, so he got back up and began to run another bath for her.

"Let me help you clean up," he murmured, picking her up and holding her as if she were precious. Tears welled up, but she kept them locked away, knowing he'd be uncomfortable with them, knowing she couldn't tell him adequately just why they were good tears.

He put her down as gently as he'd picked her up, testing to be sure the water wasn't too hot. He got to his knees next to the tub, ministering to her without words. The washing cloth slid over her skin, not too hard, just enough to prove pleasant.

When she stepped out, he wrapped her in a towel and tried to usher her back into the bedroom.

"Wait. Let me wash *you*. You fought those men off. You carried me back and you worked very hard just now. Please, let me."

He took a deep breath and stepped into the tub. The water was nearly drained, so she ran more. "Sit on the shelf there." She watched him, this man who spent all his time protecting and taking care of her, yet so utterly unfamiliar with this sort of care toward himself. How strange that was!

"You shouldn't overdo it. You'll be sore after. It's the first time."

He hung his head as she washed his hair, loving the way his scalp felt against her hands. His words were gruff, but she knew the Daniel beneath that attitude. Oh, that one was gruff, too, but toward her, it was blunted, softer, and he made an effort to be that way.

"I hardly think I'm straining my vagina by washing off a big, gorgeous man and keeping him naked just a bit longer."

He snorted. "Vagina. That's another word I'd wager came from Earth."

"Did you expect my mother to teach me *pussy?*"

"I'd rather not think about that."

"Me either, because then I'd worry about her. Stand up so I can rinse you better. Do you have to be so tall?"

He looked down at her, his normally arrogant face softened with emotion. "I keep telling you, no news is a positive thing. If she'd been executed, chances are it would have been announced."

"I know." She soaped up his shaft and balls, liking that he began to harden again. "This is very handy."

He groaned and stepped away, rinsing himself off.

"We need to get moving. I'm going to give you some topical ointment for that cut and for your very sweet pussy." His grin made her shiver.

"You do that on purpose."

"Sure I do. Do you think you're the only one who can work the sexual charm? Now, we need to get out of here at dark. We'll hire a private ship. I know a few people who will book our passage."

"Why didn't you say so before?" She wandered into the bedroom where he loomed over her. Unfortunately, now he had underwear on.

"They're not contacts I wanted to use unless I had to. It's that time now."

"Ow!" She flinched when he spread the cream onto the cut on her side.

"Don't be such a baby. You made it worse when you seduced me. I told you that would happen." He then wrapped linen strips around her body, keeping the wound closed around the medicine and dry. "Choose a simple enough outfit that you can change out of. We'll switch transport at the next 'Verse. I can't risk having you out there like this."

"I'm not a baby." She started to snap at him again until he spread the cream on her pussy, getting her all worked up again even though a bit of soreness had settled in as he'd said it would. "Oh, my. I think perhaps that may need more application."

"Good gods, what have I unleashed?" He continued to mutter as he got dressed, strapping his ridiculous and yet obviously useful arsenal to his body.

"You have lots of weapons. I only have one. I need more."

"Have you always been like this?" he asked, stuffing the last few items they'd need into a pack.

"Witty? Intelligent? Charming? Oh, I know, sexy!"

"Annoying. Yes, that's the word I was looking for." He handed her a pack, and she hefted it up on her good side. "Hold still while I wrap your hair."

Expertly, he wrapped her hair in a covering cloth, twisting it until she looked like any one of the women whose hair she'd admired on the street. "Very handy. A killer who can dress hair. I don't know if I ever plan to let you go." She grinned, and he turned away, reaching up to tuck something behind a loose wall board.

"A note for a friend?"

"We'll need to keep my people apprised of our movements. Are you ready? We'll eat once we get settled."

It was her turn to snort. He ate every meal as if he hadn't seen food for days. And yet he was hard and fit, and it annoyed her because if she ate that way, she'd look far from hard and fit. She also realized her pack was very light.

"Hey, there's nothing in here."

"You don't need to carry all that. Now let's go. Here." He handed her two more weapons, a small personal blaster and another knife. He bent, strapping the sheath on at her ankle.

"Good thing you're wearing these pants." He indicated the long, loose-legged pants she'd picked up the day before. They enabled her a far better range of movement and were warmer than a skirt.

"Who knew I'd need better access to my knives, hmm? Why are you Mister Angry Face again? Also, I can carry a few frocks. You don't need to do everything."

He took her upper arm and hauled her close. "*I need* to keep you alive. I will do whatever I have to, to make that so. Now move that pretty ass and let's go."

Caught between vexation and preening, she opted for a sort of flirty flounce as they left the room. The man was infuriatingly sweet, and he didn't know it. But if he thought she was staying away from him now, after he'd made love to her the way he had, he was fooling himself. She meant to have Daniel Haws, and that was that.

He examined her closely, clearly suspicious of her expression. "That look makes me nervous."

She walked next to him, the pace quick but not rushed. "It should."

As they walked into the common space near the entrance to the guesthouse, they saw a group of people had gathered. There were arguments and some tears.

Daniel sighed. "Wait here. Let me see what's going on."

She walked right along with him. "I'm not a pet for you to order around."

"That's true. Pets are obedient," he hissed as they approached the throng near the front doors.

"What's happening here?" Daniel asked. His Imperial standard was quite good.

"There was an explosion on Krater. Scores dead. No one is talking any details. How'd this happen? Who did it? What did it?"

The woman next to the man who'd spoken looked scared and yanked on his arm. "He's just upset. We have family in Krater. Miners. Just worried, after all. No offense meant. We're good citizens."

"Time was a man could ask questions of his government and still be considered a good citizen."

Two security officers came in, homing directly on the man who'd been talking. The clerk made eye contact with Daniel and bustled away. They needed to get out of there before anything else happened and they started hauling people off to lockup.

He pretty much grabbed Carina and swept her from the room, not letting her feet touch the ground as he did. Many others did the same, not wanting to get involved. Daniel hated it, but there was no way around it and nothing he could have done to help.

His job was the pissed-off, beautiful woman he'd just manhandled out of the building.

$\mathscr{O}$nce they arrived two turns later at the next 'Verse, Andrei had met them at the portal city, dressed as a public conveyance driver. He'd driven them away from the portal and into the Lake District, which had also been above the snow line.

He'd shared some information. The Skorpios were still on the loose. People had been caught up in mass arrests and interrogations. Daniel knew Carina would feel guilt over that, but there was nothing to be done. They couldn't help in any other way but to get her and the data safely away.

The explosion on Krater had been hushed up, and no one in the Imperium was commenting. All traffic to and from Krater had been suspended, the portal decommissioned. The Federation had reason to believe that the event was connected to whatever data Carina carried.

Impatience to know the total sum of the data rested against his unease that it put her in even greater danger. In a very short time, she'd become important. Not just as cargo but as a woman. It was the last thing he needed, to be developing feelings for her in the middle of a fucking life-or-death mission. But, as he reflected on it, it seemed that everyone close to him had fallen for someone they met during some unusual circumstances. Figured that he, of all people, should have such a regimented life according to his rules and have a woman like Carina come in, turn it upside down and leave him wanting more. Her safety was far more than just about that data.

He'd moved to his last option. They had to get to a private portal run by mercenaries and smugglers, and there was one nearby, though heavily guarded. Daniel hoped to seven hells the authorities didn't know of this portal. If they did, it might be a trap. He didn't like being edged into a corner, but there was no other choice. It had been eleven days since he'd retrieved her from Caelinus, and each day they didn't get her to Federation territory was a day she wasn't safe, and the longer they were out, the higher the probability they'd be recognized.

Andrei let them into the safe house where a fire already burned in the massive fireplace dominating the main room. The place was one of theirs, well kept, well stocked and one of the most secure places he could have wanted if he was caught behind enemy lines and needed to keep his head down. If things had been less urgent, he'd have holed up for a week or so until things eased. But they did not have the luxury of time.

"I'm going back down to do some reconnaissance. I'll be back shortly." Daniel knew Andrei would sweep the area, make sure they weren't being watched or followed and listen in here and there to see if the three of them had raised any attention from the locals.

"Thank you, Andrei." Daniel bowed slightly, honoring his friend.

Andrei deserved the trust Daniel granted him, and Daniel knew how few people were as worthy as the man near the door.

"Don't be gone long," Carina said with concern on her face. "You look tired."

Andrei smiled her way, a quick flash of the man who was charmed by a beautiful woman worried for his well-being. He waved as he left, promising to return as soon as he could.

She was pale, and the dark smudges beneath her eyes told him she was exhausted and probably still a little sore. "Why don't you rest for a while? Take advantage of this downtime while we have it." He couldn't resist brushing a strand of hair from her face.

"I'm all right."

"No you aren't. Just a nap, you won't miss anything." He grinned, knowing her well already.

"I'd rest better if you were with me." She let him take her toward one of the bedchambers.

"That would *not* be restful. Ravishment takes a lot of work. You rest up, I'll get some work done and then we can get to the good stuff later." He kissed her forehead and she frowned but didn't move to get up as he tipped her into the bed and took her boots off.

After covering her up with blankets, he came back out to the main room to put some food on to cook. Time moved slowly, normally even. It was a gift, he knew from doing this job for as long as he had, to take care of basic tasks like cooking or washing up. When his life was nonstop running and fighting, the luxury of taking time to have a life, to be normal, kept him human and grounded.

He needed to read the file Andrei had uploaded to the comm unit there in the safe house, but he needed to do one other thing first.

He pushed the door of her room open quietly and simply leaned against the doorframe to watch. He looked at her sleeping form, the sound of her breath calming in a way chemicals could never achieve. She was safe, at least for the moment. That counted.

She'd held up through a lot. He'd managed to book passage through his dodgy contact back on the last 'Verse, but it had been two 'Verses *closer* to Caelinus. He'd wanted to get out, but they wouldn't be looking for them going toward the Center of the Imperium. Or so he hoped. They'd left the more impoverished and chaotic environs of those Edge Imperial 'Verses with these last slips, so he hoped she got a chance to rest up. Her side was nearly healed, but she'd been set on seduction, and he'd been very hard-pressed to resist, even if he'd wanted to, which he didn't much. He'd managed to avoid her and to refuse outright when he had to. For the time being, she seemed to back off slightly. But he knew her well enough by that point to understand she'd just be back and far more irresistible.

She was something he couldn't define, but had become rather essential to his life. They would fall into bed again, he knew it was inevitable, he just needed to hold his cock in check until they'd arrived somewhere safe enough to let his guard down. He hoped that was soon; there was only so much masturbation a man could survive without wrist injuries.

He'd tried, truly had, to resist her, but he found himself opening up to her, sharing bits of his life he'd never intended to. And she had not judged. She had not pitied. She listened to him, saw something in him he didn't believe he had.

It unraveled him, and he found himself totally enchanted for the first time in his nearly forty years. It unraveled him but also fortified, he thought as he went back out to the main room to get the files and drink some kava while the meal cooked and he could plan.

* * *

$\mathscr{A}$ndrei came back several hours later. "Smells good." He hung his coat and kicked the snow from his boots, removing them before he entered the main area where Daniel had been working.

Daniel ladled up a bowl of the sturdy soup he'd made and slid it across the table. "Eat. Kava?"

Andrei nodded as he began to eat. "She okay?" He jerked his head toward the bedroom where Carina still slept.

"Knife fight two days ago. Ambush by street thugs. She didn't run or scream, didn't cry. She used her weapon and stood her ground. Handled herself well. Got a surface wound. Scared the hells out of me. But she's strong, Andrei, strong in a way I hadn't thought she had in her."

Andrei's grin was so quick that if Daniel hadn't known his friend for as long as he had, he would have missed it.

Andrei sipped the kava. "I knew the night we had her run for hours that she was made of strong stuff. Looks like a strong wind would knock her over, but she's sturdy in spirit. Doesn't give up. I like her. She's tough." He paused and looked Daniel straight on. "Pretty, too. I'd be lying if I said I hadn't noticed the way you two look at each other. Just keep an eye on the road and her, too, yes?"

He scoffed. "I've never not done my job, Andrei."

"You've never had cargo that was Carina Fardelle before either."

Gods knew that was the truth.

"It's not marriage. She means something to me, but you're making more out of it than it is. She will arrive in Ravena and find a whole world of opportunities available to her that she's never imagined. I'm a passing fancy."

"Are you two talking about me?" Carina wandered into the room. She'd changed from the lighter clothing she'd been wearing into a sweater and long pants. Her hair was still sleep-tousled, and tenderness flooded him, unbidden and unexpected. He shook it off as he continued to take her in. Thick socks on her feet and a pair of fingerless gloves completed the outfit. Smart woman.

Daniel batted away emotion with dry humor. "Of course we are. It's all we do. We already compared what we planned to wear tomorrow, so naturally we had to discuss the shoes you had on earlier."

She whacked him with her hand when she glided by, and he barely hid the way he breathed in to catch her scent. Andrei didn't miss it, though he said nothing more.

"Sit down and eat." Daniel pushed a bowl of the soup her way and slapped away her hand when she moved in to steal his kava. "Think again, princess. That's mine. There's a fresh pot right in front of you though, should you want your own."

"Yours would be better," she muttered and dug into the soup. "Very good. Did you make this?"

"I'm a fair cook. Good enough to keep myself from starving for the last nearly forty years. I'm not entirely useless."

She looked him up and down and quirked a smile his way. "Not at all."

Daniel managed to hold back his comment in front of Andrei. "So what's going on out there?" he asked, shifting into work mode.

Carina found the way he did that awe inspiring even as it annoyed her. He always seemed to be thinking about things on three different levels. All while looking as good as he did.

"Unrest. Skorpios came through here four days ago. Arrested many. Some disappeared. Population is pretty scared, but also angry.

Seems Fardelle's men have been here a lot of late. The mercs tell me their portal hasn't been located yet, but Fardelle has two of his own running the breadth of the Imperium."

"Merk? What's a merk?"

Andrei looked to Carina. As Daniel had asked him questions in her presence, he'd given Andrei permission to speak mostly freely. Carina noticed it and figured it had been on purpose as Daniel rarely did things without meaning to. She was sure there were things Andrei wouldn't tell her, but that Daniel trusted her when she'd been sure he thought she was a spy, meant a lot.

"Mercenary. They're soldiers for hire. Out here mainly they smuggle goods, but they hire to do many jobs."

"They help you for credits then? If so, how can you trust them not to turn us in?"

Daniel's look of approval was quick. She'd have missed it if she hadn't been mooning over him.

"Not all of them would do anything for credits, not if they didn't believe in the cause or at the very least, not be offended by it. I've known mercenaries for most of my life. They're more complicated than you'd expect." Andrei's face lit in a way she'd not seen from him before and knew he spoke of someone he cared about.

"These mercs have helped us several times. They're connected to some friends of ours on the other side of the line." Daniel hesitated but didn't say anything else.

"Your mother was seen two days ago in the courtyard of the compound," Andrei told her, bringing her attention away from asking Daniel what he was holding back. "She appeared unharmed but had a retinue of guards."

A wave of relief hit her, dizzying. She put her head down on the table and was surprised when Daniel ran a gentle hand up and down her back.

"Thank you, Andrei. I needed to know that." Carina blinked back tears as she straightened.

He stood and bowed low. "It was my pleasure then, my lady, to bring you some joy. I know times are difficult for you right now. But you're doing the right thing, and she knows that." He looked back to Daniel. "I need to get moving. I'll be putting the rest in place. I'll see you at the portal tomorrow. The coordinates are in the data I just uploaded."

"You're leaving? We haven't had much time to visit." Carina sat back. "Don't go. It's dark and cold. Stay, eat. I'm sure you can take care of your secret stuff tomorrow. There are extra beds, and you look exhausted. You can't be expected to do your job well if you're exhausted."

"I have some people to meet shortly, and I will find my rest after that. Thank you, dear lady, for your concern." Andrei bowed over her hand and kissed it. Carina blushed very prettily.

"Will you be traveling with us from now on then?"

"That remains to be seen. If I'm needed with you, yes. But we don't always need to travel together to be of use. It was good to see you, Carina. I will again tomorrow. Please, you rest as well and be sure Daniel does, too." Andrei flipped the collar of his coat up and pulled a hat on and down as he left.

"Did we chase him away? Make him feel unwelcome?" Carina watched Andrei's retreat before turning back to her food.

Daniel shook his head. "My guess is that he's got a woman waiting for him somewhere. Many of you seem to go for that type."

"The ridiculously gorgeous, tall, long dark hair and piercing pale blue eyes type?" Though she teased, she wasn't being false. Andrei had that dark, gorgeous and brooding personality type. Women wanted to fix men like him, deluded themselves they'd be the one to crack through that mysterious facade and capture his heart. Of course, who was she to judge as she stared at another version of that man and hoped with all her heart that she'd be the one to matter to him in ways no one else ever would.

She tried not to smile but couldn't help it when she saw the annoyance draw his brows together. Poking at a man like Daniel was silly, but it amused her greatly, and it only made him more alluring when he got ruffled.

"In any case, he'll do some work and then go to her. She'll keep him company and keep him warm, too. Andrei isn't one to want for company if and when he desires it."

Her eyes widened as she leaned toward him. "Oh! Tell me more. I want to know every last detail."

He snorted. "I'm sure you do. As my mother used to say to me, wanting things is what makes us human, it's good to want things. Andrei's private life is his own, Carina."

She waved a hand. "You're tedious when you try to be stern with me. As you so often point out, I'm a princess. If my father's sternness didn't stop me, who are you to think you can?"

He rolled his eyes and sipped his kava.

"As for Andrei, we can pass the time, and I can get to know him through you. I don't need to know how big his genitals are or what his favorite position is. Just, you know, is he a ladies' man? A shy type? What?"

He heaved a sigh. It wouldn't do to indulge her; she'd only get worse. But he simply found it beyond his ability. "I couldn't tell you how big his cock is, I've never looked, nor do we talk about favorite positions. He has female company quite frequently. I'm under the impression he's handsome enough; he certainly attracts women when we're out and about. Your reaction earlier was clear enough." He'd tried for dry but ended up sounding petulant. He tightened his mouth.

"You've never looked? Really? I would look. What's *your* favorite position?" Her internal filters about what should be said and not said were as absent as his ability to control her when she didn't want to be controlled.

"Don't you ever get tired of asking intrusive questions?"

She blinked and finished her kava. "About your sex life? No. So?"

He leaned in very close, so close his breath met her lips, tasted her breath in return as he breathed in. "I like to take a woman from behind, when she's on her hands and knees or bent over something like a table."

Her breath hitched. "Really? Why?"

"I like to be in control. I like how deep I can get into her pussy. I like dominating her with my body that way."

"Oh," she breathed out. "I want that, too."

His blood slowed; instead of the insistent pound, it throbbed. Warmth seeped through him, warmth he realized was desire of a depth he'd never experienced before. She intoxicated him in the most random ways.

He was bombarded with visions of her bent over as he fucked her from behind. Of the way her breasts would be free to sway, of what her spine would look like as she arched it. He'd be in deep and tight, able to reach around and play with her clit to make her come over and over.

Mouth dry, he tried to swallow. "I don't know if you're ready for that." Gods knew *he* wasn't ready for it. It was one thing to fuck her as he had the first time. He could control himself better, rein in his need—the insatiable need for her that lived in his belly every moment of the day.

But from behind, he wondered at just how thrilling it would be to take her in a way he rarely did with women he wanted to see the next day. It was an intensity far easier to share with a stranger than with someone he cared for.

She stood and pulled her sweater over her head, exposing her underclothes, her nipples visible through the thin, nearly transparent fabric. He mightily approved of the Imperial fashion of these silky, see-through, form-fitting undershirts rather than simply bras.

"I *am* ready, Daniel. I know you want to believe that I'm some inexperienced nitwit. It makes it easier to use me, to instruct me rather than make love to me, *with* me. You hold back. Even when you're pouring yourself into my body, you hold back so much your muscles vibrate with it. I may not have a great deal of practical experience, but I'm smart enough to know I want you to let go with me."

With a whisper, the undershirt was gone, followed by her pants. His head spun at the truth in what she said and that she understood it so well.

"Possess me," she murmured, meaning it. She didn't want to be used by Daniel, she wanted him to own her, to take her and mark her as his.

He stood, stalking to her, and without any preamble, he grabbed her up and hauled her to his body, covering her mouth with his, taking what he wanted, leaving the honey of desire in his wake.

There was nothing to be done but hold on. Wrap her arms around him, pressing herself tighter as he plundered her mouth. His taste burned into her, indelible. He would be there forever. Until she breathed her last, no matter what came between now and then, she'd know his taste; it would own part of her all her life.

His tongue roved through her mouth, tasting, teasing, seducing hers to tangle, follow. She moaned softly, and he swallowed the sound. When he pulled away, he nipped her bottom lip, pulling it, his gaze locked on hers before finally letting it go.

His expression was one of challenge, and she knew what she did next had better count. He was opening himself up to her, exposing part of his inner life, and she wanted him to understand she wanted it. Wanted him to take her because she trusted him, because the idea of being possessed by him thrilled her to her toes, and she would feel no shame about that desire.

"You're still dressed." She licked her lips to taste him anew. He saw it, watched her tongue slide across the curve of her bottom lip where he'd bitten her just moments before.

He paused, but only for a breath as he held a hand out. She took it, and he led her into the bedroom she'd napped in earlier.

"I'm going to make sure everything is secure, because I plan to give you all my attention once we get started in earnest." Pressing a kiss to her wrist, he stepped back and through the door.

She used the time to freshen up, to brush out her hair and to try to think up some pretty, artful position for when she got into bed. Her brain rushed through that kiss over and over. The way he'd handled her had unknotted something inside her. It rushed out, seeking more.

When she came back into the room, he was there, naked on the bed. He'd made a fire, and the warm light licked over his skin.

She moved straight to him, into his arms, and sighed happily. "You're very warm."

"Handy for women on cold evenings, I suppose."

She felt the curve of his lips at her neck, knew he teased. "I'm quite sure. But you're here and I'm here and you look so delicious I'm all aflutter with it." She flapped her hands about until he took them in his own.

"Are you afraid?"

She shook her head. "No. Not of you or what you do to me. I . . . you excite me. Make me feel beautiful and desired in a way I'd never imagined possible. It thrills me, titillates me until my breath shortens and my heart threatens to burst from my body."

One corner of his mouth lifted. "Thank you."

"For what?"

"For that, what you just said. I'm honored you'd trust me. You *are* beautiful, and I do desire you."

He pushed her back, looming over her with his weight on his elbow. His features were intense as she waited for him to make the first move. She wanted this so much she loathed the idea of messing it up.

"These are beautiful." He traced his tongue around first one nipple and then the other. "I think about them all the time."

She smiled, pleased to hear it. When he bit her nipple next, it was just shy of pain. She jolted, but when he swiped his tongue over it, her nipple bloomed not with pain but with pleasure.

As she writhed against him, he showered her nipples with attention. So much attention she wondered if this alone could make her climax. She held his head to her, his hair cool against her fingers. She moved her hips, needing just a bit more to tip over the edge, but it wasn't enough.

"Shhh. Let me take care of that," he said against her skin as he kissed the underside of her breast and then over each rib. Lips on her belly, a tongue flicking against her skin just below her belly button.

He was going to love her with his mouth again. She widened her thighs, her fingers grasping the coverlet as he put his tongue deep inside her.

Daniel couldn't get enough of her taste. Of the way she felt—soft, hot, creamy—against his mouth. Her clit stood up for him as he licked through her pussy, up from her gate. She arched, eagerly showing him what she wanted. She was not shy about her desires, which only made him want her more.

He'd wanted to hold this back for a while, spend more time getting her ready, but the moment he'd sucked her clit between his lips, she'd exploded, coming hard and loud so he'd continued to lick until she'd calmed.

"I'm sorry," he said, kissing the seam between her leg and her body.

"For what?" she asked, her voice lazy. When she had an orgasm, she went all loose and compliant. He wanted to laugh at that, at the idea of keeping her out of his hair and obeying his commands when they were out in the field by feeding her a steady diet of orgasms. Far more fun than having to scare her or drug her.

"I'd planned to take more time with that."

She made a dismissive sound. "You never have to apologize for making me have an orgasm. From now on, you can assume that I do want one, yes."

She'd grown comfortable enough to joke with him far more often. At first she'd been so wide-eyed and serious, but then he began to realize she had a quick and lively sense of humor beneath the cool exterior he'd first seen her wear. She teased his own humor to the surface. Made him happy.

She stretched, and he watched, liking the play in her muscles, the way her breasts heaved up as she arched her back. "Now, I think it's my turn."

"Greedy. You just had your turn."

She got to her knees and pushed him back to the bed. Straddling him again, she kissed down his neck and licked over each nipple. He groaned, arching into her mouth.

"I meant, my turn to love you with my mouth. It's obviously not eating you, or maybe it is. What is it called?"

He laughed. "Doesn't matter what it's called, only that it's done. You can suck my cock, blow me, go down on me, give me oral pleasure or love with me your mouth. I have no preference for what you call it."

"Well, you'll have to help me here."

"You haven't peeked at the scullery maid sucking off a guard or some such?" He teased, but truth be told, he found her voyeuristic tendencies quite sexy.

She blushed. "I still need some guidance."

"I *knew* it. What a naughty girl you are, Carina. Did you make yourself come right as you watched?" His voice lowered as his skin tingled at the thought.

"Sometimes," she whispered. "But it never felt like what you do to me. Your mouth on me; your hands are not the same as mine. It feels so much better when you touch me."

How she'd managed to keep alive in that family with such honesty, he wasn't sure.

She scooted down his body, leaning down over his cock. Her breath slid across the head. "What do you like?" She grasped him, angling him to take him into her mouth. "Licking?" She licked around the crown and over the slit. "You taste very good. I'd wondered what you'd taste like."

"All just fine." Really fine. For what seemed like an entire lifetime, he held himself in check, letting her explore him, learn what he liked and didn't. Her enthusiasm was far more erotic than any perceived expertise would have been.

Effective, too. He put his hands on her shoulders, pushing her back gently, but she didn't seem to want to go.

"Any longer, and I'm going to come in your mouth. Normally I wouldn't be bringing this up as a reason to stop, but right now I need to fuck you."

She pulled back, her eyes widening for a brief moment.

"From behind."

She nodded eagerly.

"I want you on your hands and knees." He settled behind her. Gods, what a sight. Nothing he could have done in life should have merited this woman here, now in this bed with him.

Being there with him behind her was so erotic she felt faint because of it. Her pussy ached, her lips tingled from licking and sucking on him for as long as she had. She knew she was totally exposed to him this way and imagined what it must look like from his perspective.

"Put your hands there on the headboard."

She complied, stretching back to try to make contact with him. One hand held her hip, stilling her movement, while the other reached between her thighs, fingertips sliding through her pussy and up to her clit.

She whimpered, wanting more.

He gave her more. More of what he wanted first, to shoot her into climax again, and as her body still trembled, he began to press into her with the fat, blunt head of his cock. Her fingers tightened on the headboard as he continued to push into her. Shivers ran up and down her body as she parted for him, slid around him as every part he touched within her sent shock waves of sensation through her.

And then he began the inexorable thrust and retreat, building up rhythm as she received his body. His hands were all over her skin, caressing, kneading, teasing her nipples into aching points, a butterfly of a touch over her clit. He controlled everything: the speed, how deep he got, how hard he thrust. He played her body, excited her senses until there was nothing but them, nothing but him over her, building her up until she felt as if she would explode from it.

He was not holding back, not this time. He fucked her hard and fast, keeping her wet and open to him as she danced on the edge of orgasm, his fingers giving just the right amount of pressure to entice and not oversensitize.

When she broke apart, his gasp against her shoulder and the hard, last dig into her pussy told her he'd joined her.

"Wow."

He pulled out carefully and left the bed, coming back shortly with a wet cloth for her to clean up with.

"Did I hurt you?" his question was quiet there in the dark. She heard the concern there, the worry that he'd frightened her with the raw way he'd taken her.

Carina snuggled up to him, pulling the blankets atop where they lay. "That was amazing. I've never felt anything like it. You didn't hurt me at all, Daniel. You gave me pleasure." And made her feel safe, cherished, worth something.

He didn't speak again as they slid into sleep, and for once, she didn't dream of disappearing.

$\mathcal{D}$aniel eased his way through the streets of a town some distance from the place where Carina slept deeply and safely. Andrei had shown up as deep of night broke toward early morning. They'd exchanged a nod, Andrei gave him an address and Daniel slipped into the darkness.

There it was. The night still lived as he crept up three flights of stairs and into the flat at the end of the hall. The place was a mess, but not so bad he couldn't find what he needed to. A dermal patch the size of his fingernail would do the trick. Those who knew the man, who hated him in secret or in public, would shake their heads and murmur about what a shame it was to be struck down so young by a random heart ailment no one knew he'd had. And then they'd go about their business, and no one would remember the dead in a week.

Daniel would remember the dead. His operative, a woman named

Leal who did her job with honor and skill, had been here to clear the way for him and Carina. She'd trusted this piece of trash who'd been her source on previous occasions, and then he'd turned on her, selling her out and getting her tortured and killed by Imperial soldiers.

He could not turn back time and bring her back. But he could be sure that source never killed another soul. Daniel had been responsible for Leal. She'd done her job and had died because of that. That the person who did that to her still lived was not something Daniel was prepared to suffer.

On his way back to Carina, Daniel had worked to slough off the darkness, to put it away deep inside himself. She was something far too precious to taint with that. He couldn't always shield her from what he did, but he would when he could.

The sun had begun to rise, and when he opened the door, the warmth hit him first, welcoming him back, and then he scented kava and something so delicious his mouth watered.

Carina looked up from the table where she chatted animatedly to Andrei when he entered the main room.

"We were wondering when you'd return." She smiled, narrowing her eyes momentarily, but refrained from asking more. Though, if he knew her, she'd already tried getting her answer through Andrei and failed.

"Now sounds good." He hung his coat and hat on a peg, left his boots in the entry.

"Hmpf. Come and sit then. I've baked some biscuits and made some sausages. Andrei brought eggs, too." She smiled in Andrei's direction, and he waved it away.

"You're the one who made them. My part was easy."

"I'll be back shortly. I just need to clean up." He slipped past them, nodding once at Andrei. He wanted to go to her, gather her up and kiss her, keep her against his body until he remembered all of himself again. Instead, he kept moving. He needed to wash up first, needed to cleanse the death from his skin before he touched her.

Bent over the basin, splashing water on his face, he wasn't surprised to hear the door open and close. Her scent would have given her away even if he hadn't felt her presence before he smelled her and that night-blooming floral scent she bore.

"You weren't in bed when I woke up," she said quietly, handing him a cloth to dry his face and neck when he straightened. "I thought you'd left me."

Without meaning to, he pulled her to him, hugging her. "I had some business to attend to. I wouldn't leave you. Andrei was here the whole time I was gone."

"That's not what I meant," she said into his chest.

He held her away so he could see her face. "Do you think so little of me?"

She shook her head. "It's *me*, I think."

He shook her once because she was being ridiculous but ruined his hard edge by kissing her soundly. "You? What would your problem be then? Too beautiful? Too sexy? Please do inform me so that I may run in fear."

Her mouth screwed into a smile. "You're a cad."

"That I am. But I'm not the man who'd fuck you and abandon you."

She nodded. "Right. So . . . beautiful, huh?"

He groaned. "Go get my breakfast ready, woman! I need to change my clothes."

"So, when we settle in Ravena, will you return home like this a lot?"

He couldn't control his flinch of surprise, not that she seemed shaken by it. "I don't know what will happen when I get you back safely."

"Daniel, if you think you can make me love you and then wander away to keep getting your clothes bloody and sleep alone, or worse, with women who don't care about you, you're quite mistaken."

"Carina, you don't love me. You don't know me."

"Don't insult me. I *do* know you. I have seen you pushed to your very limit. I have seen you at your worst and your best. I may not have known you since we were children, but don't try to deny that I know you." She put her hand over his heart. "I know you better than you know yourself."

"This situation is extraordinary. Most people, most couples don't have this sort of meeting. You're just caught up in the excitement and drama of it."

She straightened and gave him an imperious glare. *There* was the Carina Fardelle he'd met first. So strong, regal, sexy and pissed-off, too. "Now you're insulting me again. Once more, and I will kick your ball sac up into your throat. How dare you tell me what I feel, like I'm a youngling not out of tights? You have no right. I know what I feel. I may have been a virgin, but I'm not a simpleton. You think I don't know my own emotions? Can you stand there and say that to my face? After what we've shared? Think again, Daniel. I'm here to stay. Get used to it." She kissed his chin and left the room with a flounce.

He sighed, leaning back against the basin, scrubbing his hands over his face. Love? Gods, what a surprise she was. If someone had told him that he'd end up telling cargo his last name, sharing personal details and a bed with her, he'd have called them a liar.

But her scent clung to his skin; the feel of her flesh against him still lay on his memories. He couldn't remember the last time he'd slept the full night with a woman he'd had sex with. He itched for her, cared about her, wanted her, but there was a long way between that and something permanent when they returned to the Center.

The Center and the reality of their different ranks. Though she wasn't a citizen of the Federation, there was no doubt in Daniel's mind they'd offer her that, and she'd be treated as Ranked. Though many Houses had begun to rethink their policies and rules about marriage to unranked people, the perception remained, the *expectation* remained that Ranked married Ranked. She'd have to deal with that on top of losing her family, and he had no right to expect such a thing from her.

He was quite sure he didn't merit such a sacrifice when he turned to see she'd left him a clean sweater near the door.

As Daniel finished cleaning up, Carina wrinkled her nose as she scrubbed at the stain on Daniel's shirt. "Andrei?"

"If this is about Daniel's favorite color, I don't know."

"Is it a requirement of you spy types to have this sort of humor?"

He sighed, and the scent of his cigarette rose on the air, sharp and spicy.

"Who are we without laughter?" His voice was quiet and filled with an emotion she couldn't name, and she knew he wouldn't tell her.

"Does he have someone? Back in Ravena?" she burst out, frustrated.

"I have *you*, Carina. Which is more than enough for any man to manage even without half the Imperium on our tail." Daniel came into the room, brushing past her, pausing when he saw what she was doing. "Your hands are going to be chapped. The soap is harsh." He took the shirt and rinsed her hands, drying them and leaving her confused again. One minute he was pretending she was just another woman, and the next he did this sort of thing. Were all men this way? Was it standard issue along with a penis?

Did that mean she was his woman? For then? For the next while? Forever? Did it mean he didn't have a woman, but he was sleeping with her? What did it mean?

He laughed. "I have no idea how you managed to keep from getting killed. I can see everything you feel on your face."

But she didn't join him. "If I wanted to wear a mask with you, you'd never know anything but what I wanted you to. Don't make the mistake of thinking I wanted to live that way. I *had* to live that way or end up being gone one day with no warning. I am an expert at lying, an expert at being whatever I need to be to keep alive."

Andrei got up, took his mug of coffee and left the room.

"I made a vow to myself as we made the first trip to the portal. I do myself the honor of feeling and having emotions, and when those people around me deserve it, I will share that with them."

"I apologize," he said, bowing over her hands.

She exhaled, charmed by him again.

"I accept your contrition. You charm me, Daniel Haws. You catch me off guard, and it occurs to me that you know about as much about romantic relationships as I do. Though, more about sex, which I do appreciate."

A grin took his lips briefly.

"Is that what we have? A romantic relationship? Am I your woman? Why are you flinching, for the gods' sake! You act as if being with me is so terrible, but you're not acting that way when you're having sex with me, or drying my hands."

"Carina, slow down. You're right, I don't have much experience with romantic relationships. I don't have them at all. And being with you isn't terrible, even though you do talk far more than I'd prefer sometimes."

"You're ridiculous."

He drew his thumb over her knuckle. "I am. But I told you when I came into the room, I have you. What that means tomorrow, I don't know. We have a lot to deal with just now, and you don't know me." He put a finger against her lips. "I mean you don't know me as a person, the little things that create friendship and a relationship. The more you learn, the more your feelings may change."

"Still doesn't explain why you flinched like I'd hit you or something. Not that you don't need a good smack, you smart-arse."

"Gods, you're violent. I flinched because people don't talk like this. Women don't just blurt out a demand to know what they mean to the man. It isn't done."

She tossed her hands up in the air with a snarl. "Who says? That's just stupid. Why shouldn't it be done, I ask you? The woman is supposed to stand around looking pretty and waiting for the male to tell her what he feels? She can't say it first? Who made these rules? I'd risk a significant stack of credits, of which I have none, to say a man made them up and they suit him just fine. You listen here, Daniel Haws, *I love you*. I know you don't think I know what love is or that I don't really love you, that it's just the sex talking. But I know what I feel, and I'm not afraid to say it."

He opened his mouth only to close it again. She just scrubbed blood from his clothes, knew it was a product of his job and yet, with her, he was different. He was gentle and caring, it was like a secret she carried. She liked it even as she thought him utterly dim for not just admitting the inevitable.

She snorted. "Don't. You don't have to speak. You'll only ruin it with some gruff man saying about me being young or something. This way, I get the last word, and you know I'm right." She tiptoed up and kissed his chin. "I also think you should let your beard grow a bit. I like facial hair on men. Go sit. The food will get cold, and we should bulk up. Andrei says we'll most likely leave today."

She turned to make him a plate, grinning that he seemed as confused as she was, only she was better at hiding it. Ha!

"You can come back in here now, Andrei," Daniel called out. Sometime later, Andrei strolled in and got another mug of kava before having another plate of food. She may have detected amusement in his eyes, but she couldn't say for sure.

"I checked the routes out of the city. We should be able to keep to these back roads and arrive in three standard hours. They can take us two portal slips. That puts us back on Philos." Andrei smoked calmly, even as Carina's heart pounded. There were moments she nearly forgot they were in such dire circumstances, and then reality came smashing in again.

"All right." Carina watched Daniel plan, working through possibilities. "We can get at least to Silesia from there."

Silesia was the last 'Verse before the Edge and the beginning of Federation territory. It was their face to the public; it was clean and well run, food in good supply, a high quality of life. At least near the portal city. Go out a few clicks, and it was a totally different story. Out there things were a less picturesque. A poorly policed mess of a 'Verse where chaos reigned far more often than calm.

"Many times Timus Barley, one of my father's ministers, would tell him to send the Skorpios to Silesia. We can't keep settlers there, you know. They have no police to speak of. The water there is in demand, but he can't be bothered for some reason." It seemed a waste to her to only polish up one part of such a large 'Verse.

"The water there is rich with minerals used in convalescence. The mercs do big business in it back on our side. It prevents children in some 'Verses from intestinal sicknesses that kill so many otherwise. But we can't get it via trade. He won't deal with us at all." Daniel slathered another thick slice of bread with the preserves she found in a cold box.

Nausea was leaden in her belly. Infant mortality was not a problem in a great percentage of the Imperial 'Verses. But there were those, like the ones closer to the Edge, where poverty ran unchecked. The 'Verses didn't have any infrastructure, no potable water, health services were scant, starvation was rampant. That those children who died by the thousands of intestinal ailments could be saved with some water in their own 'Verse, but her father was too lazy or careless to have protection for those who would work to procure it, brought shame to her belly, crowding around the nausea.

"You are not him, Carina. Don't own guilt that is not yours." Andrei stood up. "I have weapons. I'll load the conveyance up. New papers for you." He tossed a packet on the tabletop.

Daniel nodded, looking through the paperwork. "Subtle."

She packed some food in a bag. He'd be hungry again before they reached the portal, so she'd be able to offer him a snack and please him. Hopefully. She could never tell when he'd be happy she was helping or annoyed. The man really was a puzzle sometimes.

"What's subtle?"

He looked up, surprised by her question. "Nothing. We're married, same names, Carrie and Neil. These mercs are trustworthy enough to arrange to get us a few 'Verses down the line, but that's it. Don't get drawn into conversation with them. Don't tell them anything. You can't trust them. Just follow my lead and don't do that thing you do. Not today."

Her brows flew up. "*Thing I do*? Like insist I'm not slow?"

"Don't get upset." He slung a bag toward the doorway and began to tie his boots. "I don't think you're dim. You like to talk. Normally that's one thing, but you like to share and get to know people, and these are not people to get to know. They're criminals, some of whom would sell you to the highest bidder."

"Upset? Listen here, you could use some lessons in making friends." She muttered to herself about his inability to deal with being human as she put the bag with the food near the other bags at the door.

He caught up, touching her arm. "My job isn't about making friends. It's about keeping you alive, and that's what I'm going to do. I make no apologies for it."

"Grr. Well that's a good thing. It's not your strong point. You're so bristly. Where's the man who woke me up last night to love me? Hmm? I like that man better than this one."

He moved quickly, hauling her to his body, crushing his mouth against hers until she went weak. When he broke the kiss, he pressed his forehead to hers. "Good. That man loves to fuck you in the middle of the night. But the man you need right now is the bristly one. That's the one who keeps your pretty ass in one piece."

Curse him and his ability to make her all trembly. "Oh." Still, she wasn't stupid, just love-addled. "Did you do that to shut me up?"

His lips quirked. "Yes. But that was just one of the many positives of kissing you." And with that, he began to haul things to the conveyance.

She stomped through the house, making one last pass to be sure they hadn't left anything behind. The expulsion of all that energy left her feeling better, though admittedly it was that kiss she attributed to most of her improvement in mood. Not that she'd tell Daniel so.

"Are you ready?" He waited near the door as she came through.

He held up a coat, helped her put it on. "It's cold out there. Even down the mountain it's snowing." With a kiss to her forehead, he put a hat over her hair and took the bag she'd brought down.

"Don't think you're out of trouble," she warned.

He held a smile back, but she saw the quiver of his lips. "I would never dream of it. This will just make us a more convincing married couple."

"Laugh while you can." One of these days they *would* be a married couple; he was just too male to know it. She sailed past, letting Andrei help her up and into the conveyance. That's when she noticed Daniel wearing a blaster in a holster at his shoulder. Today he wasn't trying to hide his ferocity like he had thus far.

"Let's go, Andrei." Daniel settled in on her other side so she remained in between him and Andrei. All that competent male strength in the cabin relaxed her, but she was still glad she had her weapons strapped on.

The drive was long and not always on the best of roads, but the scenery was breathtaking. They stopped midway to check for trackers and to stretch their legs after the bumpy ride.

Daniel stood looking out over the snow-covered hillside leading down to a valley. His breath misted as he finished a sandwich. She was content to simply watch him, loving the way he looked.

"When I was a boy, we lived in the middle of the desert. It would get so hot during certain times of the year that you couldn't be outside for longer than a few minutes for fear of heat stroke or skin burns the heaviest of lotions couldn't protect against. Snow is such a funny thing. A miracle."

Oh, he made her so gushy inside when he was like this. "I'd always thought Ravena was covered by metropolises broken by large swaths of natural landscape. Lakes and such."

"Ravena is a wonder. I've been to many 'Verses, and it remains my favorite. The outback, where I grew up, takes up roughly a quarter of the landmass. The vents that power the cities are hyperactive there, making it very warm all the time. Only certain kinds of plant life can grow out that way."

"What sorts of jobs brought men out there? Keeps them there? What did you do that you lived there?" She knew her barrage of questions amused him, but true to his promise to teach her about the world, he answered.

"The region has mining and some of the energy from the most active vents is harnessed for power to the outlying areas. My father was a teacher in one of the schools there for most of my childhood."

"Really?" She ducked her head. "I am, too. A teacher, I mean. Of a sort."

He cocked his head. "You are? That explains a lot. What do you teach?"

"*Explains a lot?* Pfft. The children who live in the compound and surrounding village can only attend school if their parents pay a quarterly fee. The farmers and merchants can easily afford this, and the schools are quite good. But the laborers have a more difficult time. They can't pay the fees, and their children remain illiterate. I set up a school for those children whose parents don't have the credits. It's nothing fancy. Reading and sums. I've been able to get some of them odd jobs around the area so they can make up the difference and get into a proper school."

"That's what my father used to do. He taught kids like that as well. Only schooling until age seventeen is paid for by House Lyons. He's a right bastard in most ways, but he changed a lot of kids' lives."

"Not yours?"

He shrugged. "Not in a way I'd say was positive."

"That's a shame."

"Nothing as tragic as all that." Daniel brushed his pants off. "We need to get back inside. It's too cold out here."

She allowed him to steer her back, but once they were all inside and had started driving again, she leaned against him. He adjusted her, telling her he had to keep access to his sidearm, but he kept her close.

She wondered about his father, wondered if he was like her own. There were other types of men, different than her father, she knew. There were families in her father's court. She used to study them, trying to figure out the whys of it. There were men who were kind to their wives and affectionate with their children. She saw it in the children she taught.

Of course, she had left them. Who would teach them now? What if the information she carried enabled the Federation to defeat them and they invaded? Had she just made a mistake that would harm millions?

Daniel noticed her tense up as they approached the town run by the mercenaries. "Keep behind me and never more than an arm's length away. Don't let them take your weapons."

Her eyes widened for a moment, and then her features smoothed. "All right. What do I do if they insist?"

"Kill them while screaming for me."

"Is that supposed to be comforting?"

He liked that she looked annoyed rather than scared. She had guts. "Sure it is. I'll get there before anyone kills you."

She huffed but nodded her agreement. He and Andrei shared a look. Daniel held up three fingers; there'd been three guards on towers as they entered the main part of town. As mercenaries go, this group wasn't too bad. There were a few who did military for pay, but mostly they smuggled goods and most likely weapons. Out here he was always Neil, and he'd never disclosed his marital status, so that should be fine.

"I wonder if they have gardens on the rooftops. I see people up there." She said it in an amused voice, the dry, very haughty facade she'd worn when he first met her. And she said it about the guards on the rooftops. Smart and sexy, his Carina.

"I don't know if folks around here are much up to farming. But it could be." Daniel pointed at a trailhead, and Andrei nodded, parking the transport.

Their contact had told them to head up the trail, and they'd be met by the mercenaries and escorted to the portal. Daniel didn't like that much. This particular group was only marginally connected to the one he trusted far more. But he didn't have much choice at that point. The longer they remained behind enemy lines, the more dangerous it became. Official portal transports were being closely watched. All known private portals were also being watched. It was only a matter of time before they got caught, and he wanted to avoid that outcome at all costs.

"Stay close to me," he told her. "Never know what kind of wildlife is out here." She tried to pout when he took her bag, but he didn't care. She'd already been injured in a knife fight, and he wanted to be sure there wouldn't be a repeat of that event. She was going to let him help her, going to listen to him, and that was that.

Daniel took point while Andrei took the rear, keeping Carina directly between them. The forest around them was unnaturally quiet, the only sound the crunch of snow under their feet. There were men out there, watching and waiting. He felt it on his skin. Wary, but not hostile, which suited him just fine.

"Ho there!" Ahead on the trail a man shouted to them with a lift of his hand. His walk was seemingly casual, but Daniel knew a warrior when he saw one. The man's eyes were those of a predator, and he carried weapons on his body.

Daniel nodded. "Hello. We're looking for the falls. We hear tell from a local, Duan, that they are something to look at."

Just like that, the cheery facade slipped, and the path filled with men. "All right then. We'll need those weapons."

"I'm sure you think you do. But we both know that's not going to happen. You have my word that we will not draw weapons unless we are provoked." Daniel stood tall, his feet apart, braced for violence, but giving the other man a way out with some measure of honor.

"We don't know you."

"You won't after the trip either. But you know who I know, and that's got to be enough. I'm not giving you my weapons."

Two men flanked the one right in front of Daniel and he knew behind him, Andrei had his back. He only hoped Carina took what he said to heart and stayed quiet.

And there was her fucking voice! He wanted to spin to look at her, but only years of doing the job enabled him to keep his composure and stay face-to-face with the other men.

Carina knew the look on Daniel's face, even if she couldn't see it. But this was stupid. She saw the older man standing off to the side, knew the marks on his face. "I visited Ulta once. It's quite beautiful. I'd never seen hot springs like that before."

The man's features lost some of their wariness at the sound of her voice, at the way she nailed the regional accent so perfectly. She should have, her mother was from Ulta; Carina'd heard it her whole life.

"I miss it. Get back there now and again; most of my family have scattered." He smiled.

This was moving in a good direction. The man lost some of the stiffness in his spine.

"I understand. I don't see my family as much as I'd like either. Sure is pretty out this way."

The man warmed, moving closer. Carina felt Andrei move up behind her, but he said nothing.

"What brings you here?" he asked.

"My husband and I," she paused to indicate Daniel, "are trying to get to his family. They're on the other side, you see. I've never met them." She smiled sadly. "The transports are full of Skorpios, and while we've nothing to run from, they scare me so much Neil, that's my man there, and his cousin Ander," she indicated Andrei, "said we could travel this way instead." She grinned for effect. "Now, boys will be boys, so I'd wager there will be some business on this trip, but I suppose that's safer this way, too."

"Oi, you up there, let's keep it moving," the old man called out to the other at the head of the group, this time in standard rather than his native tongue. "They have places to go; we have a transport to take them there. There are enough of us to deal with any problems should that one up there break his word and draw a weapon."

After some grumbling, they began to amble up the trail again. Andrei reached up, squeezed her hand and went back to walking.

The fact was, she wasn't prepared for what she saw next. Her father's private portal was out in the open and maintained, guarded by his troops. As they crested the hill, she saw a tree canopy, but the closer they got, the more apparent it became that the canopy was protecting the sight of the portal from the air.

Two transport ships of midsize sat, waiting to be boarded. The energy from the portal swept through the area. No wonder the mercenaries had taken the town and settled around this space.

There was no way something like this would go unnoticed by a passerby.

"Here we go. Ready to board. We've got a full complement, so once you're settled, we'll be leaving." The man she'd been talking to motioned to the ramp up into the ship. "Safe trip, ma'am."

She smiled at him before taking Daniel's outstretched hand. "Thank you."

He said nothing as they walked down the deck toward their cabin. Andrei was right next door to them. She figured he'd be in with them, so that came as a surprise. Not that she'd complain about time alone with Daniel. Unfortunately, Daniel at work was even more taciturn than Daniel was normally.

He opened the door and motioned for her to go in. He nodded at Andrei. "We'll see you after we set off. There's a cantina here; we can have a meal later."

Andrei agreed, sent Carina a brief smile and headed into his room before Daniel sealed them inside their own.

Without preamble, without words, he sat her on the bed and began his usual sweep of the room. He crushed two listening devices that must have been poorly positioned or of low quality because he made that sort of face when he found them, as if their subpar existence offended him. He put signal jammers out, set extra security on the door and at last turned to her.

"You did a good job."

She jerked, surprised. "Thank you. I thought you'd be angry."

"You saw something you could help with, and you did it. You used your skills to help get us on this transport with our weapons and without any more posturing. That saved valuable time."

"I get the feeling sometimes that you like catching me off guard." She smiled up at him.

He got to his knees and moved to her slowly, stealing her breath. "Do you?" he whispered.

She swallowed hard and tried not to feel cornered, and failed. But it was a delicious sort of not-fear. Anticipation. What would he do to her next?

"You wearing a knife on your calf makes me hot." He slid a hand up her leg, beneath her pants.

The pull in her belly was only partly due to the transport lurching forward and making the first slip through the portal.

He must have felt her muscles tense at the noise level. It was far greater than the other times she'd traveled. Portal accidents weren't unheard of, and when they happened, it most often meant the death of everyone on board.

"Shh, it's all right. Private transport like this through these rogue portals is far less comfortable than the licensed portal travel. But it's safe. These mercs probably do more maintenance on this vessel than the official vessels receive. They can't run goods under the noses of the authorities otherwise."

She looked down at him, sliding her fingers through his hair. "Good to know we aren't on the way to being crushed and dead."

He surged up and onto her, bringing her to the bed with his body on hers. He licked the shell of her ear and then said quietly, his breath against the sensitized skin, "Where did you learn to speak Ulta so well?"

She might have sounded more authoritative if he hadn't then slid one hand up her belly under her shirt, unerringly to her nipple. She arched, and he took advantage of that, licking up her neck.

"Uh." He pinched her nipple, and her eyes wanted to close, but his face was right above hers just then, and the sight of his eyes so lit by emotion halted that. She managed to form quiet words to answer him, but her body screamed for more from him. "I learned as a child. My mother is from Ulta. My accent would have been different than his, but my mother's maid is also an Ultan; she speaks it just like the man out there."

Ulta was a 'Verse at the far end of the Imperium. Known for its hot springs, vast oceans and floating cities, it wasn't often visited by anyone, much less outsiders from the Federation. It was then she remembered what she'd been thinking earlier before they'd arrived.

"I'm sorry. I didn't mean to upset you by bringing up your family." He pulled back, and she sighed. "What is it?"

"Nothing. It's nothing." She reached for him, but he moved away to look at her better.

"Nothing? Really?"

"It's nothing!" she insisted.

"Fine." He sat up, angering her in the process. *He'd* been closed up and moody, but that was fine. She wasn't allowed?

"You know, withholding sex is supposed to be what women do."

He narrowed his eyes at her for a brief time. "That so? You're an expert on what women do and sex now?"

"After spending time with infuriating bastards, I should be an expert on that."

He rolled off the bed, and she made a face at his back. "Excuse my intrusion into your life. I'll endeavor not to do it again."

Digging through his bag, he grabbed a book and began to read it. Insufferable! The man was actually pouting because she wouldn't tell him all the details of why she was upset?

"I never said that," she attempted to explain. He finally glanced up at her, and guilt seeped into her gut at the look on his face. Like a stranger. He'd taken her places she'd never imagined, done it with hands and mouth and cock. He knew her in ways no one else ever had or ever would. He'd made her feel valuable, loved. Seeing that blank expression cut to the core. "Don't look at me like that! You're not being fair. I let you have your space to tell me or not about things."

Horror coiled at the escape of a small sob.

"I apologize," he murmured, setting the book aside, moving to her. "I just hate seeing you upset. I thought maybe I could help in some way. I'm not trying to pry." He took a deep breath. "So, yes, I suppose I am. But I just want to know so I can fix it."

"You can't fix this." She shrugged, and despite all her best intentions, tears came. "I'm so humiliated," she said, voice thick with emotion.

He moved to her again, pulling her into his arms and up into his lap. "Sweet, please tell me what it is. Even if I can't fix it totally, share it with me so I can take some of the weight."

She swallowed hard at the emotion welling up within. "I'm afraid I'm making the wrong choice. People will be hurt, and I'm the cause."

She rushed the telling, not sure if she told it slowly if it would all release from her conscience.

He listened, and she waited, growing more nervous with each passing moment of silence.

Finally, he said, "Whatever you did, people would have died. That's an unassailable fact, is it not?"

"Maybe. I don't know."

"Really? You don't know? You're far more intelligent and politically savvy than that, sweet." He waited, and she sighed.

"I thought you wanted to fix it."

Startled, he laughed and kissed her. "You can't have it both ways. If you had stayed quiet, what could you have done? You'd have been kept a virtual prisoner. You and I both know he wouldn't have allowed you to teach children. And whatever else you have, do you truly believe your father would have used it for good?" He kept his voice low, but she heard it just fine.

"No matter what you did, people would have suffered. They will. I can't erase that. I can't make it not true, no matter how I wish I could. It's all balance. Even working for good, even the right choice will hurt people."

She caressed his cheek. So silly, she'd been so silly not to see that if anyone could understand her feelings, it would be this man who made such choices every day. How it must wear on him at times: the responsibility, the awareness that no matter what he did, people would be hurt, and so he had to make the choice that hurt less people.

"You do it every day."

"Not really. Don't make more of it than it is." He tried to move his head away, to hide his face, but she held on.

"Pfft. Officially, that's my response. For the record, and don't let this feed your ridiculous ego, but you did fix it." She put her fingers over his lips to keep him from responding. "Oh, shush, you! You are hells-bent on ruining this moment of supreme femininity, and I'm not having that. You fixed it because you reminded me that nothing is simple and that's why what you do is important. The average person could not bear the weight of such a thing, and you do. You helped me with a small piece of that by being an example. So there." She moved her fingers quick enough to kiss him before he could argue.

Chapter 12

After the chaos of getting settled in, the main part of the trip was fairly calm. They had dropped their things in their cabins and had disembarked in quick order. Since she'd been tired and slightly miffed at him for his annoyance back in the clearing, she'd been quieter than usual, and of course she wouldn't consent to staying in the room while he procured food for them. Not even if Andrei stayed with her. Damnable woman.

So they'd hunted down the small cantina run for passengers and had managed to locate a table and some decent enough food.

He hid his grin as she tried to explain to Andrei why he should eat more than just huge hunks of meat. The people around them in the small cantina went about their business, but Daniel was smart enough to know some watched him, watched and wondered who they were. More a hallmark of a grifter than anything serious. Yet. Criminals always looked for ways to make credits, so he was always careful to be unmemorable. Which was difficult just then, because no matter what her hair color was, no matter what she wore or pretended to be, she was outrageously beautiful and vibrant.

She was also smart, canny. She worked her way through the transport, smiling and nodding, taking in bits and pieces and relaying it all to him in her way. Which wasn't always direct, and sometimes it took him a few beats to understand her point. But he got it, and her eye was excellent.

Not that he'd admit it out loud, but her quirkiness, the way she could be so hard and smart one moment and silly the next, pleased him. The one thing about her that was constant was her heart. She cared about people, and in that way, he was reminded a lot of his sisters, of his brother. They'd like her, he realized, knowing he'd have to introduce her to them because Abbie wouldn't have it any other way and because he wanted to share Carina with them, show them he was capable of something more than his job.

What that meant really he didn't know. But he knew he wanted her tomorrow and the day after. Knew he wanted to see what they might have once they got to Ravena, if they had anything at all.

Andrei broke out a deck of playing cards, and she actually clapped. "I haven't played games in a very long time. How fun."

"Keep an eye on Ander; he's vicious." Daniel sat back and sipped his ale, watching the two of them interact.

Andrei lit a cigarette, drawing in deep the fragrant smoke. Despite the circumstances being so tense, it was a good moment there at the table, a decent enough meal, drinking ale, watching his friends play cards. Lovely to see Carina smile, lovely to see her getting used to life with some freedom in it.

"When I was a child, my mother was bedridden a lot, so she

played cards with us when she had good days." Andrei discarded cards, Carina gasped and then growled as she had to take the pile. Daniel wisely hid his grin.

"Hmpf." Carina mused as she looked at the cards she held, dropping two. "Are you close to her still?"

"She was murdered when I was in lockup. My younger brother was taken by the authorities, and I never saw him again. My oldest sister did her best to raise us, but she was only barely older than I was. She married young, has several kids of her own now."

"I'm sorry." She said it without pity, which meant Andrei heard it, took it to heart and nodded.

"That's life for a lot of kids." He shrugged.

"Doesn't make it right. Your father?"

"Loser."

She laughed without humor. "We have that in common."

Andrei snorted and went back to his cards.

She was as vicious as Andrei at games of chance. Daniel wasn't that surprised. A woman like her had to be serious and vicious if need be. It was sexy.

Her gaze slid from the cards to Daniel's face, and he smiled. She blushed prettily, so he figured she got the message. Need throbbed like his pulse. He wanted her, wanted his hands, mouth and cock on her, in her.

"I'm tired. I think I might go to sleep early." She stood.

"Good idea." Daniel stood as well, and Andrei sent him a raised brow.

The three of them walked back through the now quieting transport toward the cabins. People watched, most of them because it was natural to look when others passed, some because they liked the way one of the three looked and some had suspicion and calculation in their eyes.

At Andrei's door, Andrei looked to Daniel. "I saw it, too. I'll keep a watch on that." Meaning the calculated gazes they'd met on the way back.

Daniel nodded once and thanked Andrei, and they went into their own rooms, locking themselves in.

"What is he watching?" she murmured into his ear as she slid into his arms.

"People."

"What will you teach me today?" She looked up at him through her lashes, and he took a deep breath. She had no real idea what she did to him. Oh, sure, she understood her feminine appeal; it was impossible for her not to. But this was more. She got under his skin in a way he'd never imagined anyone doing. She had become integral to him, and the immensity of that scared him silly.

"To sleep, because when you push a man who's got pent-up energy, you might get something more vigorous than you expect," he murmured, meaning it. He wanted her. Badly. And he wasn't sure he could hold back all the intensity he felt just then.

"I want that. Show me. Make me feel what you do." She took a step back and pulled the sweater she wore over her head. "I'm right here giving myself to you. *Take me.*"

He groaned, lost to reason, only wanting more of her skin showing, wanting to touch.

"Show me." He leaned back against the wall, trying for patience. "Show me what you like."

"How?" She wasn't nervous, just interested. He enjoyed that about her.

"Take your clothes off and touch yourself. I want to see you, want to know what you like."

"*You* do what I like."

He grinned. "I like to hope so, yes. But life is a learning process. Help me learn more about how to give you pleasure."

"If you're trying to scare me, it won't work." She tossed the rest of her clothes to the side, putting her weapons near the bed where she could reach them if necessary. He liked that, too.

He dimmed the lights in the room and placed a chair within reach of where she'd settled on the bed. Totally naked, her skin flushed with excitement and a bit of embarrassment, he wagered.

She slid her hands up her belly to her breasts, flicking her thumbs back and forth across her nipples until her hips started to churn. The air seemed to still as it warmed, her scent built as she became more and more aroused. His pulse hammered in his head.

One hand left her breasts and moved back to her pussy. His mouth watered as she parted her labia and dipped her fingers inside that glistening space. The sound she made jerked his attention sharply until his focus narrowed and narrowed. Her body, her hands, the way he struggled to breathe was all he knew.

Finally she sighed and turned to him. "Nothing I do feels better than what you do to me."

But he was up before she'd finished her sentence, need raw on his face, and she lay there, looking up as he stripped off his weapons and moved them to a neat pile near the bed. Fully naked and erect, he turned quickly to be sure his alarms were on and then moved to her with purpose.

"Torture. Beautiful torture watching you touch these," he said around a nipple.

Ha! Torture? He was so very handsome and commanding, and the sex just sort of oozed from him and *he* was tortured?

"I'm glad I wasn't alone then. You torture me just by existing. You're just so much, it's hard to take in sometimes."

He began to move down, kissing her belly, but she yanked on his hair when he wouldn't stop at her request. "Hey, no. I want you in me. Now."

"I want you to be ready."

"Ready? Are you making a joke? I'm so wet I can feel it on my thighs. I'm ready for you right now, so put it in me!"

"I've clearly created a monster." He smirked down at her as he teased his cock around her gate.

"I'm going to kill you and hide your body if you don't hurry up." She tried to squirm to take him deeper.

"I'm not going to be able to fill your request if you keep at me. I'm going to start laughing."

"You need to laugh more. After you fuck me."

He laughed then, and the breath whooshed out of her as he thrust into her in one movement. His laughter died as his eyes slid halfway closed and he stilled.

"You're bossy," he grunted.

"You're controlling."

He managed a good shrug. "I am."

She burst out laughing. "You make me happy. Despite all this insanity, you make me happy."

"I want everything, sweet. Give it to me." He stared into her eyes and began to move. He'd taken her wildly and sweetly; this was intense on a different level. He demanded everything of her in those minutes they spent in bed. The look on his face brooked no stifled gasps: he wanted to hear it all, he wanted arching and moaning, he wanted her to experience every last breath of the pleasure he gave her. And he wanted to see it.

So she gave it to him, jumped off the edge of her self-control and let loose. Let the maelstrom of this desire between them suck her under, trusting him to keep her from losing herself entirely.

Her nails dug into his hips as she urged him closer. He adjusted her thighs and calves, opening her up. She rolled her hips, demanding more. His muscles flexed and relaxed, the sheen of exertion seeming to make him glow. The scent of him, sexually aroused male at work, made her giddy, drunk with his masculinity.

When he leaned down to kiss her, the wiry hair on his chest abraded her nipples, bringing a gasp he eagerly swallowed. Skin to skin, rubbing against each other, intertwined legs and arms, she felt it all, gave it back to him as he never tore his gaze from her face.

And then he pulled out, bringing her right up against him as she tried to hold him in place. "What?"

He pushed her back and descended on her pussy with his mouth, bringing her so much intense pleasure she yelled out with it, pressing herself to him unashamedly as he ate her, licked, sucked, rubbed against every bit of her until she nearly sobbed to come.

That's when he sucked her clit, in and out, in and out, and she tripped into an orgasm so hard and deep she was sure she'd never felt anything so exquisitely pleasurable. She barely even registered it when he rolled her over and put a pillow under her hips. And then his cock was back, pressing deep, firing up another wave of pleasure, prolonging her climax.

"Gods, so fucking tight and wet. You're the most perfect thing in creation," he said into her neck as he began to thrust harder and faster. The heat of him blanketed her back.

She managed to get her ass higher, up to her knees, her nails dug into the blankets until with a guttural groan of her name, he came.

When he rolled off, he kissed her hip and then the small of her back.

"I like it that way," she said, meaning from behind. "Now I can sleep." She grinned and turned over to look at him better.

He shook his head as he got out of bed to clean up. "I've been told I'm better than warm milk."

"I'm quite certain I don't want to know who said that. In any case, I certainly have more fun with you than I ever did with a mug of warm milk," she said as he got back in bed. She snuggled against him before getting up to clean up and get dressed herself. Being naked with Daniel was one of her favorite things, but it was too cold for that just then.

"What's your mother like?"

"She runs a bakery. She's a nice woman, a good woman who loves her children and has terrible taste in men."

She got back in with him, pulling the blankets up and gluing herself to his body. "Four children, that's a big group."

"We're all pretty good. I knew . . . well, we all stuck together and tried to keep things calm."

She pressed her head into him until he finally turned over so she could see his face when he spoke. "I had a dog once who did that. Butted me with his gargantuan head until I paid attention to him." He raised one brow at her.

"Are you saying I have a gargantuan head?"

He heaved a sigh, and she couldn't hold back her laughter. "I'm sorry, you're just so very fun to tweak. Now, back to our topic. You started to say something else. You knew. You knew what?"

He dragged a breath into his lungs. "She was fragile for a large part of my early childhood. Sick a lot. She has an immune disorder that she can treat, but the heat and dryness of the outback sapped most everything from her. She was just worn down."

His voice was quiet, filled with emotion, and she hugged him tighter.

"I knew she had enough to deal with in my father, who was, *is* a giant, selfish, cheating prick. I just never wanted to be the reason she looked sad, I guess. So Abbie and I, that's one of my sisters, we just sort of kept everything running. We didn't really have much of a chance to get into trouble."

What a man he was.

"Is she still ill? You said she owns a bakery."

"She got very bad, so bad I thought she would die. My father, he didn't really care. He'd stopped coming home, and when he did, he often brought his little protégés with him. She'd cry and cry. When I was small, they were so close, always laughing together, kissing and touching. He barely looked at her, didn't care that she was fading. So I confronted him and demanded we go. I'd have gone anyway; she needed to be away. He gave in, and we moved to the capital. The neighborhood was not a dream come true. We were freezing cold for part of the year, sweltering for another part. But she got better. She got better and put her life together."

"I'm glad to hear that. It sounds a lot like my mother's situation. Except my father has a second wife. My mother probably wouldn't leave him, even knowing what he is. My gods, my little brother. I'd forgotten until this moment."

Not that he'd died; she never forgot that. But how. Her father was a monster. A murderous bastard who would be the end of everything if left unchecked. Simply because he could.

"He has to be stopped," she murmured against his chest.

"I know." He didn't apologize, didn't say more, and that's what she needed.

"Tell me about your sisters."

"You should sleep."

"I will."

"I'm the oldest of the four as I've said. One of my sisters runs a café, she's in business with my mother. The other is a pain in the ass." He grinned, and she laughed.

"Do tell."

"She's a barrister and a rabble rouser. Has to *know* everything. My gods, the questions she asks. She's also strong, intelligent, funny." He angled his head to look at her. "A lot like you that way."

She sighed happily. "Is she married? Does she have children? Do you live near each other? Your family, that is?"

"Speaking of endless questions. She is married, yes, and she's pregnant with her first child. She lives in the city, we all do. I see them all, including my youngest brother, who is *also* a professional rabble rouser, regularly when I'm home. You'll like my brother. At first glance he seems shallow and pretty, but after you know him, you real-ize he's got immense talent with people because he's insightful and brilliant. He's been told he's stupid for so long by our father that it's only recently that he's accepting just how amazing he is."

It warmed her to hear so much love in his voice. "I'm very excited to meet them. Not your father so much, but the rest." She paused. "I will, won't I?"

"What are you asking exactly?"

She leaned closer, pressing her lips to his ear. "When we arrive, will you be with me? I mean, not just physically, but romantically, relationship-wise?"

"I'm so wrong for you," he whispered. They'd been keeping their voices low; even with the jammer, she knew he didn't want to risk anything.

"I'll be the judge of that," she said vehemently. Men were so dumb sometimes.

He snorted. "Indeed you will. I have no doubt you'll do what you want. It's part of your charm."

"Don't think I don't understand sarcasm, *Neil.*"

"Good night, sweet."

She leaned up and kissed him, meaning to be quick, but he caught her, holding her in place while he kissed her, took over, devoured and devastated. She surrendered to it, giving herself to him until he was satisfied, pulling back with a feral sound, holding her close. Now *that* could put a girl into happy dreams all dark long.

*D*aniel lay there in the dark as the fabric of space-time hugged the transport, creaking and humming, creating a sort of lullaby he'd heard more than once in his life. These private transports weren't as luxurious and silent as the ones that carried passengers from 'Verse to 'Verse via the official portals, but he always felt that estranged people from the wonder of just how the portals worked.

He couldn't quite believe he'd told her all that about his family. But she'd asked, and he'd liked sharing it with her. Maybe it was the fact that he'd lived in a state of anonymity as a member of Phantom Corps, but being known by someone other than family or coworkers meant something to him. It meant something to him that she pursued him, that she wanted him as more than just a man to keep her safe and teach her a few things about sex. She understood him in a way most people never did.

It was that, he thought, that touched him the most. She was interested in all parts of him. There was no subterfuge with her, which was funny, given the state of their situation, but she wanted the real Daniel. He was not just the sexy special ops solider, though she did seem to enjoy that, too. She looked at him and saw more. Very few people did, which he hadn't really known bothered him until he'd met her.

The rest, what he'd do when they got back and the reality of their different social status made itself clear, he didn't know, nor did he plan to waste any time worrying about it. It would be whatever it would be, and there was no use working himself into upset over it. Until then, she was his, and he'd keep her safe, teach her about sex and enjoy her for the wonderful woman she was. If he'd been a better man, he'd have stayed away from her, would have created a gulf of anger between them so she'd keep those sweet, soft thighs closed. But he wasn't a good man; he was a man who did what it took to get the job done.

Enough of that. He needed to keep his focus on the mission. He didn't like the looks on some of the faces of those mercenaries back in the glade. He didn't like it that a few times, he'd seen speculation in the eyes of people he'd seen on the transport either.

He knew cowards pretty well. Anyone who'd turn someone in for credits was a coward. But cowards did desperate things, and that made them dangerous. No one would make a move while they were traveling; it was too dangerous to the transport and to the others on board. He and Andrei would need to be sure their departure was done right.

It was at times like this one that he wished they'd opted for the implants some of the other special forces operatives had. Mental communication between team members would be really helpful right about then, but his people already had enough distrust of the system, and so many of them had refused or voiced fear, that he'd put it off.

Now, when he got back, he'd have Ash Walker or Sera Pela come to speak to them about it. They used the implants on their three-person team with a lot of success. He figured his people would better understand what it did and didn't do from people like them, people they felt closer to rather than the scientist who'd created the implant.

"You're thinking about work," she murmured against his back. Sleep lay heavy in her voice, and he smiled in the dark.

"How'd you know that?"

"You were relaxed, and then you began to tense up more and more. I've noticed you must run through a mental list of things you have to do at night. It's part of your routine."

She knew him better than she could understand. "It helps me to start each day when I'm prepared. I work through the things I need to do."

The arms she wrapped around him brought him back to her, back to her body against his in the quiet of night, the scent of sex on the air. In a short span of time, he'd gotten very used to her body against his each night. It felt good to be with her. It eased him.

"All right." She kissed him between the shoulder blades. "I trust you'll share if you need help."

Chapter 13

Carina awoke to an empty bed, but not an empty room. Daniel was already up and getting dressed. She watched, content to simply soak in how handsome he was, even as she wondered about each and every scar he bore.

"What's your favorite memory?" he asked, turning around.

She smiled at the sight of his face. "You're good. How did you know I was awake?

"Your breathing changed. You make a lovely—very feminine, of course—snuffle when you're sleeping."

"Are you saying I snore?"

"Of course not." He grinned and strode to her, dropping a kiss on her mouth. "I said you snuffled."

Hmpf. She sat, drawing the blankets about herself as he went back to grooming his beard. The one she'd asked him to grow.

"My favorite memory is the first time you, we, well you know."

He laughed. "That's one of my favorites, too. How about one that doesn't involve me?"

He had no idea how deeply she felt for him, silly man. All her favorite memories were of him.

"Let's see. My grandmother used to sneak me into the kitchen and let me roll dough with her. It was far more that she let me into her world than the treat part, though, of course, who doesn't like treats? She was a good person, a lot of fun. She and my brother, my older brother, were very close. I don't think she trusted my father, but she adored us and always took up for us, even when she couldn't win."

Even when it got her disappeared.

"Another time, one warm season, we left home and went to Duim. There's a great sea there, have you visited?"

He shook his head. "I haven't. But I've heard that it's beautiful."

"It is. Overfished, sadly, so now there are bans against any netting at all. The economy has been destroyed by itself. They do expect it to rebound. Anyway, the beaches are beautiful. We played and played, swam, had picnics each day. It was the last time we were all together as a family before my older brother . . . died. I can still smell the air, so crisp and clean."

"It sounds like a good memory. I'm glad for that. And you don't know that he's dead, he's just gone. He could have survived if people helped him. Don't lose hope."

She sat up, well aware of the constraints of just how much she could say. "I suppose you're right. I always felt like if he was truly dead, I'd know it. But then I told myself that was silly."

"Sometimes, you need to listen to that inner voice."

He'd just told her Vincenz was alive, hadn't he? The excitement of it built. She hadn't really accepted that he'd died, but believing him alive was one thing, *truly* believing it, bringing it from a silly hope she harbored deep inside to reality was something totally different.

It meant she had family on the other side; she belonged to something larger than herself, and that made a difference to her.

He dried his face and turned to her. "Are you hungry? Would you like to get dressed and get something to eat? I have plans for you later today." She smiled, getting to her knees, and he laughed. "Not those kind of plans, though I'm certainly always open to those kind of activities with you."

"Oh. Well, all right then." She got out of bed and cleaned up quickly with barely tepid water.

"Wakes you up, doesn't it?" He winked, and she snorted. He was very cheerful just then, and she wasn't sure why.

Andrei knocked on the door just moments later, and they walked to get a meal. The cantina was crowded, so they managed to find a place to sit and eat just outside where a small common area existed.

Her attention immediately snagged on a group of children. Children who should have been in school or at the very least supervised by an adult or two.

Carina held out a piece of fruit to a little girl nearby. "Are you hungry? I have an extra purri, fruit, and I'm stuffed."

Her eyes widened and she grabbed it. "Thank you, miss."

"Of course. Thank you for helping me not waste food. I'm Carrie." She nodded at the little girl, who neatly halved the fruit with a foldaway knife and gave the other part to another child nearby.

"I'm Kell. This is my sister Darla."

Daniel shifted but said nothing to interrupt the scene. She knew he kept watch for her safety and trusted he wouldn't interfere with her unless it was necessary. Since he was a control freak and a bossy one at that, she wasn't entirely certain what he would classify as necessary though.

She sat on the ground where the girls had a pick-up game with metal spirals and a bouncy ball. "Oh! I think I know this game!"

Kell grinned at her, and the other two children who had been a few feet away, came over to watch. At her back, Daniel pressed a small loaf of sweet bread and another piece of fruit into her hand.

She distributed them carefully and casually as her insides melted at his sweetness.

"It's called springs, and it goes like this." Kell bounced the ball and grabbed the little metal springs. "First one, then two, and so on. You have to grab the springs when the ball is in the air or you lose."

"I'll watch you play until I understand it better," she said, watching and smiling. There were few people he knew who seemed to be as sweet and giving as she was. Probably no one else more so than her.

*N*ow that they'd made it through that trip and were waiting for the next, he watched her as she sat on a bench in the sunlight. On the last transport, he made a mental note to see if Abbie could help Carina find a way to work with children when they got her settled in Ravena. She had a way about her, a gift, and he wanted her to be able to use it. Gods knew she could make a difference in the lives of many children if given the chance. And it would give her a purpose, roots in her new life.

They were one slip away from getting the fuck out of the Imperium, and he couldn't wait. It still wasn't totally safe, he'd have to watch closely until they got at least to Nondal, but it wouldn't be nearly as bad as it was just then. He jammed the rest of the sandwich he'd been snacking on into his mouth and crumpled up the wrapping.

"We've got friends," Andrei murmured.

"I noticed." Two men had followed them from the transport to the main portal. They'd been watching Daniel, Andrei and Carina for some time, and he didn't like it. At the same time, they were already dodgy people, so it was possible they were just looking to rob them instead of sic the Skorpios on them. Robbery would get one type of response, betrayal and attempted murder would be a whole different reaction.

"Still hungry?" she asked, looking to him with a smile. She held out another sandwich.

"You got an extra?" He warmed as he took it and made quick work out of unwrapping and eating it.

"I got *two* extras. I gave you three to start with." Her smile was mischievous. "Knowing your gargantuan appetite, a girl has to keep on her toes."

Andrei snorted but said nothing. Daniel poked his ribs with his elbow.

"I like to stock up when I can. As long as my pants button, I can't see why anyone should be so fascinated with my eating habits."

She put her head on his shoulder. "Don't pout. I'm fascinated by most things you do."

Without thinking, he put her knuckles to his lips and realized it was okay. She'd won through his defenses in such a short time, but he enjoyed that she teased him the way she did. It meant she wasn't afraid. He wasn't sure what it would do to him if he ever saw fear of him in her eyes.

"We'll need to board soon," he murmured after finishing his food.

"Why don't you go ahead and take the bags. We'll be here when you get back." Andrei knew Daniel would want to handle the recon himself, knew he'd want someone with Carina at all times.

Daniel stood, grabbing everyone's bag, knowing, of course, that Andrei had everything important on his person. They could walk away and be fine, if necessary.

Carina's eyes widened for a brief moment, but she didn't argue. If they were going to make something of whatever they had, she'd have to accept the inherent dangers of his job, even if she was unhappy about it.

"I'll be back shortly, sweet." He didn't bother to resist bending down to kiss her. Her happiness rushed through him when she threw her arms around his neck. "Stick with him, all right?" He indicated Andrei, and she nodded solemnly.

He deliberately took his time, ambling along toward the line of transports in docking bays, readying to leave. The security presence was high outside the inner ring of the departure decks. Mobile lock-ups had been installed at every portal city across the Imperium, their sources had said.

Their papers had held up at each stop so far, and Daniel thanked the gods for such good connections. But their luck may not hold for much longer; he knew that. He'd already had to take out several people, had nearly been arrested twice and Carina had been knifed. Just because they were nearly out of the Imperium didn't mean it was time to let up on vigilance.

The populace was more resentful than he could remember in the other times he'd been there. Broken, too. Polis and private contract security had been arrested themselves after terrorizing the locals in some 'Verses. There was a feeling of lawlessness in the air, even as the streets were filled with troops.

Instability was wearing on the Imperium, and he wanted out before it all crashed down around them.

He'd paid bribes, and they'd been able to get through the checkpoint without a hitch, but just outside those high walls, Daniel could hear the loudspeakers and the shouts of the soldiers. There had been rumors of more explosions and scores of stories about relatives who'd been hauled off by the authorities, never to be heard from again.

Focus. That's what he needed just then. So he pushed all the other stuff out of his head as he approached the decks for their transport. Theirs was a decent-sized cruiser. Not a crate with eight people to every cabin, or worse, warehoused in giant rooms with bunks to the ceilings. Not luxurious either. Either extreme would be out of character for their cover. But they fit right in the middle.

He showed his ticket to the woman at the ropes, and she passed him through, giving him the room assignments and sending him a smile that said she'd be happy to show him other things, too.

Instead, he smiled back, but kept going, taking in the area, where things were, who was supposed to be where and what, if any, weaponry the ship's crew had. His and Carina's cabin was small, but not as bad as it had been on the private transport. A bed, a chair, a table secured to the wall.

He ran a sweep for listening devices. Found two and left them in place for the moment. He'd wait until they began to enter the portal, and he'd jam the signal to make it look like a system glitch.

He knew this particular transport was owned by a company friendly to Federation interests. Knew they had smugglers' holds, too. Even better, he knew the location of several, including the one just above his head right that moment.

This would suit just fine. He locked the cabin door behind himself and headed back out, catching sight of one of the men he'd seen earlier. It seemed they had a tail, which did not please him, though he was not surprised.

As he rounded a corner going down the ramp out to where Carina and Andrei waited, he halted, lashed out and threw the man who'd been following them against the wall, Daniel's forearm pressed to the other man's throat.

"Just what do you take me for?" Daniel growled at him.

"Get off me! What are you doing?" the man wheezed as he struggled fruitlessly.

"If you continue this, you will die. Now, my question." Daniel's focus was on this man, on his pulse, on the sweat on his brow and on his dancing, darting eyes. The roar of calm slid over him, and he pressed harder, cutting off the man's air to underline his first threat.

He stood as people walked past without even a second glance. Daniel pressed, taking him close enough to blacking out before finally letting go as the first tendrils of death curled.

"Shall we do this again?" Daniel kept his gaze burning into the tail.

"Just, you looked soft." The man's panic stank.

"You meant to rob me and my family?"

"Just looking. You can't blame a guy for looking. Now I know, right? Now I back off and look elsewhere."

There had been nothing but this path, Daniel thought as he continued to hold the man in place. He had to show the man that he would not tolerate being targeted at all and had driven the point home in the only voice a man like that would hear.

"You so much as look in my direction, and I will be very vexed with you. If you even *think* about my wife, I will gut you while you watch." He pushed back, pressing on the man's throat one last time before turning and stalking away.

Carina saw him coming, felt the wave of his rage, saw it on his face. Andrei squeezed her hand once and stood, bringing her with him.

"Is everything all right?" she asked, feeling rather breathless at whatever show of masculine force he was exhibiting. He was so very large and threatening, and she found her knees a bit wobbly. She liked it.

"Fine." He put an arm around her, and she pressed her face into his chest. She felt alien in her skin just then, never so completely lost in another person like she was at that moment. She was sure he and Andrei shared some pointed looks and sneaky communication about whatever had brought all this protective instinct to the surface, but she didn't care. He'd protect her, and that's all that mattered. She trusted him to get her to Ravena alive.

He began to walk toward the transport, stopping here and there at the stalls, grabbing food, of course, and—she stilled—a scarf for her.

"I know you've been getting cold." He handed it to her in its vibrant blue glory. "Is it all right? I can get another one if you don't like it."

She sent him a watery smile as she wrapped it around her neck. No one had ever been this nice to her. This man was not related to her; he wasn't trying to get something from her father. He was a man with a job to do, but the way he treated her was above and beyond that job. He bought her a scarf. Because he noticed she got cold.

"It's perfect. Thank you."

He smiled. "It pleases me to see you happy," he said against her lips as he kissed her.

"The two of you are going to make my teeth hurt," Andrei grumbled, but Carina caught the edge of his smile. He wasn't as hard as he wanted people to believe. Beneath that smooth exterior, a sort of darkness lived. Lived in Daniel, too, she knew. But both men were far better than they believed themselves to be.

"You could have had Nyna, you know. But you waited too long." Daniel kissed the top of her head as he teased Andrei.

"That rat Marcus stole her out from under my nose." There was no heat in the words, just a bit of regret.

"Nyna is one of my sisters." He'd begun to simply answer her questions before she asked, knowing her so well. That made her weepy, too.

"I take it Marcus is her beau?" She looked Andrei up and down and wondered what man could outshine that.

"Her husband. They really are good together." Andrei shrugged. "She's too good for me."

"I doubt that. Not that I'm not sure Nyna is lovely, but you're a good man, so I doubt anyone is too good for you."

He ducked his head, letting his hair, which he'd left loose, fall forward to cover his face.

As they went up the ramp to enter the transport, she noted Daniel's posture had changed. He stood taller, spine stiff, and his gaze moved around the area, taking in everything and everyone. He was her protector now on a completely different level.

One man caught sight of them, the same man who'd been on the mercenary transport, and paled. Daniel sent him a raised brow, and the man scurried away in a hurry. She had a feeling this was the cause of Daniel's earlier anger.

"You see him again anywhere near you, and you tell me. Understand?" Daniel demanded after they'd fully boarded and headed to their room. Andrei was right behind them. She was surrounded by a wall of maleness bent on protecting her. She breathed easier for that.

Andrei said he wanted to take a nap, and Daniel wanted to get in their cabin to hole up, so she followed dutifully, not minding the fact that they'd be alone at last.

He paused and turned her around, her back to his front. Bending down, he spoke in her ear. "Look over there, across the bay. Do you see that couple near the water tanks?"

She obeyed and saw them. A shiver bloomed, turning warm and loose. They embraced, the man pressing the woman against a wall in the corner. They wouldn't have been visible to most people, but where she and Daniel stood provided a perfect angle.

One of the man's hands slid up inside the woman's uniform shirt, and she arched into him. Carina could see the woman's mouth open on a gasp as she lifted her leg, her thigh at the man's hip.

The man pressed forward; Carina imagined he was grinding himself against her, cock to pussy. Knew she'd been right when the woman's fingers dug into his shoulders as he continued to grind.

Her breath shallowed as she watched, her nipples hard, her clit sensitized. Daniel spoke, his lips at her ear. "Does that make you hot? Is your pussy wet? He's going to end up in pain that way; a man can't come like that. Well, most of us can't. She can, though. Look at her. His hand is in her shirt, his fingers are on her nipple, tugging and pinching. Drawing her closer until she comes. But she can't make any noise, or they might be heard."

Across from where they stood against their own door, the woman arched more fully, her movements frenzied, and then her head fell on his shoulder. He kissed her passionately, and they broke apart, hands held until they had to go separate ways.

"Her cunt will be juicy now. All for him. Every once in a while as she works, she'll remember those stolen moments, and when they come together again, she'll be ready, open, wet."

Her hands fisted and relaxed as she tried to control her breathing. Watching had always been her secret pleasure. It hadn't always been sex; she'd loved to observe people without them knowing it. But this, this with him speaking in her ear, saying all those deliciously dirty things as his hard cock pressed against her ass? This was breathtakingly sexual.

He stepped back and keyed the door open. "Let's go in. The departure lights just went yellow."

On shaky legs, she preceded him into the room, happily moving into his embrace.

"One more jump, and we'll be in Silesia," he murmured in her ear. She held on tight, wanting the whole trip to be over but also being afraid of what would happen when they weren't forced together this way. Her skin tingled with a new sort of awareness.

"I want it to be over, but I don't want to be away from you. I like having you to myself, even if we are being chased by brigands and soldiers."

He laughed softly, kissing her temple.

"Take me." She tore her clothes off, leaving her totally naked and shockingly beautiful.

He double-checked that he'd locked the door and motioned her to the bed with a tip of his chin. As she moved to obey, he did all his usual stuff, setting personal alarms and laying out the jammer he'd use once they began the slip though the portal.

Something about how he looked, how he'd been that whole day drove her need. After that scene they'd watched, she wanted to rub herself all over him, wanted to lick him, kiss every part of his skin.

She sprang out of bed. "I changed my mind. I want to take *you* instead."

"I'm all yours. Do with me what you will." He held his arms out and smiled at her.

Her hands shook a little but got the job done as he bent to let her pull his sweater from his body. She paused to breathe in the scent of his skin, warm, and uniquely him.

Caressing every part of him she could reach, she managed to get his pants, undershorts and boots off. Once he stood totally naked and unashamed of his body, she circled him. Inner bells sounded on the transport signaling the impending slip.

He sighed softly as she pressed herself to his back, encircling his waist with her arms. The moment was perfect, clear, right, and she knew she'd never forget the pulse of love within her belly, spreading through her system like a drug. Just Daniel and Carina, naked to each other.

She circled to face him and pulled him back to the bed. Her gut pulled at the entry into the portal, and he reached out, hit the jammers and his hands were back on her before she could protest the absence of his body. He picked her up, devouring her mouth. She wrapped her legs around his waist, plastering herself against him.

Daniel's head spun at how good it felt with her there, squirming against him, her naked, hot flesh stroking against his. Her power was heady, she owned it, owned her desires and took what she wanted. That appealed to him greatly.

The way she'd been as they watched the couple had ripped away everything left of his distance. He was in her, on her, she was under his skin in a way only she could be. How a woman could watch a couple getting each other off and still seem refreshingly . . . good, he wasn't sure. But she was, she was everything good, his light, and he held that tight.

He took three steps, carrying them to the nearby wall, and set his legs just right to hold her weight.

"Sweet, should I fuck you now?" He teased around her gate with the head of his cock. She was hot and wet, ready for him.

"Why are you asking? Do it!" Her nails dug into his shoulders as she arched.

He laughed, thrusting up and shifting her weight down to fill her completely. "I asked because you said you wanted to take me, not the other way around."

"This is . . . oh my gods."

He pressed her against the wall a bit more solidly, relishing the way her pupils expanded and her breath gusted from that seductive mouth of hers.

"Yes?"

"I am taking you. Sort of. Whatever, whoever is taking, this is just perfect with me. I have this need"—she stretched the word out on a gasp of pleasure—"for you. It itches over my skin, I need you so badly. The moment you touch me, look at me, put me in your attention, things ease. I should feel shame for what you make me crave, how you make me feel, but all I feel is sated, and desired in return. You answer my need."

He fell, tumbled into the abyss that was what he felt for this woman. Deep, bottomless, open as far as he could see, and he could not feel bad.

"There's no shame between us. You *are* my need," he murmured, continuing to fuck into her hard and deep.

She sank her teeth into his shoulder to muffle her cry, grinding herself against him as he thrust.

"That's it, take it. Grind your clit on me," he whispered, loving it when her pussy clutched around him, superheated and creamy. She groaned in what sounded like assent, so he kept going.

Her cunt superheated, tightening around him until he had to gasp in a breath at how beyond deliriously good it felt. She used her hands on his shoulders to lever herself up, to change her angle so she could get the friction she needed against her clit.

The heat of her stuttered breath against his neck drove him on, the sweetness of her body against his, the press of her nipples against his chest, the way her inner thigh muscles rippled as she moved herself against him, all worked together to drive him witless.

When she came, she knocked her head against the wall at her back, a hoarse cry pulled from her lips as she vised around his cock. He tried to hold on, tried to hold back, but the way she clenched around him, fluttering, wet and hot, he couldn't resist and found himself on his knees, buried deep, as wave after wave of climax stole his breath.

The knowledge that in the short time he'd known her, he loved her, kept him on his knees searching for breath.

She kissed his cheek. "Each time I'm with you I can't quite get past how it's different than the last, but still intense and amazing."

He opened his eyes to see her face, glowing and pleased, as she squirmed to get off his lap.

"Sorry, I must be squishing you." She held a hand out, and he took it, kissing her palm.

He stood, smiling down at her, and she wondered just what he was thinking about. Probably more sex, which was, admittedly, just fine with her.

"I'm afraid that while we have more room here, the washing up will still be less than perfect."

It was that he'd handed her a cloth, that he'd drawn the basin with warm water just for her, that wisped away any remaining ability to keep between herself and this enormous thing welling up inside her when she thought about Daniel Haws.

She was left there, bare to her emotions, bare to his gaze, and she was nothing more, nothing less than his woman. Whether he wanted it or not, it wouldn't change what she felt, what she was.

He looked down into her face. Well, *looked* wasn't the right word, it was as if he was committing every single bit of her to memory. She closed her eyes a moment, trying to paddle through the waves of emotion.

"I suppose you're hungry?" she managed to say at long last. "Let me make you something to hold you until the evening meal."

It gave her something to do with her hands at least, something to take her attention so she could get herself together.

He settled in, examining something in his pocket comm, so she left him alone, putting the food nearby. It surprised her when he took her hand and drew her down with him, arranged her into his side, all without a word.

She burrowed in, letting herself feel safe and adored. He stroked his fingertips up and down her arm, idly, as if he wasn't quite thinking about it but didn't want to not be touching her. She liked that. Felt it herself most of the time.

She wanted to talk to him. Openly. To speak of her past and her future in a way she didn't feel she had to constantly monitor. She looked forward to that, to having a normal relationship with him, or the closest approximation to that they'd ever get, given his job.

It was on that thought that sleep came, that deep, dreamless sleep the body needed to truly rest and regenerate. Safe in his arms, his scent on her body, she slept.

Chapter 14

"Wake up," Daniel murmured to her, shaking her gently. She'd dropped off shortly after they'd left and had slept through to the next day. She'd been sleeping fitfully on and off, and he knew she needed that rest, so he hadn't bothered her, just checked to be sure she was all right and let her be.

Andrei had come by as they'd neared the portal. They'd exit in Silesia, the last Imperial-controlled 'Verse before the Edge. The Edge, while technically a buffer between Imperial and Federation territories, was solidly under the dominion of the Federation, though not always with total allegiance and safety for her citizens. They'd be on safer footing, or at the very least, have more access to their own people and intelligence far more readily once they left the Imperium behind.

She smiled and stretched.

"We're going to be arriving soon. Get freshened up. We saved you some food from last evening." He pointed to the wrapped bundle.

"Last evening? I slept all this time?" She pushed the hair from her face and got out of bed.

"You must have needed it." He tried to sound matter-of-fact, but to his ears, he sounded a lot more like a lover than a keeper.

Andrei turned his back while she quickly washed up and changed, but Daniel knew he'd heard the tone.

"Cover your hair today." He said it from instinct. As he did, she moved quickly to obey, wrapping her head in a nondescript scarf, knotting it effortlessly. He warmed as she wound the blue scarf he'd given her the day before around her neck.

Andrei quickly braided his and tucked it into the back of his shirt so that he appeared to have short hair. Daniel had let his go back to its normal color, and he was glad he had.

Something was up. He casually went outside their room and looked around as they coasted into the portal docks and were assigned an arrival bay. People seemed overly nervous. The tenor of the energy on the inner decks of the transport changed. No one looked anyone in the eye. Ducking back into the room, he sent a look to Andrei. There wasn't time to play at hiding their conversation.

The feeling sharpened, ripened into urgency and he listened— acted.

He turned to Carina. "I need you to listen and *obey* me. Andrei is going to help you hide. Don't make a sound. Get your weapon out, and don't hesitate if you have to use it." He kissed her hard. He could see it in her eyes; she wanted to ask questions, but she didn't. Instead, she nodded and took Andrei's hand, letting him boost her up into the smuggler's hold.

He needed to focus. Methodically, he set to erase their presence.

Down came his alarms, up went the listening devices. He wiped surfaces down with DNA wipes. Enough cross data to confuse anyone.

In the background he heard Andrei come back into the room. They'd play at having a conversation still in their cover. Now that he'd taken the jammers down, chances were they'd be overheard, so it was crucial to sound like the people they were supposed to be. "We should go and wait to get off. I know she's anxious," Andrei said it as he tossed their packs up into the hold.

He laughed, feeling only numb as he did everything he needed to. The noise came from down the hall, a few cabins away. Yelling, some screaming. A child's cry.

He ruthlessly shut off his pain at hearing a child in fear. He could not help. He had a job and someone he *could* save. He got up and into the hold just as the door banged open and soldiers swarmed the room.

She trembled behind him but made no sound. He squeezed her ankle to reassure her. This wasn't the first such incident like this he'd been in, so he found that quiet place in his head and went there. Normally it would have been easy, but normally he wouldn't be in a cramped crawl space with the woman he was head over ass in love with. And she was scared. And the men below wanted to kill them all.

All he could do was keep a hand on her ankle, but it worked; her trembling stopped, and they continued to wait. The soldiers ransacked the cabin and upon finding nothing of use, they stormed out.

He wasn't sure how long they waited, but finally he poked a head from the hold and motioned for Andrei and Carina to stay. She shook her head wildly, but he went, replacing the seal, leaving them safely hidden.

He stood at the door, ear pressed to it. No more screams. The noise seemed to have died off. By that time they would have offloaded the ship, and there'd be a mandatory turnaround hold before the transport could be used again. They had to get off the transport before the new crew came on, but not so close to the offload that the soldiers might still be watching.

As he stood there, a soldier opened the door. Before he could jump with surprise, Daniel reached out, grabbed him, pulled him in, twisted his neck and closed the door quietly.

He hated dead bodies. They were heavy and awkward to move, and there was always the pesky issue of disposal.

Andrei peeked some moments later, angling out to help Daniel lug the body and secret it in the hold. Carina's face had been priceless, though he did feel bad that she had to see it. She skirted past the body, surprising Daniel when she helped shove it back into a far corner with a muffled curse.

"Clearly we have to split up!" she hissed in his ear once he'd crawled back up. He'd already figured that out but hadn't wanted to admit it to himself. The soldiers were looking for a woman and a man, or even two men.

"I'm not going to let you do that," he growled into her ear.

"You're an idiot. Stop thinking with your heart and think with your head."

Andrei shrugged, leaving it up to Daniel.

"Damn it. I'm not going to. What if they take you? It's too big a risk. I can't let you."

She put her hand over his mouth, shaking her head violently. "*Let?* Listen here, these are Skorpios. They know we're trying to leave. We have to split up to get the hells off this transport, and you know it. Why don't you admit it?"

"Because I don't know if I could survive you getting hurt or taken."

Everything got quiet. He hadn't meant to say it that way. Wasn't sure he ever meant to say it out loud to start with. But it was out, and her lips quivered as she launched herself at him in the tiny space.

"I love you, too, you big, brainless idiot. Now, find a way to make this work. I'm counting on you."

Love? He hadn't said that, but leave it to her to infer it. "Great." She grinned like an aforementioned idiot.

And yet he found himself back in the room, handing her a uniform he'd nicked from the employee dormitory. She'd pass herself off as an employee to get out of there. He'd stick as a civilian, but she and Andrei would wear uniforms. It should work. He hoped it would work, or he'd burn Caelinus down if anything happened to her.

"You go first," Andrei said, indicating Daniel. "You follow," he said to Carina, "I'll go last. That way we can stagger it." Andrei looked to Daniel. "It'll be fine. You're the best at this. No one better."

Daniel rolled his eyes and finally agreed.

Those minutes were the worst in his life. Walking out of the transport with her back there, exposed in ways he'd never wanted, broke his heart. He held on to his emotions ruthlessly, pushed them far, far down as he touched the paved streets.

He kept walking, heading to the boardinghouse where they were to meet in an hour standard. This part of Silesia was modern, sleek and wealthy by comparison to the other Edge territories and the 'Verses they'd just run through. There were parts of the Imperium like this, mainly the ones seen on vid screens and where any sort of negotiations or talks were held.

Despite the prosperity here and the higher level of freedom compared to the 'Verses closer to the Capital Center, there was an air of sadness, too. One he'd always associated with Imperial 'Verses. Even when drinking and kicking their heels up, sadness showed in every citizen's eyes. Not even hopelessness; they didn't have that much to start with, things were what they were and that was accepted for the most part.

And the shine wore off the farther one got from the portal until all that remained was chaos and lawlessness. The real Silesia and as far as Daniel was concerned, the real Imperium. Lost citizens, mistreated and left to fend for themselves, quite often turning on each other or worse, the weak who couldn't defend themselves and had no hope their government would.

There were no individual 'Verse governments in the Imperial Universes. It was all Fardelle, all the time, and he held a heavy hand through his ministers. It made Daniel angry, the way the man simply squeezed people, not caring about truly leading.

It left them all right where they were, on the verge of a war started by a man too stunted or bored to build his 'Verses up, choosing to tear those in the Federation down instead.

Enough. He needed to get himself together and appear as casually hopeless as the rest of them.

His hands trembled a moment when he sat, back to the wall, facing the door they would come through. "Smokes and an ale," he told the server when she swished over.

She laid a tin of hand-rolled smokes on the table and left to get his ale. Normally he'd take the time to have a meal, but his stomach was lead, his appetite gone.

Up to that very moment, he'd never felt fear over not completing a task. He'd simply done his job. If people got caught up in it, he'd do his best to protect them and get out, but if there had been civilian impact, he accepted it as one of the unavoidable tragedies of what he did.

He lit the smoke and breathed deeply. The sweetness of the burning herbs filled his lungs, wisped around his face. The ale arrived, and he sipped and thought, sipped and smoked, sipped and waited.

He loved her. He had not imagined being in that place so soon after meeting a woman. At the same time, he'd been with women, with enough of them over enough experiences to know the difference between a woman he enjoyed and what he felt for Carina. Yes, it was sudden; it was soon and unexpected and beyond complicated. But it was there and it was strong and he wanted it, wanted her like he'd never allowed himself to want anything in his entire life.

Yes, she didn't have the same experience he did, and he supposed he should encourage her to see some other men so she never felt cheated, but, since he was ruminating in his head and all, fuck that. No one could protect her and love her like he could, and she didn't need to fuck fifteen more men to know that.

"Lotta soldiers here today," he said casually to the server when she brought him another ale.

"Affectin' business, that is. They come through here three times already today. Every transport in and out boarded. Lockup is full of people. This is my place; me and my man run it. We can't afford this silliness. Lost a well, they tell me. Town supply here went to nothing. Can't run a cantina without water. And what happened? I asked. No one will say. We've been searched every few turns. People are afraid to travel nowadays. Portal shut down in Krater. Still. We can't get our usual supplies, so others are charging dear. I don't know what they're thinking, but like I said, it's affectin' business, and I don't like it."

He nodded. "Been traveling for a few turns. It's been this way at every 'Verse."

A woman walked in, one he knew very well. She saw him and headed straight over. "You owe me a drink, Neil." Marame Fisk, one of his operatives who'd been out in the Edge for some time, working with the local mercenaries to locate all the rogue portals used to smuggle information and weapons back to Fardelle.

She sat with a cat's grin. "My sister is around here somewhere. You should have one more before she arrives. Maybe two if she's still as mad at you as she was this morn."

"A mulled wine for my friend, please." His heart sped at the mention of this other woman he hoped was Carina.

The server sashayed off, and he turned back to the woman at his table. "It's unexpected to see you."

He looked her over. She had short, black hair that often stood up in spikes because she ran her fingers through it idly, a tic of personality, he supposed. She was unforgettable in her own way: striking, bold, with facial features that were unique rather than conventionally pretty. More important, as far as he was concerned, Marame was one of his best tacticians. A smart planner, good with people. A leader. And right now, that skill made Carina even safer.

"My man sent me. He's here somewhere. He'll be by shortly." Marame spoke cheerfully, but her pale blue eyes took in the room as sharply as he was sure his own did.

Her man? He wondered who she was with, which one of his operatives had accompanied her on the trip. In any case, it was good to have skilled hands he could trust completely at his back. Most likely Julian Marsters. He and Marame worked together quite often, and Julian was a gifted pilot and one of his very best hand-to-hand fighters. It made a solid team—Daniel, Andrei, Marame and Julian. They usually worked in teams of five, but four would do just fine. The backup would definitely help.

"And your sister?" he asked. "You've seen her? We got separated; surely she can't hold me responsible for that." He sent her a lazy grin, but he itched to know, to hear Carina was safe.

"She'll be along shortly. We found her down the way. Karl planned to take her to the house to drop her bags off. She was naturally opposed to this and bloodied Karl's nose in the offing." Marame's mouth tried to resist a smile, but lost.

"I should hope my cousin also helped?" Meaning Andrei.

"He came along shortly afterward. There was a slight . . . negotiation, and they all went together."

Andrei would have killed anyone who posed a threat to Carina, but he found himself relieved and admiring at hearing she'd managed to fight off a man as large and imposing as Julian or any of his operatives. He smiled as he inhaled the smoke, Carina was no easy mark.

Just then his heart soared as she came in. He stood, not giving one fuck what anyone thought, moving to her as if no one else existed in the Known 'Verses.

Carina had been scared beyond sanity when the big man had stepped into her path and told her he was there to help her drop her things off and to take her to Neil. She didn't recognize him, and she'd taken in every face she came across while on the transport. She'd never seen this man in her life, and there was no way she planned to go anywhere with him.

He'd tried to wheedle her, tried to reach out, and when he did, she reared back and punched him square in the nose, sending him reeling, stumbling. A woman came over then, trying not to laugh at the man Carina had punched.

She, too, had said they were old friends of Neil's and again, Carina had told them both to fuck right off. She had to be somewhere, somewhere Daniel waited for her. Carina knew he'd be worried, feeling panicked that he'd let her go this part alone. She needed to get to him, and no giant man and his pretty sidekick would keep Carina away.

Andrei was suddenly there. She hadn't even heard him approach, but he put himself between her and the newcomers. He held no weapons, but his stance told her and the people he faced that he didn't need any weapons to damage them.

It was then that Andrei must have recognized the two, because he relaxed and turned back to Carina, telling her it was all right, that they were part of their family.

They'd walked over a few streets to a small house surrounded by fruit trees, and she'd dropped her bag off. The man had introduced himself as Karl, the lady was May. It was this May who'd gone to Daniel while Carina and Andrei had briefed this Karl, who was clearly *not* a Karl, on what they'd seen.

Disorientation and doubt began to edge its way into her system. Did he send others to keep her away from him? No, he'd told her he cared about her, and she believed that. Had seen it, felt it over and over. Regardless, even if he had done it, she had no plans to let him get away with it. She finally stood and demanded to see Neil, and they escorted her to the public house where Daniel waited.

All the doubt passed when he caught sight of her, and his face changed, softened. He'd stood and began to walk over, and shivers of delight passed over her skin at the way he saw no one else but her.

"I hear you got lost." He tipped her chin up and kissed her quickly. "I'm glad my family found you."

He hugged her, and she felt his own fear melt away with hers. Everyone was all right, and after the fear she'd had since she'd opened her eyes that very morning, that knowledge left her weak in the knees.

"I'm starving," she whispered.

"Adrenaline does that. Come on then, I suddenly have my appetite back, and it'll be coming on to the midday meal. We'll see what Karl and May have to say about what's good here."

"I missed you," she said, pressing herself closer to him.

"You're all right, and that's what matters."

What mattered is that he loved her, and his arms around her, the way he looked at her, told her he did.

"We figured you might be hungry." May joined them. "We've got some meal plans, and another family member who can't wait to see you. Come on then." She led the way out, and they followed.

The trek wasn't far. The walk was quite lovely, despite the presence of soldiers all over the place. Again, Carina thought as they made their way to the little house, this 'Verse had so much potential and her father wasted it. It wasn't even that he controlled it the way he did elsewhere, it was that he took and never gave back. It was that this prosperity was possible for so few in a 'Verse where the majority suffered. His vision of Imperial rule was not working, and because of that, people suffered. It was a stupid waste.

The fruit trees at the front of the house shaded the lot and also lent privacy. Privacy was at a premium, highly sought after. She imagined this house cost quite a few credits and wondered how these soldiers had ended up there.

"Come on in," Karl said, leading them all through the front door and into the house. Carina remained silent when Daniel said nothing. He'd let her know when it was safe to talk, even though she was dying to know what was going on.

She figured these people must be Daniel's—his soldiers or his team. There was no way he wasn't in charge, that much was clear. First, she wasn't being vain when she assumed they'd only send the best to get her. Caelinus would have been dangerous to get to, and as she'd experienced, the Imperium was dangerous to get out of. More telling, though, was the way they all deferred to him. All of them. A slight drop of the gaze, the way they waited for him to set a pace and tone. Daniel was the boss here, not that this surprised her. He was a very bossy man, after all. Which made it a very good thing that she was a very bossy woman. Daniel Haws would run over a weaker woman, not out of cruelty, but out of his drive and will. He needed a woman who would push back when he went too far. A woman who could match that drive, that will, that determination to get the job done. Carina Fardelle, princess or not, was that woman.

They followed Karl through the house and down into a basement. Carina wasn't surprised to see Karl push back a set of shelves, less surprised to discover a door lay behind that. More number pads and retinal scanners existed behind the plain wooden door into another room.

"You can speak freely now," Karl called back as they entered a long tunnel, sealing off wherever they'd just been.

Everyone let out a long sigh of relief.

"I'm sorry about your nose," Carina called out to Karl, who turned and grinned.

"Hazard of the job. No permanent harm done. I'm Julian, and this is Marame." He turned to Daniel and bowed. "We're glad to see the three of you safe."

Daniel nodded, touching Julian's shoulder briefly. "Excellent job, Julian. I assume this is one of our places?"

"We liberated it from a smuggler. He happily gave us access in exchange for walking out of lockup." Julian shrugged.

They began to walk down a long tunnel, glow lights casting yellow light on them as they went, dying out in their wake.

"Julian and Marame are soldiers, too. Some of the very best," Daniel said as they continued to walk.

Marame turned and looked over her shoulder at Daniel. "Thank you. Coming from you, Daniel, that's high praise." Marame grinned, shifting her gaze to Carina. "I'm impressed with that punch, Carina. I'm glad to see you've received some hand-to-hand training."

"My father insisted. I wasn't allowed as much as my brother, but I'm proficient enough."

Daniel laughed. "Julian is one of the best hand-to-hand fighters I know. Even I'd be hard-pressed to bloody his nose."

Julian snorted without turning around. He called back, "Please. I've seen you knock Ellis on his ass a time or two, and the man is wilier than a fox and thicker than a tree trunk. Still, it's best we don't test that. Besides, your pretty princess there caught me by surprise, but she didn't hesitate or pull it. It was very nicely done."

Carina was ridiculously pleased by that praise. She'd been told she was beautiful, smart, cultured, a good rider and those sorts of things her entire life. But no one other than her trainer had ever said she was good at combat; it wouldn't have been done, given her position.

"Thank you very much, Julian. I would be very pleased if you would give me tips on technique sometime."

Daniel, who'd taken her hand, squeezed it once, a ghost of a smile on his face. This made her even more proud.

"After things die down, I expect we'll be seeing you around. We can work something out then." Julian had turned, walking backward to deliver that last bit, and she thanked him. They would of course, see her around after they returned to Ravena, because she would be with Daniel. It pleased her on some perverse level to be teasing him in her head. He was probably annoyed for no reason he could figure out right then.

She snorted a laugh, and he looked to her, cocking his head before turning back to the trail.

"We have a ways to go. Another five clicks or so. Mostly flat terrain but there's one steep ascent at the end. We'll have a meal when we arrive and talk about how to get you out of the Imperium and into safe territory on the other side," Marame continued.

Carina wondered what it would be like to work with Daniel like this every day. Part of her would be relieved to know with her own eyes that he was alive. But seeing him in danger all the time might begin to wear, and she knew well enough to understand asking him to stop would be tantamount to asking him to simply give up on what he believed in.

Without too much thought, she dug into her pack and handed him a piece of fruit, tossing another one back to Andrei.

"Thank you," Daniel said, kissing her quickly.

Now that the danger had passed, she remembered to ask Daniel about her brother. "Daniel, is Vincenz alive? You made it sound—on the transport, you made it sound like you knew he was." She stopped in the passage, hoping she was right.

Daniel nodded, and she threw herself at him. He caught her up in a hug and without any effort, they began to walk again as she clung to him. "I'm sorry I couldn't say so before now, it's a, well he's helped us a great deal, so we try to limit any exposure."

She nodded. "I understand. Oh my gods, he's alive and making a difference. I'm so relieved. I'm also heavy." She squirmed, and he held her in place.

"Watch it," he said quietly. She didn't know what he meant until she felt his cock brush against her ass. Ah. He put her down, and she returned to her place against his side, his arm around her shoulders.

"Any news on my mother? On the search for whoever may have helped me escape?" Carina asked as they began, yes, a steep ascent.

Marame answered, "Your mother appears to be fine. Someone was executed for helping you. I'm sorry. But it wasn't your mother."

Relief warred with guilt. "We know about my maid. Is that who you mean?"

"No, and I'm sorry about that. Claira was a brave woman. No, a house assistant found your former intended dead. He'd committed suicide, left a note saying he'd helped you. Your father then executed the head of his Skorpios guard for letting Alem's treachery go undetected for so long." Julian said it dispassionately as he keyed in a code and used another retinal scanner.

"Alem? Please, the man is incapable of helping anyone but himself!"

Daniel grunted beside her. "And now he's dead."

Yes. She paused, realizing she felt nothing but relief. "Everyone is better off because of that."

"Depends on who takes his place, but yes, I'd agree."

That was that. She looked back at where they'd come and then toward where Julian stood, unlocking the doors. "I can't believe all this exists." She indicated the tunnel they'd just traveled through.

"Smugglers and mercenaries." Marame shrugged. "The whole tunnel is shielded so it can't be detected from the surface. Eavesdropping programs can't find it. Never underestimate man's desire to make credits and move merchandise. The house we're entering now also has shields against eavesdropping, just so you know."

The house was spacious and appeared to be built into a cliff face. Darkened, plasglass windows showcased a view of the canyon and valley below, of the cities in the distance.

"This is magnificent." Carina turned in a circle.

It was then she saw him leaning against a table nearby, grinning. Her mouth dropped open as she dimly heard Daniel speak to Marame just behind her.

Chapter 15

"It's you." She dashed toward Vincenz, and he caught her up in a hug. He was a man, not the just barely man he'd been when she saw him last.

"Carina, gods, it's so good to see you." Vincenz kissed her cheeks and held her back so he could look at her. "You've grown up into a woman. A beautiful woman who has been in a lot of danger." He shook her once. She saw the fear in his eyes, understood it because she'd felt it for him.

"It's on my list of things to avoid in the future," she assured him, hugging him again. "Oh, Vincenz, I've missed you so much. So much. They said you were dead, but I never believed it all the way. There were days I did, just because it hurt too much to think otherwise, but always in my heart I had hope you'd escaped. YaYa helped, didn't she?"

He nodded. "She helped get me out. Used all her influence, all her saved-up credits, everything. Between YaYa and Mai, I was able to get over the line, and when I made it, Wilhelm Ellis himself was waiting with Daniel."

Daniel snorted a laugh behind her. "Vincenz, it's good to see you."

Her brother turned to her . . . lover? Her man, yes, she decided, her man. Her brother turned to her man, and they both eyed each other warily for a moment until they clasped forearms.

"Daniel, well met. You have my thanks for helping my sister."

Daniel shook off the praise. "It's my job, and your sister did much of her own saving. Resourceful, you Fardelles."

"Some of us anyway." Vincenz turned back to her. "We have so much to catch up on."

"Why don't the two of you go on, take some time. Vincenz knows the place, this was his idea. So go on and visit while we plan some." Marame smiled at them, and Carina saw the look in the other woman's eyes when she looked at Vincenz. Smitten perhaps, but he didn't return it. Didn't seem to notice it. He hadn't changed very much then.

Carina turned to Daniel, took his hand. "Does that sound all right? I'll be back shortly."

He smiled, warmth in his eyes. "Of course. You two catch up."

"You'll be here when I return?" It was, she knew a silly question to ask, but it was a fear that she'd wake up or turn around and he would be gone.

"Will you all excuse us a moment?" Daniel said it, but it wasn't really a question. He drew her aside. "Why would you ask such a thing? I'm not leaving you. Don't you know that by now?"

"I don't know. Yes, I do. I do. But I'm scared, and you make me feel safe, you make me happy, and I don't want that to go away."

He sighed, still holding her hand. "Carina, I don't have any plans to do that."

"Do you want to?"

"What? Abandon you to your fate?" The incredulous look on his face told her a lot, but he dodged the real question, and that annoyed her. Men.

"You know what I mean, Daniel. I love you."

He smiled. "This is not the right place or time to have this discussion. Your brother is right over there waiting. Go and be with him, enjoy him."

She narrowed her eyes, and he laughed. He squeezed her hand before he brought it to his lips. For him, in front of all these people, that was as much a declaration as if he'd dropped to his knees and shouted to the heavens that he loved her.

"I'm not going anywhere. It would take three armies to wrest you from me. Go. I'll be here when you return, same as yesterday and tomorrow."

She tiptoed up and kissed him before he could give her any distance. "Good. Because I've decided to keep you." She twirled, still smiling, and tossed back ever so casually over her shoulder, "I love you, Daniel."

Vincenz said nothing until they'd reached a small garden area just below where they'd entered the house.

"YaYa's gone, isn't she?" Vincenz asked as they sat together. He'd been the one to start calling their grandmother that in the first place. It had been his first word.

"I'm sorry you didn't know. Disappeared. Just a few turns after you'd gone. We weren't allowed to speak of her again. Mai tried to find out what she could, but there was nothing." There was a catch in her voice. She tried to stop it, but it was there.

He put his arm around her shoulders. "I never could have gotten out without her. She risked everything."

"She did it willingly. You know that. YaYa had her own mind. She wouldn't have done it if she hadn't wanted to. *Where have you been? Does Mai know you're alive?* She was never quite the same after you left. And then Petrus." She turned to him. "Did you know what he did to our Petrus? Vincenz, did you know?"

The pain in his eyes told her he did.

"Not until long after. News takes some time to get to the Edge, and then we didn't know for sure about the true nature of it until later. He has to be stopped. Our father has to be stopped, Carina."

She nodded. "I know." Putting her head on his shoulder a moment, she let herself relax, let herself know he was alive and safe, he was her family. She was not alone in this new world she'd tossed herself into. Well, apart from Daniel. She smiled a bit just thinking about what his face must have looked like when she told him she loved him upstairs.

"Daniel Haws is a dangerous man, Carina."

She didn't like the warning in his voice. "Thank the gods for it. You have no idea how many times that's saved my life since he got me away from Caelinus. What are you doing, Vincenz? Where do you live? Daniel says you're helping them."

"At first I lived in Ravena's capital city. You'll like it there. Beautiful, massive city for as far as the eye can see. Bustling with life all the time. The people are different than they are at home. They're open. Not all the 'Verses in the Federation are that way; some are like Nondal, which is far, far more like home than most other 'Verses I've been to."

She waited, but he kept quiet.

"You're considering lying to me. Most likely because the last time you saw me I was a lot younger and most likely far more frivolous, though don't tell Daniel I admitted that." She laughed, but he sighed and pushed his long, lanky body from the place next to her, ambling to the wall of windows.

"What is Daniel to you, Carina?"

"Where do you live now and what do you do?" she countered.

"I live on the Edge, sometimes in Asphodel, sometimes in Caldara. Officially, I run a brokerage of sorts. I work with the mercenaries and smugglers. In turn, they give me information I need."

"And you pass it on to the Federation."

"Yes. When I first arrived, they debriefed me. They'll do that to you as well, but you know more, and it is a time of great stress. This concerns me, though I do trust Ellis and Lyons. They're good men." He shoved a hand through his hair, hair she noted needed a trim.

"I'm doing the right thing," Carina said quietly.

"You are. I don't know what data you've got in that chip, but the way he's sending out his dogs after you, the massive outpouring of resources to get you back or kill you tells me you're the key to giving the Federation the upper hand in this war."

"Can't it prevent war?"

"It's awfully late for that. I'd like to think it can. You know our father. I'd wager to say you know him better than anyone. Will he simply just give up? Even with whatever you have?"

She blew out her breath. "Probably not. He's building something bad. Have you heard about all the explosions and cover-ups? The portal shut down? I can't help but think it's connected. He's worse, you know. Once you'd gone and then Petrus"—she choked back a sob and continued—"once Petrus was dead and he had no male heir, he brought on more advisors. He's not the only one in control of his office, Vincenz."

Her brother's shoulders froze, rigid, as he spun. "You're very observant. You'll need to be sure to tell this to Ellis."

"I will. Daniel tells me this Ellis is a brilliant man. I gather they're a lot more like father and son than boss and employee."

"All the Phantom Corps are that way with him. They're way out of your league, Carina. These men and women do dark deeds."

Phantom Corps? The name seemed to fit the people she'd met so far. "How do you mean?" Alarm slid up her spine, broke over her skin.

"These Phantom Corps your Daniel owns and runs, they're shadows. They're that dry, deadly wind that crops up, and all the animals run and hide. This loyalty they have to Ellis, the way he is, yes, like their father, what is it he does that makes them so efficient?"

"How is that dark? Any more dark than anyone else that carries out orders most people wouldn't have the courage to do? Are you insinuating Ellis harms them? Forces them?" Their father quite often used the people and things his soldiers cared about to keep them in line.

"I have absolutely no reason to think that. Ellis is a fearsome man. Tall, broad, you can see the intelligence in his eyes, always thinking, examining, planning. But he has, as far as I've seen, honor at his very core. His people respect him because he deserves it."

"Then why the comment? If you know something bad, you need to tell me now."

"What is Daniel to you?"

She didn't bother playing games, she knew what he asked. "I love him."

He growled low in his throat and began to pace. She watched

him, thinking how much they were alike though they had not been in contact in so long. He thought about it; she saw the edges of his warring emotions all over his body language. He disapproved; she saw that clearly enough in the rigidity of his spine. But not wholly. She saw the softness of his mouth, had heard the admiration in his voice when he'd spoken of Daniel. His eyes narrowed as he puzzled out how to say it.

He stopped pacing, pausing before the windows again, giving her his back. "So you said upstairs, though I'd hoped it was just a taunt. You're in love with a man who kills for a living,"

She folded her hands in her lap. "I am. Are you shocked that I know this? I saw him kill men to save me. More than once. He's also a man who saves lives for a living, too. What do you do, Vincenz? Do you rescue small furry animals now?"

"It's not the same! Can't you see that?"

"You're right, it's not, but not in the way you're insinuating. He does a job many others, *most* others won't do. But it needs doing nonetheless, and you know it. You may find it distasteful, but neither one of us would be here now if it weren't for Daniel Haws!" She stood. "He's a good man, a strong man who cares very much about his people and his world. He has the courage to take a step into darkness so you and I don't have to. I love him for his heart, for his strength and yes, because he walks into places I can't imagine, all so I don't have to."

"I don't want to see you get hurt."

She hugged him. "Life is full of hurts. What I feel for Daniel is beautiful, and I can't regret it, no matter how it turns out."

He sighed. "How can you even know if what you feel is real?"

"Is that a philosophical question? Because I'm quite certain you would never have the gall to suggest I didn't know my own mind."

He laughed. "You've grown up well. I'm proud."

"What is it that brings the envy to your voice when you talk about them? Is it something between you and Daniel?"

He shook his head. "No. He's been a friend to me. He's a professional. I had thought one day to be an operative with them, too. I had wanted that when I first arrived. Ellis said no, and guided me out to the Edge. I'm still there, and he was right in many ways. I've come into my own, built my own skills, and I'm good at what I do. I suppose I want someone normal for you. A man who is home each night to tuck your children into bed."

He was different now than he'd been in his youth. She supposed she was, too. What they'd lived through had changed them. She realized it would take time for them to know each other again.

"I don't know that I've ever been destined for normal." She smiled wanly. "But what I have, well, it's good and right. and I'm grateful for it. I hope you can see that. I hope you can trust me and Daniel, too."

"I'm working on it." He held his hand out. "Come on, I imagine they're working hard on a plan to get us the seven hells out of here."

$\mathscr{D}$aniel sighed, shaking his head when she called out her I love you. He held a hand up, cutting off any questions as he walked into the kitchen area, poured himself a mug of kava and took a sip before he spoke.

"Thank you for bringing him in. I'm sure she'll feel better, and he has good contacts as well." He knew Vincenz would want to talk to his sister about everything, including her parting shot to Daniel as she'd left the room. Daniel considered Vincenz a friend, though not one he saw often. He trusted the other man, respected him. In his place, Daniel had been hypercritical of his sister's relationship with Roman Lyons.

He knew Carina loved her brother, and he couldn't help but give in to a tiny spark of fear in his belly that she'd let him convince her Daniel was wrong for her. Even though he was. But wrong for her or not, he loved her.

"She loves you?" Marame asked.

"She thinks so." Daniel sipped his kava, searching for calm, finding little.

"She does," Andrei interrupted. "He feels the same. Now, how do we get the hells out of here?"

Grateful for his friend's words, Daniel pushed away from the counter and headed into the common area and sat at the large table. He drew out his pocket comm. "Let's get started."

"We got word you'd been unable to break through. Looked into the pattern of Skorpios and other military on the watch. They're out this way now because you were sighted by some mercs who sold you out. One turned up dead; imagine that." Julian shrugged.

"I expect them all to turn up dead before the end of this standard year. Every. Last. One."

Andrei nodded at Daniel. Such betrayal couldn't go unanswered, or they'd all do it for the highest bidder. If they had no honor, fear would do just as well. In his seventeen standard years doing this, he'd always found the threat of death, underlined when it had to be, was an effective tool against a coward.

"We've got a private transpo at the portal. Top-of-the-line. If we can get to it, it'll be approved to leave immediately." Marame had her own comm out, projecting several routes from their bolt-hole to the portal.

"Then let's be sure to get to it."

"What we face is two full columns of Skorpios." Julian looked at his comm. "Data just popped up. They know we're here."

It wasn't so much that Daniel doubted he could get Carina out of there, but he feared what she might have to see to make it happen.

There would be death in great, heaping servings, and his aim was to be sure he served it rather than became it.

"We need heavy weapons. Full magazines. This will not be a stealthy trip, so we need to be able to get through."

Marame did her job well, outlining the two best routes and setting multiple contingencies should those not work. Their biggest point of exposure would be once they hit the inner core of the portal city. No vehicles were allowed, so they'd have to be on the streets, far less protected, far slower than they'd be in a conveyance.

Daniel did his job to keep his focus off whatever they were discussing downstairs. Her life was paramount, getting her out and to a place where the data could be extracted. If he had to move mountains to make that so, he would. For her.

*S*he came up sometime later, and the look Vincenz gave him told him her brother had mixed feelings about whatever she'd said.

She moved to him, touching his shoulders and squeezing herself onto the bench where Daniel sat so she could be next to him.

It was then she saw the data about the people who'd been caught in the roundup to capture them. The people her father had executed. She looked at it, saw the faces, the files, the names.

"Is there a place to clean up and rest?" Daniel heard the strain in her voice, the emotion. His gaze slid to Vincenz a moment, and the two men shared their concern.

"We should stay low for the next day or so. There are rooms here." Marame stood and pointed to a door at the end of a hall. "Sleep chambers with a bathing suite located in between. There's food. Our host may be a smuggler, but he has many fine things to eat in his larder. Enough to forgive many transgressions." Marame winked.

Daniel grabbed their packs. "Let's get you settled. There are facilities here for us to wash clothing, I've been told. I'm sure those around me would be happy about that."

Her smile was there but tense around the edges.

"Would you like me to sleep in another room?" he asked once they were in the bedchamber with the door closed.

She looked up, startled. "No! Why would you do that?" She grabbed his hands, and he slid his thumbs over her skin.

"I just want you to be comfortable. With your brother here, I—I didn't want you to feel uncomfortable."

She sighed, shaking her head. "Trust you to make me feel better, even when you don't know it and are acting like you have fluff for brains. I would feel uncomfortable with you elsewhere. I'd be wondering if you were trying to distance yourself or if you were angry. I like you near me, haven't you figured that out yet?"

"I have no idea what you're talking about, but I'm just fine in here with you." He looked through drawers until he found some soft, warm clothing that would serve until theirs was clean. He handed it her way. "Why don't you give me your clothes, and I'll set them to wash with mine?"

When she did, handing it all over and retreating into the bathing room, he knew she was deeply bothered by that data. He left the room, put the clothes to wash and returned.

She'd escaped into the bathing suite to work out her emotions. But once she turned the bathwater on, Daniel strode into the room like he'd been invited. She opened her mouth to order him out, but he began to strip off his clothes, and who was she to deny herself the glory of his body?

The smile playing on his lips told her he'd done it on purpose.

"You're distracting me with your nakedness and your penis." She slid into the water, dunking herself and surfacing to find him in the water with her.

"It's not on you."

She considered making a joke, but then decided not. "Do you have a chip in my head? Do you know how I feel?" she snapped.

"I've been doing this long enough to have had innocents get caught up in the mission. But Hartley Alem was *not* an innocent, Carina. He hurt tens of thousands of people. He would have used you, broken you and not cared. That cannot stand. Just knowing someone existed who wanted to harm you made me crazy. Now that I know he's not a threat, I feel better, and so should you. I'd rather have him and your father's pet Skorpios die than you or your mother."

"It's not him. I don't care about him. It's the others. All those people who got caught up in something they had no part of. I brought that into their lives."

"Your father brought this all on, not you. It is not necessary to kill the numbers he does, but we both know he does it for his own plea-sure, to keep people so afraid he can keep them down. For no other reason than to show them all he can. He has no plan. Even your grand-father's version of leadership had a point. Those deaths are not yours; it lies with him. *All of it.*"

She sighed. He was right, but it hurt nonetheless. Seeing how many people had died because she'd run. It wasn't her intention, not what she'd wanted. "I hate it when you're wise, Daniel." She settled against him as he began to lather her hair.

"Sorry, sweet. I'll dumb it up just for you."

Eyes still closed as he rinsed, she smiled and rested against him more fully. "And while we're discussing your attributes, I need to add a few things. You have honor, true honor, and you have no idea how rare a quality that is. You're also very handsome and strong, and you have kept me alive this entire time when the weight of the Imperium is trying to hunt me down and kill me."

"Were we discussing my attributes?"

"You're messing up this moment," she said, trying pinch his thigh, finding nothing but muscle.

"Thank you," he murmured quietly into her ear before straightening. "As for the saving? It's my job. And, admittedly, I like it that you're alive. That way I can have sex with you and make you laugh. The difference between that cool, regal voice and your very fine lusty laugh is enough to make a man hard as iron."

"You're a flatterer." She thought back on something that she'd wondered since the first moment he touched her. "Have there been others?"

"I'm not a virgin."

She snorted and dunked under again, coming back up and pushing on his shoulder so he'd turn around so she could return the favor and wash his hair. "You know what I'm asking. I don't know why you're being so silly and making me work hard for it."

"Ouch! I think my scalp is just fine without the hair pulling, sweet. Ask me what you want to ask me. I don't want to play games with you." He froze a moment, obliging and tipping his head back so she could rinse his hair.

"Do you do this on your missions? Ever? You know, having a woman?"

He sighed and stood. She watched quite happily as he soaped up and rinsed. He took the drying cloth she handed him as he stepped out.

"I've had women on missions. As in I've had sex with women when I was on a job. I've never had sex with a woman who *was* my job. But to answer the question you're afraid to ask me, no, I don't use women on my missions for sex and then dump them without a word when I get them home."

She narrowed her eyes at him as he got dressed and then moved to her. He buttoned the back of the simple but very warm winter dress he'd given her earlier, all without waiting to be asked. She liked that. A lot.

She sensed he wanted to say more, so she remained quiet while she brushed her hair out.

"I don't normally have anyone with me on missions who isn't already on my team, anyway, much less romantic or sexual liaisons. I have a job to do, and there's usually nothing to be done afterward but be sure I'm not connected with the body."

"If you're expecting me to wince because your job is different than other men's jobs, you're going to wait a long time. You don't shock me."

"I know." He shrugged and leaned back against the counter. "It's one of the many reasons you get to me in ways no one else ever has. You, Carina. No one else has ever come close to meaning to me what you do."

"You love me." It wasn't a question, and he didn't answer. Stubborn man. "You love me, but you have this barmy idea that you shouldn't say it out here where this silly female can't really know her mind."

He rubbed a cloth over his hair to dry it, eyes on her, mouth closed.

"I love you, too. Are you scared?"

He leaned back, wearing only loose pants hanging dangerously low on his hips. His feet were bare, a sight that she couldn't quite puzzle out the appeal of, but she felt it full force.

"You scare me on many levels." He grinned, and she socked him in the belly, which was rock hard and impervious to her little jab. Taking her fist, he brought it to his lips for a kiss, and she was undone again.

"I should not be saying this or doing this, but I can't seem to stop breaking rules where you're concerned. Loving you doesn't scare me. I'm nearly forty years old; I've waited long enough to know what I feel and to accept it. But you are not my age, and you don't have my experience. People will try to tell you you're wrong and need to see other men. That worries me to a certain extent, because I can't be with you every moment when we return. I have this job, and I don't plan to give it up. I go away, and I can't tell you where. Sometimes I'm gone for a while, others I return in a day or so. I'm afraid I'm selfish for not encouraging you to see other people first."

She studied him for a while. Men were odd creatures, she realized. But his fear, that he'd voiced it, meant a lot to her. Almost as much as the admission, at last, that he loved her.

"I knew you loved me." She kissed his chest and then snuggled into him, hugging her arms around him. "I know people will say I'm too young, or that it's only the danger of this mission that made me mistake lust for love. I know I will be told to see others because I can't possibly know my own mind."

She tipped back enough to look at his face. She wanted him to see her eyes when she told him the rest. "I come from a world where I was traded to a man I neither consented to marry nor wanted to marry. My entire life has been about people telling me what to do, what to think and believe. I have had little space to express my own wishes. I must tell you I choose you. *Choose*, Daniel. It's important to me that people understand that. I haven't had a lot of opportunity to choose things in my life. I stand here before you, naked in body and soul, and I tell you, I love you. I don't need another man's cock in my body to know that. I don't need to go to meals and be wooed by men who I know right now will not measure up to the one I want: you."

He nodded once. "All right then."

"I must confess I'm dubious about how quickly you've assented." She eyed him warily, and he laughed.

His grin was sneaky at the edges, but so sexy and handsome, it disarmed her.

"The raw fact is, I want you. I want you, and if you want me, too, I'm not going to advocate you doing anything else but being with me." He shrugged, kissed her forehead and left the room, leaving her amused and weak kneed.

Her brother was alive and helping the Federation. She wouldn't be alone. And she had Daniel, really, truly. After wishing for someone to love, he'd shoved his way into her world and set it on end. Despite all the bad, good lived in her life, too.

Daniel, smiling, pulled on a shirt before striding out into the common room where Vincenz had joined them all at the table. He met Vincenz's eyes straight on. "Good to see you. You've made your sister very happy at a time when she needed to know she had someone on the other side. And I suppose your skills and connections will come in damned handy, too."

Vincenz thought for a moment and finally nodded, raising a glass his way. "It's good to see you, too. My sister is in love with you."

Daniel noticed he said it with finality. Not *my sister thinks she loves you*, but that she did. That was a good step.

"I know."

"I'm just going to go check on the meat in the oven." Julian stood, dragging Marame along with him.

Andrei didn't bother with an excuse; he just got up and left the room, leaving Daniel and Vincenz alone.

"If you have a problem, let's hear it." Daniel leaned forward, took one of Andrei's smokes and lit it. He rarely if ever smoked at home when we wasn't working, but one of these days Andrei was going to present him a bill for all the ones Daniel had pinched off him over the years.

"My sister knows her own mind."

That surprised Daniel. Not that Carina had her own mind—he knew that quite well—but that Vincenz would admit it so easily.

"Among many fine attributes, yes, your sister does indeed know her own mind." Daniel snorted, thinking of her.

Vincenz looked to his hands and then back to Daniel. "Do you love her? I'd never assume you would take advantage of a woman, any woman, but especially one as vulnerable as Carina."

The words came after an internal struggle. He was not a man prone to talking about his emotions, much less with brothers of his women, but he owed it to this man who'd just found his sister again.

"I could tell you it's none of your business, but it is. I've been where you are, so I'll be clear. I've never met anyone like your sister." Both men paused to snort. "She fascinates me, impresses me, she's beautiful, intelligent and brave. Of all the women in the Known Universes, she's that one for me. I love your sister."

"Any fool could see." Carina swept into the room and put the bread out on the table. "He positively moons over me, Vincenz."

Startled, Daniel laughed. "She does tend to listen to conversations she was not invited into."

Vincenz rolled his eyes. "She was like that as a kid, too. Always in everyone's business." He ducked when Carina flicked the towel that had been over the bread at his head.

The two men gave each other one last considering look, and understanding passed between them. She was theirs to protect, and they expected the other to always keep that foremost in mind.

Once the all clear had been declared by Carina and the delivery of the bread, everyone else came out, bringing food and ale with them.

Carina laughed with them, passed out plates, told them funny stories about things Vincenz did as a child, all while she'd ensconced herself in Daniel's lap like nothing at all was wrong with that.

Marame just stared, openmouthed, for long moments before smiling and shaking her head. Daniel felt a bit uncomfortable with it, this crossing of business and professional lines. He'd never had this experience before. It intoxicated and confused him. Much like everything about falling in love with Carina did.

He'd had work, and then he'd had his personal life. But this was different. He'd never quite imagined the sort of glory of this connection he had with her, with the feeling that he could do anything because of her. Until he'd met her, it hadn't been something he'd understood, or perhaps nothing he'd even wanted for fear of losing himself so entirely.

And there he was, his life in a warm, sexy bundle perched on his lap, her fingers intertwined with his. There was no loss of himself, though. Just a sense of union.

"Now that we've gotten all that silly boy stuff between my brother and Daniel out of the way, how are we getting off this 'Verse?"

"It's going to take some work." Julian pointed at the maps again. "A lot of ammunition, too."

"Good thing everyone has enough weaponry to run their own security force, then, eh?" Carina sat back. "Just make sure I have a few blasters and plenty of charges. Point me, and I'll go."

"Here's what we're going to do." And they began to plan how they'd make their way to the portal.

Chapter 17

A hand shoved her to the ground. Shouts rang out, wrapped in the *pop, pop, pop* of weapons fire. She stayed, her arms clutched around his ankle. He changed his stance so that she rested between his legs, changed his stance to protect her better. And he did it all automatically.

She did not look at the men in the trees, did not look at the men crouched at the next corner shooting round after round, all set to kill her. They would not harm her; she knew that instinctively. Knew Daniel Haws would kill a thousand men to save her, knew he'd give his life for her. This last bit scared her more than the men trying to kill her. This last bit was a bigger threat than any, because he was her everything, and she would not survive losing him.

So she looked up at Daniel, into his face, and held on to her certainty that no one was better than he.

Spent shells showered around her head, glittering in the sunlight with a sick sort of beauty. The ones that touched her bare skin burned as they bounced, hitting the ground, still smoking. Their metallic *ping* sounded over and around the other sounds, all chaos. The stench of the powder within the shells hung in the air, stinging her nose, making her eyes water.

His face was stark, a mask of furious, righteous anger, a vengeful angel. Each shot brought the energy rebounding through his upper body, and she watched, fascinated, as it bounced against him over and over, but he never lost his focus.

All around her she heard screams of rage and pain, the percussive thump as bodies hit the ground. The thick, coppery scent of blood mixed with the stench of the spent shells, the acrid wash of fear coating it all.

They'd been ambushed as they neared the portal and had fallen back into a small garden off the main street. Julian, Vincenz and Marame had split off as Carina grabbed her blaster. Andrei had melted off, disappearing like smoke, only to appear for a moment in a splash of red and disappearing again.

Daniel, brooking no argument, had shoved her down and begun shooting at the men trying to close in. She curled into a ball, not wanting to choose that moment to push back. He was the expert. She wasn't so stupid she didn't understand that when an expert gave you instructions, you took them.

She wanted to help, but she wanted him to live, wanted to live herself. So she stayed at his feet, looking up at him as the light glinted from his hair, dark like roasted kava, so beautiful, even as an avenging angel, he shone.

The paving stone she rested her elbow on splintered, driving shards of rock into her skin. She barely held in her cry of pain, but it sang through her system nonetheless.

Moments later, he said her name, hauling her up to his side as she struggled to get to her feet. He didn't drag her, he simply held her with one arm, shooting with the other as they rounded a corner and Julian came out, pulling them both into the building and slamming the door in their wake. If she hadn't been so terrified, the sheer gallantry and skill he showed would have wowed her.

The silence settled in, deafening after the chaos outside.

Daniel set her down in a far corner, patting over her, holding his bloody hand up as if she'd done it on purpose. "Are you all right? Did you get shot? Tell me now!"

"I—I don't think so."

"Blood! Carina, you're bleeding." He tried to rip her clothes back to look, but she slapped at his hands. His face was set; he was on a mission.

"The rock splintered. It hit my arm. I'm cut, not shot. Stop! Stop it!" She yanked his hair, hard, and finally he seemed to hear.

He froze, blinking several times until he pushed her sleeve up with a hiss. "Stay right here. Do not move."

As if she would with him in such a lather! "Bossy," she managed to say, and his shoulders eased a bit as she'd intended.

Marame looked over and grinned. Andrei was suddenly there, kneeling, looking her over, a question in his eyes. Vincenz stood near the windows, out of sight but watching the street. Every once in a while, he looked over at Carina, and she smiled, reassuring him.

"Move," Daniel said to Andrei. He settled at her feet and began to clean her arm when Andrei moved to the side.

Andrei tweezed the small shards of rock out of the wounds.

Julian came back in. "We have to move. They're not too far away, going house to house. Can she travel?" He indicated Carina with a tip of his chin.

"I'm fine. Just some cuts." She stood, and Daniel stuffed the first aid kit into his pack and shouldered it, not moving more than arm's reach from her.

"Where the fuck did they come from?" Daniel snarled, looking angrier than she'd ever seen him.

"A bullet hit the—"

He turned to her, the fury gone, gentleness in its wake. He slid a thumb over her bottom lip. "No, sweet, not that."

"I don't know where the soldiers came from, but I know we need to get the fuck outta here right now." Vincenz slid his sidearm back into the holster. "We knew there'd be Skorpios here, and the population is under his thumb enough to want to make a quick credit and do them all the favor of having these raids stop. I can't blame them, I suppose."

Marame looked up from where she'd been working on her personal comm. "The portal is not far. Some of our people are working on a diversion. Slip forty-two. Papers cleared, it's ready to go at any time."

"Let's go. Weapons hot." Andrei poked his head out the door. "We're clear."

Daniel hustled her out, keeping his body in front of hers. They could hear the soldiers just a street or so over, breaking down doors, shouting orders.

A block up, and they could see the portal just in the distance. Close enough to get there at a run if they had a clear way.

"You will stick with me." Daniel put a hand on her cheek. "I won't let anything happen to you."

"I know."

He seemed satisfied with that answer as they paused at a corner.

"Soldiers are filling up the streets." Marame jogged up to them.

"Run. Shoot anything that gets in the way." With that, Daniel bent, tossed her up and over his shoulder and began to run.

Funny how the world seemed on a man's back when a girl was upside down. Nicely, his butt was in her view, and a fine butt it was, she realized not for the first time. Other butts were fetching, she knew, but this one she'd had her hands on, urging him deeper as he'd fucked her. This one was hers.

"They're coming," she shouted, holding on and trying not to impede any of his movement.

Soldiers flowed out behind them, running, shouting into wrist comms and at them to stop. The streets this near the portal were closed to vehicle traffic, save for trams that ran from the portal to the part of town where visitors could find lodging and travel on 'Verse.

She saw the uniforms and knew they were her people, Skorpios, mixed with elite soldiers from across the Imperium. She knew this even as she raised her arm and shot at them. Knew this even as one of them fell, a bloom of blood on his chest. Knew they never had been her people, knew they were her father's tools with which to maim and torture others to keep the populace in line.

Up steep steps toward the sleek private transport they'd need to get out of the Imperium and into the Edge, one step closer, one step safer.

At the top, Andrei had the doors open, and Carina didn't even have time to object when Daniel tossed her to him. Tossed her! Andrei caught her with a laugh and quickly canted her upright, tipping her through the door so she could land on her feet.

"I know how to get the ship started," she called, moving toward the flight deck. Thank the gods for her father's paranoia. He'd never trusted his transport captains, so she'd been trained to operate his transports for him. In the end, he'd been convinced that it was unseemly to have his daughter doing his manual labor, and he'd stopped her, but all the time she'd spent in the operator's seat on his transports came back as she slid into the chair and began to warm the ship for the slip into the portal.

"Let me know when everyone is in. I have green light for departure," she yelled out over the sounds of battle behind her.

"Go! Now!"

"Strap in." Suddenly Daniel was next to her, strapping her into her seat as he settled in one seat over.

She heard the door slam, and the panel lit all green, indicating that they'd achieved a seal and it was safe to go. She punched the button to release the clamps holding them to the dock, mumbled a quick prayer for safety and hit the accelerator.

"We're clear." Vincenz flopped onto a nearby bench. "You're both unharmed?"

Daniel stood. "I got a blaster burn on my calf. I need to go clean it up and get some gel on it."

Carina turned and saw the bloody mess on his leg. "You dumb prick! Why didn't you say so? How long did you have that?"

He sent a smug smile her way. "Hey, I'm not dumb." The kiss he pressed on her lips sent relief surging through her. "It's not the first time I've been injured on the job, sweet. It happens. That also means I'm a whiz at battlefield dressing. Since we're safely away, I can take my time and even put it up until the gel does its work. If we were back there still, I'd have to walk on it for a while before I could fix it."

"Is this supposed to make me feel better?" she asked after setting in the navigational markers.

"Yes." He kissed her again and disappeared back into the ship.

"It's going to be hard." Marame spoke from her place to Carina's left.

"What is?"

"Each time he goes to work, you'll worry. People want to harm him. It's terrifying to imagine losing someone who has become as integral to your life as breathing."

"Were you . . . are you with one of your squad mates, teammates, whatever you call each other?" Carina liked Marame and hoped she didn't answer that Daniel had been hers at one time.

"I was." She looked to Andrei briefly. "For a time."

"Did it make it easier when you were with him on a job?"

"Sometimes. Or I convinced myself it did. But the fact of the matter is, it doesn't. I can be there, but I have a job to do as well. Just as you will. I can't imagine you'll sit around like a princess when you get back. Though there are many who will insist you do just that."

The transport safely on track, she turned to face Marame. "Why do people assume I'm useless?"

Marame grinned. "Who would dare?" She laughed, and Carina relaxed a bit. "Oh, honey, I don't mean *I* expect you to do that. I expect you to tear shit down and toss your weight around to stay with Daniel. I'm just telling you what to expect. If you've ever been strong willed, you'll need to be now."

"How so?"

"The Imperium has much the same attitude about Rank that the Federation does. That won't be a surprise to you, I'm sure. You're, as far as many will be concerned, one of the highest Ranked people in the Federation. They'll want to brand you with that. And to a certain extent you'll be protected by it. But that Ranking will rip you away from Daniel. He can't have a princess. He can have an unranked woman. Like me."

Carina spun, baring her teeth for a moment at the very idea.

"What fuckery is this? He can't have you! He's mine, and I will carve your heart out of your chest if you make one move toward him."

Marame laughed, waving a hand toward Carina. "I'm done with soldiers, thank you very much. Daniel is a beautiful man, strong, loyal, courageous. He's one of the sexiest men I've ever known. But he's ass over head in love with you. I've never seen him look at anyone the way he does you. What I meant was, our world is ruled by Rank. You are, he's not."

"I don't care what anyone else thinks. If Roman Lyons wants the information I carry, he'll have to take it knowing I have no plans to play along with the same sort of system that drove me over to your side to start with."

"Roman won't expect that, by the way. Roman nearly gave up his seat at the head of the Governance Council and of House Lyons for Abbie. Abbie is now, in what amuses me greatly, the highest Ranking woman in the Federation."

"Abbie? Daniel's sister Abbie? She's married to Roman Lyons?" She slumped back in her seat. How could she have not picked that up!

"I'm sure he didn't have a lot of opportunity to share with you, without fear of being overheard. But yes. She'll love you, by the way. Just trust her, she'll protect you from those who want to shove you into a pretty little box of Rank."

Around the corner, Daniel had wrapped his calf, adhering the special healing gel to the blaster burn. The nanites would clear out the dead, burned flesh and replace it with fresh, healed skin and tissue. It was something similar to what all the Phantom Corps carried with them, that the doctors used to heal the wounds on his sister's back so many years before.

"You okay?" Andrei sailed into the common area outside the communal bathing rooms.

"Yeah. Not too bad, considering. Those are not odds I like. If it had been just us, we've have been fucked ten ways. Marame, Julian and Vincenz tipped the scales." Daniel shifted to put his leg up on a nearby chair. He wanted to see after Carina, but his emotions were very raw just then. She'd seen the darker part of him pretty much daily since they'd met. Had seen him kill and step over bodies that got in the way. He didn't know how to begin to process that.

"That and your fury that anyone dared to harm Carina. You were five men out there, Daniel. I'm fair convinced you could have done all the damage yourself if you'd had to."

"I didn't. Thankfully." He looked to Andrei.

Andrei shrugged, acknowledging the gratitude, and the subject was closed.

"She did a great job today."

Daniel couldn't help the grin at the mention of how she'd been that day. "Our little princess is quite the feral cat in a corner, isn't she? She was using her blaster as I ran, shooting while upside down." He shook his head at the memory of it. He was so proud of her, of how courageous and clever she'd been. She didn't give up, she listened to orders and she saved them all by having the transport ready to go once they'd all gotten inside.

"You're good together." Andrei lit a smoke.

"She fills something inside me." Kept the darkness away, made him remember he was human first. "I know I'm not right for her. I feel guilty. She has so many options now, and if I don't move aside, she'll lose that chance. How can I do that to her and say I love her? What do I have to offer her anyway, Andrei?"

"I never knew you were such a girl." Andrei raised a brow. "A teenage version. Hand-wringing and all. You do love her, Daniel, you thick-headed dunce, or you wouldn't even be thinking of that stuff. You listen to her, you respect her, you'd give your life for her, and not because she's your cargo. As for what you have to offer her? A man who adores her. I hear women like that."

Daniel grunted. "She's Carina. Who *wouldn't* adore her? She's beautiful, smart, funny, she can shoot and drive the getaway transport. Really, how can any man resist that?"

Andrei snorted. "No man will, you stupid fuck. Daniel, you are consistently the highest performing member of the military corps. You outscore, outshoot, outrun, out everything. Why are you being so dumb over this?"

"Yes, I'd like to know, too." Carina stepped into the room, immediately poking at his bandages. "What is this?"

He couldn't help but laugh. "It's nanite gel for the burn."

"Really?" Her eyes widened. "Is this widely available? This could save so many lives."

"It's been an extreme trauma treatment for some time now. My sister had it when she was a young woman. They've managed to put it in med kit size, so it's standard issue for all special operations teams and military. I'd guess they'll work on getting it into home medicine kits after this. It's expensive, but yes, it saves many lives."

Despite his innate distrust of authority, which was ironic, given his job, he understood just how much good those Families who ran the Federation did. Abbie would only make them better.

"I'd love to talk with someone about it when we get to Ravena."

He nodded. "Of course."

Andrei had left, Daniel noted as he looked around the room.

"Now, back to the original question."

"Which was what?" He licked his lips.

She crossed her arms over her chest and glared at him. "Are you hungry? Stupid question, of course you are." She made a move to head into the kitchen, but he grabbed her hand, pulling her back to sit in his lap. When his arms encircled her, she sighed softly and melted against him. The world felt all right again.

She sent him an exasperated look. "No one is going to convince me to be with anyone but you, so you should just get that into your thick head. Yes, I eavesdropped. I heard a lot of what you said. If you love me, you'll hear me right now. I may have been a virgin when we first met, but I wasn't a dumb virgin. I plan to claim my right to Rank, and then I plan to make you marry me. You did despoil me, after all."

He took a breath, started to argue, but the look she sent him told him she'd never allow it.

"It's going to be hard for you. They'll start lining up eligible Ranked males the moment it's known you're in Ravena."

"Daniel, my sweet man, I've had that my entire life. If I can hold my father off for as long as I did, I think I can handle Roman Lyons. Who is, I hear, your brother-in-law. If Abbie is good enough for him, you are sure as the heavens good enough for me."

He knew Abbie would insist on helping. It was her way. He knew, too, that once Abbie appointed herself Carina's guardian, it didn't matter how many males wanted to get a crack at Carina.

"You'll like him. Roman. Knows what it means to lead in all the best ways. Almost good enough for Abbie. Abbie is . . . well, I begin to wonder about the safety of the fabric of space-time with the two of you in the same 'Verse. There's only so much headstrong, bossy female the world can take." He winked, and she pinched him.

"Ouch. Vicious." He rubbed the spot on his side and then grabbed her wrist gently. "How is this?"

"Fine, fine. I'll clean up in a little while. Vincenz says this trip is quick, just a matter of hours."

"This part is, yes. There's a waypoint first. Have you ever been out of the Imperium?"

She shook her head.

"Welcome to the Federation then." He stood and carefully avoided putting too much weight on his leg. The gel was working already, the pain less severe, but he didn't want to make things worse. "The waypoint is on a pretty desolate 'Verse. No lodging but for the workers who staff the portal station. We'll file papers there but keep going toward the Core."

"In this? We'll stay on this transport?" She snuggled into him, her fear clear in her voice.

"Yes, in this. It's fast and light. If we push it, we can be in Ravena in two more days."

"So we're finally safe?"

He shrugged. "As safe as we can be under the circumstances. Once we arrive, they'll process our papers. That's the last big thing. The governance of this way station is supposed to be independent, but it's where a lot of information got through in the scandal rocking the Federation right now. Treason trials of Family members. Hundreds died. We pay our bribes like everyone else. Hopefully that'll be enough. If not, well, we'll work through it."

"I trust you."

He hoped so.

Chapter 18

Carina waited up for him, snuggled in their cozy bed in the tiny room. They'd had trouble some hours before when they'd reached the waypoint station, but they'd listened to Andrei's gut and had hidden. It was a good choice as they'd been boarded, searched and held up for hours until they had no choice but to let them go.

They'd gotten out of the portal and headed toward the Core as soon as they'd been allowed to leave. By that point, her leg muscles had begun to cramp at the close quarters, and poor Daniel, at a head taller, was twisted up like punctuation by the time they'd tumbled out of the compartment.

A meal had lifted everyone's spirits, and then Daniel had urged her to rest while he sent a coded transmission to his commander. She'd tumbled into the warm nest of blankets, trading her shirt for one of his.

He'd shaken her that day. Not for the reasons he believed. Oh, she knew he thought he was too violent for her. As if she were some precious flower! But he'd been so male, so ferocious and had not let anything stop him from getting her to that transport. Never had she felt that sort of attention and focus. All these things made him who he was, the kind of man she couldn't stop thinking about, a man she trusted with her heart and her life. But from the things he said, she had the distinct feeling he may have felt as if she would judge him for killing men.

And she did judge; she judged that he would move mountains for her. Moreover, he would because he would do anything on her behalf.

How could she *not* be in love with that man?

She knew she faced some problems with the differences in their social status, but she didn't care. None of them had any power over her. The coded data on that chip was her protection. If they didn't *want* to let her be with Daniel, she'd insist or not give them the data.

She may have detested her father for many reasons, but she'd learned how to control people, how to manage them with fear and love, and if she had to play a hard game to get what she wanted, to be with the man she was meant to be with, she'd do it without guilt.

He'd brought Vincenz back into her life. Part of her saw the difference in him; he was a cynic now where the boy and teen she knew had been far more idealistic. But he still did work he knew was important, and for all his talk about the Phantom Corps being different, she wondered if part of him wasn't envious that he was not in those ranks. There seemed to be a story there, and she hoped they got the chance to visit a lot more once they'd arrived in Ravena.

She worried Daniel's family wouldn't like her. Worried about all sorts of things she knew she couldn't control. This thing she had with

Daniel felt so precious, the threat of losing that lurked in the back of her mind all the time.

She drew the blade of her knife across the sharpening stone over and over, the way Daniel had shown her earlier. Chances were she wouldn't have to use it now that they were in Federation territory, but a girl should always have a sharp knife.

She laughed out loud at how much her life had changed in such a short time and in turn, how much she felt like it suited her. Did she want to do this all the time? Seven hells no! She couldn't imagine how Daniel managed all the fear and worry with such calm. But she did like the idea that she could protect herself. She knew it now. Before, she'd had training but not real testing. And she had a man, a man and love. She'd taken a leap and had been terrified, still was many times every day. But she'd survived and she continued to. That was something to be proud of.

Sometime later, the door opened, and he stepped inside, hair still wet from bathing, skin scented with the clean soap he'd used. A towel hung low on his hips, leaving her breathless because she *knew* what was beneath.

"Did you walk around the transport like that?" she asked, smiling when he tossed the towel aside and climbed into the bed with her.

"Just from the shower to here. No one saw me. Andrei's seen it all before, and Marame is too busy arguing with Vincenz on the best kind of ammo for blasters to notice my towel."

She rolled atop him. "No one is too busy to notice your towel, Daniel. It's a very impressive . . . towel."

"I appreciate your protecting my honor."

He had such a sexy grin. It sent shivers through her body as she rocked against his cock. They fit together so well, perfectly. She'd always been curious about sex, had snuck around to watch what she could, but she'd never quite imagined how all-consuming it could be, and not just the actual physical act while it occurred. He mesmerized her, had charmed her, had become essential to her, and she loved that.

"Take your panties off." He nearly purred it as he touched gentle fingertips over the bandages on her arm.

"You're so irresistible." She smiled down his way, leaning in to kiss him. When she bent to do that, he grabbed the waist of her shirt, of his shirt, and whipped it over her head. "And sneaky."

"My mother tells me this all the time. Usually after I liberate a pie or two. She bakes when she's worried or happy or sad. It's all to the good. Your panties are still on, Carina."

"My. Top of the class for you." She undulated, teasing him until he simply ripped them in half, exposing her pussy to his cock. Both of them let out a ragged moan when he made contact with her bare flesh.

"You're so wet. I could slip in you right now." He teased around her gate, pushing in just a small bit and pulling back out.

"And you're not doing that why?"

"Because teasing you is so much fun."

"Is it?" She scooted down, settling between his legs. His cock was hard, and she simply took the time she wanted to look at him, to rub her cheek from his sac to the head. It was when she decided to lick across the slick bead at the slit that they both shivered through a moan of pleasure.

He tasted so good.

Using her hands and her mouth, she set a rhythm, licking around the crown, then sucking him in as far as she could before pulling back again. She knew some women disdained this act, but she couldn't seem to get enough of him, of his taste. He was masculine and salty, spicy.

He tried to hold back; she felt the tremble of his muscles. "Don't hold back with me, Daniel."

He groaned, his head thrashing from side to side briefly.

"Do you like this?" she asked, licking over the head while her eyes were locked with his.

"Fuck yes. What clued you in? The moaning? Begging?"

"I could make you beg? Really?"

His face lost its tension as he grinned and then laughed. "Carina, there's no one like you. Not anywhere, not ever. Please, please suck my cock."

"Certainly. I can't say no to such a lovely request."

This time when he got close and he tried to pull her back, she refused to move.

"I'm going to come. Let me be inside you when I do."

"You will be. First in my mouth, then in my . . . pussy. I want this, Daniel, please."

His groan was desperate, and he stopped trying to hold her back. Instead, he rolled his hips, meeting her when she moved her mouth down him. Not too much but just enough that his need rode her as well.

When he came, she tasted the essence of him, what he was to her. Surprising that she could evoke such a response from such a man.

"Give me a few minutes. Once I recover, I'll return the favor, and then we're going to fuck."

She moved up, fitting in that spot against his body, her head resting on his shoulder. "So I was all right then?"

He laughed. "Sweet, you were far more than all right. You're perfect."

"Good." Silly, how safe she felt against him just then. But she did. "So you were able to get your message to your boss?"

"Yes. I also sent a brief note to my sister telling her to expect a visitor at their home for a while when you arrive."

"I'll be with *you*! Are you going to do this forever? You're being unfair. You say you want to be with me, and then you foist me off on someone else."

He had the audacity to roll his eyes at her. "Stop jumping to conclusions, for fuck's sake."

"What else can I do when you toss these barriers up between us every chance you get?"

His sigh was very nearly a growl. "When we get there, you'll be taken from me instantly. They don't care that you'll want me to be there. They're going to be about the business of saving the citizens of the Federation from more war and bloodshed. When I checked in, I found that there'd been two more attacks, this time with biological agents. Faelene has been quarantined, her citizenry hugely affected by an ailment they eradicated, or thought they did, on Earth generations ago, called dysentery. It made the water undrinkable. The elderly and children are hardest hit. It's a simple and devastating illness that renders populations useless from bowel issues and dehydration. They have teams there now, treating the sick, cleaning up the water, disposing of the dead."

She sat up, her hands over her mouth. "My father did this?"

"We have every reason to believe so, yes. So when we arrive, I'll have to go and be debriefed, which can take a while. They'll use scans to see what I saw, to pick apart every image." He must have seen the panic on her face. "No, that'll be filtered out. No one but the scan operator will see. It's their job; that data gets expunged instantly." He traced down her neck, and she relaxed a bit.

"You'll also be debriefed and be taken to a place where they can access the data without harming you. I may be sent on another mis-

sion, depending on what they find. I just want you to be safe and
with people I trust while I'm gone. Part of my job involves me being
gone, I told you that. None of that changes how much I want to be
with you. None of that changes the fact that when you get there,
when things have calmed and a routine of sorts settles in, you might
change your mind. I can't refuse to deal with reality because you
don't want to."

"See, you had me until those last sentences. Why does everyone
keep doing that? As if I'm so shallow I'd walk away from you once I
see shiny things and men with Rank!"

"Someone really should have told me about this "women being a
huge pain in the ass" thing before I fell for you." He sighed, and she
contemplated kicking him for a few moments.

"I'm certainly not your *first* woman, Daniel. I'm sure those before
me had female attributes." Still, she didn't miss the comment about
falling for her, and she warmed before she realized it and snapped out
of it, firming her resolve.

He snorted then. "Get that look off your face, Carina. Imagine if
you froze that way, and all your life from now on people would think
you just ate something sour or were about to lecture them about your
religion."

Oh him and that humor! She tried not to be moved, not to smile,
but failed. "You be quiet. You're making it seem like I'm a freak or
something."

"Did you know the term *freak* came from Earth? There used to
be these traveling shows, and they employed people with various
physical defects to entertain the crowds. They were called freaks."

She froze, looking him over, finding herself yet again disarmed
and charmed. He was a menace.

"Why do you do that? I'm set to be angry with you and you do that and I can't be because you're charming and funny and damn it all."

"You forgot right. You know I'm right. I'm not trying to push you away, you infuriatingly beautiful pain in my ass. I'm trying to tell you what to expect. I'm trying to be sure you're safe and in a place where you can withstand all of that. Your presumption is incorrect."

Well, maybe it was a bit presumptive of her. But if he thought she was going to take any more of this nonsense about how he wasn't right for her, he was wrong. It was pretty sweet of him to take care of her, though.

"I've asked Abbie to represent you, or to at least be your advocate during the process. Wilhelm is a good man, but he has a job, a job that comes before everything else. Roman will keep you safe, but it's Abbie who will advocate for you. They're all afraid of her, which will serve you well. Anyway, they live in a compound. I figure you'll be at home with the sheer immensity of the house and grounds."

She pouted; she knew it, but she didn't want to be with anyone else; she wanted to be with him. Period.

"If I have to go off on another mission, it will ease my worry to know the most powerful people in the Federation are on your side and will protect you. When I am done with work and once they release you from debrief, we can talk about where to live. I have a flat, but it's not a place for a couple."

She scowled, and he laughed. The fear that he'd been trying to foist her off on someone else passed, and she rubbed herself against him shamelessly.

"I see you're feeling better now." He flipped her so he was on top. "Shall I eat your pussy then? Make you come so hard you scream my name?"

She nodded enthusiastically as they both laughed.

His mouth on her belly was hot and wet. But that's not what she wanted. "Wait. I have something else I need instead."

"And what's that, sweet?" He nuzzled her belly, sending pleasure skittering through her enough to nearly make her forget what she was about to say.

"Over! On your back."

He grinned and flipped. She loomed over him, taking in how unbelievably gorgeous he was. All that strength and courage, and he was hers.

"You're my reward. I've decided." She settled in astride his lap.

He swallowed, his cock hardening against her pussy as she rubbed herself over him. "How's that?"

"Well, I mean, I left a lot behind. Hartley Alem actually grabbed my breast when he thought he'd be the one to rid me of my virginity."

Daniel tensed, baring his teeth.

"I'm not sorry he's dead. Though I don't believe for one moment he was part of any conspiracy to get me out of the Imperium."

Daniel shrugged but said nothing. He knew something, she could tell.

"Would you care to weigh in on the matter?" She arched a brow at him.

"I'd prefer to fuck you."

"Grr." She rose up a bit, grabbing him around the base and guiding him straight into her body as she lowered herself.

"Sweet levels of heaven, that's so good."

The power of making him feel good rolled through her. That a man like him would be attracted, no, that he'd find her irresistible, that he'd want her as much as he clearly did, made her feel like a queen.

"Ride me then, Carina."

She braced herself, resting her weight on his biceps as she began to rise and fall on his cock. Each time she got him all the way in, she swirled her hips, surprising them both with how good it felt.

Body to body, interconnected heart and mind. This was all sex could be and more.

"I'm spoiled." She sat up, arching her back to get him deeper.

"How so?" he croaked.

"You, of course! Look at you. My first experience is the best one I ever could have asked for. You've ruined me for all others."

He laughed. "Good to know."

She could see the effort in his muscles, the effort to let her be in charge of the pace. She appreciated it very much and secretly it delighted her to test his control.

"Tell me something. Teach me."

"You're going to kill me," he muttered, sweat sheening on his chest.

"Piffle. You're a tough man, hard. Strong and fit. Teach me something about sex."

"I thought that's what I was doing. Though, to be honest, you're doing more than fine on that score."

She beamed at him, making him laugh.

"I've noticed you like this." She pressed all the way down, circling her hips with him deep inside her.

"Yeah," he wheezed. "That works. If you want to continue to kill me, try tightening your inner muscles."

"Oh! That hadn't occurred to me at all." She did it, and he moaned, holding her in place before sliding his palms up her rib cage and cupping her breasts. The grin he wore told her they had engaged in a game to see who could make the other the most insensible.

"Let's see here," he said lazily, one hand tracing down her belly, his fingers spreading her pussy open. "So lonely there, all shiny and wet."

When he slid his fingertip over her clit, round and round, increasing his pressure, she knew he was winning.

Laughter shook her, and he tried to frown. "What? Since we're learning things and all, laughing at a man when he's trying make you come is considered bad form."

"I was laughing"—her breath came shorter now as he drew her toward climax—"about how you were winning, and then I remembered that either way, I win."

"Okay then." He grinned and made some special secret agent moves on her clit, and she shot into orgasm so hard she probably drew blood when her nails dug into Daniel's arms where she'd been hanging on. With him inside her, it felt different, the orgasm was bigger, more intense. It felt as if it would never stop as she arched her back to get more.

He gave a ragged groan and unloaded deep inside her. She felt each spasm of his cock as he came.

"I always knew I loved school," she mumbled and fell to the side. He chuckled, holding her as they surrendered to sleep.

Chapter 19

"We're nearly in Ravena." Daniel paced, worried about the future.

"Abbie and Roman are going to meet the transport. She'll take care of Carina, you know that." Marame patted his arm.

"I'll be here awhile, to help her transition, too." Vincenz spoke from his place at the table where he pored over some reports of recent border violence.

"I don't need taking care of! I'm an adult. What I need is Daniel to not be sent off on some other mission so fast after we arrive."

Daniel looked to Carina. "They could decide you're lying to them and put you in lockup, or worse, send you back. Don't take this lightly, Carina."

"Why would they do that? Daniel, I'm helping them." Carina sat nearby, her gaze only leaving him occasionally. "They didn't do that to Vincenz."

"They didn't trust me for some time. Not all the way. It was Ellis and his support that helped me so much. Don't give Daniel a hard time, Carina, this is his world. My world now. Hells, your world, but this is politics. You know it. Don't let love cloud your brain. You're smart; you'll need those skills." Vincenz looked at his sister, and Daniel realized right then just how much he'd wanted Vincenz to approve of him, not as a soldier, though he appreciated that, but as a match for his sister.

"Politics makes for bad choices sometimes." Daniel was going out of his mind imagining all the possible outcomes. Though he did trust Wilhelm and Roman, and he knew his position would protect her, it was impossible not to be concerned.

Wilhelm had inferred there was something else brewing, and he'd need to hit the ground fast on it. If at all possible, he'd assign one of his teams to it and stay in Ravena with Carina.

"If you thought that, you'd not be taking me straight to them."

"He doesn't want you to be rational, sweetie. He's a big, protective male, and he has to let go of control over the thing that means more to him than anything else. It makes men crazy to have to do that. They get far more panicky and absurd about this stuff than women do. It's also his job. He protects us all: me, the rest of our teams, the Federation. A more protective, bossy and controlling man I've yet to meet." Marame, clearly amused, winked at Carina, who laughed.

"Oh. I hadn't thought of that, but you're so right." Carina winked at him.

Daniel sighed, trying not to be amused by this female banter and nearly failing. "If you two are finished mocking me and my worries?"

She frowned a moment and then moved to him, pushing her way onto his lap, which he was sure made his tough leadership reputation laughable. But when she did this, he couldn't remember why he'd care.

A want of her, of all he could be with her, sprang up from deep inside him, taking hold with such powerful entirety he was momentarily shaken. He'd never really allowed himself to want like this; the ferocity of it was entirely new.

He realized, as he buried his face in her hair, he'd wanted her before, but he'd not expected her to stay; he'd held back part of himself to prepare for the inevitable when she walked away. And now, with her there against him that way, there was no holding back.

She tipped her head back and then quickly popped up to kiss his nose. Gods.

"I love you," she said as he breathed her in. This woman had laid him low, and he would never be able to refuse her anything. She got to him in a way no one else could.

"I'll do everything I can to escort you to Wilhelm's offices where you'll be interviewed. Don't be afraid."

She cocked her head. "Daniel, I do so love how protective you are. It's overwhelming and flattering, and you make me feel so feminine. If you trust Wilhelm Ellis and Vincenz trusts him, he's trustworthy."

Sitting up, she moved to the space next to him. She reached out to smooth her thumb over the frown line between his eyes. "You can't do everything for me. I lived in Ciro Fardelle's court my entire life. I had to keep my face blank as people were executed so close to where I sat, blood spatter got all over my hem. I'm an adult who can handle herself quite well when she needs to."

"Here we go," Julian called out from the deck where he guided the transport through the extensive portal docking process to Ravena.

"I will be so glad to sleep in my own bed," Marame said. "You're all great and everything, but it's like the second to last day of a trip back home to see your family at a holiday. You know?"

The laughter of the group lightened the mood a bit, but the tug in his belly when they'd been allowed through reminded him he now had something important. And something important to lose.

She didn't want him to know it, he was worried enough, but Carina was scared. Scared they'd do exactly what he was concerned about. She'd be Universes away from a home closed to her anyway. Adrift with no one to go to.

Standing tall, his hand at the small of her back, she waited just inside the transport doors for Roman Lyons to enter.

Instead of a man, what launched itself inside was a woman, a small one with dark hair just like her brother's. "Daniel! You went to enemy territory! Without telling me?"

Daniel frowned for one long moment and then relaxed with a smile. He bent, hugging his sister and kissing each cheek. As he drew back, he placed his palm over her belly, just a brief moment. Carina's heart melted a bit more, knowing he probably hadn't even noticed he'd greeted the baby in his sister's belly, too.

Daniel glanced up to the man who stood just on the other side of Abbie, the man who looked at Daniel's sister with so much love Carina almost felt as if she'd stumbled into their bedroom at an intimate moment. "I told you it would be wise to keep that information in a folder where certain people couldn't see it."

"I'm afraid this one is my fault."

Carina looked up, and then up some more until she met the handsome and imposing face of the man who'd spoken.

He bowed low, surprising her with his innate grace. "Ms. Fardelle, please accept my welcome to Federation Territory and to Ravena.

I'm Comandante Wilhelm Ellis, and it's my great pleasure to meet you."

She blushed as he kissed her knuckles.

"All right then, shouldn't we be going? I don't like being out there so exposed." Daniel stepped up.

Abbie's gaze sharpened on her brother for a moment and turned back to Carina, speculation in her gaze. "I'm Abigail Haws Lyons. Officially, I'm here as your representative. That means I'll keep them on the right side of the law and of your needs as much as I can. Do you accept my representation?"

Daniel reached out briefly and slid a hand across her shoulders.

"Yes, thank you." Carina didn't know what she should do but hoped it was enough.

Abbie lost the formal manner then and gave her a genuine smile. "Now that that's out of the way, I'm Abbie, Daniel's sister. You'll be staying with us for as long as you want or need."

Carina blinked, grateful and pleased his sister seemed to like her, but also still unhappy that it meant Daniel wouldn't be with her.

"I'd like to be wherever Daniel is. I appreciate your offer, I do, but I want to be where he is." Right up front with it. She wanted to let them all know what the situation was between her and Daniel, so there'd be none of that Rank nonsense.

The area got suddenly very quiet for a moment.

Daniel began to speak again until the other man stood forward. "I'm afraid Daniel has some off 'Verse work to do shortly. I'm Roman Lyons. We are grateful to you for this service and offer you sanctuary."

"Thank you." She did appreciate it, and it would have been rude not to reply, but now she had other things to say. "Why can't someone else do that job? He can't be the only one with the skills to do it.

I need him here. He risked his life and saved mine on multiple occasions. It seems silly to send him off when he's the man who made my being here possible."

"Sir, this area is exposed. We really should be moving out." Daniel spoke softly to Ellis, who nodded agitatedly.

"Let's move this conversation to a more secure location," Ellis called out before turning to Roman. "Sir, we agreed this would be a very short turnaround, if you'll recall, after I voiced my sincere and strident objection to your and your wife's presence. There are several prime targets in this transport."

Roman eyed Carina carefully, and Daniel groaned.

"I ask him that question all the time, you know." Abbie squeezed Carina's hand conspiratorially.

"Moving out now," Daniel said tightly.

"My guard is outside as well," Ellis called out.

Daniel did some finger talking with the others, and they took their places around Abbie, Roman and Carina. The mood became more solemn as they opened the doors and began the walk down a set of steps to another platform.

She wanted to see the outside! All this time she'd had this idea of Ravena, mainly via other people's memories and viewpoints, and she wanted to see if it could possibly match those tales.

Daniel wanted to be next to Carina, but he knew Marame was far more than capable. He kept a watch, trying to pinpoint anything out of place in the crowd below as thousands of people milled around, arriving and departing. Freight moved along a ramp just below the travelers. Vendors sold their wares, children played in the drop-off for departures so their parents were able to manage any cargo to be loaded.

The energy of the portal played along Daniel's skin as they continued to move. He wondered what Carina would think of this place. This was the grandest the Federated Universes had to offer. Not just this portal city, but Ravena itself. Would she, too, love the scents of the spicy kabobs wafting up from the carts? They were so different, he thought, not for the first time.

Alarm pricked the back of his neck, and he turned, looking through the sight of his weapon and saw it on the freight ramp, a male busting from a box, pointing a blast rocket in their direction.

"Down!" he screamed. His personal comm registered the order, and Ellis's guards began to fan out on the platform below.

The blast hit as he threw himself over Roman, still shouting out orders to the soldiers to apprehend the shooter and his location. On his other side, Ellis crouched over Abbie. Weapons fire sounded as he pushed himself up to get a visual. Reports sounded in over his comm: the shooter was dead, the area secured.

A medical team came up, and Daniel twisted, her name on his lips as he checked Roman over for injuries. Roman wasn't interested, shoving Ellis aside to get to Abbie.

"Carina!" he screamed out. Behind where they'd stood was total carnage. Vincenz pulled himself to stand with the help of a medic. His arm appeared to be broken, his clothes partially scorched.

Julian pulled a soldier away from a pile of bodies. Daniel sprang over debris to get to them. *Carina was there*.

He began to pray in his head. It could have been out loud, he didn't know. She couldn't be gone, not after all they'd experienced to get her here. His hands began to shake as he continued to give orders to his men.

"Marame, fuck, fuck!" Julian said, shock in his voice. Daniel stepped through the rubble. Saw what happened to Marame. Grief struck him to his core.

That's when Daniel caught sight of that pale hair. Something pinned her in place, and he sprang forward to help. Relief rushed through him as she sat up slowly, appearing unhurt.

"Marame?" Carina leaned forward as Daniel pulled her to him.

"She's gone," he murmured.

"She pushed me out of the way." Tears rolled down Carina's cheeks as he picked her up. "You yelled, and she turned and shoved me backward, toward the doorway. She saved me."

"We've got to get her out of here and to safety, Daniel," Vincenz said, his arm in a temporary sling. "We don't know if they have another ambush set up."

Daniel had known Marame for a very long time. His team, his life wouldn't be the same without her.

"Julian, stay here with her. Can you do that?" He knew Julian and Marame were as close as siblings. Julian would keep her body safe, would handle the removal and the contact with her family. It would help him process the pain.

Julian looked up, relief on his face, and nodded. "Yes, sir, of course. I'll report to you as soon as we've . . ." his voice sort of wandered off track for a moment. "As soon as we've taken care of her."

Feeling torn a thousand ways, Daniel headed down to the platform and out of the station where the military vehicles waited.

Chapter 20

"*T*here were three separate attacks today at the same time," Ellis spoke as he poured himself a drink and pushed a tumbler toward Daniel. "Here in Ravena. Elsewhere, forty-eight miners were killed in a bombing in Nondal. He's escalating."

"In my fucking 'Verse. In my fucking control, and on my fucking watch. These animals could have killed my wife and child. They could have killed my men. This must be dealt with in such a way that they understand never to do it again." Roman turned his gaze back to Ellis and drained his glass in one last swallow.

"This is about the chip, Roman. We have to get that data from the chip. What we know is bad enough. The rest of the data is imperative." Ellis began to pace.

"Carina is resting right now. The doctor said it would be better for her health if you waited until tomorrow, and I'm telling you right now that you will have to get through me to harm her any more today." Daniel said this through clenched teeth.

Ellis cocked his head, studying him before he spoke again. "It's bad business, Operative Haws, to develop attachments to cargo."

"With all due respect, Comandante, fuck you."

That got Roman's full attention as he set the glass on a low table, watching, but saying nothing.

"She's not cargo. She risked her godsdamned life to come here and help us. My operative lost her life to protect Carina's. I won't have her health compromised any more than it is just now. And that's far more than I'd prefer as it is. Your precious information can wait until Carina has rested."

"I'm afraid I'd have to agree." Abbie swept into the room.

Roman sprang up, his hands tossed into the air with frustration. "Gods damn it! Abbie get your ass back into bed."

"You're going to go gray with all that upset, Roman. Sit down. I'm all right." She pushed her husband into his chair and then climbed up into his lap. Not that she was giving in. "I'm her advocate, and I'm going to tell you I will heartily disagree with any plans to deal with that chip today. I have official documentation from your own doctors advising that, and I will make your life at least a few levels of hell if you disturb her before tomorrow." She yawned a bit, undercutting how scary she might have been otherwise, but all in that room knew she would do everything to upset any plans but the ones she endorsed just then.

Daniel kept his face as blank as he could, but he winked her way when no one was looking.

"You're not all right. Someone might have easily killed you today. Or the babe." Roman put a hand over her belly, and Daniel's stalwart sister leaned into her husband, her eyes dropping closed a moment as a shadow of grief crossed her features.

Daniel had had those might-have-been moments all day long, had relived them time and again. His sister could have died, his love could have died. Roman could have died. His friend *had* died.

"Marame," he said, standing. "I have to go make a comm, be sure her family has been informed and her interment is taken care of."

"It's done. My aide made the call some time ago. Her family will be here soon to claim her remains. They'll take care of her flat. Her mother insisted it was something she had to do, so I've ordered it sealed until they arrive." Ellis poured another drink. "I take it very personal when my people are killed."

"Me, too. Julian will need some time away. My people will need a memorial of some sort. I assume she'll receive a posthumous commendation for her service and valor."

"It'll be done. In the meantime, you'll need debriefing. I'll do it myself, and then you can go to her. You won't heed my advice on this and have already gone and fallen in love with her." Ellis glanced at Abbie, affection clear on his face. "You Hawses and your total lack of respect for the rules of Rank."

"They're dumb rules, Wil, and you know it." Abbie moved to stand, and Roman did, too, bringing her up with him.

Wil?

"I'm putting you back in bed." Roman moved to the door, his arm holding Abbie to his body. Daniel liked seeing how protective he was, even if he disapproved of bringing her to the portal in the first place.

Then again, telling Abbie something and expecting her to obey if she felt differently was a losing game. One Daniel had played his whole life.

It was all his fault anyway for asking her to be Carina's advocate. Of course she'd felt as if she'd had to go to the portal.

"Don't think I don't know you're all going to talk about me when you get me upstairs."

"You are always the topic of our conversation," Daniel called out. "If you don't do as Roman says, I'm comming Nyna and Mai. Your choice."

"You all gang up on me so." She pouted as Roman guided her out of the room, closing the coded entry as he did.

"I'm going to record this." Wilhelm tapped a few keys on the comm. "Start at the beginning. We'll get the scan when you bring Carina to the med center tomorrow for the extraction of that chip."

He relaxed, as Wilhelm had intended, and the questions began in earnest. He opened himself up and began to speak.

*C*arina was awake when Daniel came into the huge suite of rooms they'd told her would be hers as long as she desired. She'd been sitting in a chair, pretending to read a book, and stood, going to him.

Only when he held her, only when she was sure he was solid and real and alive, did she heave out a long breath.

"How are you feeling?" he asked, gently but firmly putting her back into the chair. "You should be sleeping."

"I've slept. I've cried. I've taken a pain draught, I've paced, looked out the windows over this lovely inner courtyard below and I've worried. I'm done sleeping for now."

He put his boots in the closet and slid off his various weapons, placing them on a shelf above the shoes. "I suppose I'll have to break myself of that between now and the baby's birth. Can't have weaponry lying around for little fingers to get hold of."

Carina watched him as he spoke for the sake of making sounds. There was much there, lurking below the surface, so she waited for him to reveal it.

"Are you hungry? Warm enough?" he asked as she allowed him to steer her into bed, but she grabbed him, pulling him down with her.

"I'm glad you're alive," she whispered, looking up at the pale blue ceiling.

He took her hand, her uninjured hand; the other had been broken, and she'd had severe burns on her wrist and lower arm.

"I'm . . ." His breath choked from him, and alarmed, she rolled to face him, pressing her body to his, nearly crying when he cradled her arm with care, all while he sobbed. She didn't know what to do. This outpouring was gut deep, and most likely decades built up. A man like him didn't cry on a regular basis, even at horrible things, and she had no doubt after today that he'd seen more than his share of horrible things.

The desolation in that sound, the anguish and fear, the rage, sounded as he let it all out in great, shuddering gulps. She held her own tears in check, knowing he needed her to be strong just then, to let him be the one who broke down, if only for this once.

Some time later, he cleared his throat, dragging the back of his hand over his eyes. She'd held on to him the whole time, trying so hard with her body to tell him he wasn't alone and she was there and alive. What they had together was there and alive.

"I'm sorry."

"For what?" She kept her face buried in him, breathing him in.

"For everything. Fuck, this is all just fucked sideways."

"You do have very strong shoulders," she mused.

He paused. "What?"

"For all that guilt you've taken on. You have broad shoulders, so I suppose that must help."

"It's not a joke, Carina. People are dead. My people are dead, civilians, twenty-two children who were waiting to get on a transport with their families who were emigrating to Sanctu."

"And so, you're sorry."

He groaned.

She leaned up, got nose to nose with him. "For saving my life today? For loving me? For saving Abbie and Roman? For getting me through Imperial territory with leagues of Skorpios at our backs? Huh? Sorry for the blaster burn on your calf? For Marame? For taking a young girl with no prospects in life out of a vermin-infested settlement on the Edge and giving her a chance to be one of the finest soldiers in your military? She told me her story, Daniel. So you tell me again, what the seven hells are you sorry for?"

"It's my job!" he burst out, sitting up and getting out of bed. "And I failed."

She sat, using the pillows behind her back for support as she watched him. "What you do is inherently dangerous! You can't possibly blame yourself for this."

"Of course I can! Don't you see, Carina? It's my job to be sure this stuff doesn't happen. She's the second operative of mine to be killed on this mission. My orders brought them out, put them in danger, and I did not do my job in protecting them and now they're dead."

"I'm sorry, Daniel. I'm sorry about Marame and your other friend. I'm sorry about those children and the others who were killed today. If anyone is to blame, why not me? If I hadn't run, no one would have been after me."

"That's ridiculous."

"No more than what you're saying."

He paused, his brow furrowed, such a fierce moment as he wrestled with logic and emotion. She hated that he thought he hadn't done his job. She'd watched him with awe and respect since the moment he'd taken her hand and told her to run. It had been nearly fifteen standard days, and her life had been turned upside down. Her one constant, the thing that anchored her, was Daniel.

"You're good at your job. My father is a bad man; you're trying to stop him for a reason. He doesn't care that children get caught in the middle of his war. You're not that. You could never be that. You got me here, and hopefully this information I have will help. All this will be worth something."

His eyes widened, and he fell to his knees next to the bed where she knelt. "Do you think this is about that?"

"What is about what?"

He took her upper arms and hauled her closer, this time his nose to hers. "You could have *died* today. If Marame hadn't thought as fast as she had, you'd be dead. I can't—" He shook his head.

It washed over her then, nearly knocking her back. It wasn't the job—though that was part of it—it was her. It was losing her that scared him so much he'd broken down and wept. She threw her arms around him, sending them both tumbling to the rug.

"You love me."

He growled, sitting up and making quick work of getting her into bed again. "Stay there! You could have injured yourself just now."

"Again."

He growled again and spun away, pacing.

"I'm not dying. Just so you know, I have far too much to do to die. Anyway, you love me."

"I have to leave in the morning."

Her grin fell away. "Why?"

"Things are very bad. I need to head back to the Edge, just a quick trip."

"Someone need killing, or is there another woman you need to smuggle? If it's the latter, I'm coming along." She crossed her arms over her chest.

"You have nothing to worry about in that department. One woman is more than enough worry. And to be frank, it's rare my job entails human cargo anyway."

She nodded once, burning to ask more but seeing on his face that he wouldn't tell her anyway.

"I won't go until I'm sure you're all right. They'll remove the data chip when I go in to get my scan. I'll be as fast as I can to get back to you. Vincenz is here as well, resting. He'll stay until I return. Perhaps longer, though he's needed, too. He made it very clear that he wanted time with you, and I think it's good you two will have it."

"At least get naked and in bed with me. Hold me so I have this until you return."

His face lost the tension as he moved, quick to divest himself of his clothes. She managed to get her robe off, and he helped her get beneath the blankets, sliding in with her. His heat warmed her skin, made her feel home again. She sighed, breathing him deep, risking a quick lick of the hollow of his throat.

He started listing off all the safety features, all the procedures in place to keep her unharmed, and she didn't interrupt. She figured it was his way of controlling what he couldn't while he was away. She would make sure he had sex with her before he left. His cock was already beginning to show signs of life against her thigh.

"I'm going to miss you. I don't want you to go." She tried not to sound whiny, but she didn't manage it. She couldn't get it out of her head: flying backward, Daniel yelling, watching in horror as a ball of flame hit, tossing Marame into a nearby support beam. The beam fell, white-hot, onto Carina's arm and hand. She tried to crawl to Marame, to see if Vincenz was alive.

"It was your voice. Today, it was your voice that kept me sane."

He held her tighter for a moment.

"I didn't know if Vincenz was alive, I didn't think Marame was. There was all this noise, the smell"—she shuddered violently, remembering the smell of death, of burning flesh, of blood and dust— "choked me. And there was your voice, calm even as you shouted orders. I knew you'd get me out alive. I knew you were alive, and that's all that mattered to me. I feel sort of guilty about that."

"It's a thought you had after you nearly died. With the stink of death in the air. You're allowed a selfish thought now and again."

"And so are you, Daniel."

He flinched, and she knew she'd hit home with her comment.

Daniel exhaled. "All I could think about was you. Even as I had to do my job, even as I gave orders and pulled people from the rubble, I was on my way to you. I shouldn't have been. I should have trusted my men to get you out of there safely. But I had to see you, to know myself, to hold you and get you out of there."

It wasn't his job to do that. He *should* feel guilty for it, but at the time, he didn't. Even then, in the pale, fading light, he felt triumph that she lived even as devastation hit that he'd lost a friend like Marame.

If he'd lost her . . . Though he knew it wasn't something he should obsess over, he couldn't quite let go of the fear, the fear in the pit of himself that she was dead. He'd faced his own death more times than he could count, had accepted on some level that his life was more expendable than others. But she was different. Her life wasn't expendable, and to see her there, crawling from the chaos, pinned by a support beam that had to be pulled from her, all as he made his way over to her, trying to rein in the need to rush, to run over the dead to touch her and know she was real—it had unraveled something within him, a line he'd always held fast on: duty first.

She changed so many things, and he wasn't sure how to process it. He'd always had a direction, still did, but love changed things, shifted priorities.

"I don't want you to go."

Her voice was so small, lonely. He hated to go, but he had to. This target was high-profile, and he couldn't simply hand it off to another operative. He was the best man for the job, knew all the terrain, the target, and had the best chance of success. Knowing that was academic when he cradled his heart to his body.

"I don't want to go either. If it could be avoided, I'd send someone else. I don't want to leave you so soon after nearly losing you."

"I suppose I have to get used to it sometime. This is your job, and you'll be leaving a lot."

He laughed. "You don't sound very sincere."

She held on tight. "I'm working on it. Before you go"—she nuzzled his neck—"I need you."

"Knock it off, Carina. You're hurt. I won't be gone that long."

"Now which one of us doesn't sound sincere?" she teased, reaching down to grab his cock.

"You're hurt! You could have died. Damn it." He let go of her hand with a groan of surrender.

"I am, and I could have. But I'm here, and I need you. I need to reconnect with you. I need to feel alive. You make me feel alive when you touch me."

"Your arm."

"Unless I'm really not catching on to how this sex thing works, you don't put your penis in my arm."

He wasn't going to push her away. She wanted those memories before he left, wanted him to have her on his skin as he went off to do whatever he needed to.

"Please," she said, kissing his throat.

"You're a menace."

She tried not to smile victoriously when his hand slid down her side, taking her breast into his palm.

"I am. Apparently I need to be taken in hand."

He groaned again, pushing her gently onto her back. "Lie back and let me love you." He said it softly against the hollow between her breasts. "Close your eyes." She obeyed on a gasp as he licked and then bit a nipple.

Behind closed eyes, her senses took over. Each touch of his fingertips, each kiss, every lick and nibble radiated through her with powerful force. That he was so incredibly gentle as he touched her brought the sting of emotion to her. A man who could easily kill with his hands but who'd never done anything but cosset, that was a man worth grabbing and never letting go of. She planned to be with this one until she ceased to draw breath.

When he parted her legs, slipped inside her in one thrust, she gulped in air and her eyes flew open to catch his gaze lingering on her face with such intensity she felt as if she'd caught him in an intensely private moment.

"I love you," she said, because there was nothing else she could say with him so deep inside her, wrapped around her, filling her physically and emotionally.

He touched his forehead to hers briefly. "I love you."

The sound of it, so quiet but rife with emotion, filled her, up and up, up until she felt as if she'd burst with it. She flew apart, and he rebuilt her, each stroke, each press and pull he made, his body over hers, around hers, inside hers, he was everything, and she never wanted to find a time when that wasn't so.

Chapter 21

Daniel had gotten up early, before the light began to wash over the horizon. He filed his trip plan, he took care of some bribes and tributes and he began to dress. He needed to be out of there early. The earlier he went, the quicker he'd return. He needed the space to put that skin back on without her, needed to keep that Daniel away from her presence. There was no room for her, for softness and love, when he had to deal death.

Before Carina came down, he sought Abbie out. She was where he guessed she'd be, sitting in Mercy's kitchen, looking through a book of designs for a nursery.

"I like that one." He pointed.

She leaned back into him a moment. "That one is at the top. Roman likes this one better." She flipped through to another design, and he nodded.

"That one is nice, too. Abigail, you'll watch over her?"

"Of course. I see how you look at her. Why didn't you tell me you were in love with her?"

"It wasn't appropriate conversation via link, Abbie." He shoved a hand through his hair, frustrated at not having all the words he needed.

"When I fell in love with Roman, it was when I thought I couldn't have him. It was the most bittersweet feeling ever. I imagine you worry about the Rank bullshit, which you do know will mean nothing to her." She laughed. "Or me, and I'm—as Deimos said yesterday—the head bitch of House Lyons now."

He grinned at Roman's oldest son's words. "You certainly are. Just, you know, she has to make her own choices, but she's been forced enough. I don't want her being pushed into anything, and I'm sure the Families will start sniffing around once they all know she's here."

"It's quite a pity that you don't know how worth loving you are."

"Don't analyze me; I don't have the patience for that now."

She waved him off. "I don't care what you think you have time for." She kissed his cheek. "Come back safe and soon."

"I'll do my best. I have plenty to make me want to."

Abbie insisted on accompanying them to military command, where he had his scan done, and then they waited for Carina to finish with the chip extraction.

One last hug before he left. He needed it to keep him going. "Abbie will protect you, Roman, too. My mother and sister will most likely come over before I get back. You'll like them. Be safe, and don't go anywhere without Ellis or Roman knowing. Andrei and Vincenz will be your guards while I'm gone."

"I'd rather it was you." She looked up at him, and he kissed her forehead.

"I'll be back by the end of this week. Enjoy yourself, enjoy getting to know Ravena. You and Vincenz have a lot to catch up on. You'll hardly notice I'm gone."

She huffed. "I want to go with you. To see you off."

He took her hands, kissed the tips of her fingers. "No more trips to the portal for a while, Carina. I can only take so much before my heart simply gives out."

"Your heart? Pfft. Daniel, I hate this," Carina hissed at him as they began to walk down the stairs and out into the plaza. The complex looked out over the city. It was one of his very favorite spots.

Carina hadn't noticed much on her way there that morning, but now she took a moment to look at the city spread out all around them. It was then she realized how very small she felt.

"Beautiful, isn't it?" Daniel murmured as he followed her gaze.

"I've never seen anything like it. It's stunning."

And it was. Buildings spired up, dizzyingly high into the air, all in multihued shades of glass. The sky above was brilliantly blue, as blue as the deepest water. It stretched on to the horizon, and she hungered to see more, to get to know Ravena so she could know more of Daniel.

"I can't wait to show you more of it." He said it sweetly, but he was fully in work mode, his eyes narrowed as he took in everything around them. It was impressive the way he moved with utter confidence, as if to say to anyone even *thinking* about doing something bad, *Think again or I will grind you into a greasy spot.*

He helped her into the conveyance where Abbie already sat with Vincenz. When Daniel stepped back, she grabbed his wrist. "Now? Already?"

He softened his tone, leaning close so only she could hear. "Sweet, you know this is my job. I can't turn it off, especially just now. I'll be back, you know that."

She got back out of the conveyance. "Daniel, I love you. Don't get killed."

He laughed and kissed her quickly. "I'll do my best. You, too."

With a last touch on the back of her hand, he melted away, leaving her annoyed.

She slid back in, this time across from Roman, with Abbie beside her and Vincenz up front in some sort of protection mode.

"He's the best at his job, Carina." Abbie spoke as they finally began to move.

She took the other woman's measure. "I understand that. But is it too much to ask that he stay with me? He risked his life over and over to get me here."

Roman looked at her for some time before speaking. "He's one of the most highly ranked officers in the military, higher than those with Family Rank. He is feared for a reason, and that reason is he's merciless in the pursuit of the goals of this Federation. You can love him, he can love you, but he will be Daniel Haws, solider, just the same. We all have our duties."

"Roman, be quiet." Abbie waved a hand at her husband as she angled herself to better see Carina. "I know he must make you feel safe. I know when I'm frightened or worried, I want Roman." She laughed. "Or Daniel. I know this is hard for you, leaving everything you knew behind the way you did. I admire that greatly. As you may have noticed, Daniel protects people. It's who he is. Always has been. Even when he was a small child he took care of us, of my siblings and my mother. That's why he's good at what he does, and that's why you have to find a way to deal with having to share him with his work."

Abbie looked at Roman for a moment, and Carina noticed the hand on her belly. An ache, sharp and sweet, sliced through her. Want. She wanted that with Daniel. A life. A family. Carina knew she was being childish. It was his job, and he did have to do it, even if it meant he had to be separated from her for a little while. He wouldn't be Daniel without that loyalty to his Federation, to his people.

"I apologize. I don't have tantrums. Ever. I don't know what's come over me."

Abbie held her hand. "You've just had to turn your back on your people, on your family, even if they aren't perfect. You've been on the run and fallen in love with a man like Daniel. That's a lot for a very short period of time. You're allowed a bit of a tantrum. We'll have to keep you busy while he's gone."

She needed to get hold of herself, to be Carina Fardelle again. She sat taller, held her spine straight and nodded. "Thank you."

She watched part of the city go by through the windows, watched the looks on the faces of the people on the streets. Vincenz had been right; there was so much here, so much energy. Their features held such a dizzying array of emotions!

"Daniel said I'd be debriefed today?" Carina turned to look back at Abbie.

"I've negotiated for that to take place in our home. Silly to drag you all the way down here when Wilhelm can just as easily come there, and we can be comfortable." Abbie said it cheerfully, but Carina got the sense she was a hard-edged negotiator. And she was thankful for it. "My position as your advocate is really symbolic, you know. Wilhelm, despite being as big as a tree trunk, is quite sweet. Roman, too, even though sometimes he can be extra fussy House Lyons. Grrr." Abbie's mouth twitched.

Roman sighed heavily but didn't look up from his comm.

"All right, thank you." She nodded her head.

The rest of the drive was uneventful as she gawked at the city. But the house, the manse, compound, whatever it was called, where Abbie and Roman lived was the most impressive thing she'd seen. She hadn't taken it in the day before; there had been so much chaos with the attack at the portal. But now she had the opportunity to take it all in and be, in no small amount, impressed by the glory of the Federation as it was embodied by this place.

It was a house, a physical space fit for a ruler. Tall, imposing, surrounded by beautiful gardens that, she realized as they drove past and then exited the conveyance, would be in bloom across the seasons.

Stone stairs led the way to doors easily thirty feet tall, and the entry foyer stole her breath. Where her father's idea of power had been black and red, *true* power and glory lived in this house. Ceilings soared, held up by columns of wine-colored wood as big around as the conveyance they'd been in. The floors gleamed, first in polished stone a deep green and then in warm toned hardwoods with mosaics set within.

The art on the walls was an eclectic mix of old and new, of styles across cultures. Tall windows let in light but appeared to block heat and cold. A grand staircase marked the south and north walls.

Roman looked his wife over, kissed her quickly. "You'll tell me if you're feeling poorly today." It wasn't a question. Carina liked Roman Lyons. Despite his short, brusque, even formal nature, he was a man who cared about his family and his people. It was something she wished her father had learned.

Abbie sent him a soft smile. "I promise. Go work; I know you're itching to."

"I love you, Abigail Haws, you beautiful, pregnant troublemaker," he mumbled as he went back in for another hug.

"I love you, too." Abbie grinned, and they both watched him walk away.

"Vincenz, if I may speak with you for a time?" Roman called out.

"You have my comm; ping me if you need me. You and I have a lunch date; we'll eat in the gardens near the greenhouses." Vincenz clasped her hands and followed Roman's path out of the room.

Carina turned back to Abbie. "I didn't get much of an opportunity to look well yesterday, and this morning I was distracted. This is a magnificent home, and at the same time, it has heart."

Abbie smiled. "Thank you, Carina. There are still days I find my-self surprised I actually live here. Would you like some tea? I have a chill, and it's always a good way to have Mercy offer me some special cake she's made me."

Carina followed Daniel's sister through the house into the kitchen. She turned and knew it was the heart of the house immediately. She felt embraced by the space as she sat across from Abbie at a small table bathed in light from high windows.

"I'll be wandering around in the greenhouses and remember that a year ago I lived in a flat that was never quite warm enough. Roman brought a lot of unexpected changes to my life. Good and bad. But the Roman part is always good."

Carina liked her, liked Abbie and the love shining so openly in her eyes for her husband and her family.

A woman caught sight of them and made a sound in her throat. "Abbie, have you eaten?"

"Of course I have, Mercy. You made me breakfast, remember?"

The woman kissed the top of Abbie's head. "Well I did put by some of that spice cake you like. Don't tell your mother; she and I have a difference of opinion on the recipe." She turned and took Carina in slowly. "Ah, I can see what he sees in you." She nodded once and bus-tled off to a nearby cabinet and began to rustle through it.

"Mercy, this is Carina." Abbie winked at Carina.

"Of course she is," Mercy called out as she brought a tray with tea and cake to them.

Carina didn't know if Mercy's nonchalance was good or bad, so she just took her cues from Abbie, who didn't seem alarmed.

Abbie sipped her tea and goggled at the gargantuan slice of cake Mercy put in front of her. "Mercy, you really don't need to give me a slice as big as your head. I'm not in danger of blowing away anytime soon."

Mercy waved a hand as she moved away.

"Mercy has been with Roman since he was a child. She helped raise Roman's sons after their mother died. If you need anything and you can't find me or Roman, go to Mercy. She knows everything."

Mercy snorted but kept at whatever it was she was doing. "Just come to me straightaway, Roman will frown you to death, and Abbie will talk you to death."

"She's such a lovely woman; as my grandmother used to say, butter wouldn't melt. Did you know that was a saying they brought from Earth?"

Carina laughed, relaxing for the first time in a long while. "Your brother would often tell me this sort of thing. He told me you had to know everything, said I was like that. I see it was a compliment."

Abbie cocked her head. "He made a good choice."

Daniel felt her absence acutely. He walked through the crowded, dusty streets of Parron. The 'Verse on the Edge was basically one large series of mining towns. Canyons, much like those on Mirage and Asphodel, cut through the landscape here and there, offering some respite in the sameness of dusty sidewalks and men in mining clothes.

He'd done his planning on the way. Surveillance, some investigation, and if he was lucky, he'd get out with a minimum of fuss. He also realized Wilhelm had most likely sent him to get him out of the way while they debriefed Carina.

It agitated him to be manipulated that way, even if he did understand the reasoning behind it. She was there, and he was a world away, and he could do nothing but put his faith in Abbie and Vincenz.

Good thing he had such good judgment when it came to people. Abbie would never allow anyone to take advantage of Carina, even if Carina had been silly enough to fall for any tricks. Between Abbie and Carina, if Wilhelm thought to try to maneuver Carina anywhere she didn't want, he'd never try it again.

A savage smile marked Daniel's mouth, twisted his mouth with the surety that he'd done well. The women in his private life, those he loved without reservation, were strong, smart and vicious if need be.

Vincenz was a different story. Daniel knew details most others didn't, including Vincenz's desire to be part of Phantom Corps, but there had been initial distrust of him when he'd first come to them. And then, once they knew he was trustworthy and a good operative, he had too much pride to ask again.

Wilhelm did not miss details, even minor ones, and so if he hadn't asked, there had been a reason, and as in most things, Daniel trusted his boss and whatever master plan he had in that head of his. Didn't mean Daniel wouldn't tear a strip off him when he returned if any harm had come to Carina, though, even if she'd merely been upset.

He caught sight of his quarry: a tall, beady-eyed man with gaunt features and a stooped back. Most people would have kept on, not understanding the wrapping was merely a guise, a mask he wore over a blackened heart and a craven soul.

This man was Henry Sessions, third in line to the leadership of House Sessions. A Family member had yet again betrayed the Federation. Cold rage built within him as he stalked his prey, following him into Parron's only establishment any Ranked would lower themselves to stay in. Parron wasn't known for those sorts of fancy digs, so their attempts to mimic what the Ranked would expect in most other 'Verses were a profane twist on reality.

It also meant the place was absent the kinds of security measures that would impede Daniel's movements as he trailed Sessions back to his room.

He locked the door at his back, baring his teeth.

"What do you want? Get out!" Sessions, though afraid, stood his ground.

"Henry Sessions, I am here to pass your sentence."

Two steps as he raised his hands, faster than Sessions could track. "Traitor," Daniel hissed, poised in that moment before he'd flex to twist the other man's neck.

He dropped the body to the carpet, stepping over it like the offal it was. The coin he left bore a lion's head. Roman Lyons was done fucking around and trying to get these people to do the right thing.

He'd told Daniel when he'd given him the assignment, "Leave the body. Leave the coin. I want them to know I will find them all and kill them." But at the time they hadn't suspected it would be another Family. That news was particularly serious.

The portal loomed ahead as Daniel passed through the last part of town. It was time to go home. Before he entered the transport, he hit a code on his personal comm. A smile touched his lips for a brief moment at the sound of an explosion. The warehouse Sessions had been using for his weapons smuggling operation sat just outside of town in a complex owned by House Sessions. Two, three, four, five more explosions as the entire compound burned.

By the time he stepped off the transport in Ravena, House Sessions would be no more. Once Roman learned the identity of the smuggler, he'd strike just as hard as the explosions and the death of Henry Sessions.

Chapter 22

*I*t had been eight entire days since Carina had seen him last. Eight. Days. She missed Daniel desperately, making her even more sure of her decision to be with him. Wilhelm had told her, kindly so, that Daniel would not contact her while he was gone, that they never did on a mission outside extraordinary circumstances.

In his absence there had been a major disaster. A bomb had gone off on a large passenger transport as it had been in transit between Borran and Ravena. Nothing could survive an explosion like that, and when it happened in the portal space, there would be no cleanup, no rescue.

Her father was behind it, she knew for certain.

Despite Daniel's absence, Carina had begun building a life there in Ravena's capital city. Abbie had kept her out of the public view; only a very select group knew she was in Ravena, and Roman appeared to want it that way, at least until Daniel came back. She realized, during these conversations she had with Roman and Wilhelm, that Daniel was a lot more powerful and influential than he'd ever let on to her.

Carina was proud of that. Proud that she'd chosen to love a man with so much to be proud over.

Not that it stopped the comments, even from the preapproved people in the circle who knew about her. How many times did she have to tell people she was not interested in marrying a Khym or a whoever else? She wanted one man, and that man would marry her, even if he didn't realize it just yet.

She grinned at herself in the mirror in her rooms. She'd lost the dark circles beneath her eyes and didn't look so tired these days. She wondered when Daniel would return and wanted to be sure to look lovely every day just in case.

She had an outing planned with Abbie and Vincenz in just a short while. Abbie had connected her with the staff at a community center in the second circle of the city. They were looking for a teacher, and she certainly wanted to work as one. She'd met, though under guard, with the people in charge, and after she'd taken their entrance exams, they'd offered her the position. She'd accepted, building the foundations of her future there.

When she went downstairs, she called Abbie's name rather than use the location system. It seemed so silly to have a machine do the work she could easily do herself.

That's when she saw Alexander Lyons in the common room having tea with Deimos, Roman's oldest son and the next in line to lead House Lyons.

"No, Alexander," she said as she entered the room. The man was a ridiculous flirt and had propositioned her every single time she'd seen him. She got the feeling it was because people expected it of him. He was a lot smarter and kinder than one thought when they first met him. But that didn't mean she tolerated any of his silliness.

"You wound me." He grinned, his hands over his heart in mock devastation.

"She might. But I can assure you Daniel will if you don't stop it." Deimos shook his head at his uncle.

"Daniel isn't here," Alexander teased.

"Be quiet, you. You and I both know Daniel is one of your friends. Stop it." Deimos seemed to constantly steer his uncle into behaving. It was sweet, and Carina had no doubt there were dozens of women who closed their eyes each night thinking about Deimos Lyons. Alexander, too, was a stunningly handsome man. Roguish and sexy, if not far more work than he would be worth.

Too bad she already had her heart set on a stunningly handsome man who said a lot less than Alexander, but when he did, it meant something.

"See, she's thinking of Daniel right now." Deimos raised his teacup toward his uncle.

"I am. You two behave. Have you seen Abbie or Vincenz?"

Abbie rushed up, spectacles perched on her nose, a sheaf of papers clutched in her hand. "I'm sorry, I got caught up in this speech."

Carina smiled as she pushed Abbie's spectacles up her nose with a fingertip. "Now then." She hugged Abbie and stepped back to look at her again. "Don't apologize. I know you have a job to do. Vincenz will be by in a bit. If you need to finish your work, you can come along on another day."

"I'm done now. I can't wait to see it. It's so thrilling. Perhaps afterward, we can stop in and you can see my mother's bakery and Nyna's café?"

"I'd love that."

"Excellent! Oh, and Nyna tells me there's an opening in her building. A large flat on a corner. Perhaps the perfect size for you and Daniel."

"Daniel is going to kill you for doing all this while he's gone. Like an ambush. He'll return and find himself contracted to marry, a few kiddies in school and you behind it." Alexander stood and kissed Abbie's cheek.

She swatted at her brother-in-law but wore a smile doing it.

"They have to live somewhere, and Daniel's flat is not meant for two. Nyna moved to Marcus's building so it's safer and nicer even than her old one. Daniel will appreciate these small details being taken care of in his absence. He's a busy man." Abbie's mouth firmed.

"I'm going to blame you when he gets mad," Carina teased. "You scare him."

Abbie's face lit with amusement. "I know! I think I heard Vincenz down the hall, near Roman's secret fortress office thing." She snorted. "I'm going to run and get presentable. I'll meet you back here shortly."

Vincenz had only agreed to let her do it if she had him along as a guard and that he be allowed to check out the security in the area. She'd argued, but he'd told her Daniel would insist anyway so to just agree now and get it over with. In any case, it would be him or Andrei with her at all times when she left the house, so she may as well spend some time with her brother and let him guard her, too.

Funny how one could be separated from their sibling for long periods of time and still fight as if you'd never been apart a day.

"Don't run!" she called after Abbie. "Roman will shove me out into portal space if you get hurt."

Restless, Carina moved to the windows overlooking one of the myriad courtyards just outside. She'd been debriefed the same day Daniel had gone, had agreed to serve as a sort of consultant on the Imperium. Her goal was educating them about what the inner workings of the Imperium were, how power moved, that sort of thing. It hadn't felt traitorous, and she believed that with some more information about what the Imperium was and wasn't, the idea of peaceful coexistence was possible.

They watched her still; she knew that. Vincenz told her they'd watched him for two standard years before they began to trust. She hoped in time, they'd see she had no ill intent toward anyone, was pretty sure they did now, but Roman Lyons wasn't a fool, so they'd be on their guard for a while.

With a soft sigh, she turned at the sound of Vincenz's laugh. He walked out into the large entry where she waited, still talking to Roman. Both men turned to her with smiles. Roman was ridiculously handsome when he wanted to be, and Vincenz was more than aware of his own appeal.

"Vincenz tells me you three are off to look at the community center classroom? Wonderful. I wanted to tell you before you left. On behalf of the Governing Council of the Federation Universes, we offer you sanctuary and citizenship as Family Rank. You will be considered, for all intents and purposes, an associate member of House Lyons."

She relaxed a tiny bit. "Thank you, Roman. I must tell you I do not plan to accept that offer unless I am allowed to marry Daniel Haws."

Vincenz exhaled hard, and one of Roman's eyebrows slid up. Abbie burst into the room at Carina's back.

"Did he ask you, and neither of you bothered to tell me?" Abbie's fists rested at her hips.

She grinned at Abbie a moment. "He didn't ask me. He's not here. Anyway, he will ask me, because he loves me and that's his nature."

Abbie shook her head, still smiling. "Oh, of course he will. He probably wallowed around in his *I'm not good enough for her* place for a while. But what's the alternative? Letting someone like Alexander grab you up? Pah! My brother is one of the most competitive people I've ever known. He's won you; he won't give that up. Especially as he's beyond in love."

"Carina, as you can see"—Roman tipped his chin at Abbie—"our Family does not hold to any marriage rules."

"I'm as base as they come." Abbie's face was solemn.

Roman clucked his tongue and quickly moved to help his wife into a coat. "Stay warm and safe. I ordered a conveyance for you. Vincenz, can you handle these two?"

Her brother sighed. "Yeah. But I may want a rise in my credits after today."

She and Abbie linked arms and went out.

Vincenz got them settled in the back and joined the driver up front.

"Your brother is avoiding us back here."

"He may believe we're discussing our monthly bleed or what happens when you go into labor." Carina shrugged. "What is it with brothers, anyway? Roman's brother is a pain in my behind with his constant, mocking flirtation. Your brother has been gone eight days, and I miss him. I want him to see this classroom."

"Daniel will be back as soon as he can. Sometimes he just goes. I know that's not what you wanted to hear. But he'll always come back. Daniel is too good to get killed. Roman told me Wil says Daniel is his finest pupil in all his time at the corps. As for Alex, he's an idiot, but a pretty harmless one. He loves the attention, even negative attention."

"Family." Carina shrugged.

"Wait until you meet Roman and Alexander's father. Now *he*—well, I'm trying to avoid him while I'm pregnant because he's best digested after a glass or two of wine—also has a good heart, but he's a grumpy pain in the ass. Oh, and don't start feeling relieved. You've only met my siblings. But my father? He and Daniel do not get along. Mainly because Daniel is a man. What a man should be, and his existence only shows my father what he's not."

"My father is a tyrant and a despot who had my younger brother murdered for research. I win."

Abbie groaned.

"He's an overachiever, my father."

They took the rest of the trip in sociable silence, broken occasionally by Abbie pointing out the sights. Her classroom was simple but colorful and, Carina thought, filled with potential. She'd begin the training that all new teachers went through and start teaching right after that. The school administrator was helpful and friendly, and Carina realized she'd been waiting her whole life to mean something to someone in a way totally not related to who she was born to.

"Still up for lunch at Nyna's café?" Abbie asked as they traveled back. "We can celebrate and then sneak off to look at the flat."

"If you're sure that would be all right."

"Don't be nervous. Really, they both love you. Even if they didn't love you already, they'd love you simply because Daniel does."

Carina relaxed. "All right then. Daniel must have his own chair at the café. He's probably your sister's biggest customer with all the food he eats."

Abbie grinned and then sobered. "When we were young there were times when we didn't have a whole lot to eat. It was . . . hard, being that hungry all the time. Daniel often gave up his portion to my mother or to the rest of us."

Carina closed her eyes a moment. "I hadn't imagined. I've teased him about it, and now I feel horrible."

Abbie took her hand. "No. Don't. He would hate it if he knew anyone realized why he eats like such a hog. He would never want pity, not ever, especially from you. We all have our scars, our buttons and issues. I don't know if he even realizes it. It's just something I put together a few years ago. Everyone teases him about it. You know Daniel, he'd prefer that to pity."

"I suppose." But her heart hurt anyway. Knowing he had lived with the sharpness of hunger in his belly like that.

"Here's what Daniel says about the rest of us. He says Nyna and my mother find a way to heal through their food, I do through my work and Georges does by mimicking me. He's right of course." She smiled. "But he misses himself in the equation."

"He'd say he was a killer."

Abbie looked at her carefully. "And do you agree?"

"I would, though not how he means it. He thinks I don't under-stand. That I don't know what that darkness he fends off all the time feels like. But I know it takes a toll on him, and yet he keeps on doing it because he believes in it. Because it's what he was ordered to do by Wilhelm Ellis, and he'd just as soon hack off an arm as to disobey.

"The darkness he carries around is his toll, I suppose. The price he pays to save us all from that darkness. I find that impresses me far more than his silly idea that he's a killer, therefore blackhearted and not good enough."

"You're going to be good for him," Abbie said as she got out of the conveyance.

* * *

$\mathcal{D}$aniel rushed through the disembarking process and began to send all the information he'd been jammed from over the last two days. The transport had suffered repeated problems, and every transmission he'd attempted to send back to Wilhelm or Roman had been scrambled and bounced back. He'd tried to send, at the very least, a status message via other points of access, but nothing worked.

As a result, Roman didn't know a thing about Henry Sessions or the destruction of the warehouse complex. Unless House Sessions had reported it themselves, but somehow Daniel doubted that. Especially if they'd found Henry's body and the coin.

"Daniel, we've been anxious." Wilhelm's face showed on the screen of his personal comm.

"I need to speak to you immediately. My signal has been jammed the entire trip. A quick check with the docking monitors tells me this was not isolated. Transports of this type, leaving in the time frame I did, were all jammed."

"Come to the corps HQ immediately." He heard Roman's voice over Wilhelm's.

He showed his credentials to a soldier who'd been acting as a driver for someone. "I'm commandeering this conveyance. You may report to your superior."

The young soldier looked from the credentials back to Daniel, awe on his face. Very few people had that level of clearance. He nodded and stepped away. "It's keyed in, sir."

"I'm on my way," he said, slamming the door and speeding away from the portal.

"Daniel, straight to me, please. Your lovely lady has to wait," Wilhelm said.

He snorted. "Of course. What do you take me for?"

"A lovesick fool, which is amusing to watch most of the time. It's not an insult, Daniel." Wilhelm delivered those words bluntly, so Daniel believed that. Still, being thought to be soft wasn't a good thing in his business.

He nodded and signed off.

He'd missed her so much, had felt wrong in his skin being away from her. At first, the time on the transport had made him overthink. Doubt. Why would a woman like Carina Fardelle want a man like him? She was educated, refined, powerful, connected at a level Daniel could barely imagine. What would she see in him?

Once he'd gone, she'd be around other men, men like Alexander Lyons, Roman's brother; Deimos and Corrin, Roman's sons. Men who were like her. Men nothing like Daniel, with his rough edges. He was *not* refined or elegant. He was a dirt hopper who ended up in the corps because of the darkness that lived inside. Daniel was good at his job, but he sure as seven hells wasn't a smooth-talking prince like Deimos.

He'd driven himself crazy with it. Imagining her being charmed and realizing Daniel's difference. Finding that difference lacking. Imagining coming back and seeing her face and knowing she'd moved on.

But as they'd traveled and he'd had so much time alone to think, he continued doing it until he realized none of that mattered.

Daniel Haws knew he was in love with Carina Fardelle, and he meant to grab at that happiness. Whether she'd lost interest when he'd been gone, he had no other course but to hope that didn't happen and if she was still in love with him, snatch her up and make her stay with him.

So he'd do his job, debrief and then go to her. He'd hold out his hand, and if she took it, he'd never give her a reason to regret it.

* * *

"*D*aniel, please come in before Abbie sees you." Roman beckoned from behind his desk. "Or before you and Carina get behind a closed door with a horizontal surface."

Daniel stepped inside after waving to Marcus. "I do have self-control, Roman." Daniel sent his brother-in-law a look as he fell into a comfortable chair. "Anyway, even my sister can't hear me from across town. Her powers are mighty, but not that mighty."

"They're here. Abbie stopped in just before you showed up. They've been to the school where Carina will teach."

He grinned. "Nicely done. She made quick work out of securing a position."

"Yes, yes. It's all lovely. Now, your report?" Wilhelm indicated he should speak. "By the way, this signal jamming situation is being investigated. My people are ripping that transport apart."

Daniel nodded. "I found the smuggler. I'm surprised they haven't reported the loss of all their warehouses on Parron."

At that, Roman's eyes widened and then narrowed dangerously. "You're telling me this was another Family?"

"Sessions. I monitored the broker who led me back to a hotel where Henry Sessions was staying. I have a recording of the deal." He tossed a disc onto the desk. "It's attached to my report as well. Should be in your personal comm files by now. I sent them when I was still in the portal yards."

"Fill in the details." Wilhelm leaned closer.

"Millions of credits for small-scale tactical explosives. Their warehouses held stolen military material. Also on the disc. Stacked to the ceilings. I've assigned Andrei to work with one of the comandante's other special teams to figure out what depots are missing their munitions." Daniel had contacted Andrei right after he'd spoken to Wilhelm, and he had no doubt Andrei had probably already mobilized and was on his way by then.

"Whoever they are, *wherever* they are, they're missing enough material to severely curtail their ability to repel an attack. Roman, in part of the conversation I overheard, Sessions went on and on about you giving rights to those who didn't deserve it. The unranked. I imagine Sessions isn't alone in the sentiment."

Roman held up a finger to stay the rest of the story. He called his assistant. "Marcus, call an emergency meeting of the Governance Council. Attendance is mandatory. I'm on my way to the chambers now."

Marcus's voice shook a moment but firmed as he clarified and got to work.

"How do you want to proceed with this, Roman?" Wilhelm asked.

"They will be stripped of status. There's no way Henry's brother was unaware of his actions. I want them arrested and *brought here*. The entire top tier of Sessions is to be arrested and taken into custody. Max security."

He put on a suit coat, smoothing down his clothing. "I want them, every last one of them, to be turned out of Sessions holdings. They are now *my* holdings. They will surrender every factory, every shop, every piece of land and home. All of it is to be in House Lyons hands by the end of the day. I don't care if you send every last fucking soldier available to Lumina, it will happen, and it will be done."

Wilhelm nodded and stood. "I need to get to work then."

"What do you need me to do, sir?" Daniel asked Wilhelm. This was serious shit; he needed to keep his focus.

"You're on call. You know the procedure here. You've been out, and now you're grounded for a solid twelve hours' mandatory rest. You went on two high-profile missions in a row. Sit your ass down and sleep, or have sex with your lovely lady. Whatever. If I need you and no one else will do, I'll contact you."

Roman called Abbie's name as they all exited the office.

"What? Seven hells, Roman Lyons, don't bellow at me." Abbie came down the stairs, Carina right behind. "There you are, Daniel! I have a grievance with you. We've only now learned of your return. We learned from Marcus. We love Marcus, of course, but expect better of you. And oh my, what happened?" She came to an abrupt halt, her affectionate frustration with Daniel replaced by her attention to her husband's face.

Carina rushed around Abbie and into Daniel's arms. "You. You're here, and you look so handsome and a bit tired, but still handsome."

Even in the seriousness of the moment he had to take her face in his hands and kiss her softly. "I'm back, and I missed you."

Her eyes widened, and she blinked several times. Her bottom lip even quavered a moment, but she held it together and sent him a smile.

"We need to go to the Governance Council right now. House Sessions has been trading weapons with the Imperialists," Roman told his wife.

Abbie's shock slid away, replaced by outrage. "What will we do? I mean, I have my own ideas on this, and you know I'd be happy to expound on that. But I know this is tenuous, and you have my support for whatever direction you take."

Roman paused a moment, cocking his head. "Tell me. What do you think, Abbie?"

"I think you should burn Sessions to the ground and, as the old saying goes, salt the earth after. They need to know."

"Know." It was clear Roman understood what she meant.

"We're on the verge of war. This sort of succor to the enemy cannot be tolerated. You've tried to be gruff, you've levied fines and put people on trial. *And still they continue to put this Federation at risk.* These are our people; we can't let this sort of egregious offense against us go without the kind of response that will put a stop to anyone else thinking they can get away with it."

Roman's smile was bloodthirsty, and Daniel understood. He understood this was exactly what Roman had planned from the start. If she'd been too far the other way, he'd have perhaps softened or worked it through with her.

"I agree."

"As do I," Wilhelm grunted before going back to his personal comm, where he'd been issuing orders since they'd left Roman's office.

Carina stepped forward . "You have to. I know you've decided this, but if you waver, let me tell you my father will not respond to mercy. To kindness or compassionate second chances. My father knows the lash; that's the language he speaks, and it's what he will hear."

Roman nodded. "Thank you, Carina."

"Would it help you if I said as much? At the Governance Council?"

Daniel turned to look at her. Seven hells! She did not just volunteer to head into the heart of what would surely be a firestorm of controversy. He shook his head, but she just patted his arm.

"We can be united. It'll bolster your position as well."

"Can you not say anything else?" Daniel grumbled.

"She's right, you know." Abbie shrugged. "Come on, we may as well all go together."

"I'm not taking twelve off," he told Wilhelm, who looked at him long without speaking.

"Fine. If you're working, you can change into a uniform on the way." Wilhelm turned on his heel, heading for the doors. Before Daniel could follow, Marcus came jogging up and handed him a uniform, freshly pressed.

"I overheard and took a chance you might need one. I had it rushed over from your office."

"Marcus, I can see why my sister loves you so much. Thank you."

"I'm in whatever conveyance Daniel will be changing his clothes in," Carina called out.

Daniel groaned inwardly. Being with this woman would probably teach him a few things about keeping his composure in public. Or something. She was lovely to look at. And to know she was his.

"We don't have time for that, young woman. We'll be at our location in short minutes." Wilhelm frowned at her, and she rolled her eyes.

Still, Wilhelm got into their conveyance, and he nearly laughed aloud at both of them.

"You left it? The marker?" Wilhelm asked, meaning the coin.

"Yes. They know. And they know we know."

"Only men could ever use those words in a sentence," Carina muttered, looking out the window. She reached out and took his hand.

Chapter 23

Carina smiled as she watched Daniel shrug out of his clothes and into his uniform. He and Wilhelm were discussing what Daniel had found, and his attention was solidly with his boss. Leaving her free to fantasize about him and think about their future.

She'd had a lovely afternoon with Nyna and Clementine Haws. Daniel's women, she'd come to think of them all as. Clementine was a lot like her own mother, and it had been bittersweet to sit and enjoy a meal the way she'd most likely never be able to again with her mother.

It had been an impulse, but she spoke with the building's owner about the flat, and Abbie had insisted on paying a good faith deposit. In the end, she'd decided to lease it for her and Daniel. Carina hoped he came back still in love with her, because she'd drag him home every night by the hair if he thought he was going to leave her behind.

They pulled up near a side entrance. Wilhelm held an arm out. "You two have a few minutes alone. Not *too much* alone, mind you. But I want to check security myself, and you are off duty until I say otherwise." And with that, he got out, leaving them blessedly alone.

A rush of love nearly knocked her over as he turned, and she shamelessly jumped into his lap for a fierce hug before she leaned away enough to look into his face. "You're back."

"I am." He hugged her again, bringing her back against his body. "You feel good."

"Not nearly as good as you feel. You're here." Happiness pooled in her belly, spread outward, until her lips curved into a huge smile.

"I'm sorry I didn't contact you the moment I got back. This was so important, and my signal was jammed. I had to get that information to Roman."

"I understand." She sighed happily. "You're here. I missed you so much."

"I missed you, too."

"Do you still love me?" she asked.

"Do you think me so shallow I'd fall out of love with you in just eight days?" He tried not to smile.

"I shouldn't tell you this—it'll only go straight to your head—but you look so dangerous and handsome right now. I've missed that. I've missed being able to reach out and touch you. To know you're real and mine."

He kissed her forehead. "I'm real and yours."

"I can't wait for you to show me." She fluttered her lashes, and he laughed.

"Hold your panties, Carina. I have work to do first. Then there will be showing. Lots and lots of it. You're not the only one who missed touching the other."

"Oh, good! We'll go to your flat then? After we finish this madness this afternoon?"

"I don't know what will happen after Roman makes his speech. As soon as it's safe, we'll be together. As for my flat? We've gone over that. My flat is too small for us, Carina. The rooms at Abbie's are what you need. Spacious, safe, luxurious. You need that."

She sighed, patting his chest just a bit too hard. "If that's what I needed, I'd have accepted Alexander Lyons's repeated social invitations. I need *you*. I need a place that's *ours*. I have a salary now!" She grinned up at him. "We can get a nice place on the vents, with plenty of room. I looked at a flat in Nyna's building. It'll suit us just fine. The owner says we can move in any time we like. Abbie put a deposit down. She told me you had credits in savings. I assumed you'd be all right with that. I'll also have credits soon, once I start my job."

That line of his formed between his brows as he scowled for a moment.

She smoothed it with her thumb. "Such a handsome face to mar with those nasty frown lines."

"First let me congratulate you on the job. I heard the news from Roman."

She flushed with pleasure. "In the second circle. Vincenz went with us. He says it's very safe. I start training in the new week. Then I'll begin teaching once that's finished up."

"I'm proud of you."

She blinked back tears she swore to herself she would not shed. "That means so much," she whispered.

"You deserve it. Those kids are lucky to have you."

The warmth on his face hardened into annoyance again, and she tried hard not to laugh.

"Now, back to the other thing. You and my sisters have gone flat hunting together?"

She laughed and hugged him again, only then realizing she'd only thought she missed him a lot. Right then, with his scent in her nose, his arms around her, she realized she'd missed him far more than she'd realized. She missed his steady, calming influence on her, the grumpy but totally sweet way he dealt with her. He filled up the empty spots without pushing everything else out.

"I really do love your sisters and your mother. Georges is such a lovely man, too! You're so blessed to have them. They love you so much. I've heard so many wonderful stories over the last few days."

He growled low in his throat, but she knew he didn't mean it. "Stop trying to steer the conversation elsewhere."

"Pish. It's a very nice flat. I just wanted us to have a place of our own. I've never had that."

He groaned, and she ruthlessly held her smile back. He was really was so softhearted. It was a pity so few knew what an adorably sweet man he was. Though she did suppose it was safer for him that his reputation was that of a stone-cold warrior.

Just not with her.

"Nyna and Abbie said you'd like it. Abbie even tried to arrange with Wilhelm to have your things moved. Wilhelm got very gruff with her though, said you'd want to handle that yourself. It was only just a short while before you arrived. We were at Roman's offices to pester Wilhelm, and Abbie wanted to get something from her office. It's very cute that they have adjoining offices."

"Seven hells, Carina! I have weapons in my flat. I don't want you poking around and getting hurt."

"Shush, you! I didn't go. Wilhelm refused, and Roman agreed. Even Vincenz gave me a dirty look. Your precious dirty underpants and scores of blades are untouched by me. But I'm not thick. I can actually see something dangerous and not poke myself in the eye with it."

"Hmpf." But he relaxed a little. "I'll look at it with you later."

She tried to resist but gave in, bouncing around a little, making him laugh. She'd pretend not to notice the way he kept watch on the world outside the conveyance. She knew it was ingrained into him, and she couldn't complain about being safe. "You're back, and things all feel better. I just want to be with you, and you're letting me. Thank you."

"Gods above and below, you undo me." He said it not as a complaint but with wonder, and she threw herself into his arms again.

She burrowed against him so tightly it was like she tried to get inside his skin. Where if he had the right words he could tell her she already dwelled within him. Holding her like that, so small and totally, utterly resilient, he let himself breathe, truly just let go of his anxiety.

This was what he had been missing: the sense of return. Not just coming back to Ravena but returning to someone, something bigger than simply himself. She was his place to come home to, the reason to return.

"I love you."

She sniffled. "You said it first. You said it."

"Yes. Well, I was gone. You smell good."

Tipping her head back, she smiled up into his face. "I do?"

He leaned down to breathe her in. "Mmm, yes you do." He stiffened as he suddenly registered what she had said earlier about Alexander. "Wait. What?" He jerked, anger making him jittery for a moment. "Alexander Lyons did what?"

"Now, Daniel. Do you think I couldn't put him in his place?"

"His place is with my fist in his nose," Daniel all but snarled. She looked very pleased with herself, and amusement at what she would have done to Alexander did temper his anger. But Alex was supposed to be a friend. Daniel had thought Roman's brother was finally growing up, but this sort of thing was something the old Alexander would have done. And damn it all, he had to go debrief and his cock was hard; he needed to be with her, and this whole thing about Alexander had riled him up.

"You're very attractive when you're jealous, but there's no need. As if some pretty boy could ever be more attractive and wonderful than you. Anyway, I don't think he truly meant it."

He groaned, shoving a hand though his hair. "Wilhelm will be back in a moment. Please follow my instructions and let me keep you safe. I'll be right behind your chair. I'm proud of you." He kissed her, meaning for it to be quick, but there was never quick when his lips touched hers.

She fitted herself against him, throwing her arms around his neck. Her mouth opened on a soft sigh he greedily took into himself. Her tongue met his boldly, sliding along in a sensual dance, inviting him in, and he followed.

Sweet. Her taste greeted him, taking hold, rooting, making him crave more. Need roared in his ears as he fought for control. He had to get his head back on keeping them all safe, shouldn't even have kissed her, but he needed that.

With a groan and a nip of her bottom lip, he set her away and as an added measure, took a step back. "We'll finish that later."

She touched her lips with her fingertips. "I love you, Daniel. I love that you came back to me. Ah, and there's Wilhelm."

"Let's go. Everything's in place." Wilhelm opened the doors, and Daniel stepped out, the soldier first now. Things were going to change. He felt it in the air.

Chapter 24

Carina tried not to gape as they strode through the halls of the Grand Council building. It was difficult enough with the inlaid marble work and the columns rising up to soaring ceilings.

And then she'd gotten a look at Daniel in his uniform. Not sitting in a conveyance speeding through the streets to the meeting. She hadn't gotten the full effect in the cramped space. But now he stood tall, back straight, eyes inscrutable but missing nothing. He was pressed and crisp and very authoritative. She'd never seen a more breathtaking sight.

"When we finally have our own flat, you and I are going to play prisoner and the interrogating soldier," she murmured, leaning into his body.

Daniel pinked and then bit his lip to keep from laughing. He narrowed his eyes her way, but amusement and interest lit them, not anger.

She gulped, sneaking peeks at him as they walked. Vincenz caught up with them as they reached the massive double doors to the Council Inner Chambers. Her brother looked handsome and solemn as he took a place behind Daniel, shielding Carina even more.

Nothing could have prepared her for the sound of that room. Roman hadn't opted to have his arrival announced, so they entered through a side door, and the moment they did, the noise hit her like a slap. Arguing all around, yelling via vid screen, slamming of a gavel as the sergeant at arms shouted for order.

Roman slid into a role right before her eyes. He was The Lyon, he was the leader, *their leader*, and took the highest dais, Abbie at his right. Deimos came in through a side door with a group of younger men who all sat on a lower level.

"Associate Council: they're the next in line to House leadership. Deimos is the chair," Daniel murmured as he held a seat out for her and then stood behind it, his hands clasped at his back.

Though he hadn't said a single word yet, the entire room noticed Roman's arrival. All eyes lay on him, including her own. When he spoke, she was unable to tear her attention away from him. He held the room by sheer force of personality as he told them to be quiet and come to order.

"I call this extraordinary session of the Full Governance Council to order. Proceedings will not be recorded. Any House without representation at this meeting will lose their vote on any issue that comes up."

And then he turned them all upside down.

"I hereby proclaim House Sessions has been divested of their Rank. Their property will be stripped from them, their coffers claimed. All Sessions members will lose any Rank-held jobs. They will quit their residences on all three 'Verses they hold. Lumina, Kyff and Alia have now returned to control of House Lyons until such time that the Governance Council decides under which House these 'Verses will affiliate."

Stunned silence fell over the room as Roman let them fully digest what he'd said before continuing.

"Henry Sessions is dead after being found a leader in a weapons smuggling scheme he led from Parron. I have a disc filed and available for those House leaders on the Law and Justice Committee. On that disc, you will find photographic and video evidence of Sessions arranging an exchange of tactical small explosives for credits. This exchange took place with a known member of the Imperium. Further review of Sessions's financial documents has uncovered a trail of credits tied to more than a standard year's worth of such dealings. Those weapons have been involved in several attacks on Federation citizens.

"House Turgev will be questioned after this body adjourns, so please stay in this chamber until you are told you may go." He looked down at a man sitting just a few rows away. "Parron is your 'Verse, and I will know just exactly how this happened under your control."

The chamber erupted again with shouted questions and official complaints about Roman's tactics.

Roman ignored it, instead cutting the sound amplifiers off and tweaking a button so a piercing wail came from the sound system, and they all quieted again.

"I'm going to make some things clear to every last one of you. Nearly two standard years ago now, we discovered Families had engaged in treasonous actions against the Federated Universes. As a result, thousands of lives were lost and more risked by the instability it created. *We are on the verge of war.* This is not a phrase I use to grab more power. I've led with a fair hand my entire tenure. This is not business as usual; we are all in peril, and I will use all the powers granted to me to protect my people."

He outlined some of the recent skirmishes on the Edge, including the bioagents used.

"Why do we care about the Edge?" someone shouted out. "If we let the Imperialists have those 'Verses, they'll leave us alone. Why are we killing our own people and dissolving Houses for a handful of dirt piles?"

Carina was pleased to hear a number of disgusted murmurs in reaction to such comments.

"Because, House Moander, we are the Federation. We signed treaties and gave our oath to protect those 'Verses that are ours. Those 'Verses on the Edge are Federation 'Verses, just as Kwen Lun, Ravena, Nondal, Borran, just as each one of our 'Verses is. I will not be a liar and a coward."

"And because Ciro Fardelle won't stop at those 'Verses," Carina said in a loud, clear voice.

All eyes turned to her.

"This is Carina Fardelle. She escaped the Imperium and has sought sanctuary. Her brother, Vincenz, known as Vincent Cuomo, has been in the service of the Federated Universes for seven standard years." Roman indicated she address the group.

She decided to stand. She put her mask back on and addressed them all in a cool voice. "You will gain nothing by letting the Edge 'Verses go. You think he cares about the territory? You believe this is why he has shown no hesitation to blow your citizens up? Use viral agents on them to make them ill and kill them?" She sighed, as if they were all silly children. "Ciro Fardelle doesn't care about those 'Verses. He is not throwing the Imperium into chaos for a number of Edge

'Verses. This is not about territory. He cares about power. If you turn tail and abandon your people, he will see that as weakness, and he will continue forward, toward the Center. Because to abandon those 'Verses will mean you are afraid, and he will punish you for that. He responds to one thing and one thing only: more force than his own. Not the threat of force, not the menace of force, but brute force delivered with swift hands."

She sat back down and looked out over the room.

"How can you be trusted? You're a filthy Fardelle! You're not fit to be in this chamber."

"House Stander," Daniel murmured, knowing she could handle the retort on her own.

"House Stander, isn't it? Whether you trust me or not, I'm up here. I brought information out, risking my own life and the life of my remaining family and friends back home. I have proven my loyalty, and I'm telling you how my father will respond. You can trust me or not, but the fact is, he's a man who puts in practice his belief that humans need the lash frequently enough to keep them from having any ideas about getting away alive. Ciro Fardelle doesn't care about you or anyone else here. He cares not for minimizing loss of life or negotiated peace. He cares to destroy and maim. You are prey, or you are predator."

Roman stood. "We are predator. Enough. Let it be known that from this day on, any treason will be met with force. It will be eradicated under my boot heel if those of you who have no honor can't learn one way . . ." Roman looked to Abbie.

"If you can't learn one way, we will destroy you. This treason will end one way or another. How it ends is your choice." Abbie spoke softly but clearly. She met the eyes of several House leaders.

"House Walker stands with Lyons. Our recent experience with our members participating in this mess has underlined the importance of standing unified now."

It followed over and over. Each House leader standing up and supporting Roman. Two houses dissented but agreed not to interfere with Roman.

"Look to your Houses, people. This is our land; these are our citizens to protect. We took an oath. Let us not break those promises."

Wilhelm's people swept in and escorted House Turgev into a side room to be interviewed.

"You did what was necessary," Deimos said to his father.

"All my life I've been taught the ideals of fairness and justice. These people helping these bastards, this is about giving more rights to the unranked. But by doing this, they'll speed up that process, only turn it on its ear, create an angry populace who feels so betrayed and threatened they turn on us. This is bad business. I hate them for making me do this. How else can I handle it?"

"How you are handling it, Dai. Like a leader. A true leader doesn't just lead when things are easy and decisions aren't life-altering." Deimos shrugged.

"So let's do something about that," Abbie interrupted. "We've taken all the House Sessions holdings: land, dwellings, large farms on Lumina. Let's give it to the unranked. No, not all of it. I understand whatever House takes over will need to pay for services and salaries of employees. If you split it, one 'Verse each to the three most affluent and progressive Houses on the agreement that citizens are offered a certain amount of Sessions-held land to farm. On Earth there was a history of this. Governments encouraged people to move and settle places. To work the earth, build civilization again. They gave them a certificate of ownership to some land and a beast of burden. We can give them that and perhaps a small stipend to build dwellings."

"Roman, doing something like that would threaten the Houses." Vincenz spoke from behind Ellis.

"Yes. And they should be. I've got millions of unranked upset right now. Betrayed by the people who are supposed to protect them. They have no voice, and their protectors have not spoken for them. I'm putting down near riots every quarter now. All across the Federation. They are angry, and they have reason to be." He paused. "Abbie, if you mean this, have your office look into it. Present me with three versions of a plan to do this. Do it officially as the liaison to the unranked. Your office can benefit from this, and it should. Don't skimp. I want all financials worked out. Make this thorough."

"We have Turgev in interview now. I'll inform you when we finish. I don't believe they were involved with Sessions. Negligent in their holdings, yes. Treason? No." Wilhelm sighed.

"I agree. Let's go home. I've made enough people scared for now." Roman indicated the doors, and they followed.

Chapter 25

*C*arina had done such a great job. Daniel would tell her that in private once they got the chance to escape for a while. Unfortunately, he wasn't done working, and that twelve hours' rest seemed very distant indeed. He couldn't concentrate until he knew she was safely away.

"I have work." He touched her cheek. "I'm sorry. I need to . . ."

She nodded. "I understand." She laughed at his expression. "Yes, I truly do. This is important. You're important. You have a job. You'll come to me? When this is done?"

"I will *always* come back to you when my work is done." He needed her to understand that. "Question is, Carina, will you always be there?" He put his fingers over her lips for a moment. "Don't answer that yet. Think about it carefully. When I come for you tonight and if you agree, I'm taking you and I'm never giving you back. It won't be easy loving me, being with a person whose job lies in secrets. I want you. I want you so badly that I'm willfully ignoring all other reasons not to be with you. But my part is easy. You're easy to love. So think, and if you take me, you've got me forever."

She nipped at his fingers. "You're slow. I've told you my answer a hundred times. Just know this, Mr. Haws, you're already mine. Be careful." She turned and moved toward the conveyance. "I'm in love with you. I want to have your taciturn, grumpy, serious-faced babies, and you have to marry me. I'll give you some time to think *that* over."

He put his palm over his heart. Leaning down, he spoke into her ear. "You really are the most infuriatingly bossy woman to ever draw breath." She stiffened, and he chuckled. "It's one of your best qualities. I'll come to you when I can."

He straightened, and she tiptoed up quickly to kiss him. "I'll be waiting."

After the conveyance pulled away, he turned to Wilhelm. "I'm going to walk over to the offices. I don't want to be jammed into a conveyance; I've been on a transport for days."

"We'll see you there. Meet me in my office. We've got some data from that chip."

He jogged, needing the exercise. The cold air pumped through his body as he ran, waking him up, helping him push out doubts and anything else not to do with the problem at hand.

By the time he'd cleaned up in his office and changed out of his dress uniform, he was less jittery and more focused. Being back home had been the first important thing. He'd seen her, knew she was well and now he had work to do.

Wilhelm's assistant waved Daniel through when he arrived.

Roman and Wilhelm were already inside, sitting at a large table, looking at a screen.

"They haven't unlocked the data yet?" Pulling up a chair, Daniel looked at the flow of information on the screen, still encoded.

He could see the blocks of information that had begun to unravel, the code broken, revealing whole data beneath it.

"My best people have been on it, and it's been slow going. Layers of encryption so dense and complicated it's taken two teams working half a day each to get this far. Today was the first time we've seen any actual data behind the coding. We have some places, but not much more yet."

"Esta told Carina she didn't have the programs to untangle his security. She must have taken it directly from Ciro's personal files. That takes guts," Roman said.

"You can tell she's pretty extraordinary. Look at that daughter of hers." Wilhelm continued to look at the data. "Asphodel, Parron, Mirage."

Daniel wished he had it within his power to get Esta Fardelle out, but he feared it was impossible. Their intelligence had indicated a heightening of security on Caelinus. So severely they couldn't get any word at all from inside the Fardelle compound.

"The Edge is clearly the key here. We know that from our own intel and what little Esta was able to tell us before we got this chip. Other than being the buffer between us and the Imperium, what makes the 'Verses mentioned similar enough?" Daniel pulled up a map. "Not even the three closest 'Verses to the waypoint."

"Whatever we've got here, it's big. Teams are on the ready, I trust?" Roman asked.

"I've sent two teams out. Sera, Brandt and Ash will rendezvous with Andrei and Julian. I have another special team on the ground in Mirage." Wilhelm turned his attention to Roman. "Sessions has given my people some trouble. It's not going to be as clean as I like it, getting them here."

Roman snapped his teeth shut. "Get them here. Dead or alive.

Make that clear to them. I'm not having this silliness. Not for one moment more. We're on the verge of all-out war, and Sessions played us false. They expect mercy now?"

"Sir, it's been fairly clear in the investigation I did before I locked in directly on Henry that at the very least, the top tier of the House knew what had been happening. The credit trail is proof that this had brought way more capital into their House structure than ever before. Even the warehouse workers knew."

"This is what mercy gives you." Roman stood up and began to pace. Daniel didn't envy him just then. The weight of this would rest on Roman's shoulders above all else. He had to balance so many things, people would be hurt and there was no way around it. That sort of power wasn't something Daniel ever craved.

"Mercy is underrated, but not in this case. We'll get them here," Wilhelm said. "Sit down, Roman. There's a course here, we're on it and we have to stay true to it as we learn more. I've got my people working with the code breakers, and the trackers are on the data flow between the three 'Verses in question and toward the Imperium. We'll figure it out.

"Vincenz has been invaluable with this. Not just on the data coding, but the knowledge he has of the Imperium and the contacts he's built up over the time he's been with us. He's sped this up immeasurably."

"Perhaps you can let him come on board then." Daniel rarely interfered with Wilhelm's vision of Phantom Corps. While Daniel ran most of the program, Wilhelm had handled recruiting in his own unique way from the start. It had worked, bringing exactly the kind of men and women on as operatives that the program needed. Wilhelm created Phantom Corps, and he had a specific vision. Daniel had no trouble with that.

But in this case, a reminder might suit.

"Vincenz Fardelle as a Phantom Corps operative? I wasn't aware he was interested. He's doing quite well in his current capacity."

Daniel scrubbed a hand over his face. "He's wanted to be one of us since the beginning. He's proved his loyalty and his capacity to excel in the corps." Daniel shrugged.

"He has?"

And that's when Daniel realized Wilhelm knew everything Daniel had told him. He knew it already and was leading him somewhere with it.

"Wilhelm, he asked us back when he came over. You told him he wasn't right for this job, and that's how he ended up where he is now."

"I do remember that. He was so young then. Not just young in the way you all were when I found you, but young in his heart. He was not"—Wilhelm paused—"hard. Even with all he'd seen. You were hard. Andrei was hard. Marame was the hardest young girl I've ever seen. It's what you all use to keep the kill from tasting good."

Daniel didn't quite know how to process it all. He was proud Wilhelm had chosen him, proud of the job he did. But being so hard that killing people became one's living didn't seem like something to aspire to.

"He's received excellent training. I've seen him in the field. His investigatory skills are quite good. I think he would be an asset to Phantom Corps. Living on the Edge, watching one's father decimate your home and try to do the same here? That'll harden a man." Daniel knew Vincenz well enough to know what motivated him.

Ah, that was it all along. Ellis was waiting for Daniel to step out from his shadow, to lead more within Phantom Corps.

"I trust your judgment on this. Why don't you speak to him about it?" Wilhelm asked.

He appreciated the way Ellis had left the door open, but in this case, Daniel felt it would be better coming from Wilhelm. "If you're sure it should be me."

Wilhelm's eyebrows shot up briefly, and Roman dropped into a chair to watch their interplay. "You don't think so?"

"Since the beginning, you have made the choices. You have brought them on in your own way. I know he's not your usual recruit. But he'd want it to be you. He asked. You said no. And yet, he didn't turn tail. He could have taken Ranked status and sat around doing nothing since he arrived. But he took your rejection and made himself better, made himself invaluable, and has proven himself loyal over and over. He deserves the same honor as the rest of us."

Wilhelm nodded. "Point taken."

*C*arina sipped her mulled wine and pretended to listen to Corrin while he played piano. Abbie sat next to her on the cozy couch, her head leaning on the pillows.

"Are you all right?" she asked quietly. "No nausea?"

Abbie blinked and sat straighter. "Yes, yes, I'm all right. I haven't had much trouble with sickness this week. Mercy says I may be done with it now. Thank the gods."

"Good."

"Are *you* all right? You did a good job today, Carina."

"I want Daniel," she said with a smile. "I know he's working. I know he's coming for me. Selfishly, I wish it was now." She shrugged.

"I've told you about how Roman and I fell in love. I would wait for him, we'd steal time whenever we could to see each other, even knowing it was doomed. Love works that way. And love finds a way. My brother is"—she sighed, thinking about what she was saying— "he's intense. His focus is intense. It's why he's so good at his job. You're in that focus. He'll be back for you. Always. Other than Roman, I don't know anyone who is more loyal and sure of his course in life. Sometimes it'll make you . . . I don't know." Abbie shook her head. "It's big. Being loved by a man like that. Sometimes I come into a room and he'll look to me and there's no one else there. I never imagined that's what love would feel like."

"Sometimes you feel as if you'll drown in it. All that focus. Not negative, like I feel like I'm dying. But just lifted up by the tide of it, consumed by it. It's powerful. I've known people in love, and other than you and Roman, I've never seen that sort of intensity before. I'd begun to wonder if it was just me."

Abbie grinned. "It's rare. I believe this sort of connection we've found to our men is rare. You can have love that's less intense but no less enduring."

"But I'd rather have this." Carina laughed, meaning it with all her being.

"Gods above and below, me, too. I sure can't imagine doing this baby making thing with anyone else."

"That's good to hear, darling." Roman glided into the room, not looking like a man who'd had the weight of millions of lives on his shoulders. "Come up to bed. You look tired, and the doctor said you need more rest."

Carina didn't want to interrupt this lovely moment between them, but where was Daniel?

"I've been lying on the couch, listening to Corrin play piano just for me and gabbing with Carina. It's not like I'm working hard." But her eyes were on her husband as she moved to him and into his arms.

Carina watched them, loving that Daniel's sister had such a connection with someone who clearly adored her.

"You're still awake?" Daniel came in and made everything better.

"I waited for you."

He held a hand out, and she rose without hesitation, moving to him and taking it. "For you and only you. I'll always wait."

"I love you, Carina."

"I love you, Daniel." She smiled up at him.

"In my front pocket there's a marriage application."

Before he could say anything else, she'd reached in and grabbed it. "You did!"

"You ordered me to." A smile hinted at his mouth.

"Pffft. Daniel, I order you to do all sorts of things."

"Come on upstairs with me. I'll explain to you how I'll obey you sometimes."

The echo of Abbie's laugh followed them as they escaped upstairs.

$\mathcal{S}$he yanked at his clothing while he laughed. "Come on, Daniel! You're not naked. I've had to wait all day for you to be naked. You should obey me right now."

"It's a good thing I appreciate bossy women."

"*Woman*. Not more than one." She tried to pinch his side, but he was all flat, tight muscle. Not that she was complaining.

"Other than the women I came with, Abbie, Nyna and Mai, you're the only one. I'm fairly sure you'd kill me if that weren't the case."

"You have to sleep sometime. Just remember that."

He tumbled her back to the soft rug, his arms around her taking her weight to soften her fall.

"I won't forget your vicious threats." He didn't sound very threatened as he licked up her neck, his nimble fingers unbuttoning her pants and shoving them down her legs.

He reared up, resting on his haunches, looking down at her. "You have the most beautiful legs."

"You're marrying me? When?"

"Impatient, too." Smoothing his palms up her legs from ankle to thigh, he leaned down to kiss her belly, inching her sweater up as he did.

"Don't think you can just show me papers, and I'll back off at this point. You've despoiled me, after all," she said, ending on a squeal as he deliberately slid fingertips over her panties, pressing just hard enough to remind her she wanted him so badly.

He laughed, letting go long enough to pull his coat and shirt from his body, tossing them in the room behind them without a glance.

She took a deep breath, looking at him. "Wow."

"Now you." He pulled her sweater over her head, and she shook her hair from her face.

"More beauty. Every inch of you is so beautiful." He kissed one nipple and then the other. "You're not despoiled. You're loved."

"Oh, you're so good at this." She smirked. "I say we need about three weeks or so to plan. We'll need to move in all that time, and then we can have the ceremony here. Abbie said you often spent time in the colored glass gardens. I love it there, the way the light dances over the flowers through all the colored panes."

He groaned but didn't pause as he got rid of his pants and boots, lastly tossing his underpants away.

"Come to the bed. You shouldn't be taken here on the floor."

She rolled over onto her hands and knees. "But you like it."

It had been the right move. His eyes glazed over. Over her shoulder, she watched, her stomach tightening, as he licked his lips.

"I'm not going to break if you fuck me like this, Daniel. I thought we went over that before." Feeling daring, she reached back between her legs and opened herself. A ragged groan tore from him, making her feel beautiful and desirable.

He pressed a kiss to the small of her back. Heat and gooseflesh rose from the contact, spreading outward until it consumed every part of her.

"I need this as much as you do," she whispered. "Take me how you want. I'm yours. It's love, no matter how you touch me. What use is this thing between us if you can't take what you need from me? When I'm offering it freely? This is about you trusting me enough to know I love you. I accept all of you. I *like* how you are with me. Rough, soft, whatever. "

He didn't know how she could. She was so beautiful and soft. He wasn't. He didn't deserve her. He breathed in deep, licking her hip. Not that he planned to be a better man and walk away.

She'd taken his hand, had accepted his offer of marriage. She had ordered him to make it happen, after all, so he'd expected her to be pleased. But she was a woman, so he half expected her to make him beg. Which he would have.

He wasn't giving her back. He snorted and nipped one of her perfect ass cheeks. She yelped and started laughing.

"Daniel!"

"What? Sweet, have you seen your ass? It calls out to be nibbled. I'm a slave to my urges, you know. Just a mere man enraptured by his love."

She shook, still laughing.

"You're utterly full of it."

"I am." He slicked his fingers through the folds of her pussy, so wet and ready for him. She arched back, and he went to her clit.

"Thank gods." She groaned, her laughter dying. "I've been waiting for that for what seems like forever. I've missed your hands on me. I'm quite used to being serviced by you regularly. It's a horrible thing to get me used to that and then to just go away and deny me this pleasure."

It was his turn to laugh, squeezing her clit between his thumb and forefinger. "I do apologize terribly for being so selfish. Let me give you this little present to begin to atone." As he said it, he ramped her up with relentless intensity. He needed her, needed to give her pleasure, needed to touch her and steal every gasp, moan, cry, every bit of her desire.

Her head dropped forward as he tugged and pinched her left nipple in time with his movements on her pussy.

And then she exhaled sharply, climaxing in a hot rush against his fingers, leaving her ready and open as he began to enter her, pushing his cock into her gate, settling all the way in.

"I accept your apology," she mumbled. "Please don't hesitate to err in the future. Your way of atoning is more than acceptable to me."

"I'm just getting started, sweet." He pulled out and shoved back in over and over. His pace was fast and hard; need threatened to crawl from his skin. Her body answered his need, gave to him what he craved.

Around him she was hot and wet, holding him, caressing his cock as she pushed back at him to meet his thrusts. He gave in to his urge to control her just then, to ravish and pay homage to her.

Then he'd slow things down and enjoy her for hours.

Carina had never been happier in her entire life. His cock deep within her, his hands all over her body, holding her to him as if he couldn't bear not touching her. Her muscles were loose and warm from the delicious climax he'd given her, and their rhythm matched.

When he was like this, overwhelmingly male, dominant even, it was as if every cell in her body was supersensitive. The rug at her knees wasn't comfortable, but it didn't hurt, and somehow it only *added* to the entire experience. That same rug knotted around her fingers as she searched for purchase. The scent of them rose around her, her body welcoming his, clean sweat, his own unique smell, all these married together, heightening her need.

Each time he couldn't resist another moment and made a sound it drove her crazy. A sort of frenzy built in her bones, her muscles, because she needed all of him.

He kissed her shoulder as he pumped into her. His breath ragged, the muscles on his arms corded with strain. He was all around her, over her, behind her, inside.

Inside so deep and hard and then his entire body hardened as he groaned her name, coming at last and tumbling them to the floor, cradling her in his arms.

"Welcome back."

He panted for breath, and she kissed his lips, not wanting to move for a time.

"Does this mean you're going to marry me then?"

"I've only been pestering you to marry me since the day we met, Daniel. What clued you in that I'd be interested other than that?"

He stood, pulling her up against him. "Come with me. I've stayed here, so I know the bathing tub is spacious enough for two."

She watched him as he ran the water and fetched drying cloths. She sat on the edge of the counter and looked her fill because he was hers. That pleased her straight to her toes.

"I never expected you."

He turned and held a hand out to assist her into the water. He followed, settling in at her back.

"You didn't?"

She laughed, because he made everything better.

"I didn't expect you, either. Thought you were useless and shallow that first time I saw you. I wanted you even then, even as I looked and judged you as a cold and remote beauty. You've proven me wrong ever since."

She was so relaxed there in his arms, the warmth of the water all around, her body's call sated for the time being.

"You don't think I'm beautiful now?" she teased, her eyes closed.

"You're not cold and remote. You're not useless or shallow. Your beauty is like that of the hours after a heavy snow. Brilliant, covering everything it touches with that beauty. You are pale as moonlight and just as luminescent. Like a pearl. You are strong and intelligent, and what you did today took a lot of strength. I'm proud of you."

"Oh Daniel, you're so"—she licked her lips—"I don't know how you do it, but you say exactly the thing I need to hear."

"Not when I tell you no."

She laughed again, joy always so close to the surface when she was with him. "You're very gruff to tell me no. But I suppose I'm hard to handle and all those things men say about women with their own minds. You must like us all well enough. I've seen how Roman looks at Abbie. Seems to me, bossy men like you need women who hate to hear no."

"Trust you to make that into a virtue." He kissed her temple, and she felt the curve of his lips as he smiled.

"Things are going to get very bad, aren't they?"

He paused before resuming sliding his soap-slicked hands all over her, getting her worked up yet again.

"I think so, yes. We're getting the data translated. Vincenz is helping. Your father is up to something unimaginably horrible judging by the lengths he went to, to protect this data."

"I'll help however I can."

"Wilhelm told me you'd been a lot of help already. Thank you for that. I'm trying to get word about your mother. I assigned Vincenz to a plan to get her out. It can't happen for a while. I'm sorry. But as soon as we can do it, we'll get her away."

Carina looked out the windows above the tub. The sky above was lit with a thousand stars. Totally different stars than the ones she'd grown up seeing at night. It still caught her at times, realizing she was so far from everything she knew.

"I'm not even sure she'd leave. I appreciate you working on it, but I trust you to wait until it can be done safely, or at least the safest way possible.

"Tomorrow we can get started on moving into the new flat. I saw what you make. For goodness' sake, Daniel, why do you live in such a tiny flat? You can afford to have a far bigger abode."

He sighed. "How did you see that?"

"Abbie did it. She had to tell the owner of the building what your salary was so he could lease to us. We'll need furniture. A bed. Abbie tells me you sleep on a narrow one-person bed. Why do you torture yourself so?"

She'd risen to face him, and he rinsed her off, setting her outside the tub, joining her and tossing her a drying cloth.

"I haven't had a reason for a bigger bed until now. All I've done in my bed is sleep. I don't move much when I sleep. Why waste time and money on a big bed? By the way, in the inner pocket of my coat, on the other side from where the papers were, there's something for you."

She squealed and ran out the door, not caring that she was naked. Rifling through the coat, she found a soft pouch with a drawstring in the pocket.

She didn't want to open it without him present, so she scampered around the corner and found him settling into bed. He'd started a fire, so the room was toasty. She leapt up next to him, snuggling against his body. "I love presents."

"I suspected as much." He tipped his chin. "Open it."

She did and found a ring with brilliant blue stones inside. It fit her, but it was the way he slid it on her finger that touched her the most. It was his way of marking her, a public declaration.

"It's beautiful. I've never seen such amazingly deep blue stones." She looked at her hand, loving the sparkle the stones made in the firelight.

"I was stuck. Away from you and I had to spend a lot of time wandering around and pretending to be casual while I looked into a few things. Each day, several times a day, I passed this shop. Little more than a junk shop, so I didn't think of you when I passed.

"And one of the afternoons, I paused, turning to keep from being seen, and I was in front of that shop. In the back there were scarves and things for hair. I thought of you then and went inside. At the back, on the other side of the scarves there was a jeweler's stall. Behind a locked grate, of course. I didn't expect to find anything, but when I looked closer, I saw this ring. I knew it was meant to be yours."

"You tell me I undo you. But you're wrong, Daniel. It's you who undoes me."

He grinned, and she took a deep breath, kissing his forehead before sitting back.

"You've wanted to marry me since then." This pleased her greatly.

Until he shook his head. "No. I've wanted to marry you since that night in the bolt-hole. Deep within that mountain where it was just me and you."

"Again with the undoing. Daniel, you are the sweetest man to ever live."

He threw his head back and laughed. "That's the most ridiculous thing I've ever heard." He swooped in and ended up on top of her, looking down into her face. "I'm not sweet. I'm not good. But I love you so much I'd tear the fabric of the 'Verses apart if you but asked. You're my mate, my heart and soul, and you remind me I'm a man."

She blinked away tears. "I waited my entire life for you."

He kissed the side of her neck, and she held him tight, not ever wanting to lose the warmth of him against her.

Vincenz looked at the data and his eyes, eyes that had been losing focus just a short while ago, focused in sharp.

He connected through to Daniel and Wilhelm's personal comms. "I've found it. You both need to see this."

Just minutes later, Wilhelm came in. "Daniel and Roman should be here shortly."

He'd felt bad about calling Daniel out. Vincenz knew he'd asked Carina to marry him that evening. Daniel had spoken to him about it before heading over to Roman's. He'd been skeptical at first, but Vincenz had to admit he thought they were a good match. Carina would keep Daniel on his toes, and Daniel would adore Carina the way she was meant to be. And he'd keep her safe. In the end, he'd given his well wishes and had meant them.

"Before they do, I want to speak to you about something." Wilhelm took the seat next to Vincenz. "Daniel and I were speaking about you today, about how invaluable you are to us. I'd like to bring you on as an operative."

"A Phantom Corps operative?" Vincenz had wanted that for as

long as he could remember. He'd hated that he wanted it, hated the envy he had for Daniel and the other operatives he'd worked with. Had wondered why he had been passed over when he knew for a fact he was just as good, especially after the years of training he'd endured.

"Yes. Daniel and I both think you'd be an asset to our team. Daniel is a sub-commander. He runs Phantom Corps. You'd be assigned to him here on Ravena. I'll let him fill you in on all that. That is, if you're interested."

Vincenz was proud of the way he'd stayed calm and nonchalant. First at the invitation to join Phantom Corps and now at the news that Daniel ran it. Oh, he knew Daniel had high rank, he knew he was influential, but Vincenz had no idea just how powerful. He could work under Daniel. He respected the man, trusted his skills.

"I'd be interested, yes. Now that Carina is here, being on the same 'Verse would be good for us both."

"I'll get the papers in play. You'll report to Daniel from now on."

He heard the noise outside and then Daniel came in with Roman, and they settled around the table with him.

"Let me just say it. From what I can tell, and the analysts agree, it appears that this data is a discussion between my father and his military research division. The bits and pieces we've translated appear to be about attempts to build a machine to collapse a portal."

The room got suddenly silent as that settled in.

"Fuck." Daniel leaned in to look at the data more closely.

"They may have already done it successfully. That portal explosion back while you two were on the way back here shut the 'Verse down totally. We still can't get any intel about it other than the basics." Wilhelm sighed. "The best we can hope for was that it was a test that failed. But we can't go by that assumption."

"What all is in there? Is it done? Do they have them? How can we stop them? Why the mention of the other 'Verses?" Roman sat forward.

"We don't know yet. We don't know anything more than I've told you. Each letter we translate comes painfully slow. There are traps built into the code so if you don't take it just exactly right, it re-encrypts the entire document."

"I doubt he'd have that level of security if they didn't at least have a good chance of developing it." Wilhelm shook his head.

"What would be the result? What would collapsing a portal do?" Daniel asked. "In the long term?"

"We don't know." Vincenz sat back.

"Let's get people on it. I want every single engineer with top-tier clearance on this. Have your people spread out among the teams, Wilhelm. We'll get some troops out to those three 'Verses. Get the special teams on it immediately."

War was coming on heavy feet . . .